The Guarded Circle

Ahna and the Goddess of Sustainability

by Taille Weaver

Published by Studio On A Hill

Copyright October 2011

all rights reserved

cover art by Heather M. Thayer

www.studioonahill.com

www.tailleweaver.com

Foreword

More than twenty years ago I read Riane Eisler's The Chalice and The Blade, an archaeological compilation of data and interpretation of the known prehistoric cultures in and around the Mediterranean. I was, and am, fascinated by her description of the little known culture of the Old Europeans, a peaceful, sustainable agricultural society that developed all across Europe and Anatolia and the Middle East, the "land of milk and honey," the earliest evidence of which is dated to as long ago as 9000 BC. This culture was apparently completely wiped out, Eisler argues plausibly, by a male dominant nomadic culture or cultures somewhere around 2500 BC.

Most of my story is imaginary. There are very few hard facts available for either of these cultures. The nomadic one left us nothing, really, except some piles of potsherds that date to the same period as the end of the settled culture. These only attest to their original ownership by their crudity compared to those of the settled culture, a trait of pots commonly found associated with nomadic cultures. We assume that they were horse nomads because so many later ones were, and such a life-style would have made it much easier to overrun the bronze age settlements that did not ride horses.

As to those towns and villages, they were so thoroughly burned and destroyed over such a wide area that there is little beyond bare foundations and a few very durable artifacts left. The excavations that have been done, however, have shown that they were a slowly evolving, peaceable and probably essentially egalitarian agricultural people for thousands of years. Four or five thousand years ago they had just begun to use the potter's wheel, and, it is thought, to make the first wheeled vehicles.

I have used details from later similar cultures or better documented similar, contemporaneous cultures found in other places. It is believed, for instance, that the so-called Minoans (my Kaphtori), about whom the archaeological record is not nearly so shy, came originally from the Neolithic Old Europeans of Anatolia. Because there was never any loss of contact between them thanks to the seagoing trade of the Minoans, I have hypothesized that their basic cultures would have remained fairly similar throughout the long centuries of their habitation of both the mainland and the islands.

Although there is a wealth of artistic and archaeological data on the Minoans themselves, one still has to interpret the finds to come up with a picture of how the people lived and what they believed. I am again going on Eisler's interpretation of the data. Some later writers have tried to discredit her, claiming that of course the Minoans were a stratified society, with some people and some towns ruling others, starting very early. Being products of their own culture, and having been very successful in that culture, these scientists simply can't imagine a successful society that follows a very different pattern. At least until the so-called second palace period, when the influence of the stratified, weapons-using Mycenaeans began to be felt on Crete itself, the evidence all points to a sustainable, nonhierarchical, inclusive society. A tablet found in contemporaneous Egypt has been interpreted to read that the Kaphtori (a reference, it is believed, to the people of Crete, and the source for my name for them) 'are the wisest people in the [known] world.'

My other source for details is contemporary knowledge about how things are done, like creating waterproof baskets from materials that grow in swamps, building pots without potter's wheels and firing them without kilns, making fermented mare's milk, or making felt for tents. If you follow the directions in the books, you can make pots and fire them, or make felt and stitch it into a tent. You could even build a seaworthy boat to the Minoan model out of a couple of trees (although I suggest that before you try it you Google for the very detailed directions and photos on the web), or carve an alabaster platter from a slab of stone. These are all simple tasks accomplished with the skill of one's hands and common local materials, yet they add up to rich, complex, and fascinating cultures. When I do rely only on my imagination for details, as I did to create a portable communications system for the nomads based on color codes and called 'yard sticks', I have tried to stay well within logical parameters.

I have been very careful to leave out the impossible. There is no magic, no improbable fantasy, nothing more inexplicable than the coincidences that we meet with every day. Whether you want to read my books as pure fiction, or you want to go along with me and say, 'it might well have been that way,' I hope you will enjoy reading about my characters and their long ago lives as much as I have enjoyed writing about them.

Taille Weaver

Prologue

2500 B.C. They swept down from the high, arid steppes, their individual attacks sudden and overwhelming, completely devastating, their overall progress more like that of the glaciers: slow but inevitable. The destruction they wrought was total, irrevocable. Their beliefs, their paternalistic, warrior oriented culture, their horses and weapons, their language, their nomadic life style, even their looks were as alien to the peaceful, egalitarian, nature-centered farmers and craftspeople of the northern Mediterranean lands as glaciers would have been in their temperate climate, heavily forested hills and wide, deep-soiled valleys. Driven from their own lands by their own excesses, the barbarians came, and the world changed.

Chapter 1

Ahna expected a night of secrets. She fasted all day, drinking water from the spring, eagerly attacking her multitude of chores, hurrying the sun. Each time she had a few moments to spare she turned her thoughts to the Goddess, asking for acceptance and understanding.

The work was not light. In the morning she cleaned up after preparing and serving breakfast, then carried water from the drinking spring to the tents, refilling the large jars that stood in the shade between the double felt walls. She milked the mares next, her task because she had a light hand with them and they gave her more milk than they would give her mother. Vladia milked the ewes and nannies. The mares' milk went into the large skin that hung outside the work-tent flaps to ferment, after Ahna skimmed off the cream that had risen to the top from the previous day's addition: it had different uses and went into a smaller bladder nearby. Then she helped her mother make the yogurt - they would not make cheese this morning - and then prepare the midday meal for her father, brothers and foster-brothers, and clean up again before she approached her hardest task. She saddled her mare and a pack horse and rode past the nearby hills, now stripped of most of their trees by the clan's incessant need for firewood. They had been more than a full turn of the seasons in this location and were having to go further and further for fuel. When she reached the area where trees had been cut down and left to dry during the winter past, she picked up a day's worth of firewood and bundled it for the cooking fires, then loaded larger pieces and brush on top until her pack horse could carry no more. The greener and larger pieces would be left on the piles for the perimeter fires, lit and tended every night around the home pastures to keep predators and evil spirits away from their livestock and their camp.

In the early evening, after they served her father and brothers their supper, her mother sent Ahna to the stream to bathe. When the girl returned, Vladia gave her daughter new clothes: an undergarment of plain cream colored linen and a simple shift of tightly woven cotton that flowed straight from her shoulders to below her knees. It had no sleeves, and it had not been dyed, retaining the natural off-white of the raw material. The only decoration was a narrow embroidery of daisy-like flowers, white petals, pale yellow centers and delicate green leaves with stems twining around the edge of the slightly scooped neck. There was no sash. She'd begun wearing the brightly colored scarves with which unmarried young women covered their heads in public when her moon times had started. Tonight she would go bareheaded. Her mother helped her brush her thick, slightly curly red-blonde hair until it flowed smoothly to her waist. Vladia also told her to leave off her bracelets and her earrings and to wear her felt house slippers rather than her boots or leather work shoes.

It was traditional for young women to come before the Goddess silent and naked. Ahna could neither ask questions nor comment during the rituals. She must not make a sound until they sang their songs. Her mother would tell her when she was to take off her clothes.

Vladia herself wore one of her prettiest ceremonial outfits, blouse and skirt of woven linen in a panoply of gorgeous blues and greens lavishly embroidered with flowers and baby animals, a sash of a deeper, almost ultramarine blue at her waist and a matching scarf sewn with small gold beads. Her lustrous blonde hair, still pale enough that the grey in it did not show, was usually worn in an ornate braid around her head. Tonight it, too, was loose and cascaded far down her back. She wore multiple bracelets and rings, hoops of gold in her ears, and a double chain of gold set with deep blue stones at her throat. She had soft leather slippers stained a rich blueberry color and trimmed with more gold and silver beads on her feet. Her daughter thought she looked like a goddess.

Ahna was of marriageable age. Some girls of the clans were betrothed by their fathers when they started bleeding, or even earlier. She did not want to think of leaving home; she knew she was luckier than many of her peers that way. She dreaded having to obey without question a strange man, or most of all having to be of use to him in the way that the mares were for the stallions or the bitches for the dogs. True, the female animals did not seem to worry about it much. They actively sought such attentions when they were in season, but she could not imagine wanting it herself, at least not with any of the men she had met. Still, it was important to learn how to please a man.

When her father went to her mother's sleeping place, Ahna knew essentially what transpired. Unlike the female animals, her mother could never deny her mate access to her body. A young woman had to learn how to keep her husband contented in their private quarters, perhaps even more so than with her cooking and the making and keeping of their home tents. It was also vital to learn how to carry and birth healthy children and how to ask the Goddess of women and fertility to give her sons and help her be a good mother. That was what she thought the initiations were all about. That was what most of the folk of her clan thought their formal meetings and ceremonies were about.

On this night the boys who were old enough, usually around fourteen summers, and who had shown themselves adequately skilled at war games and horse mastery were being initiated into the warriors' society. The ceremony lasted all night and into the next morning, and was followed by feasting and celebration well into the following night. All the men and boys down to the youngest herd boys, and especially all the priests, would watch or participate; this was an important milestone, both religious and secular, in the lives of every man of the clans, and equally important to the future of the clan itself.

The women had no more part in the men's rites than to prepare the food and drink for the parties starting the next afternoon. The priests' wives took care of the specially prepared and blessed meats that were eaten during the ceremonies. Since the beef, lamb, and game that the rest of the women were to cook for the celebrations would not be available until after the ritual sacrifices had been made and blessed, and that didn't happen until after the individual initiations were all complete, the women were free to spend the intervening night as they would. It was the best, most surely private time to introduce the newly adult young women to their own secret society.

Ahna was surprised, curious, and a little apprehensive when her mother walked right through the tent village and out into the surrounding fields, holding her hand. It was deep dusk, almost dark, the second moon of spring a tiny new sliver that cast little light, and they had no lamp. All her life Ahna had been taught to fear the dark. Her people, especially the men, were superstitious. The priests warned that evil spirits had power after nightfall and that, except for the warriors who kept the guard fires and protected the herds, wise folk stayed in the safety of their tents. This evening there were other women and their daughters moving in the same direction as Ahna and her mother. No one had a light and none of the adults seemed concerned about spirits of any kind.

They continued across a meadow and into the woods. All the women and girls were together now, pair by pair following closely behind one another. It got darker and darker, until in the shadow of the trees they could see almost nothing at all. Despite herself Ahna's grip on her mother's hand tightened. They climbed fairly steeply among rocks and trees beside the unseen music of a brook, its rippling voice increasing once to the splashing commotion of a waterfall, which then receded behind them. Progress was slow; they had to step carefully to avoid tripping over roots or slipping on rocks that were mostly invisible. When the ground beneath their feet leveled out and the surface changed to dead leaves and short spring growth they turned away from the sound of the water and went on more quickly through closely spaced trees burgeoning with new leaves, holding up their hands to ward small limbs away from their faces.

After several more minutes of walking the way grew lighter ahead of them, and they came out into a space free of trees, a small grassy arena above which they could see the stars and the new moon. It was almost bright by comparison. They followed the shadowy figures ahead of them until they were moving in a circle, and then they stopped, more than thirty girls each holding her mother's hand and facing toward the center, where a misty figure in white appeared to be standing on air a few feet away.

"Take your clothes off and place them on the ground behind you, then take the hands of the girls next to you, her mother whispered close to her ear, so quietly she almost didn't hear. Ahna removed her shift and undergarment and even her slippers and, turning, put them behind her, then turned back and reached for the hands of the girls on either side of her. Their mothers had disappeared without a sound. They looked at one another, and one or two tried to whisper something, but were silenced by firm pressure from a neighbor's hand or a quick shake of her head.

They turned to the white figure that seemed to float in the middle of the circle, ethereal, almost ghostly in the faint light. She wore a pale, loose robe that covered her from neck to feet, with full sleeves spilling from her raised arms and very light hair that made a nimbus around her body and fell below her waist. She neither moved nor spoke. Minutes passed, and more minutes. The night was calm and full of spring, but it was still very dark. In the silence the shadows held a hint of menace, a nebulous warning that kept Ahna's nerves on edge. She concentrated on standing, and keeping, still.

The girl to her right, a girl of twelve summers whom she knew only slightly, started to fidget, then tried to let go of her hand. Ahna glanced at her, caught a glimpse of her lower lip gripped in her upper teeth and trembling, and tears glinting in the faint light on her cheeks. She squeezed the child's hand gently a couple of times, trying to be reassuring, but she said nothing. Still, the younger girl seemed to relax a tiny bit.

Time stretched out. The figure in the middle remained so still that Ahna began to wonder if it really was a person, though the hair and clothing seemed to stir a bit in the slight, fitful breeze. Around the circle a very few of the girls broke the silence. Nothing happened. No one answered them. One started calling for her mother, but, apparently obeying the vigorous head-shakes of the girls around her, quickly resumed her silence. A second began by complaining of the cold. Ignoring the shaken heads, she tried to get the attention of the figure in white, rebuffing the restraining hands of her neighbors, stepping forward and asking a little belligerently what they were expected to do. She received no response. The figure did not turn or even look at her. "This is stupid," she finally said, facing the circle of girls. "Nothing is going to happen. They have just left us here to work it out for ourselves. I'm really cold. We should get dressed and go home!"

Ahna recognized her voice, though she was not close enough to see her features, as belonging to the daughter of one of the most overbearing and opinionated women in the clan, a girl who took every opportunity herself to instruct, not to say boss, her peers. When no one answered her except by shaking their heads again, when the two girls who had been standing on either side of her mutely held out their hands, and when a quick search for her clothes revealed that they, too, had vanished, she finally stepped back into the circle and subsided into sulky silence. A few more minutes went by. No one made a sound.

"Who among you can keep a secret?" a low, sweet voice suddenly asked. The figure in the middle began to rotate in a slow circle, and each girl in turn felt that she was being examined. "I represent the Lady, the Goddess who brings the lambs and calves and foals in spring, who sends the fawns and cubs to their mothers in the forest, who causes the flowers to blossom and the leaves to unfold and enables all living things to be renewed every year. The Goddess wants to know who among you can keep a secret. Look into your hearts. Step forward if you cannot keep a secret."

Some of the girls looked at each other, some of them took a half-step back, some of them looked down at their feet. Ahna and several others stood their ground and looked back at the woman in the center of the circle. No one stepped forward.

"Good," said the woman in white, "for you shall learn the secrets of your mothers, tonight and in the weeks to come. These secrets are not to be spoken of except in meetings of the women's society, and are never, never to be shared with the men. They do not share the secrets of their societies with us, and we do not share ours with them. Do you all understand?" Around the circle a few heads nodded. Soon everyone was nodding.

"Good," she said again. She seemed to walk down the air until she was only a step or two above them. Then she sat down on something unseen.

"Come here," she said. "Sit in front of me." The girls approached, the ones who had been behind her coming around to face her, and suddenly they were walking on bedding instead of grass. A few surprised gasps accompanied feet meeting unexpectedly with cool fur, but no one spoke. "Sit down," the woman in white repeated. "Take a blanket and wrap it around you. It is chilly, and we have much to talk about. The Goddess wants you to listen and learn, not to shiver."

When all the girls were seated in front of her, Ahshela, for indeed it was the Eldest, although Ahna had never seen her with her hair loose or wearing such a curious outfit, spoke again.

"This is a secret and sacred place of the Goddess," the most revered of their women began. "Here our voices are strongest in Her ears. Whenever we move camp, the experienced members of the women's society seek out the place nearby where Her voice is the loudest, where it is easiest for Her to hear our voices. It is usually a secluded and fairly high place like this one, often surrounded by trees. Such places have been dedicated to the Goddess over and over for thousands of years by thousands of women. They are holy, and if you use them correctly you will receive the help offered in them. You may come here and to all other such places whenever you wish to ask the Goddess for help or to thank Her for help you have received. The only rule is that you bring no man, nor any uninitiated girl or child old enough to talk. Babies are always welcome before the Goddess whatever their sex. Your mothers and foster mothers will teach you more in the moons to come, and you will be welcomed at our meetings, where I or one of the other elders will try to answer any questions you may have if your mothers have not done so. Now I have a story to tell you." There was a rustle of anticipation among the girls, although most knew that this story were already familiar to them.

"In the beginning was the Great Goddess," Ahshela said. "From her womb the waters of the earth gushed forth, filling all the low places, making the clouds and the rain, the rivers and lakes and the great sea itself. She gave birth to the Sun, and to his mate, the Moon. Then was there light upon the land and the waters. Then did plants grow, and trees, ferns and fungus in the forest, grasses and herbs in the open places, and all the flowering and fruiting things on the earth.

"Next from her womb came all the living and moving things, the insects and crawling things, and those that swim and fly and run, animals of every kind large and small, some to eat the plants, and some to eat other animals. She created the balance, put each plant and animal in its proper place, and made them all to depend upon one another for their existence. She gave birth to the Gods, Her sons, and finally She gave birth to the People. That is why she is called the Mother of Life, the source of fertility. That is why we pray to Her for children and for many lambs and calves, foals and fawns and rabbit kits. She fills the rivers and lakes with fish. She regulates the sunshine and the rain, the cycles of the moon, and the passing of the seasons. Her sons watch over the People. They have given us our laws. They guide and support us in our endeavors, but it was She who was First. She is the Mother. Praise Her for all She has given us. Praise Her for our beautiful and bountiful world."

Ahshela began singing the songs of learning and praise. The first, the song of beginning, repeated what she had just told them, with the girls responding to questions like, "From whence came the waters?" When they finished that song the eldest had them stand up, leaving their furs on the ground. They formed a line, dancing around her while she sang the second song, and they responded. This one was about birth and death and the cycle of the moons through the year: the little death that was winter, and the rebirth of all species with the coming of spring. It was a very old teaching song, with many verses that gave practical information for hunter-gatherers. The wisest of the women believed that they or their daughters or their grandchildren would always have need of that knowledge, but as she sang it with the initiates, Ahshela left out some of the key verses.

They ended with a verse in which they promised to remember and pass on the song to their daughters. Then they returned, a little breathless, to their furs.

"Sit, now, and be quiet," she told them. "Listen to the voice of the Goddess. Let Her fill you with the knowledge of all the blessings She has given us and the expectation of those that are to come." The silence that swelled around them then felt no different from earlier, a void that demanded filling, although the hint of menace, the feeling of danger lurking at the edges was gone. Then, as the sounds they had themselves been making faded to memory, the voices of the spring night returned and swelled in their ears. Insects sang. An owl called and received responses. Leaves moved and whispered. A twig snapped softly. A nightingale began his courting song, etherial and beautiful, soaring, solid as the dark.

When the bird finished his anthem Ahshela lifted her clear voice in another, asking the Goddess to bless these young women and accept them into adult society and into Her presence. This time the responses came from behind them; their mothers had returned. The song became one of thanks, rising gloriously into the clear night air as the women's voices grew stronger and more joyous. It ended, as they all did, with praise for the Goddess.

Finally Ahshela told the girls to come forward one at a time and bow their heads, asking silently for the blessings they particularly wanted from the Goddess. After each one had done so, the Eldest greeted her by name, saying, "The Lady hears your prayers. If you are true to all you have learned, in time they will be answered." She gave each girl a fervent hug and a kiss on the cheek. "Go now and dress yourself, and depart for this time with your mother. Know that the Goddess welcomes you and blesses you and has joy in your coming-of-age, and that your entrance among us as a member of our society brings us joy as well."

When Ahna's turn came she approached the eldest with reverence and a feeling of lightness and exultation. She knelt and bowed her head, not even noticing the chilly breeze on her bare flesh. When she raised her eyes an indeterminate time later she did not even really know what she had asked for, but she knew that she had been answered, that the Goddess welcomed her knowledge of Her and blessed her entry into adulthood. Words of thanks and praise formed on her lips, but she did not voice them. She presented a radiant face to the Eldest and was answered by a smile as joyful as her own. "I'll see you later," whispered Ahshela when she hugged the girl, then intoned aloud the words with which she was dismissing each initiate in turn.

Ahna turned away as one of the few remaining initiates came to take her place. Her smiling mother greeted her with a kiss and her clothes. She donned them quickly and they started back down the path by which they had arrived. It was obvious that the older women all knew the route very well, because although they were now traveling in pairs separated from each other, and although it was still just as dark, no one tripped or blundered off the path. They walked without talking. Crickets and other night insects sang their various mating songs. A night-jar called, and they heard the owls again. Sometimes an animal rustled in the undergrowth, but there was no threat in any of the sounds they heard. The faint light of new moon and stars penetrated fitfully through the canopy of leaves, a patchwork of dark dappled splendor. The air smelled sweet and fresh, the scent of new growth and spring flowers occasionally punctuated by the odor of evergreen boughs someone had brushed against, or that of herbs crushed under foot. The dark seemed to Ahna to enfold them in blessings and to promise them safety, which struck her as very strange; the warriors and older men delighted in telling tales of ghosts, demons and other dangers that awaited the unwary nocturnal venturer. She gave a passing thought to wolves, but even the memory of some very real hazards of the night didn't have the power to disturb her new sense of calm certainty.

As they came out of the woods into the starlit meadow Ahna murmured to her mother, "What did Ahshela mean, she would see me later?"

"You will know soon," Vladia replied as quietly. "We are going to her tents now." As they came into the village, where many tent flaps had been left open, spilling light from the mutton-fat lamps within onto the walkways, Ahna saw the girl who had complained during the ceremony and her mother turn into a tent where the mothers of tiny babies and the girls who were old enough to babysit but not yet women were watching all the younger children from their neighborhood. She looked at her mother in inquiry. Several other pairs were heading in that direction as well.

"They are picking up the children in their family, on their way home," her mother commented. "They will celebrate the initiations with their friends and neighbors."

"Aren't they…" began Ahna. "Shh," warned her mother, "no, they're not. Patience, Dearest, all will be explained."

Chapter 2

The warriors were expected, but the ferocity of their attack was more than anyone could have envisioned. They came out of the pink and gold sunrise, out of the bright clear blue and green of a fresh autumn day, hundreds of them howling unintelligibly, death in their voices. The newly built palisade might as well have never existed. While most of the barbarians galloped their horses along the barrier dispatching a storm of arrows from their bows, the first ones wreathed in pale flame and followed by flight after flight tipped with killing bronze, the noisiest contingent threw ropes with hooks to the top of the wall and swarmed up them right off their horses' backs, long knives ready in their teeth and swords sheathed behind their necks for instant access over their shoulders. They were dressed in thick leather vests, many with the fur still on, their heavily muscled arms bare except where circled with guards of bronze or gold. They had thick leather leggings doubled to protect their thighs and groins and close-fitting helms or headbands of layered embossed hide often studded with disks of silver or bronze. Every one wore an identical expression of teeth-bared anger, hatred, an insane intentness on killing, and kill they did.

The defenders tried with increasing desperation to push them back, but the invaders didn't seem to care if they themselves died as long as those they were attacking did. Holding the height, the townsfolk managed to knock off a number of the nomads at first, and even to kill a few. Not enough. The horse fighters seemed strong beyond the limits of ordinary men, and ruthless. As the raiders came over the wall the Others died, male and female, cut down without mercy, many without even scratching one of the enemy.

Only minutes after the first arrow flew the gates swung back, opened from within, and the rest of the horsemen swarmed into the town. Jaromir led them, as was his duty. He rode into the open, stone-paved space in the center of the narrow streets of one and two-story houses, his stocky short-necked brown war mare picking her way fastidiously around the bodies that already littered the bloody ground. He gave his companions permission to leave their horses and loot at will, then sat alone, his back straight, the high leather boots on his long legs snug against War Bird's sides, alert for action. There were no longer any living others in sight; his blue eyes closed momentarily at each despairing scream that rose, only to cut off abruptly, from within the surrounding houses.

There were occasional fires already starting around the edges of the village. A spell of dry weather had made a few of the blazing arrows more effective than their usual intimidation and distraction. When four warriors came out of a house right in front of him Jaromir instructed them to leave their bulging hemp bags of treasure and go put out the fire that was blossoming in one end of a large building with imposing double doors and no windows that stood by itself at the foot of the green; it was probably a storehouse or granary. He did not want it to burn until they had a chance to determine the usefulness of its contents. Monyin started to object. He dragged a slim, dark-haired, dark-eyed girl, clear skinned and attractive despite her torn-open blouse and the blood on her cheek, by her wrist, and was obviously reluctant to leave his prize.

"Sit her down here," his chief instructed, pointing to the ground. "I will watch her for you."

"What if she runs?" the warrior demanded. "Will you chase her?" A faint trace of derision hung in his voice.

Jaromir glanced about him at the mayhem and destruction, listened to the ongoing echoes of death. This quiet spot in the middle of it all was a haven.

"She won't run," he said.

The young warrior pushed the girl to a seated position in the shadow of War Bird's shoulder, made an unmistakable gesture that she should stay there, and followed his fellows down to the storehouse, where they efficiently smothered the nascent blaze with heavy pieces of tent felt pulled from the rolls behind their saddles. The child of the others, no older than Jaromir's daughter Ahna, put her hands on the ground and looked around as if considering whether or not she should run, then glanced up at him. He shook his head. She slumped, put her face in her hands, and started to weep.

When the men came back Monyin, who carried a still-burning brand, glanced at the girl and nodded to his chief. The warriors then joined their fellows, who had carried their finds out of various buildings and were now throwing the bodies of the others into them, after divesting them of jewelry and anything else they thought worth keeping. Here and there a warrior tied a hemp rope to his saddle and used his horse to drag a heavier corpse to its final rest. When all his comrades had finished in the houses Monyin used his torch to good effect, then tossed it aside, collected the girl and his bag of loot and mounted his horse, lifting his new concubine up before him. As the men of the Lion clan rode back out of the square, smoke from the cremation houses behind them began to sully the deep blue sky.

Jaromir and his men gathered the flocks of sheep and goats and a small herd of cattle from pens inside the walls where the townsfolk had hoped in vain to protect them, driving the animals back to their temporary camp. The priests who waited there sacrificed a massive hump-shouldered bull and a pair of heavy-fleeced, curly horned rams in thanks to their Gods for the successful raid. The meat was set to roast over great fires; it would serve for the feasting that night.

Even before the main body of attackers had finished their looting, small bands of the Dedicated, the warriors who first went over the walls, ranged out into the countryside. It was their duty to be sure that there would be none of the others left to present a threat to the clan in the future. Their rage was still potent, their self-induced blood lust not yet satisfied. They searched for likely hiding places, aware that there had been far too few women and children in the town for the number of men, and they found them. In caves, in copses, in orchards and vineyards, in the middle of thickets in the woods. The nomads were hunters as well as warriors; their tracking skills rivaled their violence. Except for the most desirable young women, not many because their clan already had a good supply of women, they killed all that they found.

In a large open cave above the river some three miles south of the town a handful of the Dedicated found an altar, carved of wood with symbols, flowers, and plants, and niches in the walls that held human bones, thousands of them. The barbarians suspected that the cave hid more than just bones. A cursory search of several side passages yielded scores of women and children and a few elderly men whom the invaders dispatched without ceremony, the victims' terrified cries, even their prayers and death songs like distant echoes in their murderers' ears. By now the sun had passed its zenith and the killing lust was wearing off, descending into lethargy.

The fighting men carried water and dried meat in their saddle bags, but they wanted to be off their horses, to share a fire with their fellows, to feast and brag of their deeds and imbibe more potent beverages, to drink themselves into a stupor. They left the area, headed back to camp. They would tell the priests of the sacred cave; this, too, was one of their duties.

Chapter 3

Ahna and her mother went into their own tents first, and Vladia
lit a couple of lamps in the main living area. She then disappeared
into the work area and returned with baskets of strawberries that she
and Ahna had picked just that morning. Ahna held hers away from
the unsullied front of her shift. They stepped back outside and walked
quickly but quietly along a shadowy path that cut diagonally across
the camp to Ahshela's tent. When they entered through the open tent
flaps some of the other girls and their mothers were already there,
along with at least forty more women ranging in age from fifteen
summers to fifty or more, all dressed in their best, chatting about the
ceremony just past. There was plenty of room; except for the
gathering tent near the priests' compound, this was the largest
enclosed space in the camp. After a few minutes Ahshela came in
with her own daughter Reova and her granddaughter Luliana, married
for almost a year now and heavily pregnant. She asked them to bring
tea and the food that had been prepared from the work tent, then set
about getting all the women seated in a broad circle on the rugs, the
new initiates in the front beside their mothers. Vladia and her
daughter placed their baskets of berries among numerous other
baskets and plates of wild spring foods in the central area.

"We will eat before the meeting," said Ahshela. She smiled
around at the nine fresh young faces among them. "These girls, at
least, must be famished. It is time they broke their fast and celebrated
this glad occasion with some of the best flavors the Goddess has
granted us! While Reova and Luliana are bringing in the hot food and

the drinks, I believe there may be some questions to be answered."
Ahna nodded along with the others.

Ahshela's countenance took on a more solemn cast. "Did it strike
any of you as odd that the first thing I did in the holy place was to ask
who could not keep a secret?" Most of the girls nodded this time.
"Why?" asked the Eldest.

After a moment for thought Ahna said, "Because it was unlikely
that those who could not keep a secret would admit it, so it was a
question that even if answered would not tell you anything."

"You are absolutely right, Ahna. It was not meant to tell us
anything. It was meant, rather, to give you all the impression that we
were about to reveal the secrets of the women's society, secrets that it
was vital everyone keep. Now I have another question for you. Are
there any girls among those who were initiated tonight that you
would not trust with a secret?"

Nearly all the girls nodded this time. Another of Ahna's friends, a
tall blond named Maezian, said, "There are many that I would not
trust with a secret, but they are none of them here now."

"You're right," praised the Eldest. "You see, the women's society
really does have some secrets, secrets taught to us by the Goddess,
secrets that all our people once knew. But now if it were known to
the men, especially the priests, that we are teaching them and using
them, these secrets would get us in very serious trouble. They are
important. They are the most basic lessons and commands given us
by the Goddess, and they must be handed from generation to
generation for the well-being of our clan and indeed of all people.
You who are here now have shown yourselves mature and
responsible young women, not only ready to take your place as adults
in the society of our clan, but strong enough and trustworthy enough
to start learning these secrets. Once this group was made up of
priestesses of the Goddess. We are no longer permitted to call
ourselves priestesses. Now we call ourselves the inner circle of the
women's society, and even our existence is a secret; you are here to
be welcomed into that circle."

"The sacred knowledge that was shared in the holy place tonight
does indeed represent secrets of our society," Ahshela continued, "but

they are not secrets that can hurt us. If, as happens every year, they are told to the boys or men by the less reliable new initiates, they will not be used against us, and they will help convince the priests that our 'secrets' are known to them and are harmless. Those who want to limit our activities and beliefs will be less likely to suspect that we are hiding any 'secrets' that they would consider unacceptable.

"I want you to think seriously about this while we are eating. All of your mothers are or were members of this group. Some of the forbidden knowledge you may learn in the months to come could cost you your place in our clan, probably would get you and your family banished if the wrong people were made aware that you have such knowledge. A few of these secrets, especially certain of those about fertility, childbirth, healing, death, rebirth, and the sacredness of all life are so powerful and so feared by the men that using them or teaching them is considered witchcraft and could lead to your death if you are caught. These secrets are not witchcraft. They are simply an understanding of the natural world which has been taught to our ancestors by the Goddess, no different from knowing which mushrooms are good to eat and which will make you sick. Some of this knowledge can be used for evil purposes, it is true, but that would be to go against Her laws, and remove oneself from Her favor. Still, if any of you do not want to learn these secrets, you have only to tell your mother. We will all understand. You will be excused from the meeting after supper, and no one will think poorly of you. Our only requirement is that you keep silent about this meeting, and our group. Ah, here is the food."

The Eldest got up to help her daughter with a large basket-weave platter bearing two whole roasted lambs, carefully carved into manageable slices without disturbing their form, while her granddaughter had brought pitchers of hot tea spiked with wine which she set down beside a basket full of tightly woven, waterproof reed cups. When they were all seated everyone joined hands and bowed their heads while Ahshela gave thanks to the Goddess for the wonderful foods of spring, for the bounty of this particular feast, and for the blessing of so many bright new stars in the sky of their society. When they raised their heads she reminded the newest members of the society again that such blessings could only be asked for silently and privately in any company other than that made up exclusively of members of this group. Then with a smile she gestured toward the food. "Eat now. Eat!" Everyone was hungry, so there was little talking while they enjoyed the succulent meat and the fresh, flavorful spring vegetables and fruit, washed down with cups of the hot herbal tea and wine.

When they were finished the remaining food was put away, a task that took only minutes, there were so many helping hands, and the cups were refilled. All the girls waited, some eagerly, some with a bit of fear, for the revelations to come. Not one had told her mother she wanted to go home. Another of the grandmothers, a woman of fewer years and darker hair than Ahshela, took up the recitation.

"You have heard the story of how all things came from the Mother Goddess's womb, and how last of all She gave birth to humans. Most of that story as it was repeated earlier tonight has been known to you since you were small, but that is only part of the story. We are here to tell you the rest.

"Some of the story as you will now hear it contradicts what you have learned in the past. Please listen without interruption unless you absolutely must ask a question; the reasons for the contradictions will be explained as the story goes on.

"We refer to the Goddess as 'She,' but She is both female and male, and listens to the voices of men as well as those of women. Because women and female animals make babies, and She is the creator, we think of Her as female. However, no woman can conceive a baby without the help of a man any more than a mare can have a foal without first being intimate with a stallion. To create life the Goddess, who has no mate, *must* be both female and male.

"We also think of the Goddess as being a mature woman, as befits One who has given birth to all creation, but She has two other very important aspects. Of course She is the matron, the Mother of all, but she is also the Maiden, the bringer of spring and the symbol of rebirth, the object of lust and the image of love. And finally she is the Elder, the wise one, the giver of knowledge, including our understanding and acceptance of the gift of death."

There was a stirring among the girls; death was a *gift*? For *women*? They had been taught that they were born only to serve their men, and that for females as for all animals death was an absolute ending with nothing beyond.

"The Goddess tells us to study the world around us. In order for there to be renewal, in order for the cycle of life to continue, there must be death. Some creatures have short lives, some have longer ones, and some of the great trees live for many generations of men, but everything that lives dies. Everything and everyone must die in order for the new generations to have a place to live, to have sustenance, to keep the balance and continue the pattern. Everything that lives is recycled. All plants return, are reborn, some from the roots of the old plant, others from its seeds. Those plants are only healthy because other plants and animals before them have died and rotted and put food into the ground which the new plants can use. The same is true of all animals. The Goddess teaches us that we, too, are reborn. These are the verses that have been left out of the teaching songs, the verses to which the men object. Our bodies are given to the earth, the materials in them reused over and over again. And our spirits, which the Goddess also created, are given new bodies and a new consciousness, another life in a long succession of lives. This is the reason we must obey the precepts of the Goddess, those that you are about to hear and others. This is the reason we should take the same care of the place we live in and the other living things around us as we do of our own families. As surely as we will die, we shall return. Not only our children and our children's children will have need of the resources the Goddess has given us. We will have need of them.

"The Gods, according to the priests, teach that the spirits of men go somewhere else after death, that they are rewarded for valor and sacrifice while they are in this current life with a place in which they will forever be feasting and carousing, and have everything that they desire. This place is, of course, for men only. Although there will be women there to look after their needs, they will not be women who once lived on earth. According to them, the spirits of animals and women and the others, any human not male and of their own clans, vanish when their bodies die, and are gone forever. These beliefs do not make sense, but they do allow, even justify, our current way of life. The men have no stake in long-term protection of their territory, or in keeping the balance, because they are not going to need that territory once they die. They are going to a 'better place,' and never coming back! By adhering to these beliefs they have freed themselves of all restraint. There are no consequences inherent upon their taking anything they please, doing whatever they want, unless others have the will and the strength to impose consequences upon them. The most powerful of them will always prevail, so all they seek is power.

"These beliefs are directly contradicted by the teachings of the Goddess. This is the first reason the men deny the Goddess, claiming She is dead, except for the limited part of Her that brings the moons of spring and confers fertility on women and animals. She represents a real threat to them. The Goddess as we know Her teaches that our present way of living is wrong because it destroys the balance and will bring disaster, starvation, and permanent death upon us eventually. So you must not talk about the Goddess or Her teachings. The wrong person simply knowing of your belief in these aspects of Her is enough to get you and your family banished, designated non-clan and sent away at the least." She stopped talking, and another woman took up the refrain.

"The story as we told it earlier said She gave birth to 'men,' but of course She created both men and women. In the eyes of the Goddess, men and women are equally important." There were gasps around the circle as the girls realized this statement represented another radical departure not only from all they had been taught, but from the realities of their daily life.

"If the Goddess created us to be equal, why does She let the men rule us as they do?" asked one of the girls.

"The Goddess does not interfere in the lives of Her creations," the grandmother answered, "not directly. Along with life She has given us the gift of self-determination. She will give guidance through example and through Her laws. Most creatures follow Her laws by their very nature, but humans are able to take actions which are contrary to those laws, even when such actions are not in their best interests. The choice is ours. She did not want to create puppets.

"The Goddess gave birth to all men and all women, not just those of our clan or the clans," she went on. "She has no favorites among us. The people who have inhabited these lands for thousands of summers worship Her and try to follow her laws. It is they who originally found and have kept up the holy places where we now go to speak to Her. Among these people, both women and men use these places to communicate with the Goddess, and both sexes listen to her equally."

"What is more, She values the animals and plants as She values us. She commands us to share our territory with them, to thank them when their bodies provide for our needs, and to have a care that we do not overuse any one kind of animal or plant so that it becomes unable to renew itself. She teaches us that the long-term health of our people depends on there always being enough animals and plants born every spring to see us through the next cycle of a year, and that means not taking too many away; not, for example, keeping so many animals that they overgraze the land available or crowd out the wild animals. It also means not having too many children."

The gasps that greeted this last statement were much more general and much louder. "How can that be?" one girl asked. "Everyone knows it is our first duty to have as many children as possible."

"Why would the Mother make such a requirement?" asked Ahna. "Does she tell the other animals and plants not to have too many babies?"

"You will learn as you get older that sometimes what 'everyone knows' is not right at all," said Ahshela to the first questioner. Then she looked at Ahna. "As for the other plants and animals, in a way She does tell them just that. The number of babies they have is regulated for each of them by their nature and the world around them.

"The eagle usually raises only one chick each year, because she is a mighty predator. She needs a big territory with many prey animals and fish. If she had large broods, like the sparrow or the rabbit or the field mouse, and if she were able to feed them, there would soon be too many eagles. They would kill off most of the animals and fish upon which they prey, and then they would die of starvation. Therefore not only does the eagle have only one chick, the eagle parents drive that chick out of their territory when it is old enough to fend for itself, so that there may be enough prey in their home range for the parents to raise another chick the next year. If the land has a full complement of eagles and the young eagle cannot find a territory of his own, he will not mate or make a nest or have babies. As long as the balance that the Goddess designed is kept, there is a natural limit to the number of eagles.

"The mouse, on the other hand, breeds rapidly and has as many babies as possible; she and her children are food for many other animals, and she must hurry to have enough babies so that some of them will survive to have babies in their turn. The same is true for other animals and many plants that make far more seeds than can ever grow. Still, if the balance gets upset, if something happens to the predators for instance, so that too many baby mice grow up and have more babies, the population of mice can outgrow the food supply that is available, and then many, many mice will die of starvation and disease.

"People are the same, if they follow the guidance of the Goddess. We are like the eagles. We prey on many other animals and eat plants as well, and there are not many creatures that prey on us. Each family or clan or town of people takes a certain territory as its own, large enough to support it. The eagles generally respect each other's territory, with only occasional disagreements, as the Goddess made them to do. For most people it is the same."

"The Goddess has also limited the number of children we can have naturally. For example, a woman who nurses her own child as the Goddess created us to do will seldom have another child until she has weaned the first. This alone means that she will usually have only one child every three or four years, but the clans have changed those rules. Our men want more children so that they will have more sons to fight with them and to pass on their characteristics, their blood. To them many sons are a mark of wealth and power. They usually demand that a woman of the clan wean her children early, or else give them, especially the girls, to another woman, preferably a concubine, to nurse, so that their first wives can get pregnant every year. In this way a woman is able to have many more children. The men bring home extra women from their raids, to do the work for the child-bearers and to have even more children for them. In this way the population of any one of our clans can grow very rapidly indeed. When we do not follow the laws of the Mother, it is inevitable that we will outgrow our food sources.

"We used to live in territories of our own as the rest of the animal world does, but now, the priests say, the Gods have changed the rules. Instead of starving to get the numbers back in balance, as most of the rest of the Goddess's children do, when the clan's food sources run short we are told to move into some other people's territory, kill them and take their food and their grazing for our own. As long as there are rich new lands tended by others who are weaker than we to move into, this strategy for increasing our numbers and living well will answer beautifully, as it does now. The problem is, as the Goddess teaches, that not keeping the balance has inevitable and disastrous consequences. We women who listen to the Goddess fear that our people will be at risk of destruction when there are no more rich Others to conquer.

"Now you know the main reason that our men deny the Goddess, worshiping instead Her sons, whose laws are much more in tune with their own desires. It is also why you must keep the secret of Her continued presence as a primary force in our lives, and of your use of the knowledge She offers. It is a threat to all the men hold most dear, and as such they will destroy it wherever they find it, and those who teach or use it, as well." She stopped talking, and took a sip of her tea. Vladia took up the story.

"Among many other things," she began, "the Lady has taught us ways to avoid having too many children. She has created herbs that can prevent a woman from conceiving, just as She has given us herbs to ease pain, to make childbirth easier, to ease congestion when someone has a cold, to help broken bones heal, to prevent rotting and heal wounds. Knowledge of these gifts is also forbidden by the men, especially the priests, not only because of the birth control herbs, but because all such knowledge, they believe, gives women power and thus reduces their own. You will learn of these healing herbs from your mothers, each to her own abilities, this coming summer. The Goddess has blessed this region with many of Her most useful plants. What we wish you to learn now, and never forget for a moment, is that you must keep this knowledge secret. You must gather and prepare the plants with the utmost care, in privacy, and keep them in a way that will make them seem innocuous to anyone stumbling upon them. You must not discuss them among yourselves except when you know yourselves to be alone; it is best to keep such discussions and any questions you may have for secret meetings of this society. You must reduce the importance of the herbs, and direct your patient's attention to prayer when using the Goddess's healing gifts, so that those who are not members of our group do not become aware that you have this knowledge.

"Some healing herbs and methods are so common that everyone knows of them. Willow bark for pain is one, as is camphor to clear the nose. Using clay to make poultices to draw down swelling is another. You will learn other, more effective herbs for some kinds of pain, but you will have to make those you are tending believe that you are using only the commonly known herbs. Likewise, you will learn of herbs that may be added to poultices which will greatly increase their effectiveness, but you must not let anyone except other members of our society see you adding them, and you must not tell anyone about them. Discretion in all cases must be foremost in your minds.

"Inevitably there will be times when you know how to help someone, but will be unable to do it because there is too great a chance that you will be caught. I know that feels wrong, but it is not only for your own welfare that these secrets must be kept, it is for the welfare of all our people both now and in the future. It would be a terrible thing if our contact with the Goddess, limited and secret as it now is, were to be severed and Her knowledge lost because the priests learned what we were doing and purged our people of all those women who have it. Do not doubt that High Priest Zynjaar and his son Srogaraad would do so without a qualm, should they learn of these activities, just as if we were no more than a group of the Others. Even if they were to banish, or kill, all of us, they would say it was ordered by their Gods, and believe it a necessity to protect or increase their own power."

"That is everything we wanted to share with you tonight," said Ahshela. "I know it is a great deal for you to think on. Before you go home, we will each individually and before all the others promise the Goddess that we will keep everything which has been said here tonight locked in our hearts, no matter what provocation or pressure we may feel to reveal it. Each new initiate will make this promise as 'repeat-after-me' this once, because you have never heard it before. Then you will memorize it, and be able to repeat it without prompting at the end of each meeting." The adults and older initiates present began in chorus, stopping after each line so that the new initiates could repeat it.

"Thank you, Great Goddess, Mother of All, for accepting me, Your humble daughter."

"I promise that I will keep faith with You, that I will never reveal Your secrets."

"I promise that I will keep faith with You, that I will do my best to live by Your laws."

"I promise that I will keep faith with You, that I will use the knowledge with which You have blessed me only for the good of others."

"I promise that I will keep faith with You, that I will deny the use of Your healing knowledge to no one, unless such use will endanger me or Your other daughters, or may result in the permanent loss of Your knowledge."

"I promise that I will keep faith with You, and trust in Your help that I may do so."

Chapter 4

Zynjaar approached the mouth of the sacred cave of the others a little warily. The warriors had told of finding the women and children here, and insisted that all were dead, but there was something odd. There were no bodies lying around. It was not the habit of the Dedicated to go to the trouble of burning bodies unless they were in an area to which clan members meant to return, such as near full barns or warehouses. Nor were there any signs of recent fires.

The priests entered the cave. The entrance was high and wide; there was no shortage of light in the main chamber. The huge space was too quiet, too vacant. There were no bodies here, either. The altar with its carvings of plants and animals crouched on the left. There was some dried blood on it, and evidence of much more in places on the packed clay floor. Zynjaar hid a shudder as he caught glimpses of bones in the deep niches and crevices around the sides of the cave.

"Here," he commanded of his followers, "start getting rid of those bones. This is a good place to dedicate to our Gods, but They will certainly not want bones of the Others in here when we do!"

One or two of his underlings moved hesitantly toward the nearest niche, but most of the fifteen priests with him hung back. One spoke up, his eyes showing white. "Wha... What about ghosts?"

"You fools," their leader sneered, "these are bones of the Others. They are not sons of the Gods. There can't *be* any ghosts; it is no more possible than that a collection of animal bones could have ghosts. Now get rid of them! Dump them all over that ledge outside into the river."

Most of his minions obeyed slowly, their reluctance and doubt showing in hesitant movements and frightened eyes, but Srogaraad, less than two years a priest and already believing himself second only to his father in their hierarchy, a fancy the high priest did nothing to dispel, showed no inclination to assist in the task.

"There may be no ghosts," he said to Zynjaar instead, "but I think there are still some living others here. Someone had to have moved those bodies. I don't think the warriors did a very thorough job of searching yesterday. Let me and a couple of my friends make sure we don't have company."

Some of the lesser priests thought this was very brave of their leader's son given that priests, alone among all the men of the clans, were not permitted to use violence unless they were attacked. Since it was against the laws of the clan and grounds for banishment to even challenge a priest, and the penalty for attacking a priest with a weapon was death, the priesthood was a great refuge for those who feared or abhorred violence. Still, one could hardly count on the Others to obey the nomad's laws.

At a nod from his father, Srogaraad spoke to two other young priests. They fetched torches from their saddle bags, lit them with the coals the fire keeper carried in a small closed pot, and began a systematic search of the passages, small and large, that led out of the main chamber of the cave.

High on the side of the cavern, in a niche that was hidden by a jutting ledge from any vantage in the main cave, a small group of the Others huddled in fear. They had avoided the carnage the previous day not because they had made it to their current refuge, but only because the Dedicated had indeed not searched the lower passages thoroughly. They had stayed after the killers left because they thought the barbarians would not return, there being no further goods to loot or food to be found here, and because they needed to care for their dead. They had spent all the afternoon and evening and much of the night carrying the bodies to the top of the hill above the cave, a holy place where the town's dead were always exposed until the Mother Goddess through her creatures took their flesh back into Her body, leaving only the bare clean bones to be interred in the sacred cave.

This morning, when they saw the priests approaching along the river, a route which was observable for some distance, they hurried to climb the ropes they had put in place as a precaution, the only means of access to the high ledge with its secret recess. There was some trouble with getting the children among them up, and they didn't all make it. Their leader, the Eldest, high priestess of their town, had insisted on being last. When the priests arrived outside and began dismounting from their horses, she fled into one of the most inconspicuous side passages while her people pulled up the ropes.

Now the Others above dared make no sound, dared not even peek over the edge to see what was happening. All they could do was listen to the strange language below them and the noises the priests made hauling away the bones of their ancestors, and pray silently but fervently to the Goddess that they be protected from discovery, and that their Eldest and Most Holy not be caught.

She was. Srogaraad himself, searching his third and last passage, and thinking he had reached the end, was turning back when he caught a glimpse of something that seemed to show alternately white and dark in the flickering light of his reed and mutton-fat torch. He propped the torch between two boulders, pulled his long bronze knife from its sheath at his waist, pressed himself flat against the rock wall so that he would throw no shadow, and inched silently toward the outcrop at the end of the passage where he thought he had seen something move. When he reached the rock he leaped out into the open where he could see behind it, his knife held ready to repel an attack. An elderly woman, much slighter and darker of skin than his people, crouched there. When he appeared before her, his bronze priests' robes at odds with the knife held threateningly in his hand, she stood in resignation, shook out the full flounced skirts that had given her away, and spoke to him with dignity. He stared a moment, knowing she was a priestess by the richness of her dress and jewelry, by the simple coroneted headdress that crowned her long, loose and slightly disarrayed silver hair, and by the open front of her tight bodice that displayed her aged bosoms. She spoke again, a question in her tone.

The young priest laughed shortly and gestured with the knife. She walked ahead of him, her back straight, her step firm. She said nothing more.

When they came out into the main cavern Srogaraad stubbed out his torch on the floor of the cave and dropped it. His father approached and looked his prize over. "Is that all you found?" he asked.

"That's all," his son confirmed, seeing that his cohorts had returned from their explorations empty handed. "There were probably others. She is not strong enough to have moved the bodies alone. The rest must have left the cave."

He glanced around. The old bones had been removed, and most of the priests were watching them, awaiting further developments. An unpleasant little smile curled the young priest's lips. "We need a sacrifice to rededicate the altar and the cave to our own Gods. What's wrong with her?"

Zynjaar looked a little taken-aback. Human sacrifice was not something they had hitherto practiced. On the other hand, they had no sacrificial animals with them, there was no warrior present to kill her and they were not themselves allowed to take life unless for a sacrifice, and he had just finished telling the rest of the priests that the Others weren't really people, anyway. What more appropriate offering could they have to propitiate their Gods than a priestess of the discredited and dying cult of the Mother Goddess?

"A fine idea," he said. "She is even dressed appropriately."

"I have never performed a sacrifice, Father," said Srogaraad.

"Then it is time you took that step in dedicating yourself to the Gods," responded the High Priest. "You shall do the honors this very day." The cruel anticipatory smile in the corners of his son's mouth spread a little wider.

In the high hidden niche, sitting in frozen silence against the back wall, the Others listened to the unintelligible conversation and movements down below. Soon they heard the priests begin a low chant, statement and response. The male voices swelled slowly, somehow ominously, and then they were all singing together. Suddenly through the building volume of sound the hidden folk heard a high quavery voice beginning a song of praise and dedication, a prayer for rebirth sung by or for their people when they died. An elderly man started almost involuntarily for the high opening, but the younger man held him back. He swallowed a shout of anger and despair. A young girl, Ester, her short blue shift torn and muddy, her dark ringlets tangled, buried her dirt-streaked face against her mother's bare chest. Silent tears made new tracks in the grime on her cheeks. The female voice grew stronger, the quaver disappearing, but the voices of the priests rose to a triumphant climax and her grandmother's song ended abruptly.

"Just so did the Mother Goddess die," proclaimed Zynjaar, turning away from the bloody form on the altar and the strangely disturbing look of ecstasy on his son's face. "Our Gods will always reign alone!"

Chapter 5

Redwolf and the rest of the boys his age were playing at war games with their practice weapons in a field which had been grazed nearly bare and was now reserved for exercises when the incident occurred. A tall boy of twelve summers, exceptionally well developed for his age and bidding fair to become an impressive man, he still displayed the freckles and rust colored hair for which his father Jaromir had, rather whimsically, named him. He was not the oldest present. Nearly all the boys of fourteen summers had been initiated into the warrior society in the spring, and were now on their first raid, although it was unlikely they would take part in the fighting, but all those who would be initiated next spring were working hard on the skills they would need as warriors. Still, a good many of them looked on Redwolf as their natural leader despite his tender years. He was not only well spoken, thoughtful of others, and very good at everything from hunting and riding to wrestling and war games, he was the son of their chief.

The retired Dedicated assigned to oversee the boys' practice while the warriors were away was in his tent, drunk again, so when the shepherd came pelting over a low rise and into their midst on a wild-eyed pony with blood running down its shoulder, there was no adult present, no one with real weapons or real authority, to respond to his extremely urgent summons.

"Lions!" the boy shouted. "Hill lions after the sheep! They killed two of our dogs, and even attacked my horse when we tried to scare them away!"

"Let's go!" called Redwolf.

"But we only have practice swords," protested his friend Ahruset.

"Drop the toys," suggested Redwolf, following his own advice while he gave Rain Cloud, his father's retired war mare, directions with his knees and heels to go after the herd boy, who was already racing back the way he had come. "Get out your hunting bows. It would be foolish to attack lions with swords if we had them!"

All the young men of the clan were required to make their own first hunting bows and arrows, although for most these would be the only weapons they ever made themselves, so many of the youngsters did not have bows yet. The whole group, more than fifty strong, bolted after Redwolf anyway, those with bows stringing them and notching bronze-tipped arrows as they rode.

They topped the hill and galloped yelling and screaming down into the midst of havoc. Well over a thousand sheep milled around, some running in all directions, some huddled in tight bunches facing the action, others stumbling back and forth almost aimlessly. Those furthest away still picked grass, apparently undisturbed. A lioness and a nearly grown cub had an ewe down and were tearing at the meat, on the side of the flock nearest the steep, once-forested hills to the east, now stripped bare of anything usable for firewood. Two more cubs had hold of a large ram nearby, one by a hind leg and one by the thick, newly grown-in fleece around his neck. With fierce kicks and bucks and violently tossing horns the ram was managing to give the inexperienced predators a hard time. All the big cats were ignoring the yells of the seven young shepherds, who had called off their remaining dogs and could not get close on their terrified ponies.

The stampede of approaching horses and yelling boys was too much for the female cubs that were trying for the ram; they let go of their prey and turned tail, racing for the wild country whence they had come. The lioness and her male cub stood their ground, defending their kill.

Most of the boys, those whose mounts would approach the cats at all, got as close as they dared, and several started shooting at the lions, who faced them with their front paws on their kill, tearing off great chunks of flesh between snarls. Redwolf meant to shoot, too, but he noticed a number of his friends who had no bows riding around behind the lions. He called them back by name; the rule was always to leave an open escape route for large predators. If the cats felt trapped they were much more likely to attack, and they were perfectly capable of killing horses and humans. While he was making sure he was being obeyed, some of the other boys' arrows found their marks. The lioness took two arrows, one in her shoulder, and one in her back. As others whizzed by or glanced off, her snarling increased in volume. It appeared for a moment as if she might attack despite the odds, but then her cub went down; two of the boys shooting at him had been luckier. One arrow had enough momentum to penetrate his chest, and another went into his open mouth and on into his brain. He didn't make another sound.

The lioness snapped at the arrow in her shoulder, then turned to her dead cub. She nuzzled him, then nudged him hard. When there was no response and another arrow grazed her side she turned with one last snarl to follow her two remaining cubs into the hills. A few of the boys started after her and Redwolf called them back; the only thing as dangerous as a trapped predator was an injured one. The adult hunters would undoubtedly have pursued her, but the boys had all been warned it was no job for them.

Redwolf turned to speak to the shepherds, but they were already scattering to collect their charges and move them to a part of their pasturage away from the slaughter, with the help of the dogs and some of the older boys. He spotted Ahruset nearby and sent him to the tents to bring women to determine the ownership of the sheep that had been killed, and then to butcher it and the dead dogs and distribute the meat. He was headed for the ram that the cubs had been worrying, to decide how badly it was injured and whether it needed care or perhaps to be slaughtered as well, when his attention was drawn to a loud altercation behind him. He spun Rain Cloud and she leaped to a gallop, sliding to a stop after only a few strides next to the dead sheep and lion. Redwolf landed on his feet between two young men who were facing each other, their expressions furious, their stances aggressive, their argument already having passed the insult stage.

"Put your knives away, Stepan, Darius!" he demanded. "You both know you cannot fight with weapons! If you must fight, use your fists. That might get you extra chores, but it won't cost your fathers blood price!"

"The cursed other insulted me," snarled Stepan, a chunky brown-haired boy a year older than Redwolf, but he put away his knife. Not so Darius. The slight, dark-skinned, black-haired concubine's son tried to dodge around Redwolf, his eyes squinted tight in anger, his knife aimed for his rival's throat. Redwolf disarmed him with a quick twist of his wrist, tossing the knife behind him on the ground and blocking the blow the smaller boy aimed at him.

"You're insulting him, too, Stepan! Enough, both of you. Your fathers will be ashamed of you." He shook Darius, who hadn't taken his hate-filled eyes off his antagonist. "Stop glaring at him and tell me what this is all about," Redwolf insisted. Both boys started to talk at once, and again the leader's son rounded on Stepan.

"I asked Darius," he pointed out. "You can tell me your side of the story after he tells me his."

"He's a nobody!" spat Stepan. "*My* parents are married, and *my* father's on the council; his father doesn't even acknowledge him *or* his mother. By law he doesn't *have* a father! And we're older than you and *you* aren't initiated, either, Redwolf. You have no authority to tell us what to do."

Redwolf had to tighten his grip on Darius's wrist, but he continued to speak to Stepan.

"*Your* father, and the entire council, will hear how you have been trying to provoke Darius to fight with you, Stepan," he said sternly. "Now shut up and let him tell me what happened, or I will ask some of our friends to keep you quiet!"

He glanced around and saw that Yashihar had ridden up on his cream-colored gelding, another of the older horse masters beside him. They were sitting their mounts looking on along with the rest of the boys. Stepan, realizing as well that there were now adults present, and a council member at that, took a step back and shut his mouth. But the tension remained in Darius's body, and Redwolf did not let go of his wrist. Instead he looked at the senior Horse Master, expecting him to take charge.

"You're doing fine," said Yashihar. "Go on."

Redwolf looked back at Darius, who was finally looking at him instead of Stepan. "What happened?" he asked, releasing the other boy's wrist.

"I killed the lion," he answered. "My arrow went into his heart. I dismounted to determine that it was my arrow and claim the pelt, and Stepan jumped off his horse and told me to get lost, that he had killed the lion and the pelt was his."

"That's my arrow in its mouth," said Stepan loudly. "A head shot kills faster than a chest wound. *I* killed the lion; the prize is mine!"

"Which arrow hit first?" asked Redwolf of Darius.

"Mine did!" both boys declared.

"Who among you saw both arrows hit?" Redwolf then asked the assembled riders. Hesitantly several of the boys stepped their horses forward, but at first they did not seem sure which arrow had hit first. Finally Redwolf asked one in particular, a boy of only eleven summers whom he nevertheless trusted to speak the truth. Neither Stepan nor Darius was well liked among their peers, but there was no question that Stepan came from a family with more status in the clan, although his mother, too, was originally a concubine. His father took her as his second wife after she produced the only son he had who lived, so Stepan could legitimately lay claim to his father's surname. Both boys were often in trouble for their aggressive, and in Stepan's case, sometimes underhanded behavior, but few of the other boys were willing to antagonize Stepan just to help Darius, who had no status at all even if his father was Dedicated.

"Just what did you see, Paicis?"

"Darius's arrow hit first," the slender blond boy answered from the back of his dark brown pony. "At least, the arrow that went into the chest hit first. The lion was snarling, and when the arrow hit he opened his mouth, and the second arrow went into it. They were very close together, but I'm sure the chest arrow was first."

"Thank you," said Redwolf. "Is that what the rest of you saw?"

Some still said they were not sure, but three of the other boys agreed that they had seen the lion's mouth open when the arrow hit its chest.

"Then the pelt belongs to Darius," decided Redwolf. "His arrow hit first, according to the only witnesses who are sure what they saw. Our custom is to give credit for a kill to the man whose killing arrow hits first, not," he said pointedly to Stepan, who was about to protest, "by which shot killed the animal, since most of the time that is impossible to determine."

"You have no right to make that decision!" objected Stepan. "You aren't the chief, or the council! And I'll remember *you*," he said to Paicis meaningly.

"That *is* enough, Stepan!" said Yashihar with finality. "Redwolf has done a fair job of finding the facts and making a decision in your dispute, and I will lend him the authority necessary to make it official. I will also report your actions, including the threat you just made to a younger boy, to your father and the rest of the council. It is not at all the proper way to behave, and there will be consequences."

The horse master sent one of the other boys to fetch Darius's mother to skin out the lion. He knew the youngster would not want to leave his prize; even a poor pelt such as this would be welcome in his mother's tent, and the killing of the big cat in itself would give the boy some stature. Redwolf watched a clearly disgruntled Stepan ride away, then remounted his mare and looked down at the dead cub. It was so thin. In the last two years the clan's hunters had about wiped out the game in this area; probably the starving lions had been forced to attack the livestock, even though it was guarded. He hoped the warriors' raid would go well; the clan needed to move on to fresh territory. Then he shrugged, thanked his father's friend Yashihar, and rode after his peers, back to the practice field. Clan warriors, especially the Dedicated, were unbeatable. The raids always went well.

Chapter 6

A solemn procession, no less significant for its shortness,
accompanied the naked body of Ester's grandmother to the top of the
holy hill, where it was gently laid among those of her neighbors and
kin, many well on the way back to the Mother already. The black
feathered vultures with their ugly wrinkled red heads and great
hooked beaks had flown reluctantly away at the humans' approach,
and now were circling like a restless cloud high overhead.

Ester's mother, wearing her formal priestess' dress and headdress
and all her jewelry, led the prayers for the dead, thanking the
Goddess for the grandmother's long life and returning her body to the
earth, her spirit to the deity's care. There were so few voices that the
responses seemed to disappear on the breeze.

The moment the ceremony was done Wilam, who had been
watching the sky more than his partner, said, "We must go, Mariana.
Anyone who sees those birds circling will know they have been
disturbed. Some of the barbarians may come to investigate. We need
to leave and let the scavengers get back to it!"

"An observer is as likely to think they were disturbed by a lion or
wolves as by people," said his father-in-law. "There is no reason for
anyone else to come to this place." He was having trouble leaving his
mate of more than forty summers alone with the rest of the dead,
though he knew the important part, her spirit, was already with the
Mother and would not return until it was time for her to be born
again.

"We will go, my husband," said Ester's mother, forestalling an argument. "There are plans to be made. We cannot stay here; already we have stripped the nearest land of most of the wild edibles. We need to be where there is fresh water and an adequate supply of food that can be easily collected after dark and eaten, if need be, without cooking."

They returned to the sacred cave, more sacred now because so many of their people had died there. They were only two women, two men and three children; Milli, who had five summers, Josan, seven, and Ester, eight. They sat in a circle and passed their lone water skin around. Ester's grandfather thought they should go back to the town. There might still be food in the storehouse.

"We dare not go there," said Wilam. "The barbarians will set up their camp somewhere fairly nearby so that they can use the grain and dried fruit and wine in the storehouse: everything we have saved for the winter ahead. If the tales of those refugees from the North are true, the barbarians will stay until the stores have run out, maybe a year, but then they will move on. If we can remain hidden until they have left, we can have our homes back. Let's hope some of our friends and neighbors have also managed to elude them, and can continue to do so!

"They are supposed to be notable hunters," interjected Natali, mother of Milli and Josan. "Won't they find us no matter where we hide, even if we only go out to forage at night?"

"I think we need to find somewhere to stay that will have many old traces of people, so that ours will be less noticeable," said Mariana. "We will need the Goddess' protection for sure if we are to avoid their notice for a year or more. It will not help to go further away from the town; their hunters will undoubtedly scour the hills and valleys for game." She nodded to Natali. "They would be too likely to find traces of us, and hunt us down. At the same time, if they think they have found all of us, perhaps they will not be looking close to our homes any more. It is much easier to avoid notice if you are not expected to be in a certain place. They will undoubtedly come to the storehouse, and maybe even to the communal gardens, but they will not hunt near the town because they would not expect to find game there. Since every report of them indicates that they never travel or fight at night, keeping strictly to their own camps when it is dark, we should be able to move around safely between dusk and dawn.

"There is a farmstead a half mile north of the town," she went on. "You know it, Father. There is a good spring there, with a pool among some rocks right near the barn. The house was burned because all the family that lived there died of a fever several years ago, but the barn is still standing. A neighbor of ours keeps - kept - his pigs there. The gardens have been maintained, too. The land is rich and productive in that valley. I think we could hide in the barn if the barbarians have not destroyed it. Nothing is stored there; the grain and vegetables that have already been harvested went to the storehouse in town. But the gardens should still have most of the winter vegetables: onions and cabbages and turnips - oh, many things we could eat. There are fruit trees and olive trees nearby, too. If the pigs are still there…

"Won't the barbarians have taken the pigs?" asked Natali.

"It is said they do not eat pigs or chickens," said Wilam, "that instead they avoid the animals. If it is true, that may be the saving of us. I know that farm, Mariana. It may just be close enough to the town that they will believe no one would hide there. We will have to be very careful to stay out of sight during daylight, and to leave as little trace as possible of our activities. No hunting, and no traps or snares. No obvious tending of the gardens, and we will have to take care to cover any sign we leave while harvesting what is left in them. Still, I think it might work. It seems like our best chance."

Moving that night with an extreme caution engendered by the knowledge that discovery meant death, they made their way back to the town. Circling it, noting that most of the fortifications and houses had been burned, but the storehouse was still standing, they continued north until they came to the farm they were seeking. They found two dead guard dogs, undoubtedly trained to keep predators away from the livestock, at the edge of the farmyard. They were already partly eaten, probably by the hogs, who would eat anything animal or vegetable. The dogs must have come running to greet the wrong people.

The barn was a ruin. It had been burned, but the arsonists were apparently careless, having found no one there. The fire had done damage only to the end near the road; the roof and rafters had collapsed into the interior. The other end was still standing. The pigs sheltered there at night, entering through a half-open door that hung drunkenly on warped leather hinges, and the chickens roosted in the rafters. There were at least 20 pigs; the season for killing pigs had not yet arrived. There were a good many chickens, too, enough to provide more eggs than the little band of refugees could possibly eat, and meat in the winter when the egg-laying tapered off. The gardens, fenced with slim logs stacked waist high to keep the pigs out, were apparently untouched, with rows and rows of onions, carrots, turnips, kale and other cool weather vegetables. If they decided to stay here, they would not lack for food.

The refugees hid in the barn the following day. That night they set about making it more livable, using materials from the ruined end to deny the hogs access to a corner large enough for them all, grateful that pigs were neat creatures who did not soil their sleeping quarters. They did not dare make any alterations that would show on the outside, not even to close the cracks between boards or patch the leaky roof, so the hogs would be welcome companions as the months got colder. Their body heat would help keep the very drafty barn warm.

The problem of bodily waste had Mariana and Wilam worried. Whether they used just one spot or tried to scatter it over a wide area, even if they made a point of going into the nearby woods, they feared that the waste from this many humans would eventually give them away. In the town they had had a drainage system; rain or wastewater from the cisterns washed the offal down open sewers into a nearby swamp, which seemed able to deal with it nicely. There was no swamp near the farm.

Ester's grandfather came up with the answer. He had once visited a village where the people had little houses in which they deposited solid waste, with pits dug under them. When the pits filled up, they were covered with a couple of feet of earth, and the little houses were picked up and shifted until they were above a newly dug pit. The refugees could not build a little house, of course. He suggested that they dig a small pit, as deep as they could, next to the ruined end of the barn, and cover it with some partially burned beams placed haphazardly as if they had fallen there, with spaces between them that opened into the pit. They could put soil from the many pig wallows in as needed to cover the waste and disguise any human odor. The pig wallows were well dug up already, and were often used, so removal of some soil from them would not be noticeable. If their first pit filled up they could dig another.

The refugees had no proper tools for digging. They had a couple of small pots for cooking which the women had had with them in the cave, but they had only their knives for tools. Everyone knew how important it was to take care of those; they could not get any more. The knives would not be used for digging.

"Tonight I will go into the town to the storehouse," Wilam said finally. He held up a hand to stay his wife's protests. "We cannot dig a pit with our hands, and we need the pit. I will be very careful. It is unlikely that there will be guards; these barbarians are too afraid of our ghosts. We need tools, if they have left any behind, and some grain would be very welcome, too. We are safe, I think, with small cooking fires well screened, lit only inside during the middle of the night. We will have to gather only dead wood from the forest, and take care that we leave some to hide the fact that we are taking it, so I don't think we can have fires often. Nights with bad weather would probably be best."

He headed out about two hands after dark. The half moon dodged in and out of scattered clouds, providing all the light he would need. The children were asleep, but the adults saw him off, with a kiss from Mariana and murmurs of 'the Goddess be with you' and 'may the Mother guard and guide you' following him.

He returned a couple of hands later saying that, except for having been momentarily scared silly by one of the storehouse cats, his trip was uneventful. He brought a large sack of barley and another of rye, tied together with one end of a good length of hemp rope and slung across his shoulders. In his hands he had two bronze shovels with wooden handles, a deer horn garden trowel, and a large, badly dented bronze kettle. In the roomy side pocket of his tunic he had a treasure: a linen bag waterproofed with beeswax and containing at least two pounds of salt! He apologized because these things were all that he could carry.

Wilam regretfully reported that he had found no sign that any of the rest of their people had survived. They dug their latrine in what was left of that night. Over the next few days they settled in to their new, nocturnal routine. They were lucky no one came by for a while because it took repeated warnings before the children could be trusted to remember that they couldn't just run outside any time they wanted. The refugees would wait out the barbarians.

Chapter 7

Ahna's fourteenth summer was well along toward fall, busy with further learning of healing herbs and techniques, the birthing and care of children and animals, and even some lessons in how to please a man when her comfortable routine abruptly ended. The Lion clan had moved after the successful raid the previous fall, and was now camped near a little river, two miles upstream from the remains of the destroyed town. The community had been rich, yielding a treasure trove of cloth and household goods and animals to add to their herds, a few lithe, healthy, dark-haired young women to be taken as concubines, and great stores of grain, pickled vegetables, honey, dried fruits, and wine and beer.

There were now no Others to plant the fields and orchards anew, or to tend the hives and vineyards. But the gardens, though weedy and beginning to revert to the wild, still produced some vegetables, abundant fruit and many useful herbs. The concubines knew how to get honey from the bee hives, how to make beer from the hops, and when to harvest other perennial crops that, though untended, were still producing. The wide pastures along the river bottom were not yet overgrazed. There were stores of food and drink enough remaining that the council voted to stay here after winter blossomed into spring, and on into the summer, and now had decided to spend a second winter here as well.

One late summer morning the women returned from collecting plant materials to set out the midday meal for their men. As they served the food all the talk was of the racing that was planned during the annual horse fair to be held later that ten-day. Ahna was determined to run her beloved filly, Firefly, now four years old.

Jaromir, having three healthy sons born before her, had been charmed by his only daughter from the start. When she insisted on learning to ride like her older brothers although she was no more than two summers beyond first talking, he laughingly presented her with a shaggy little mare, then watched in amazement while she managed to pull herself up onto the animal's back. The mare proved to be one of those who look after fools and small children, and the child herself cared nothing for the inevitable tumbles, but only for the freedom that riding bestowed, further impressing her father. Before many years passed Ahna graduated to mounts as spirited and courageous as herself, and she was allowed to ride with her brothers and their friends well beyond the age when most girls were confined to the tents and female company.

When she was ten her father gave Ahna a foal to raise and train for her own, as he had each of his sons before her. The filly was out of one of his best war mares, a typical strong, low-to-the-ground steppe horse, and by a stallion the men had taken from a conquered town, a fine-headed, arch-necked bay horse with bright intelligent eyes, long legs and a thin coat; the Horse Master said he had come from far to the South.

When the stallion's first few foals arrived, though, Jaromir did not like them, thinking they were weak and spindly. He gelded the stud, though now he was beginning to think that had been a serious mistake. The double handful of 'weak' foals grew into long-legged, long-striding, exceptionally good-tempered horses that were very strong and agile, easy keepers with amazing stamina and even more amazing speed. Firefly had grown up taller than the steppe horses if somewhat slimmer, mostly clean-legged where they were shaggy, a light-stepping, dish-faced beauty with a burnished fox-colored coat, shiny black mane, tail and stockings, a small white star on her forehead and a pink snip between her nostrils. Ahna had trained her entirely on her own; the young mare followed her around like a dog.

Ahna's love for her horse had a lot to do with her success at her lessons. She learned to work well because her mother would make her do things over if they were not done to the best of her present ability. She learned to work rapidly because she wanted as much time as possible when her chores were done to ride, usually with one or more of her brothers and their friends, but sometimes alone, either in the fields and meadows or up across the hills that surrounded whatever place they happened to be camped that particular season.

Ahna's pride in her filly was justified. Firefly was fast, had already beaten all her brothers' and their friends horses in the impromptu races they often held on sunny afternoons. When their trips out into the surrounding countryside became cross-country competitions, she and her horse arrived home first, no matter how long the agreed-upon course. Girls just didn't ride in the formal racing, but what other girls didn't do held little interest for Ahna where Firefly was concerned.

Jaromir and his sons were seated on the luxurious rugs that covered the floor of their main tent, having finished their meal, and the women were present because they, too, would have preparations to make for the holiday, though their actual participation was normally peripheral and brief, when Ahna broached the subject. At first her father said, unequivocally,

"No. Your mare may only race if one of your brothers rides her. All the older ones are fostered out, Redwolf has his own colt to ride, and Ahndru is too young, so put it out of your mind."

"*I* will ride her!" declared Ahna mutinously. "She is my horse, and she will take care of me." Vladia's brows snapped together in sudden concern. She looked a warning at her daughter, but Ahna had no fear of her father. She ignored the look.

"I will be entering Dark Streak, of course," interjected Redwolf. Her next brother was in his thirteenth summer now, but he looked older, tall and already broad shouldered, despite the freckles that still peppered his skin. His horse was also four, one of the crossbreds like Ahna's, a fiery nearly black colt, no taller than the more solidly built steppe horses but with a proud carriage of his heavily crested neck and remarkable quickness and stamina. "I can look after her, too." He smiled at his sister, his closest sibling, whom he treated as a pal.

"I'll be there, too" said Moshel, the oldest of the three young men from other clans that were fostered with them and the only one who lived in Vladia's tent, enjoying his seventeenth summer, a little shorter than Ahna but considerably broader, blond, blue-eyed and very good-natured. "I'm doing extra chores every day so I can take the time to participate. My Fleetfoot lives up to his name and I want to show all the visitors what kind of horses we breed at home. Ahna will be all right."

They were both used to riding everywhere in the area surrounding the camp with their sister, did not really think of her as a girl, and did not realize what an unusual, even provocative thing it would be for her to race against strange young men. But her father knew. Jaromir opened his mouth to voice his final refusal, and his wife spoke softly.

"It will be her only opportunity to show what her mare can do," Vladia said. "Ahna is getting too old to ride with the boys and young men. Soon you must be seeking a match for her." She, too, smiled at her daughter, who had started forward in dismay at the part about a 'match,' but sat back again without speaking as she met her mother's eyes. "Her husband will expect her to tend to household duties rather than spending time with horses," Vladia continued. "She has mastered all her lessons; she will be an excellent wife."

"That doesn't surprise me," commented Jaromir. "You are her mother."

Vladia blushed faintly at her husband's steady appraisal. Compliments for women were not common.

"Thank you," she said.

Jaromir glanced at Ahna thoughtfully. He was very fond of her and he knew how much she wanted to race that really quite remarkable young mare. What's more, everyone knew the horse was of his breeding; if she did well the value of his stock would increase.

"All right," he said. "You may ride her in the races, just this one time." Ahna's lovely face lit up, and again she opened her mouth. "But," her father admonished, "you must ride her over to the horse fair, you must stay with your brothers, and you must not dismount to mingle with the young men, not even if you win. I expect you to come straight back to the tents after your last race, no matter which heat it is. These affairs get rowdy when the racing is over." He looked at Moshel and Redwolf. "I do expect you to look after her, and at least one of you is to escort her home afterward." They both nodded.

Ahna tried to control her triumphant smile. "Thank you, Father," she said. "Thank you! I will obey."

Chapter 8

At midmorning on fair day, their chores all finished, their horses groomed until they gleamed and wearing freshly washed saddle clothes and newly cleaned and oiled equipment, and themselves decked out in festive fashion, the three young people set off for the long level field between low hills near the river where the races were to be held, perhaps a mile from the tents. The racing hadn't started when Ahna and her escort came over the rise and rode down into the open meadow. Low, rocky hills surrounded the field, affording a good view of the course. When the clan arrived they had been covered with olive groves and vineyards. Much of the wood had been hauled over to the camp for fuel, but there were still some surviving trees scattered across the slopes, with grass and stumps between, where spectators and their horses could find comfortable spots from which to watch the racing. The course itself was being laid out on an extensive flat area where the sheep and cattle had been grazing for a moon or more, resulting in a smooth expanse of short turf. The herds had been moved elsewhere a day or two earlier, and showers the previous night had somewhat softened the summer-hard ground. The meadow was perhaps two hundred paces across and nearly a thousand paces long, with only slight undulations that would not unbalance a speeding horse or interrupt his stride: the perfect place for racing.

The younger men and older boys were out on the course demonstrating their riding skills, bouncing off and back on running horses, standing up on a galloping back, swinging down from the saddle to pick an object from the ground as they passed it at full

stride, trying to unseat one another, putting their horses through mock
battle maneuvers. All were wearing bright clothes that usually
included at least one clan color. Many had shirts with bold patterns,
or sleeves of a contrasting color, or some other distinguishing feature
that would make it easy for their friends to pick them out in the
crowded fields. Most of the horses were bays or browns, with a
generous smattering of feral striped duns whose coloring harked back
to their wild ancestors, native to the clans' original home. There were
a few chestnuts, grays, and other colors that, like Ahna's filly and
Redwolf's colt, indicated blood from horses not of the arid northern
steppes.

The horse masters on their favorite mounts, referees for the
proceedings and informal but all-powerful police for the day, wore
black and white shirts, or at least a black and white armband, and
had black and white ribbons fastened to their horses' saddles as
marks of their office. Since it was the speed and stamina of the horses
that was being tested on this day and not riding ability, excessive
roughness, such as trying to unbalance or trip another's mount or to
push a competitor off his horse, would get a rider disqualified if a
referee saw it done. Those activities were among the milder practices
in war games, but were considered unsporting in the more formal
races.

Dotted over the length and breadth of the meadow, the horse
masters inspected the placement of the posts that defined the inside
of the course. They were ensuring the alignment, to make the long
sides of the course absolutely straight and the turns at the ends
smoothly curved. There was nothing between the markers to prevent
a rider taking a short-cut and reducing the distance his horse had to
run except the rules; the referees would be watching, and any
contestant that passed inside of a post at any point on the course
during a race would be disqualified.

It looked to Ahna and her brothers as if the preparations were
almost complete. The boys explained that each heat would be twice
around the field, nearly three miles in total distance. There were three
heats, with most of the horses entered being eliminated in the first
two. That meant the best horses had to race a total of nine miles

during the afternoon. Speed, especially athletic quickness, in their horses was very important to the clans, but fitness and stamina were equally important; these races tested both.

Many hundreds of horses already occupied the meadow, including large contingents from several other clans who had been invited to the racing. They had come in the night before to temporary bivouacs nearby or had ridden out from their home camps early that morning to arrive in time. There was already much horse-trading going on in the infield. Little clumps of colorfully clothed men examining and trying horses, making deals, and leading or riding their new acquisitions could be seen everywhere. The Lion clan was famous for the quality of their horses.

Surveying the lively scene, the new arrivals felt their own excitement mount.

Ahruset spotted them as they rode down into the meadow. He turned his blaze-faced bay gelding out of a melee of boys showing off their horses, approaching his friend with a curious look for Ahna. "What's your sister doing here?" he demanded, but before they could answer a warning horn sounded. The horse masters were satisfied with the course and were calling for the contestants to make up their sets. The first heat was about to start. Ahruset went quickly back to his chosen group, shrugging philosophically, perhaps harboring some secret relief since he knew how fast Dark Streak could run, when Redwolf refused his invitation to join them.

Only the horses that came first, second and third in the preliminary races were eligible for the semifinals, so the trick for the first heat was to get yourself into a field of horses that you were reasonably certain you could beat. Ahna was not familiar with any of the jockeying involved, but Moshel quietly pointed out another group of some twenty teenage warriors who were dancing their horses around at one side of the throng. "You should be able to beat most of that lot handily, and many of them are racing for the first time, too," he said. "Tell the referee you want to be placed with them."

Ahna and Redwolf approached Horse Master Yashihar, who was riding among the nearby groups organizing and instructing them. His black and white shirt with the red ribbons that said he was the ultimate authority for the day, and his black riding leathers made a strong contrast with his cream-colored, almost white gelding and his own grizzled dark blonde hair, clubbed in back to be out of the way. He gave Ahna a searching look when she said she would ride in the set Moshel had pointed out.

"Does your father know you are racing?" he asked skeptically.

"Yes, he gave me permission," she answered. Yashihar looked to Jaromir's son for confirmation, and at his nod said only, "All right, but stay out of trouble! Redwolf, I think you should be in the same set with your sister in this first heat." The young man started to object; staying with her meant he would have to come in second or third to advance. He knew Dark Streak could not beat Firefly. Then he remembered his promise to his father and nodded resignedly.

"Good," said the horse master. "Your set will be the seventh to go." He moved on to other competitors.

The brother and sister rode up to their chosen group. Several of the boys greeted Redwolf by name, but no one said hello to Ahna, although she knew some of them. "Ha," sneered a brown-haired, stocky young man wearing a forest green and dark brown shirt with yellow sleeves that proclaimed him a member of the Wood Buffalo clan, and mounted on a sturdy buckskin with well-muscled quarters and a wall eye. "Here's one we won't have any trouble beating. What are you doing with that skinny girl and the skinny mare, Red?"

Redwolf deliberately turned Dark Streak away, greeting a friend as if he had not heard the question and thereby dishonoring the stranger, who was starting to ride after him in anger when another boy grabbed his wide sleeve to stop him.

"That's our chief's son," the Lion clan youth explained, "and his sister. Don't start anything, Khaleno, or you won't be allowed to race. I just wish they weren't in our set. That 'skinny mare' is the fastest animal in our herds!"

"Well, fastest doesn't always win," mused the young Wood Buffalo warrior. His face acquired a knowing grin. "She might not even make it all the way around."

His informant looked alarmed. "If you try to stop her, you will be disqualified." He started to back his brown gelding away from

Khaleno, glancing around to locate the horse masters. "The whole set might be disqualified if the referees think we planned something against her."

"Don't worry," the other assured him, changing his approach. "I only meant that she looks like a lightweight. I don't think she can go the distance." He continued to stare at Firefly thoughtfully.

Before long a war-horn sounded the 'get ready' again. The referees spread out around the course on their horses, inside the marker posts, where they could keep a close eye on things. The value of a horse would go up or down depending on its performance. There was enough at stake both in material terms and in the garnering of prestige to encourage some riders to cheat if they thought they could get away with it.

A procession of priests in dark bronze robes embroidered with black and gold glided across the course to the starting post, singing a round chant to invoke the Gods' blessings on the horses and riders. They placed two ceremonial yard sticks fluttering with bronze, black and gold ribbons next to the starting post as a symbol of the favor of the Gods and declared the races begun. Then the starter, a lean, sandy-haired horse master of middle years mounted on a tall black bay with a striking white blaze that emphasized his regrettably prominent nose, rode forward and called the first set to warm up.

The horses stepped out onto the course and trotted or cantered down the track to the turn, a matter of perhaps three quarters of a mile; the finish post, which was also the starting post and was painted bright red, was more than half way down that side to allow room for a long straightaway in which the horses could contest the final part of each race. Then they galloped back and lined up across the course beyond the red post. The horses danced on tight reins. There were no 'false starts' allowed. If a horse passed the marker before the starting referee said, "go," it was disqualified.

The rest of the contestants were arranged around the large oval on the inside of the course in their sets, in the order that they would race, well back from the white course markers. There would be twenty-five preliminary races with between twenty and thirty horses in each field. The first three horses in each race would be grouped together by the referees into five fields for the second heat. Only the first three horses from each of those contests could run in the final race to determine the champion. Just getting to the finals meant increased value for every horse that made it and prestige for the breeders and owners; the championship itself was a prize coveted by all and attained by only one at any given horse fair.

There were also a few spectators watching from under the trees on the surrounding hills, but most of the men present were either competing or acting as support crew for someone who was competing. The crowd of participants would diminish and the crowd of spectators grow as horses were eliminated. The rest of the men of the clan were still attending to other duties; they would come to watch the later, better heats. The women from all the attending clans would come in the mid-afternoon, with specially prepared food and drink, and often stayed to watch the final races before going back to their evening duties.

"It's an advantage to be in one of the earlier sets," Redwolf said to Ahna. "If we advance there will be time to rest the horses before the second heat starts. We will move around as the heat progresses; we'll see the sets immediately ahead of us start."

Ahna suddenly thought of something. "Firefly will need water, maybe even a bath, after the first heat! How will we manage that?"

"We'll go to the river," said Redwolf. "You can let her drink small quantities frequently if she is to race again. We can sponge her off and walk her if necessary. That's what we did last year when Dylezo got third prize with Deer Catcher."

"But I am not supposed to get off her!" Ahna's nerves, now that she was actually here and going to race, were making small obstacles loom like mountains.

"We'll deal with that," her brother soothed. "We can sponge her off with you on her if we must. You don't take up much room, and you are so light the weight will not bother her. She will probably feel safer and be more relaxed in all this crowd if you do stay on her. But you need to relax, too. If you get upset, so will she, and that will use up energy she needs for running!"

Ahna deliberately took several slow, deep breaths. Redwolf was right. Her filly knew her very well and was tuned to her moods. If Ahna accepted all this as a matter of course so would Firefly.

"You're right," she acknowledged, "and now I'm all right."

"That's the way," he approved.

The early races were run, their progress around the track traceable by the sound of yelling from both the riders and the infield crowd. They passed Ahna's position on the lower back corner, a melee of galloping horses with their brightly dressed riders crouched over their manes urging them on. The second time around the sets were more strung out, with five to eight horses still in contention ahead of the rest. The beaten riders were still galloping, but sitting back on their horses, waving their arms and yelling even louder for the sheer fun of it. The crowd near the finish could be heard cheering, too. Betting was informal and very common, mostly among friends and acquaintances of the riders, at least until the final race, when it often became more general and more serious. They bet jewelry, clothing, saddles and other gear, sometimes even leather armor and weapons, though most refused to part with these. It was not uncommon to bet the horses themselves. Many riders would have new mounts when this day ended.

Moshel rode up to them as a roar signaling the start of the fourth set went up, and they moved up around the corner. Their foster-brother was in the tenth set, so Ahna and Redwolf would be going before him. Ahna greeted his familiar face with relief.

Moshel beckoned to Ahna and rode a little away from the group. Redwolf went, too. "I thought you might like some pointers," he said quietly when they could not be overheard. "The men are all talking about you racing in this set. They know your filly is fast, but they also know you are inexperienced. Most of them think you will let her use herself too hard at the beginning and then she'll have no energy left for the end of the race."

"I know I need to save her speed," answered Ahna, "but I'm not sure how to go about it."

"I would let her start fast at first," Moshel suggested. "Her quickness should get you a spot near the front of the field and avoid the crowding and jostling at the start. Then take her in hand a little. Settle her into a pace that you know she can carry easily for three miles: a strong, but not really fast, gallop. Some of the other riders will try to get you to go too fast early. Ignore them even if they seem to be getting a long way ahead of you. They will tire and come back to you. The real threat will be from the horses with more stamina, and they will be either right with you or just behind you.

"Georha is an experienced race rider, the lean fellow in tan and green with that short-backed light brown mare over there, and he will be seriously trying to win. He will make his bid late in the race. When he tries to pass you go with him." Ahna studied the mare he pointed out, plain and somewhat taller than most of the others, though not as long-legged as Firefly, and the blond young man who stood quietly beside her, not joining in the horseplay around him. She remembered seeing him follow them into the set.

"I don't see much in this field that you can't beat easily," Moshel went on, glancing around, "so keep Firefly as relaxed as you can, and don't give her the signal to really run until you come around the last turn and see the finish. Save her speed and energy for the semifinal heat. There will be a lot better horses in that set." He looked around.

"Do you know that fellow on the chunky buckskin?" he asked. "He is staring at you."

"He is a stranger," said Redwolf, "from the Wood Buffalo. He insulted Ahna and Firefly when we arrived."

"That's just bravado," said Moshel, "but I don't like the way he keeps studying you. Look out for him. Don't stay too near the inside markers even though that is the shortest way around. If a solid horse like that bumped you in the right spot he could push Firefly off the course, and you would be disqualified."

"Wouldn't he be disqualified, too?" Ahna asked.

"Probably not just for bumping you if he stayed in bounds. There's plenty of contact out there, especially in these crowded sets. No one takes it seriously unless it's an obvious attempt to stop a horse or unseat a rider. If he harasses you, move away from him and get in between some other horses."

Ahna looked over at the stranger again, and as quickly looked away. He was watching, and when he saw her glance at him he made a quick, emphatic thumbs-down gesture. She felt a little shiver of fear, but immediately suppressed it. She would trust Firefly to take care of her.

Their group moved up again. Only three more before them. They would be able to watch the fifth and sixth sets start, and to see those races finish. Firefly danced a few steps when the fourth set raced by on their first trip around the field. Ahna patted her neck soothingly. "We'll be going soon enough," she whispered. "Save it for the race." The filly settled to her touch.

That set came back around, the three horses in the lead crossing the finish line in a gallop nearly side by side some distance ahead of the rest, whose riders came in yelling and whooping and acting as if they had won. The onlookers cheered; apparently favorites were still winning. The leaders were duly acknowledged, being given red (first), blue (second), and yellow (third) ribbons on yard sticks by the starter, and galloping back past the winning post holding them aloft. The ribbons were their advertisements that their horses had won and their tickets into the semi final heat. They would push the yard sticks into the ground nearby to show their standing while they cooled out, washed, and grazed their horses between heats, and fasten the ribbons to their saddles when they entered the next heat. The fifth set lined up and were sent off, and now the riders with Ahna's group moved to the side of the track where they could see the finish as the group ahead of them took their final waiting place on the infield near the starting post.

Moshel moved closer to Ahna, who was studying the horses in the fifth set as they milled about on the track before their start.

"Watch the way the different riders handle their horses," he said. "They are all afraid of getting off before the starter says, 'go,' and being disqualified. The horses know they are going to race and are very eager. If they are properly trained they will not start before their riders give them the signal, but some of the riders do not trust them." Ahna indicated an elegant liver chestnut with a splash of white on his forehead. He was being held on such a tight rein that his neck was bowed and his chin right in against his chest, and still he danced, mostly sideways.

"Yes," Moshel agreed. "If you want your horse to dance and plunge, there's the best way to go about it. His rider has his legs tight in his sides pushing him forward, and the reins tight on the bit in his mouth holding him back. He thinks he is creating an explosion, that he will get a quick start when he releases the reins, but he has already told the horse to 'go,' and now is preventing him from responding. When he does give the signal, the additional push of his legs will have no immediacy, and all the release of the reins will do is unbalance the horse onto his forehand. It will take him a moment to get his feet back under him and get started. He will be left behind." Ahna nodded.

"Keep your horse balanced on all four feet with her quarters well under her. A horse's instinct is to leap away if startled. The starter's 'GO' and the signal to go from your heels will 'startle' her. Your hands should move forward just a little. You won't need to 'let her go' since you will not have been 'holding her back.' Keep her calm and ready by keeping contact with her mouth, but on the lightest rein you can while she is standing still."

Ahna nodded, patting her filly's neck again. At that moment the starter called "GO," and the horses on the track plunged forward in a line. Sure enough, the chestnut tripped and nearly went down as he tried to leap forward. Several of the other horses also made awkward starts and were well behind the leaders as they raced away.

"He did stumble! He almost fell," observed Ahna sympathetically.

"Of course he did, and his owner will probably blame the colt's 'clumsiness', not his own lack of riding skill. It is all really unnecessary, too, since this race is so long that the only purpose of getting off to a fast start is to get a good position in the field. A horse could start flatfooted, be a long way behind and still have plenty of time to make up the lost ground in a race of this distance."

"The only other thing we want to tell you is that your filly will continue to rely on you for balance while she is running," Moshel concluded. "You already have learned, in the races you have had with us, to keep your weight forward and on your knees, not on her back. In a long race like this it is also important that Firefly be able to 'take a hold' on you, to lean just a little on the brace of your hands. You can even cross the reins on the back of her neck. It will help her gallop more smoothly, and she will not tire as easily as she would if you left the reins loose. Balance is everything."

Ahna looked at her foster brother. "This is so much more complicated than I thought it could be!" she commented.

He laughed. "It is different from racing with your brothers near the tents. You've done a great job with Firefly. You will both do very well today."

Ahna blushed and looked down, thanking him. He watched her watch the other riders and their horses. It made him a little sad to think she would soon be married off and gone. He hoped her husband would not try to break her spirit. Some men just did not understand that you had to handle a girl with the same consideration that you gave your horses. At least, that's what his dad and brothers said and he believed it was true. He himself wouldn't be married until next summer, so he hadn't had much opportunity to put the idea into practice yet.

The sixth set ran their race with only a slight delay when four of the horses got in too tight on the home turn, two nearly falling and one losing his rider and his bridle, then going on to 'win' the race before cavorting all around the field, playing hard to catch. They finally got him,but one of the other horses involved in the tangle managed to pass the winning post second of the horses with riders, so the referees had to confer before the ribbons were awarded. They determined that the mix-up was caused by nothing more sinister than some minor reckless riding and let the results stand.

"Good Luck," called Moshel as Ahna and Redwolf rode out onto the track with the rest of their set. Other voices were making the same wish to other riders, and Ahna heard her name called a few more times, to her surprise. They jogged down the track to loosen their mounts up, then galloped back to line up for their race.

Chapter 9

Wilam looked out through the cracks in the side of the barn. It was full daylight, so he did not dare go out, but there was another pig down near the gate to the garden. Three had died in the last few days. He felt a little twinge of concern. The family who had farmed the land for generations had died of a fever, every one, several years ago. That was why the house had been burned and never rebuilt. Mariana was quite sure that people could not catch fever from animals, but they had dragged the carcasses as far into the woods as they could. It had been a major effort where the old sow was concerned; she weighed as much as three or four big men.

They had had a fair winter. It was strange at first to live like nocturnal animals, but now it was habit. There had been no shortage of food, between the chickens and pigs, the garden and the warehouse of grain in the town. In the spring two sows had farrowed. They had enjoyed piglet until the remaining ones had grown too big, putting the bones and other inedible parts in their waste pit, leaving no evidence that might give them away. They could not eat pork now, though. It was still too warm to slaughter anything they could not eat up at once, since it would have been far too dangerous to try to smoke the meat.

The summer had been harder. They could do little gardening without giving themselves away and it was galling to be confined to one end of the barn during the warm days, especially for the children. The heat of summer made the proximity of the animals a penance. The pigs' ubiquitous wallows and the chickens' even less avoidable droppings made the air noisome. On really hot days it could be difficult to breath in the barn, but there was no escape. They tried cleaning the chicken poop up with the shovels and putting it, too, into the waste pit. The improvement was so slight it hadn't seemed worth the effort, and now they would soon have to dig another. Wilam's father-in-law had been steadily losing strength; if truth be told, they all were, but it was more evident in the old man.

They had endured, believing that the nomads would depart with the arrival of fall and they could go back to a more normal way of life. Now it was fall, albeit early yet, and their deadly neighbors showed no sign of pulling up the tent stakes. In the summer the barbarians had held some kind of games, fighting games, it looked like, in a large level field across the road from the farmstead. They had come every day for a moon. No one had gotten any sleep, so worried were they that something would make the warriors suspicious, or that one of them would decide to investigate the derelict structure. Wilam thought then that if one did come they would have to silence the visitor in whatever way they could, then leave their refuge before he was missed. Remarkably, none of the barbarians had come near them. They even went into the woods on the far side of the field to relieve themselves. He did not realize that it was the presence of the pigs and chickens, both animals that had been declared unclean by the nomads' holy ones, that kept his little band of refugees safe.

Still, the fighting practice made the refugees hope that the barbarians were soon going to move to some other unfortunate town, hopefully somewhere far away. It didn't happen. Now at least the training, or whatever it was, was finished. No more warriors came. Instead it was women who rode by on the road, fetching grain from the more than half empty storehouse. It was harder and harder to find a place from which to take grain without it being missed. The barbarians were neat, often leaving an even row at the front of the stash from which the removal of just one bag would create an all too obvious gap.

One day in midsummer Wilam had seen his niece by marriage, Sara, with a group of the passing women. It had taken every ounce of restraint he had not to call out to her, so glad was he to see another of their people alive. It was a good thing that Mariana did not see her, or, the Goddess prevent it, Ester! He hadn't mentioned it. The news would probably generate more sorrow than joy. Sara was apparently not restrained or confined, so at first he did not understand why she stayed with her captors. Then he realized that she could not know they were alive. She must believe that there was nowhere to run, no one to help her or hide her. He would have to find a safe way to get a message to her, to tell her they were here and would welcome her back, before the barbarians did depart.

He looked over at the garden, which had been generous with carrots, cabbages, parsnips and turnips last fall, and herbs and lettuce and kale for much of the winter, though now they were mostly gone or rotted in place, except for the perennial herbs, which had been well established and were still producing despite the weeds that threatened to swallow them. The fence was still keeping the pigs at bay; he kept it repaired, while making it look as if it was slowly falling down. The onions and lettuce had gone to seed last fall, and had sprouted all over the garden in the spring. There was still some lettuce and numerous onions, now round and firm. The green ones had been welcome additions to their stews of chicken or pork, and the mature ones would be even better. But he didn't think they could survive on onions and greens.

They had eaten more than a few chickens in the last weeks. Several of the hens sat clutches of eggs in the spring, but so many of the chicks had been taken by foxes and other predators that their flock was disappearing. There were still plenty of eggs, but they dared not eat so many of the birds themselves that the dwindling numbers would become obvious. And now the pigs were dying. If the barbarians stayed over a second winter, his little family would not fare nearly as well as they had these seasons past.

He made a prayer to the Goddess. She had protected them until now. He asked Her to provide them with resources and the patience to continue their slow vigil.

Chapter 10

Moshel calmed his own eager mount, watching the field approach the start. Several of the horses were moving restlessly, some sweating freely. Firefly was on her toes, but not dancing, and Ahna was maintaining a relaxed seat and a light hold on her horse's mouth. She was following his instructions to perfection.

"Go on back to your own set! You're hogging our viewing space," said a laughing voice beside Moshel. He looked over to see his friend Havad seated on his big-nosed bay gelding, Schnoz, a plain animal that was both a better war horse and a better race horse than anyone would think at first glance.

"You must be in the next set," he said, smiling. "Be quiet. I want to see this start." They both turned back to the field, and momentarily the milling horses and riders settled into an only slightly ragged line with Ahna and Redwolf side by side in about the middle. "Ready!" shouted the starter. "GO!" Twelve or thirteen horses leaped off their haunches, hitting full stride as their front feet found the racing surface, the rest getting off in a second, slower flight. Firefly was among the leaders. Moshel could see Ahna's gold and green scarf only a couple of horses out from the inside of the course as the field raced away from them.

"She made a good start," commented Havad. "I bet my silver-hilt knife against Mrovorin's gray two-year-old that she would win. I hope she does. I don't want to lose that knife!"

Moshel looked at him in wonder. "Well, hopefully you won't," he said finally. "That gray colt shows some promise. Why would Mrovorin bet him? Was he drunk?"

"Mrovorin admires my knife, too," Havad answered him with a laugh. "He might have had a beer or two, but I'm sure he thought he couldn't lose. All the men, are certain a girl doesn't have any chance out there!"

"Then why did you bet on her?" asked Moshel.

"I've seen Ahna working with that filly," his friend answered. "She really is fast and much tougher than she looks, and they are a team. And you have to admit she doesn't have much competition in this set. What's more, most men don't credit girls with any brains at all, but your foster-sister has a really good head on her shoulders when it comes to horses. She has to have guts, too, or she wouldn't even be here today."

"Here they come! Let's watch," said Moshel, pushing closer to the edge of the course as the sound of the approaching race swelled on the stretch of turf before them.

*   *   *

Ahna sat quietly, her weight on her knees pressed in behind her filly's shoulders, her balance forward, her hands feeling Firefly lightly mouth the bit, her calves resting snug against the filly's sides, but not pushing, not yet. Earlier she had seen the stranger on the heavily muscled buckskin lining up a couple of horses outside of her, but now she was focused on the starter and the course ahead. She took a tighter grip on a thick clump of Firefly's mane. The hardest part would be maintaining her balance and not pulling on Firefly's mouth when they made their sudden start. "Soon," said Redwolf, on her left, and at the next moment the starter yelled "Ready!" She tensed, and felt Firefly tense under her. "GO!"

The filly leaped forward on the word, as fast as any other horse in the line. Ahna didn't know whether she had signaled her or not, but they were off and neither one had lost her balance. Hooves drummed the turf and young men yelled all around her. She was glad she was near the front. There was a dangerously crowded mass of galloping horses and riders behind her, but she knew that at this speed she would soon be leaving them all in her dust. She eased Firefly fractionally, angling her toward the inside of the course to give her more room, then straightened her, letting her settle into an easy ground-covering gallop. Most of the other riders seemed to be doing the same. She realized then that Redwolf and Dark Streak were racing along inside of her, right where they had been at the start. Her brother, crouched low above his sturdy colt's withers, glanced across at her. They shared identical grins of pure joy.

As they approached the first turn several horses went past them, two or three on the outside and one between them and the inside markers. All were yelling to their horses to go, go, go, and one boy waved goodbye as they pulled ahead, calling "We'll wait for you at the finish!" We'll see you long before that, Ahna thought. They were definitely letting their horses run too fast, egging each other on, apparently forgetting that the race was twice around the course. Firefly lengthened her stride, wanting to go after the horses ahead, but Ahna snugged the reins. "Not yet," she said to her mare. "We'll catch them when it counts." As Firefly settled back into her former pace Ahna noticed that Redwolf was having more trouble with Dark Streak. The competitive colt did not want the other horses ahead of him. He was shaking his head, trying to snatch the bit; Redwolf was having to fight him to keep him at the slower pace. "Talk to him," Ahna suggested. "Distract him."

Redwolf felt foolish talking to his horse in a race, especially talking to him about going slower, but he tried it anyway. As they came out of the turn and straightened into the backstretch Redwolf shifted his weight and Dark Streak obediently switched leads, one ear flicking back. He relaxed minutely, no longer fighting for his head. There were other horses around them now, and suddenly Firefly increased her speed, fairly leaping forward. Surprised, Ahna took a moment to react, then with hands and voice brought her filly back to the pace she wanted her to maintain. A hundred strides later it happened again, and this time, amid the yells and thundering hooves, Ahna correctly associated the sound of a flat racing whip slapping against flesh with her filly's reaction. Slowing Firefly, not so easily this time, she looked back to discover the stranger on the walleyed buckskin coming up on her outside and preparing yet again to hit Firefly with his stick!

"Don't do that!" She commanded. Khaleno gave her a humorless grin. "Let's see if your skinny mare can really run!" he yelled, and slashed her horse on the tenderest place he could reach, the thin skin over her flank. This time when Firefly leaped forward Ahna let her go.

They blew past seven or eight horses racing in a loose group in the middle of the track, and were leaving them behind when she remembered what Moshel had said to do in a situation like this. As they rounded the turn into the homestretch for the first time, the entire field moved closer to the inside, and Ahna again asked Firefly to slow her pace, this time dropping back into the middle of the horses she had just passed and putting two of them between her and Khaleno's buckskin. "Well done," called a thin young man now racing beside her; she recognized Georha, the rider Moshel had said would be a good pacesetter for her. He nodded at Firefly. "She is fast! *And* kind. I hope you qualify."

Ahna smiled her thanks and concentrated on relaxing her filly, who was still strung up and wanting to bolt. No one had ever hit her before. Ahna succeeded in settling her into her former easy stride as they passed the finish for the first time. She kept glancing over at the buckskin, wondering why he was not coming into the pack after her. Then the yelling intensified, and as they ran down the backstretch for the second time she realized that Redwolf and Dark Streak were racing inside the buckskin, and that every time his rider tried to turn his attention to Ahna either Redwolf or his horse would do something to get his attention back on them. Finally the stranger let out a particularly angry yell and raised his whip as if to swing it at Redwolf, but Dark Streak seemed to pull away. Now they were entering the final turn and she had to concentrate on avoiding slowing horses, including the ones that had passed them with such enthusiasm early in the race. As they straightened into the homestretch, Georha called "Come on, Ahna, it's time to run!" Then he leaned a little farther forward, and his horse found a faster pace.

As Ahna copied him on Firefly, nudging with her heels, she realized it was a much faster pace! The nondescript brown mare was pulling away, but Firefly responded with alacrity and no sign of fatigue. She switched leads smoothly and began catching up, her strides getting longer and faster while all the other horses dropped behind them. Ahna glanced back to her left, where Redwolf and the Wood Buffalo warrior seemed to be making a race of it at last, their horses well separated and their riders concentrating on getting to the finish line first. The stranger was whipping his horse hard, but her brother crouched quiet and low on Dark Streak, urging him with hands and voice.

She and Firefly flew down the homestretch, catching Georha and his mare just before the finish. Even then Firefly, excited by her own speed, did not slacken her stride. She was many lengths ahead and nearly to the first turn again when Ahna finally got her slowed down. Georha was waiting for her when she trotted back toward the finish, admiring Firefly, who was tossing her pretty head and snorting a little as if to say, 'That was fun! Let's do it again!' He grinned his congratulations as Ahna came up to him. Then Yashihar loped up, too.

"You rode very well," he said to Ahna. "What was going on out there?"

"That... man on the buckskin kept hitting my horse with his whip!" Ahna's tone was outraged.

"Did he try to hit you?" asked the referee. "Did he try to tip you off your horse?"

"No-o..." said Ahna.

"He wanted to make her mare bolt and wear herself out," said Georha.

"I'm sure he did," said Yashihar. "There are no rules against trying to make your opponents' horses run faster, but there is still the question of what he and your brother were doing out there."

"Where did they finish?" inquired Ahna.

"It was a dead heat for third," he answered. "We will either have to let them both go on or disqualify them both."

They let them both advance. Neither boy would say anything beyond Redwolf's "I was telling him to stop bothering my sister."

Neither had interfered substantially with anyone else in the field, and although Khaleno had a blood-streaked bandage wrapped around his calf above his short boot and limped when he walked, when pressed he admitted that Redwolf had done nothing to cause it. Little sniggers began making the rounds behind his back. From what some of the other riders had seen, Dark Streak had bumped the stranger's horse more than once. Khaleno had hit Dark Streak several times with his whip, and finally when he rode in close enough to hit the black colt's face, or maybe try to bump them into the infield, Dark Streak reached over and bit him. A disgrace, to allow yourself to be bitten by an opponent's horse.

As the rest of the preliminary sets went on, Khaleno developed an anti-female argument in an attempt to get Ahna and Redwolf barred from the rest of the racing, and spent some time trying to garner support for it. He found scant sympathy. The Lion clan's men may have thought it was strange for Ahna to be racing, but she had been riding among them all of her life and they were proud of the way she handled the race, happy that she and her fast, sensible filly were their own. Her father's friends and subordinates made sure everyone knew that her racing did not portend future involvement by other women, and that indeed this was the only time she herself would be participating. Jaromir was a very popular chief, and everyone loved well-trained, courageous horses. Even among the visiting clans most of the men were inclined to cheer on his daughter and her unusual filly so long as they represented a lone exception, at least when it wasn't their favorites she was beating.

Havad's Schnoz won his set, and Moshel came second on Fleetfoot in the tenth. When Redwolf raised his brows at the blue ribbons, Moshel said quite seriously that the winner was trying too hard, while he was saving his horse's strength for the contests yet to come. Since there were still sixteen sets before the preliminaries would be over, Ahna and the young men took their beribboned yard sticks and rode more than a mile up the river, wanting to get away from where other contestants were watering and resting their animals. They walked, saving their mounts, since they had plenty of time.

Havad was effusive about Ahna's race and the consequences of his winning bet. She hoped Mrovorin wouldn't be angry at her because of the loss of his promising colt, but Havad assured her that his friend owned another fine young horse and, while chagrined at his own lack of perspicacity, was proud of Ahna and Firefly.

Moshel's friend showed them the knife he had bet, a beautiful weapon with a honed bronze blade more than two hands long and a silver hilt with an embossed hunting scene, the stag so realistic it seemed to be leaping off the knife even as the hunter's spear found its chest. Ahna examined it with interest, then pulled her own small bronze knife, a women's tool for gathering and preparing food rather than a weapon and a gift from her father, from its sheath at her waist to show him. It, too, had a silver hilt, this one worked with sheaves of grain and flowers so real they seemed to nod in the breeze, with a band of interlocking spirals around the base below the minimal guard and a raised spiral on the top. Despite the different subjects, it was easy to see the similarity in workmanship.

"I think the same craftsman must have made them," she said. "They are so alike." Havad examined her knife admiringly. "You wouldn't like to make a bet, would you?" he asked. Ahna laughed and slipped it back in its holder. "No," she responded. "Your luck is too good."

They stopped under some tall trees where a small stream came down to join the river. The brook burbled past a tiny meadow, a glade among the trees, thick with grass still sweet and green because of the extra moisture near the water. It was surrounded on three sides by heavily leaved brush and berry bushes. "We can safely let the horses loose to rest and eat here," said Havad. The men dismounted, and they let their mounts drink a little. Ahna asked Redwolf to get her a drink, too, and Havad looked at her curiously.

"Aren't you going to get down and give that poor filly a break?" he asked.

"Father said I was not to dismount," she responded.

"All day?" asked Moshel's friend.

"Your father said you were not to dismount and mingle with the other riders," interjected Moshel. "I cannot think that he meant you had to stay on Firefly every minute, and we are all family here." Ahna looked at Havad. The young man laughed.

"Just pretend I'm a brother, too," Havad suggested. "I would be honored to be your brother."

Ahna smiled at everyone and slid down from Firefly's back, stretching gratefully when she was on the ground. She really did need a break. She went to the brook for a drink, and to fill her hide water bottle; it seemed like many hands' time since there had been any water in it. Then she excused herself and stepped behind some of the thick brush to deal with her other problem. Meanwhile the young men, who did not need to be so reticent about relieving themselves, took the gear off the horses, replacing their bridles with braided hemp halters so they could graze comfortably. Then, taking soft shammies from their saddle bags and filling a cleverly designed collapsible leather bucket belonging to Moshel with water, they began cleaning off the horsey sweat and dirt that was an inevitable result of racing. Their saddle bags also contained grooming tools and spare strapping for emergency repairs to gear, pieces of cloth that could be used as towels or impromptu bandages, and some food. Ahna returned to find that Firefly had had her bath first and was now contentedly munching in the little meadow. She made a general thank you, not knowing who had sponged off her horse, then called Firefly and took her down to the stream for another drink. When they came back the other horses were also in the meadow, three grazing and Schnoz rolling back and forth delightedly, scratching his back by wriggling with his legs waving comically in the air. Ahna's brothers were getting food for the people out of the saddlebags.

"I should be doing that," Ahna told them.

"Why?" Moshel responded. "Don't you think men can get their own food sometimes? We would get awfully hungry on hunting trips or campaigns if we couldn't!"

"I never saw men get their own food when there was a woman around to do it for them," commented Havad. Then he grinned at Ahna. "But I don't see why we shouldn't. I brought some mead." He lifted a plump sealed bladder out of his saddle bag.

"Not for me," said Moshel, shaking his head. "As long as Fleetfoot is in contention, I'm sticking with water. I have seen men fall off their horses in the final race because they had too much to drink before it." The other young men looked thoughtful, and Redwolf and Havad opted for water, too.

Everyone sat on the ground in a companionable group - Ahna's brothers insisted that she join them - chewing on dried meat and cheese and hard flatbread, drinking and watching their horses move in and out of the dappled light as they stripped the glade of its grass. Havad watched the girl, who behaved very modestly, eating sparingly and listening to the conversation, and when spoken to, answering intelligently. The discussion was, of course, about horses.

Later they washed themselves in the smaller stream, then groomed the horses, let them drink again, tacked them up, and rode back to the course in a leisurely fashion. They arrived in time to watch the last of the preliminary races from one of the hills that surrounded the field, affording a view of the entire course. Moshel pointed out that the inside few feet of the course were now brown instead of green, all the way around, but more so on the turns, the turf churned up by thousands of striking hooves.

"Stay away from the inside in your next race, especially on the turns" he told Ahna and Redwolf. "The grass has been torn into chunks by the heavy traffic there. You can see how rough it is. It could cause a horse to stumble. At best, it will take more energy to run on that stuff than on the smoother surface further out."

"Why are you suddenly so free with advice that will help your competition?" asked Havad curiously.

"I'm not telling you anything you don't already know," laughed Moshel, "and these two youngsters can use a few pointers."

"Useful pointers!" complained Havad. "Most of us have to learn that stuff the hard way. These 'youngsters' may well use your 'pointers' to beat us!"

"They may," agreed Moshel, smiling at Ahna and Redwolf. "'Let the best horse win.'"

Havad scoffed at that, knowing how much clever riding and plain luck had to do with winning horse races. The final set was just crossing the finish line. "We'd better get down there," Moshel said. "The referees will be choosing the fields for the next heat."

As they rode across the course Moshel spoke quietly to Ahna. "I forgot to tell you that you will have to keep a tighter rein on Firefly at the start this time. Now that she's done it once today she will be eager and ready to do it again. She may try to go when the starter yells 'ready' or even sooner. Most disqualifications for early starts happen in a horse's second or third race. Best to take a little more hold when you think they are almost ready, to warn her to wait for your signal and so you can check her instantly if she should try to start before the 'go'."

"Thank you, Moshel," said Ahna. "Why *are* you giving us so much help?"

Moshel looked a little embarrassed. "I guess it's because this is your only chance at it and I don't think it would be fair if you were beaten just because you are inexperienced." He patted his horse's neck. "Firefly is so fast you probably will beat us, though we will do our best to get there first. But Fleetfoot and I have had many races, and will have more."

The course infield had emptied out as the racing progressed, most of the losers joining the spectators on the surrounding slopes unless they were helping other contestants. Now the referees sent any lingering riders without ribbons on their way, reserving the space for horses that were still in contention and their backup crews. There were seventy-four horses ready to run in the five semifinal races. The referees moved between them, conferring among themselves and separating the horses and their riders into new sets. The object was to try to have the best horses all end up in the championship heat; it would not do to pit them against each other in one or two of the semifinal contests. The horse masters were good handicappers, adept at remembering horses and judging their relative ability; they divided the contestants accordingly. Khaleno and his walleyed buckskin were not in the race with either Ahna or Redwolf, who found themselves in different sets, with Moshel in yet a third. The only rider Ahna knew in her group was Georha, who greeted her kindly although he was not happy to find himself racing a second time against a filly he was sure his mare could not beat.

One rider from each set was sent to draw straws for their racing position, an important moment because the horses running in the last set were at a distinct disadvantage in the final; those in the first set would have much more time to rest and recover between races. The riders in Ahna's set sent her, hoping she would bring them luck in the draw, and she came back with the second position straw: not bad at all, they agreed. Moshel was in the first set to go, as was Havad, but Redwolf and Dark Streak had the bad luck to be in the last.

As groups to race got organized the backup teams began setting up in the infield, with buckets of water for the horses to drink and with which to bathe them, the heat of the late afternoon guaranteeing that they would all come back sweaty and tired. There was to be a break between the last semifinal and the final race, but it would be little more than enough time to clean off and cool out the horses from that set before they would have to go back out again. There would not be time for any of the contestants who were to go in the last race to go to the river again. Elegin, a friend of Moshel's, came to tell Ahna that he and some other friends were ground crew for Moshel and Fleetfoot, and that they would be ready to care for Firefly after her race if she qualified for the final. She thanked him.

Chapter 11

Ahna did not win her semifinal heat; later her brothers would jokingly accuse her of having been distracted. While Moshel's set was warming up one horse drew every eye. He was at least a hand taller than any other horse in the field, but that difference, although striking, went almost unnoticed because of his color. His coat was a rich gold with a hard metallic sheen, his mane and tail more bronze than gold, a pleasing contrast. His nose was straight and aristocratic, his ears small and alert, he carried a high head with neck arched and chin tucked down, and he took long, fluid, almost floating strides as he trotted up the course. Ahna had never seen nor imagined any horse that looked like that.

The young man on his back was nearly as impressive: tall and broad-shouldered and so blond his hair was almost white. He seemed to have dressed to match his horse, in a glinting gold shirt and bronze pantaloons with a darker waistband and headband, both embroidered with gold. He sat his gorgeous mount easily, balance well forward, knees tight, heels down, hands low and still on his horse's neck. Ahna had never seen him before, either.

"That's Marvulf," said Georha beside her. "He's from an eastern mountain clan." He laughed as something struck him. "They're called the Red Wolves. They just moved into a winter camp fifty or sixty miles northeast of here. He's the first son of their chief. His horse came from beyond the great mountains, and they plan to use him to breed more like that. I don't know. He's beautiful and he won his first set easily, beating some decent animals, but I don't think he could stand up to my mare on a long forced march. And he probably eats as much as three or four of our horses, which would be a real problem in lean years or on campaign."

"The horse must have stamina if they came fifty miles this morning, and are racing this afternoon," commented Ahna quietly.

"Oh, they came a couple of days ago," Georha informed her. "They have a temporary camp a few miles up the river. He's not running a tired horse."

The big golden horse won easily. Moshel and Havad came second and third, so they, too, would be in the finals. There was a short delay before Ahna's set was sent out. Several horses had fallen because of the badly chopped up footing on the inside of the course. The referees conferred, then went with helpers to move the course markers on both turns further out, putting the dangerously rough ground out of bounds.

The hero of the afternoon was Schnoz. Havad told them later that he was running just outside of the group that cut the corner with such disastrous consequences when a horse ahead of him was knocked sideways out of the tangle, and went down right in front of him, legs flailing in the air. Schnoz was war-trained, and in desperation Havad gave him the signal to jump, not thinking he would be able to do it from a dead run. But somehow Schnoz did, soaring into the air at full speed to clear both the downed horse and his rider, who had rolled into a compact ball in defense against oncoming hooves.

"He landed well, too," Havad concluded. "Never missed a stride. What an athlete. Not the first time he has saved my bones."

There were fewer horses in Ahna's set. All went well until they entered the last turn and she told Firefly to run. She was on the inside, and as her filly began to fly a rider on a dark bay mare ahead of her looked back. His horse then started to drift over, closing the gap between her and the marker posts. Georha, on the warrior's other side, his own horse visibly tiring, shouted "racing room! Give her room!", but the rider gave him a blank look and his mare continued to drift over, crowding Firefly further. They were still on the corner; if she allowed him to push her over any more she would be forced to run into the next marker post or cut behind it and be disqualified.

Ahna clucked to Firefly and dug in her heels. The filly

responded with a burst of speed, straight ahead. She bumped shoulders twice with the dark mare as Ahna grabbed her filly's mane and yanked her right foot up in front of her to prevent its getting caught behind the other rider's leg or in his tack. He stared at her, shocked at her willingness to risk a fall or be pushed out of bounds; the marker post flashed past just inches away on her left, and then they were in the clear. There were still three or four horses in front of them, but all well out in the middle of the track, and they had entered the home stretch. Firefly was still striding out after her encounter with the other horse. Now as Ahna leaned further forward and squeezed her calves a little harder the young mare switched her leads, took a firmer hold against the bit and leveled into an even faster pace, her hooves barely skimming the turf, her long legs taking incredible strides. The horses in front of them seemed hardly to be moving, they caught them so fast, and suddenly Ahna could hear the crowd yelling in excitement, and knew that many of them were urging her flying filly on.

Ahna took second. Having passed the rest of the field, she remembered what Moshel had said about saving her horse for the final, and eased Firefly before the finish. She only realized that the third place horse was the dark brown mare whose rider had tried to shut her off when he came with them to collect his ribbons, and grudgingly complimented her.

"We have certainly all underestimated you," he said. "Good race, and a great young mare!"

"Thank you," Ahna managed.

"Jaromir will be very proud of you," he said in parting. "He used to be quite a race rider himself."

Ahna mulled that over while they were receiving their yard sticks and cantering back past the winning post waving the ribbons over their heads, to the cheers of the onlookers. She had not known that about her father.

The rest of the semifinal sets were completed without any further major incidents. Khaleno and his walleyed buckskin were in the fourth set and could manage no better than fifth despite the rider pushing his horse to exhaustion. Ahna knew it was not sporting, but she was glad he would not be in the final heat.

Redwolf 'declared' Dark Streak out of the final race before his semifinal set went onto the track, saying that two races without time to rest between them might be too much for his four-year-old and that he would not risk hurting him or burning him out, to the nodded approval of the horse masters. Dark Streak came in a close second to an acknowledged star. Redwolf was very pleased with his colt's showing at his first real races.

Moshel's crew worked on Firefly as well as Fleetfoot, and insisted she dismount while they cared for her mare, saying they would keep the crowds away. It didn't prove necessary. A few acquaintances from their clan called congratulations to her in passing, but no one showed any disposition to linger. Two of her older brothers did show up, however, to her delight. Oyerlyn and Fellazyn were here with their foster fathers to trade horses, and had not realized she was racing until they came to watch the semifinal heats.

"I'm surprised Father let you ride," said Oyerlyn, "but you and Firefly are doing us proud, so I'm glad he did."

Khaleno did not take his defeat lightly. He had found some like-minded friends, and as they were cooling out their horses they groused to each other about the bad luck or mistreatment they had had in their various heats. Loudest among them was Redwolf's enemy since the lion incident the previous fall, Stepan.

"I don't know why you're having bad luck," he said to Khaleno. "You aren't from our clan. *We're* having bad luck because our stupid chief and the horse masters let that girl race. My father and Zynjaar, our High Priest, say that she is shamefully indulged, permitted to do things that no woman is ever allowed to do. That makes the Gods angry. I bet the priests wouldn't have blessed the racing if they had known she was going to ride!"

A slow grin began to spread over Khaleno's face. "We should go tell them. Maybe they could stop her riding in the finals!" Stepan looked at him, then looked around. "Maybe they would stop her brothers, too, for helping her. I don't know if we have time, but we can try. I think Zynjaar and some of the other priests are over there on the hillside watching the races." He indicated a large group of people some distance away that seemed to contain a high percentage of bronze robes. "Come on!" Leaving their horses with their crew, the two troublemakers ran across the infield and out onto the track toward the crowd.

When they reached the section Stepan had pointed out they did indeed find the high priest and most of the rest of the clan's priests gathered there. Stepan bowed to Zynjaar, who nodded and took a drink from his wine glass. The group had just sat down around a fine alfresco meal, served and waited on by a number of their women.

"What do you want?" asked Zynjaar shortly. He had little patience for the young of the clan, especially when they interrupted the ritual of eating.

"We thought you should know that girl, Ahna, is riding in the races," answered Stepan politely. "You have often told us that the Gods will be angry and send us bad luck if we do not keep women in their assigned place. We *are* having bad luck; if she is allowed to race in the finals our clan may lose the championship at our own horse fair. We thought perhaps you could stop it."

The priest reached out and picked up a succulent rib of cold beef. He looked thoughtfully at Stepan's out-clan companion as he took a sizable bite, raised an eyebrow and looked back at Stepan, who was trying to keep from shifting his feet back and forth with impatience.

"The clan leaders and horse masters have allowed her to race," he answered when he had swallowed his mouthful. "You deserve all the bad luck that comes. I am busy."

Stepan's father, Councilor Jumri, who was attending on the priests, stepped up beside his son.

"Most of the men seem to have accepted this latest outrage of Jaromir's," he said. "I fear that some of our people do not yet realize the seriousness of letting women and their supporters do such ungodly things. They need to be shown the way, Zynjaar, and you are our spiritual leader."

"He's right, Father," said Srogaraad from his seat on the other side of the circle of diners. "If you allow this unwomanly behavior continue when you might have stopped it, our people will think we have condoned it. Jaromir and the women will gain power from it. Ahna is to be my wife. She must be taught her proper place. It should be impressed upon her at every opportunity. We cannot let her or her father get away with this."

"Oh, all right!" snarled Zynjaar, slamming his rib down on the woven mat in front of him and climbing to his feet. He glared around the circle.

"Come on, all of you!" he commanded. A couple of the older priests started to object to having to leave their food, but their chief looked so thunderous that they got up in silence and followed him down the slope and across the meadow to the finish post, where the horses for the final race were gathered.

When Ahna and Moshel rode up to the starting post there were ten horses in the field, three more having been withdrawn for one reason or another. The sun was westering in a sky still clear of any cloud, and the ruddy evening light and long shadows added a special patina to the colorful scene. For most of the day's participants the serious business was over; now it was time for one giant party. As the day cooled there would be bonfires, and fights, and camaraderie, and finally the men, except for the unlucky ones who had been assigned to guard the herds, would sleep it off around the guttering fires or stagger back to their tents, too drunk to remember that it was dark and there might be evil spirits.

All the women had arrived with food and drink while the semifinals were still in progress. Most would return to their own tents after the last race, before dark and before the celebration got out of hand. There was still some horse-trading going on, and of course the betting, but there was also a great deal of eating and drinking. Already a couple of fights had broken out among the spectators and some challenges had been made, but few were so drunk that they could not concentrate on the championship race, the pinnacle of the day's activities.

Therefore the attention of the crowd was easily drawn to the problem that developed at the start. Before Yashihar, who sat his cream-colored horse in the infield with the mounted contestants ranged in a semicircle in front of him, could finish his instructions, the contingent of priests arrived with Zynjaar stalking in the lead. He had worked himself almost into a frenzy of righteous anger on his way across the track. He stormed up to the horse master.

"Enough," roared the high priest, pointing at Ahna and Firefly. He had a deep, persuasive, almost mesmerizing voice which he used to full advantage. "This blasphemy will end now! The Gods have taken note and our clan will pay in blood and sorrow if that female is allowed to race. The Gods gave horses and racing, hunting and war to men exclusively. Letting a woman participate defiles their gift, and that has angered them!"

"She is just a girl and has already raced today; she has represented our clan quite competently," soothed Yashihar. He knew the high priest was motivated more by ambition than piety. "It will only be this one time. She will not do so again, certainly not once she is married. I don't think the Gods will bother to notice."

"She will not do so *this time*!" Zynjaar insisted. "I'm telling you the Gods *have* noticed, and withdrawn Their blessings. Something terrible will happen if she rides in this race, and it will be your fault. The Gods must be appeased. It might help if you disqualified her, stripped her of her winning ribbons and sent her and her brothers home right now. She needs to be soundly beaten. I make no promises, but if all that is done it might help."

Among the waiting riders, Marvulf leaned a little to speak to a dark blond man on a blue roan mare next to him, a warrior of the Lion clan with whom he had struck up a friendship. It was the first time the Red Wolf chief's son was close enough to Ahna and Firefly to get a good look at them, where they stood across the semicircle of riders from him, and he hadn't taken his eyes off of them for more than a few moments since they rode up.

"How can anything that the Gods gave that much beauty be considered blasphemous?" he asked. "What's got into your priests?"

"My father says that the women were opposed to an all-male priesthood and the priests can't forget it. Our high priests have been working for decades to deny them the right to their own society, or any rights at all. Zynjaar is determined to succeed. He uses every little thing any woman does that he can say is unholy against all women. He even claims that the fact that they bleed every month is a mark of evil, that it proves them unclean and unable to be cleansed, although it is only a part of the moon cycle of renewal found among animals as well as people. Father says that once there was a Goddess whom our people worshipped and the priests want to be sure that never happens again."

"Of course there are goddesses as well as gods," laughed Marvulf, shaking his head. "Every living creature is blessed with two sexes. The important thing is that the Gods and the men are in control. They are the stronger sex. That's what counts."

"Do your people let girls race horses?" asked his friend.

"No," said Marvulf. "It hasn't anything to do with the Gods, though. It's because women just aren't suited to racing or any other men's games. I never saw a woman handle a horse or ride the way this girl does."

"We don't have any others like her, either," agreed his confidant.

Yashihar and the other horse masters, too, were skeptical of the high priest's claim. The chief's friend in particular smelled politics, not religion; he was well aware that the high priest was jealous of anyone other than himself who wielded power, and often opposed Jaromir in affairs of the clan.

"I fail to understand why the Gods would be so concerned about one young girl riding here," Yashihar tried one more time. "After all, we ride and race female horses. Everyone knows mares are often better war horses than the males, and good in competitions as well. How could the Gods hold femaleness against a woman?"

"You can't compare them," explained Zynjaar. "Horses are animals, given to men for their use and betterment, their sex not an issue. Women, however, are human, inferior but necessary. Because they have no souls, if they are left to their own devices they turn swiftly to evil. Females are only acceptable to the Gods when they are kept to their own limited duties. They must stay completely out of men's business."

"We do not have time for these word games," said Yashihar. "We will put it to the clansmen whether she should be allowed to race or not."

"The men do not know what the Gods want," snapped Zynjaar. "I do!"

"Well," Yashihar countered, his patience exhausted, "until the Gods speak directly to me, *I* don't know what They want, only what you do. We will put it to the people." He knew that would anger the priest, but the word of the horse masters was still law over all others in equine matters.

Zynjaar turned on his subordinates. "Get out there and warn the men of the Gods' anger. Tell our people they must make the only decision which will placate Them," he said. "Go!"

Like so many rusty crows the priests in their dark bronze robes scattered out into the crowd, flapping their arms and warning of impending doom if Ahna was allowed to ride, while the horse masters went as well, to try to determine how the majority really felt about the issue.

Arguments broke out all over the grounds, but before long it was the priests who were getting loudest and most frustrated. A few men sided with them about the girl, notably some of those she had beaten, but everyone loved a fast, game horse, and most wanted to see Firefly run in the final race. The Lion warriors felt that Ahna was a credit to their clan and should be allowed to ride this one time. A slightly inebriated young man clapped a priest on the shoulder and voiced the predominant opinion.

"What I think, friend, is that if the Gods did not want her to race they would not have given her such luck, or such a superb horse!"

The priests had power, but it was not absolute. If they had spoken earlier in the day, before Ahna had made such an impression, they might have prevailed. Now even the visiting clansmen knew who Ahna was, and many from all five clans attending the horse fair admired her for what they saw as rare courage and ability.

Realizing he was losing face, Zynjaar gathered up his followers and stalked back to his supper. He thought to take the blessing sticks, thereby removing the visible favor of his Gods, but Redwolf and several other strapping young warriors were joshing each other good-naturedly around them. He decided against it. He hadn't achieved his current position by pursuing battles he couldn't win.

Yashihar jumped to his feet on his horse's back and got the attention of the crowd of men at the start, which had been growing steadily throughout the confrontation. He asked in his carrying voice if Ahna should be allowed to run. There was an instant overwhelming roar of approval.

The horse master promptly sent the competitors out onto the course to warm up and the crowd moved back behind the markers or across the course to the viewing slopes, still buzzing with talk about Ahna and the priests.

Havad was one of those who had withdrawn his horse, having found a little heat in one front ankle when Schnoz was cooled out, but Moshel and Fleetfoot were still in the running. Firefly was playing with her bit and seemed eager to go again, but she waited for Ahna's signal at the start. They got off a little slower than in the previous two races and found themselves galloping along with the last few horses rather than near the front. That was all right; Ahna was not in a hurry. With the smaller field she was less likely to get trapped behind horses and in this final heat it was more important than ever to save her horse's speed for the end.

Marvulf and Golden Boy took the lead and began to draw away from the rest of the competitors when they had no more than completed the first circuit, with still a mile and a half to go. Ahna felt a twinge of worry, but she remembered what Moshel had said about big horses not having stamina. She had no intention of wearing Firefly out early. She just hoped that Golden Boy would tire enough that she could catch him in the stretch. Several riders did shake up their horses and try to keep close to the leader, so that soon it looked like two separate races. She glanced around and was pleased to see that Moshel and Lakshi, the winner of her second race, were both in her group, falling gradually farther and farther behind the frontrunners.

Halfway down the backstretch she decided it was time to send Firefly along a little faster; the leaders were already entering the final turn. As her game filly lengthened her stride it became apparent that some of the leading group were tiring, and Ahna passed between three of them, one slowed almost to a lope, as she came out of the turn into the homestretch. That left only Golden Boy and one other in front of her, nearly halfway to the finish pole, but the second horse was beginning to falter, too. Ahna crouched low on Firefly's neck and asked her filly to change her leads and run. Firefly did, the heart-stopping speed she had shown at the end of the last heat still available. As her horse began cutting down the gap between themselves and the leaders, Ahna heard other quickening hoofbeats, and looked around to find Moshel trying to stay with her. She grinned and turned forward again.

In just moments she blew past the tiring horse, and then she was almost up to Golden Boy's flank with still an eighth of a mile to go. Marvulf looked back and saw her. He crouched lower and urged his horse to greater effort. Golden Boy responded gamely. For a few moments it seemed like the big horse would draw away from her yet again, but his size and the distance and the much greater weight of his rider were beginning to tell on him. The colt's immense strides started to roughen. Firefly gained steadily, her ears flat back and her neck stretched out, until they were running side by side, and then she had her head in front and the finish pole flashed past. She had won!

Ahna sat up, registering the incredible noise the onlookers were making for the first time, and looked back as Firefly slowed to a lope, to see that Marvulf was still close behind her but Moshel, who had got third, was pulling up and jumping down just beyond the finish. She hoped Fleetfoot was all right.

She had Firefly down to a walk and was about to turn back when the big golden colt ranged in beside her. She gave Marvulf a wide excited smile and opened her mouth to say what a great race it had been and what a wonderful horse he had, but Marvulf didn't wait to hear what she was going to say. He crowded his stallion right up next to the filly, leaned over, put a long arm around Ahna and snatched her off her horse's back and on to his own.

"Hey, what are you doing?" she gasped.

"Teaching you not to make mockery of a man," he growled. His tone frightened her and she tried to get away, pushing, then clawing at the gold-clad arm trapping her, kicking against the big horse and attempting to throw herself sideways. Golden Boy, tired as he was, was unnerved by the strange things happening on his back. He sidestepped sharply, and suddenly both Ahna and Marvulf were flat on the ground with Marvulf on top.

"Get away! Get off of me!" ordered Ahna. Her tone was low and breathy because the fall had knocked the wind out of her, but there was panic in her voice. Marvulf laughed, his temper somewhat restored by the absurdity of their situation. He shifted to get his hands under him, but of course that pushed him temporarily more against her. Not knowing his intention and beyond thinking, she reached up with both hands, grabbed his white-gold hair, and yanked.

"*Ow*!" he yelped, laughing harder. He disentangled her hands from his hair, then pinned them to the ground with his own. He moved his weight off of her while keeping her hands imprisoned. "That wasn't very nice," he said. He looked down at her, marveling at her beauty. "Get away! Let me go!" she demanded, a little louder this time. The big stranger just kept looking at her, and she looked back, anger and fear in her eyes, but she stopped struggling.

After a moment, almost as if mesmerized, Marvulf let go of her left hand to untie the laces that held her high-necked blouse closed across her chest, forgetting that she might reach up to pull his hair again. She did not. She slowly moved her hand down toward her waist instead, and as he opened her blouse, and inevitably looked down, she grabbed her little knife out of its sheath and drove it into his thigh. She wasn't aiming for his thigh, but the Goddess was looking out for her. Her future would probably have been very short and unpleasant had she not missed what she was aiming for. He leaped up, swearing. Then several things happened at once. Marvulf hauled back his arm, his hand clenched into a fist, his eyes on the girl. Ahna sat up, the knife held threateningly toward him. Firefly, who had come up behind the man, clamped his shoulder between her teeth, and from two different directions two furious male voices commanded, "*Stop*!"

Chapter 12

Ahna froze, recognizing both her father's voice and his intense anger, a chilling tone she had never heard nor imagined before. Marvulf did not stop his attack, but focused it on the filly instead, smashing his fist into her jaw. She let go and backed off, shaking her head, and suddenly there were several men, including Ahna's older brothers, gripping his arms, pulling him away from Ahna and her horse, immobilizing him in spite of his violent verbal and physical protests. Yashihar, still on his horse, stood beside them, glaring at the furious easterner.

"What do you mean by attacking one of our maidens? Are you drunk? You are a visitor here. Your behavior is inexcusable!" The outrage in the Horse Master's voice was palpable.

Marvulf started an angry answer, but Ahna heard no more. Ignoring the stranger, her father stopped in front of her. He reached down and yanked her to her feet by her right wrist, the silver-hilted knife dropping unnoticed from her hand.

"Fasten your blouse and get back on your horse and go home. *Now!*" He glanced around. Redwolf was right beside him, but looking at Marvulf, and there was murder in her younger brother's eyes. "Take her back to her mother," his father ordered. "You, too," he said to Moshel, who had arrived with Ahndru, leading a tired but sound Fleetfoot. Redwolf started to protest, then thought better of it. He had never seen his father so coldly furious before, either, and he was very glad he wasn't Marvulf.

Sure that he would be obeyed, Jaromir turned to follow the horse master, who was riding back toward the finish pole where the other referees were gathering, the tall easterner, still in the grip of two of his captors, walking beside him.

"Are you all right?" Moshel asked Ahna quietly.

"Yes," she answered. She began retying her blouse, so Redwolf went to get Firefly, who had backed out of the sudden crowd and was standing a few yards down the track facing her mistress, her eyes showing white. The big golden stallion was there, too. Every little while he tried to nuzzle Firefly, but she either lashed out at him with one hind foot or snapped at him with her teeth, her ears pinned. The rest of the time she ignored him. Redwolf had to laugh. He led Firefly back to Ahna. Now the attack was over his sister was leaning on Moshel and shaking like a leaf in a high wind, so her brother led the filly up beside her and lifted her into her saddle. Then the young men led the horses back toward where Dark Streak was waiting in the care of the ground crew in the infield. The golden horse followed them for a short distance until Marvulf's brother came and led him away. Redwolf thought that Ahna might protest having to leave without her red ribbons and the prize she had won, but she sat quietly on Firefly and said nothing. Slowly both girl and horse stopped quivering.

As they walked through the crowd, which had spilled onto the track and gone unusually silent, the men made a path for them, and a few cheers broke out. Ahna heard her name called many times. She was still too shaken to acknowledge the accolades, but as they continued her face lost its set look, and she smiled. Then she reached down and patted Firefly's sweaty neck, and the cheering intensified.

*   *   *

When Yashihar and Marvulf reached the finish post the rest of the horse masters had arrived and dismounted, questions in all their eyes. Those who had been on the backside had seen nothing; most of the rest were not sure what they had seen. The referee who had been posted at the beginning of the turn had left when the horses raced by him for the final time, along with the spectators who had been watching from that vantage, so there was no one close by to see Marvulf snatch Ahna off Firefly, and from a distance it was really impossible to tell what was going on. Many men thought that Ahna might have fainted, and that Marvulf was helping her. Seeing him brought back under restraint raised every eyebrow. Marvulf's brother approached hesitantly and Yashihar waited while Marvulf asked him to collect his horse and take him to the infield to be cooled out and given his bath. Then the horse masters, Jaromir and his sons, and one or two other of the clan leaders gathered around the stranger. Many other men crowded as close as they dared, wanting to hear what was said. Yashihar spoke first.

"I really did not like what I thought I saw out there," he said coldly to the young easterner. "Suppose you tell us your version of what was going on." It was clear from his tone that if he had any doubts about Marvulf's story, it would be checked.

"She beat us!" Marvulf began. "She and that damned fast filly caught us at the finish, and I admit I was furious. Then when we were pulling up she gave me a mocking grin, and that was too much. I pulled her off her horse onto mine. She started struggling like a wild cat - she has claws, too - and we both tumbled to the ground. I landed on top of her, but before I could get up she started pulling my hair." Oyerlyn's face lost its grim look; the corners of his mouth turned up. There were a few snickers from the onlookers, quickly shushed by others. "I grabbed her hands and pinned her down, and then..." He stopped talking.

"Then you opened her blouse, and backed off fast, and you were about to punch her when we stopped you. We saw that." Yashihar was speaking because he didn't dare leave the proceedings to his friend and clan chief. He knew how Jaromir felt about Ahna. Any father of a maiden would have been justifiably angry, but this father of this maiden... It would be a blot on the clan if their chief ended up challenging the son of another clan chief. It would probably lead to blood feud if either killed the other!

"I was not going to hurt her. At least not until after she hurt me," Marvulf amended truthfully. "You surely can't think I was going to rape her out there."

"Then what was your intention," demanded Yashihar.

"I just wanted... I wanted to get a good look at her, and to teach her a lesson. I admit I was angry that she won, but if she had been male I would have congratulated her - him - and that would have been the end of it. But even clan chief's daughters cannot be allowed to believe it's all right to show up a man. She needed reminding that men are in charge and women are meant to be obedient."

A short silence as the referees and onlookers digested this gave Marvulf the opening he needed.

"Now we have a much bigger problem," he said solemnly. "Do you people allow your women to attack men with weapons?"

"What are you talking about?" demanded Jaromir. "She has no weapon." The moment the words left his mouth, he remembered the silver-hilted knife, and vaguely recalled seeing it fall from Ahna's hand as he hauled her to her feet. In the heat of the moment he had not noticed. "Except..."

"She has her horse," interrupted Marvulf. "A war mare is a weapon, and that mare bit me!" He fingered his torn shirt, darkened with a considerable patch of drying blood at the shoulder. "And she certainly had a knife. She stabbed me in the leg with it. I saw it in her hand just before you arrived. She attacked me twice. What is the penalty in your clan for a woman who puts a knife in a man? In mine it is death, more swiftly and certainly if the wound is serious." He paused, watching Jaromir, who had gone white.

"My wounds are far from serious and I do not demand the death penalty, but you owe me blood price," Marvulf concluded, indicating the tear in his bronze-colored pantaloons and the much more substantial bloody swath that stained the opulent material.

"Does that need tending?" asked Yashihar, chagrined that he had not noticed the second wound before.

"Not immediately," Marvulf answered. "It is not deep, and it has stopped bleeding. I'm glad she didn't hit anything vital."

Jaromir thought about that, and shuddered.

"I don't believe the filly is war-trained," Yashihar began again after a moment, glancing at Jaromir, who shook his head.

"She was probably trying to protect her rider the way a mare does her foal. That, at least, can be attributed to your actions," the horse master went on. "As for Ahna stabbing you, she was undoubtedly scared, angry and beyond thinking clearly, between the excitement of the race and then your grabbing her like that. Nevertheless, she should not have cut you, or even pulled the knife. Our penalty for that is indeed severe, and circumstances do not mitigate it. Among us the decision about punishment is left to the injured party. She is lucky you have no wish to invoke the law." He looked at Jaromir.

"What is your blood price?" asked Ahna's father.

"I want her mare," began Marvulf, and after a moment Jaromir nodded. "And I want her."

There were murmurs among the onlookers and protests from Ahna's brothers. Jaromir spoke emphatically.

"No! The horse, yes. All of my best mares if you want them, but not the girl. Ahna is a good maiden, skillful at women's tasks and much esteemed by her family and all our friends. She has the right to make a proper marriage."

"You misunderstand me," said Marvulf. "She is not an outclanner, and I would not demean her by making her a concubine. I meant that I wanted her for my wife. I am past eighteen and my father has been after me for nearly two years to choose a bride. Now he says that if I do not do so soon, he will choose one for me."

"You want to *marry* her, after she cut you with a knife?" There was disbelief in Fellazyn's voice, but Oyerlyn was now grinning openly.

Marvulf looked at the brothers. "She is the most beautiful creature I have ever seen, and has more courage than any woman, and many men, I know. Yes, she is my choice."

The murmuring among the onlookers increased, but the negative tone was gone.

Jaromir looked at Marvulf for the first time without an overlay of fury. The tall blond stranger looked back at him steadily. The tense silence lengthened. Just as Yashihar appeared about to break it, the clan chief came to a decision.

"We need to talk about this," he said, looking around. For the first time he noticed the presence of his older sons, noted as well that Oyerlyn's often misplaced sense of humor was in play again.

"Marriage negotiations are not best made in front of a large crowd at a horse fair," he observed to Marvulf. "Come back to our tents with me. I want you to meet Ahna's mother and brothers. You have met two of them, already, it appears."

The Red Wolf warrior nodded as Jaromir's sons identified themselves with little bows. He relaxed minutely. He was already thinking he might yet win much more than he had lost this day. "I would like that," he said, "but could I possibly come tomorrow? Today is nearly gone. I need to see to my horse and get these wounds cleaned up. I would be embarrassed to be presented to the rest of your family like this." Again he indicated the damage to his clothing.

Jaromir thought a moment. He had been hoping that he could get a better feel for this prospective son-in-law on the ride back to the tents.

"That will do," he agreed at last, "but walk back down the course with me now. I want to retrieve Ahna's knife. It is just a woman's gathering knife. It was certainly never intended for use as a weapon."

"I'm sure of that," said Marvulf. "She was defending herself and she did not think. I'll go with you to find it if you will let me give it back to her." Jaromir was rather surprised, but he agreed readily.

"Have we resolved this matter, then?" asked Yashihar.

"I don't think it will come to fighting now," Jaromir answered him dryly, "at least not between this young man and myself. Thank you for your time and concern," he said to all the horse masters, "and thank you for managing the racing so well today. It seems to have been a very successful affair." Several of the onlookers made noises of agreement, some calling "It isn't over yet!" amid laughing approbation.

The horse masters dispersed to other tasks, including awarding the prizes for the final race, a problem given that all the recipients were otherwise occupied. Jaromir asked Marvulf to give him a moment, then greeted his sons properly and introduced them formally. As they prepared to leave, he asked if they would visit their mother's tents that evening. Both young men said they would stop briefly in the morning, before their respective foster clans broke camp and headed back, but that they had other tasks tonight, by which their father accurately divined that they wanted to party.

As Jaromir and Marvulf started back down the course, someone set up a cheer for their popular chief and the handsome blond stranger, and it was taken up by the whole crowd.

Walking beside a silent Jaromir, Marvulf made some comments about how badly the racing had cut up the rain-softened turf. The older man barely heard him. Jaromir could not get the picture of an angry Marvulf, hand raised, fist clenched, Ahna cowering in front of him, out of his mind.

"Do you like to hit women?" he asked abruptly.

Marvulf paused, staring at him. "No," he said after a moment, and walked on. "I couldn't even hit my horse," he mused, "when Ahna and that amazing mare were about to pass us, and maybe whipping him would have gotten a bit more out of him. I was sure he was doing his best."

"But you do think it is sometimes necessary to beat women," Jaromir pressed him.

"I think that if you end up beating any living thing you have probably failed to communicate in more productive ways. I know I raised my fist to her, but that was in surprise and anger at her having stabbed me. I would not hit Ahna if there was any other choice. Have you never beaten your wives?"

"Wife," corrected Jaromir. "I have not. There has never been a need. If she makes a mistake, and I point it out to her, she corrects it. She is an excellent wife." He did not say he loved her and could not imagine striking her.

"Well, I've always been told that before you choose a woman, you should find out what kind of wife her mother is. It seems I have made a good choice. Why should I need to beat her?"

"I pray you never will," said Jaromir, "but Ahna is strong-willed, has been since she was tiny, with a streak of independence and stubbornness that many men would find unacceptable in a wife. If we reach an agreement, I want it to include one thing; if you find you cannot get along with Ahna without beating her, send her back."

Marvulf was amazed. He walked along kicking at the loose chunks of sod for a few moments before he said, "You mean divorce her? Isn't a divorced woman a disgrace to herself and her family in your clan?"

"Yes, she would be forever in disgrace," agreed Jaromir, "and it would disgrace us, too. We would lose much stature, but..." he hesitated. "She could not survive being beaten. It would break her spirit, or it would make her mean and vindictive." The thought of what it might do to her made him feel sick.

"If that is really what you want I will agree to your terms," Marvulf said after a moment. "I cannot picture myself beating her anyway, as long as she refrains from sticking knives in me."

"I don't believe she will do that again," said Jaromir. If he had anything to say in the matter she wouldn't!

"Neither do I," agreed Marvulf. He had no intention of provoking her to such an extreme again.

After some hunting around Marvulf spotted a glint of silver where the little knife caught the low-angled sunlight. Jaromir swiped it through a clump of grass a few times to clean the dirt and dried blood from the blade, then stood contemplating it for a minute before handing it to Marvulf, who examined it with interest.

"It's beautiful! Where did you get it?"

"There was a town a few years back, north of here on a great river between the mountains," Jaromir answered. "The concubines said they had craftsmen who came in long boats from some land away across the water and taught them how to work the designs into the metal. I don't know if it was true, but it doesn't matter. We have found many beautiful things along the road."

Marvulf nodded, and they walked back to collect their horses and return to their respective camps, talking of nothing more immediate than horse mastery and horse breeding. Yashihar was waiting for them. He gave them a curious look, but asked no questions. He handed Marvulf the carved, blue and silver ribboned yard stick and the intricately braided leather bridle with its silver-inlaid copper bit that were the awards for second place, congratulating him and complimenting his magnificent stallion. Then he turned to his friend.

"I thought you would want to take these to your daughter," he said, holding out a highly polished yard stick of a golden wood carved with running horses and festooned with long red and silver ribbons, the champion's trophy, and indicating a beautifully embossed, silver-mounted saddle on the ground beside him. "She and her horse earned them; she should have them. Tell Moshel I will bring his prizes back to camp for him if he does not return for the celebrations."

"I will take Ahna's to her," said Jaromir. He looked admiringly at the saddle. "I doubt she will want to ride much when she no longer has Firefly."

"She will not lose the mare if she weds me," said Marvulf thoughtfully. "I will give her to Ahna for a bride-gift, and the foals I hope she will have by Golden Boy as well, but please don't tell Ahna. I don't want her to think I am trying to bribe her into consenting." Both the older men nodded. Then Marvulf excused himself to go find his horse and go back to his camp, saying he would come to Jaromir's tents at midmorning the next day.

Thanking Yashihar, who had to stay while the celebrations were going on, Jaromir took the saddle and beribboned yard stick and joined the group of friends and subordinates who were waiting nearby with his horse for the ride back to their tents.

Chapter 13

When Jaromir walked into their main living space, he found Ahna helping her mother serve supper to the boys; they had not eaten since their lunch by the river. The chief's place was also set waiting for him on the carpets, and Vladia and Ahna greeted him as was proper with water for washing and a hand towel. They both looked at him with inquiry and some trepidation. Vladia especially feared for her daughter, knowing exactly how the men would view Ahna's use of her knife on Marvulf. There would be no consideration given to the fact that it was in self-defense. She had some fear as well that her husband might have killed the young man for attacking his daughter, precipitating a blood feud between the clans.

Jaromir sat down to eat with nothing more than a curt greeting and asked his sons to tell him how the preliminary races had gone, as he had only arrived in time to watch the final set. Moshel talked, telling about the accident in the semifinals, which he had avoided precisely because he had not tried to cut the corner. He described Ahna's first two races in detail, emphasizing how well she had ridden.

Jaromir listened without comment, finished his meal, and sent Moshel and Redwolf to check on the horses. Then he spoke to Ahna.

"What could you have been thinking, sticking your knife into that young man?" he demanded severely when she stood, her expression half penitent, half defiant, wholly scared, in front of him. "Surely you know our code provides that a woman who attacks a man with a weapon may be killed? Did you think that somehow you were exempt from the law?" He shut his lips in a thin hard line and awaited her answer.

Ahna started to point out that Marvulf had been attacking her, then remembered her mother's words; by their laws and customs, nothing could excuse a woman for attacking a man with a weapon. She tried to think of something else to say in her own defense, but finally she hung her head and whispered "I wasn't thinking, I guess." She met her father's eyes apprehensively. "Am . . . Am I going to …"

"Die?" he finished harshly. He looked back at her sternly, letting her stew for a bit longer.

"No," he answered at last. "Marvulf does not demand the death penalty." Ahna sagged in relief, as did her mother, who was listening closely while quietly doing chores around the room. "What he does require is blood price," Jaromir continued, "to which he is entitled."

"What does he want?" Ahna asked, but fear clamped bands around her chest again. Suddenly she knew.

"He wants your mare," her father answered, "and he shall have her." Ahna's mouth opened, but the chief did not give her time to speak. "There is no point in arguing. You are very lucky to have gotten off so lightly for your folly." He did not mention Marvulf's second demand.

Ahna stifled both her cry of protest and the tears that threatened; smart women saved their tears for times when they might do some good. After another moment she asked if she could go back to her work.

"I trust that you will never repeat this folly," her father admonished.

"I will not," agreed Ahna quietly, her eyes lowered.

He looked at her searchingly for a moment, then, satisfied that she recognized the seriousness of her actions and had learned her lesson, he softened his tone. "You rode very well today. The prizes you won are in the equipment tent. You may go."

"I don't want them," she said, turning away. "Firefly won them. Let *him* take them, too." She grabbed a large jar and left the tent to fetch water.

Vladia brought Jaromir an evening cup of tea with a generous measure of fermented mare's milk. She did not speak, although she knew there was more to the story than he had revealed to Ahna. It was men's business, and as well as she got on with her husband, she did not dare ask until he gave her an opening. He watched her putting things away for a few minutes, drinking his nightcap. Finally he spoke.

"Marvulf will be here tomorrow morning," he said. "You should be prepared to serve him, and perhaps some of his friends, a formal meal at noon. I don't think Oyerlyn and Fellazyn will stay for dinner, though."

Vladia's eyes lit; it would be a joy to see her two oldest sons, if only briefly. She knew better than to comment, though, when Jaromir had been so offhand about their presence at the horse fair.

"So the young man is not coming just to collect Firefly," she said instead. "I thought probably he would want more than one mare, however fast. I assume he was not badly hurt, but he could demand a much higher blood price for such an injury, however slight."

"Thank the Gods he was not badly hurt! He does want more," confirmed her husband, "but it is not as blood price. He wants to marry Ahna."

Vladia's arched brows snapped together. "Marry her? When he's only met her once, and at that meeting he attacked her and *she* stabbed *him*?"

"By his account he didn't really attack her," Jaromir elaborated. "He snatched her off her horse, he says, to teach her more respect for men after she beat him in the race. *I* think it was because he is fascinated by her. Anyway, her struggles caused them both to fall off his horse and matters rapidly deteriorated from there. He says he meant her no harm, but that clearly is not how she saw it."

"He must have been besotted," said Vladia. "He may change his mind by tomorrow."

"I don't expect it. He said his father is becoming insistent that he find a wife. He seems to admire Ahna out of all proportion to the amount of time he has known her." Jaromir paused, thinking that he had known the moment he first saw Vladia. Then he told his wife about his walk with Marvulf to find the knife.

"He has it. He wants to return it to her. That feels odd to me."

Vladia thought about it. "I expect he wants to try to reverse the negative impression he made on her by 'attacking' her. He is probably very well aware, as I'm sure you are, that she would not look with favor on the idea of marrying him under the circumstances."

"She probably won't under any circumstances," commented her father, "but she will have no choice in the matter if I accept his suit, and she knows it."

"Certainly she does," agreed his wife, "but I am convinced that you would not force her to marry someone for whom she had a real aversion. That he asked to give her knife back to her argues that he, too, is aware that marrying a girl who is seriously opposed to the match might not do much for his domestic comfort. He means to woo her, to seek her consent as well as yours, and that is a good sign. What is his background?"

"Didn't the children tell you?" asked Jaromir. Vladia shook her head. "He is the eldest son of the leader of the Red Wolf clan. Their home territory was far to the east of ours, but they are forming the western edge of a horde that has been moving south parallel with us in the lands to the East. They just conquered a small town a bit more than 50 miles away, and they mean to winter there. They came a couple of days ago with horses to trade and race. They are camped a few miles away. Marvulf says they brought many horses and did not want to encroach on our grazing."

"Very thoughtful," commented Vladia.

"He seems like a thoughtful young man," her husband responded. Then he added, "Wait 'till you see his horse. I know you will be busy, but be sure to find an opportunity to look at him."

"He must be something, if he impressed you that much," she said.

"At first I thought he was *all* looks," said Jaromir, "but he proved in the competition that he has speed and stamina. I'm sure he would have beaten Firefly as well, if he had been carrying Ahna instead of Marvulf. She had a huge weight advantage. Still, that golden animal is so big I question his agility, and he seems to be hampered with the distractibility around mares of most stallions. He would not be my choice for a war mount, but he is certainly spectacular."

"He's gold-colored? How strange!" commented Vladia. "He must be a wonder."

"He is. His winter coat is starting to come in, but even that shines. Marvulf means to breed Firefly to him. He says he will give her back to Ahna for a wedding gift, but that we aren't to tell her, because he does not want her to think he is bribing her to accept him."

"Better and better," said Vladia. "He's right that we should not tell her. It would be just like her to marry him to get Firefly back, and that isn't a good foundation for a life together, either. I hope she doesn't accept just to be near her horse! She needs to think about the man himself."

"Shall I tell her that he is coming, and why?" asked her husband.

"That he is coming, yes. Tell her at breakfast. She will know that he would want to get the mare. Don't tell her that he means to ask for her. Let him try to make his peace with her first. She is not yet ready to contemplate marriage with anyone, let alone him. If she finds him attractive - he is attractive?"

"To young women, very, I should think."

"Well, if he can persuade her to form a more favorable opinion of him than she now holds it will make everything easier." She stood a moment, then asked another question.

"Jaromir, do you *want* Ahna to marry him? She will go so far away. We may never see her again."

Her husband locked eyes with her for a moment, then looked down. "I know I'm supposed to say it is an excellent match, but the truth is I don't want her to marry him. I don't want to lose her and I know you don't either."

"Then why…" she began.

"Zynjaar has been pestering me to betroth her to his son Srogaraad. I have turned him down every time, but he is growing increasingly insistent. In the eyes of the rest of the clan it would be a very proper match; the boy will probably be high priest one day, and he can pay a good bride price. There is really no one else in our clan as... suitable, but Srogaraad..." He paused.

"May I say what I think?" Vladia asked. The chief nodded.

"I think that young man is a selfish brute who likes to lord it over others, and will never be willing to admit that he might be wrong about anything. If he does not end up abusing any woman he marries, however compliant, I will be surprised. Ahna... it would be a catastrophe. It... it would kill her. *He* might kill her!" Jaromir nodded again.

"I'm thinking that Marvulf Storm may prove to be a godsend," he said, a contradictory note of sadness in his voice.

Their conversation ended when Ahna came in with the water. She should have been back much sooner, but she'd made a detour to check on Firefly where she grazed among the riding horses in a meadow near the spring. The horse came to her and nuzzled her neck. Firefly's legs were cool, her eyes calm and clear, her breathing relaxed, normal. She had taken no hurt from the day's exertions. Ahna found herself crying with her face buried in the filly's mane. Finally, wearily, she picked up the water jars and returned to the tent in the waning light. Neither of her parents said anything about her slowness, however, nor did they comment on her unusual silence as she finished her evening tasks and went to bed.

Soon after daybreak the next morning Ahna was serving breakfast to her family. She looked somewhat less than her best. Shadows stained the skin under her hazel eyes, darkened now with sorrow. The spring was gone from her step, the smile dimples from her cheeks. She had passed a nearly sleepless night, the events of the previous day and their disastrous consequences running round in her head, unable either to rid herself of the image of an angry Marvulf or to come up with a way to keep her horse.

She even considered going out in the night, taking Firefly, and leaving the clan, but she had no notion of where she could go, especially as any other of the clans would look askance on her running away, expect her to obey her father, and promptly return her to him, by force if necessary. Her situation would then be many times worse, she was sure, so she had discarded that option. She could think of no other.

Jaromir and the young men were discussing the day ahead. Her father waited until Ahna was filling up their cups, then casually mentioned that Marvulf would be coming that morning and that he would be staying for the midday meal. Ahna nearly spilled the pitcher of tea. She did not know how she felt about seeing Marvulf again, but she knew he must be coming for Firefly. She knew how she felt about that!

It wasn't long before Oyerlyn and Fellazyn came in, apparently none the worse for their partying of the night before. They greeted their mother with hugs and laughter, and congratulated Ahna on her prize. Oyerlyn started to say something about her conquest of Marvulf, but caught his father's warning look and stopped before she could realize he meant something more than the race. Then the two young warriors complimented Redwolf on his black colt and asked about his progress in weapons training. Soon he and Ahndru and their older brothers were off to the riding field for demonstrations of their newest skills, much to the flattered delight of the boys.

After the men had gone out Ahna hurried through her early tasks, then asked her mother if she could go. Vladia pointed out that there was more work than usual that morning; they had to prepare a formal meal for guests. Then, knowing that she needed to say goodbye to her horse, her mother gave her permission to take a hand-width by the sun. Ahna nearly ran to the pasture, grabbing only a hackamore and a saddle cloth to keep her divided skirts clean; she wanted one last ride with Firefly. The red mare was watching for her, as she did every morning. She stood quietly while Ahna slipped the bit-less bridle over her nose and behind her ears, tossed the saddle cloth across her back, then grabbed a handful of mane and jumped nimbly up. The filly tossed her head impatiently, but waited while Ahna straightened the cloth under her, stepping off eagerly when her rider finally tightened her calves. They trotted away from the pasture and the camp itself, across a stream and up a steep rise into an area of low, rocky hills.

Ahna just rode, letting Firefly find her own way, watching the birds fluttering among the branches, hunting bugs in the occasional scrubby trees, and clinging to the bending tips of tall grasses, picking seeds from their ripe golden heads. She noted a rabbit that vanished quickly under some berry bushes, and a brown and gold patterned snake warming itself on a rock. A light breeze stirred her scarf and Firefly's mane, chasing the biting flies away and mitigating the heat of the late summer sun. It was a glorious morning. She reveled in the feel of Firefly's muscles moving under her as the filly climbed among the rocks, and tried to forget that this was the last time she would share such a ride with her.

Just as she was thinking sadly that they had to turn back, Firefly stopped abruptly, gazing toward a low-branched tree next to the trail some thirty paces ahead, her ears pricked, her head high. She snorted and started to tremble. Ahna looked more closely at the tree. At first she could see nothing, but then as she stared she saw something like a beige snake swinging back and forth below one large branch. She shifted her weight and tightened her right knee, moving Firefly along the slope to the left so they could both get a better look into the tree. Stretched out on the branch, utterly still except for the twitching of her tail, a hill lioness watched them through sleepy golden eyes. Free and wild, the great cat was mistress of all she surveyed. Firefly tossed her head, snorted again, and backed up a few steps. Ahna stroked her neck, soothing her. The cat was not in hunting mode or they would not even have known she was there. Besides, she was too far away to present a real threat, and would probably not have attacked such a large target anyway. Saluting the lioness with a raised hand, Ahna turned Firefly toward the camp and they trotted back down the faint track they had been following.

The lion was their clan totem and the lioness was sacred to the Goddess that the women still worshiped in secret. Ahna felt blessed that the cat had let herself be seen, for she knew if the men had come upon the predator they would have hunted her mercilessly. Totem or not, lions were hard on livestock.

As she rode home, it dawned on Ahna that the encounter was a message from the Goddess herself. Inexplicably she felt her spirits rise. Changes were coming in her life, but she, like the lioness, would remain mistress of her world if she could live by the teachings of the Goddess.

Chapter 14

Marvulf entered the camp of the Lion clan at about the same time as Ahna and Firefly were turning back from their ride in the hills. He had made an early start, having slept little more during the night just past than Ahna. He had left Golden Boy at pasture to rest and was riding his best war mare, a big dark bay with a short back, long sloping shoulders and hips and a long stride. He wore a red polished cotton shirt shot with silver thread and riding pants of supple black leather tucked into tall brown leather boots and held up with a silver-grey sash; red and grey were the Red Wolf clan colors. He had a heavy gold chain around his neck and a gold band worked with running horses around his right arm below the shoulder. He carried no weapons, but a bronze dagger with a carved onyx hilt hung in a sheath at his waist. His younger brother Peatli and his best friend Svander, as dark as the two brothers were blond, rode beside him, the one on a bay mare with dark legs and a dark mane and tail, high-stepping and striking to look at, and the other on a plain-headed brown gelding, solid, perhaps even stolid in appearance, but with a light, sure way of moving that promised more quickness than his conformation suggested. Both young men also wore clan colors and their personal adornments, dressed in their best for a formal visit.

They rode between the groups of felt tents, each one decorated with the identifying patterns and colors of clan and family. They noted that this was a very prosperous clan with few decrepit or even undecorated tents. They had passed pastures teeming with fat, healthy cattle and sheep on their way into camp, the livestock watched by bright-eyed young boys and alert, well-trained herd dogs. In the village each family group of tents was flanked by yard sticks that identified the occupations of and goods offered by their owners, but some of the color codes were different from those in Marvulf's own clan; he was not always sure of their meaning. Passing the tents with the brown, gold and white ribbons, however, he could smell sourdough, and the attractive odor of baking bread; that was no different from home.

A multitude of women scurried around the camp, going about their morning work. They gave the strangers curious glances from beneath their head coverings, but did not speak. Marvulf knew that the many dark-haired young women were captured from towns the clan had razed, taken for concubines, virtually slaves that made the work easier for the women of this camp, but that also had to be housed, fed, and clothed. No wonder most of the family units had multiple tents. There were numerous babies strapped to women's backs, and many small children and young dogs playing among the tents. This was a growing clan, like his own.

The men and boys they passed did greet them, but did not ask their business. Marvulf surmised that, after the very public discussion at the race course yesterday, the entire clan knew why he was here today. As they were passing the large complex of tents marked with the bronze, black and gold yard sticks of the priesthood, they met Yashihar, who directed them further into the camp to Vladia's tents, where the gold, cats-eye green and light brown ribbons on the yard stick beside the main tent, its door flaps invitingly fastened back, proclaimed that the chief was present and available.

As they came up a young boy who looked so much like Ahna that Marvulf knew he must be another brother scrambled up from the mat where he had been playing a solitary game with some colored stones, gave them a wave, and disappeared into the tent. They were dismounting when he returned with Jaromir, flanked by Moshel and Redwolf, whose older brothers had already left. The clan chief greeted Marvulf formally, welcoming him to their camp and his wife's tents. Marvulf introduced his brother and Svander. They all smiled when

Redwolf was introduced; his personal name was the same as their clan name.

"Come," said the chief. "We will take your horses to the home pasture where they can get water and grass. I see you are not riding your golden stallion."

"I thought he should have a rest after the racing yesterday," Marvulf replied. "Besides, Dusky Lady here wanted exercise." He turned to his bulging saddle bags, pulling out two sizable round clay jugs stoppered with cork. "I brought some of the beer that my foster-mother makes from hops. There are many growing around where we are now camped. It is very good."

"It will be very welcome," said Jaromir. He turned to his youngest son. "Ahndru, take the beer in to your mother, and tell her who brought it. We will show our visitors the mares and foals before we return for dinner."

Ahndru took the jugs from Marvulf, but said, "I want to come, too, Father. May I catch up with you?"

Jaromir nodded assent, then walked away with Moshel, Redwolf, and Marvulf and his companions, leading their mounts. They stopped at the small equipment tent to remove the saddles and scrub the saddle marks from the horses with cotton shammies, replacing their bridles with halters from their saddle bags before releasing them in the same pasture from which Ahna had taken Firefly. They waved to the single herd boy, then walked over a nearby barren, stony hill toward a further rich pasturage, where the clan's broodmares with their spring foals, not yet weaned, were grazing under the watchful eyes of more of the younger boys.

Marvulf wondered where Ahna was and what she was doing. He assumed she was helping her mother prepare the midday meal; he knew that they had no other women in their tents to share the work. He wondered if she was looking forward to seeing him again, or if she feared him, perhaps even hated him, after the events of the previous day. Moshel told him that she knew he would be taking Firefly as they made their way up the hill.

"Is she very angry at me?" he asked Jaromir's foster son. They were walking a little apart from the others.

"She is very unhappy at losing Firefly," Moshel answered after a moment. He wanted to help Ahna, but he thought this privileged stranger would be very unlikely to relinquish his prize.

"Ahna is a very special girl," he went on. "She raised that filly from a foal, trained her entirely by herself. Firefly is the only horse she owns, and the only one she rides, although I don't think there is a horse she couldn't master if she wished. As for her encounter with you, I think she may be more angry at herself for losing control and pulling that knife than she is at you, though if you thought to impress her by snatching her off her horse like that it certainly didn't work!"

"I wasn't trying to impress her!" declared Marvulf. Moshel looked at him skeptically. "Well, all right, maybe I was, although at the time I was angry with her for beating us, and I thought I would teach her a lesson. You are right either way; it was a stupid thing to have done. I do not want to take her horse, not that any man wouldn't want that mare, but I don't see how I can change it now without letting her think I'm giving in to her, that she can get away with what she did. A woman who thinks too highly of herself is likely to be in trouble all the time."

"You're right, and Ahna has been indulged beyond what many consider proper in this clan as well. Even so, she is careful to keep her place. She never gets above herself. She is also very kind and capable, thoughtful, observant, and courageous, too."

"No one doubts her courage!" commented Marvulf. "Will she hold a grudge against me for what I did yesterday, or for taking her horse?"

Moshel looked at the tall blond stranger curiously. Marvulf was showing decidedly more interested in the way Ahna felt about him than he was in her mare.

"She doesn't hold grudges," her foster brother finally answered. "You might help change her impression of you if you told her you didn't mean to frighten her yesterday." He did not even consider suggesting that Marvulf say he was sorry. Men just did not apologize for anything, certainly not to women!

"I could do that," Marvulf said after a moment. "After all, I didn't." They topped the rise and looked down into a wide, shallow, valley, well-watered by springs emerging from the hillsides around it and still emerald with rich grazing at this late season, scattered thinly with trees through which a sparkling little river meandered. Hundreds of beautiful mares of many hues picked the grass while their long-legged foals bucked and played, nursed, spread their forelegs to nibble the turf, ran impromptu races, or slept sprawled in the sun. Moshel and Marvulf joined the others, who had stopped to survey the bucolic scene.

Watching the broodmare herd would have been Ahndru's duty this morning, if he had not been visiting with his brothers and then watching for Marvulf's arrival instead. He had caught up with them as they were releasing the riding horses and now walked ahead of them down into the valley and in among his usual charges, a little swagger in his step for the benefit of the other herd boys, who had not the luck to be receiving such important visitors.

They examined the mares and foals, discussing their breeding, their conformation, their dispositions, the accomplishments of various mares and their older offspring. Even Ahndru kept up his end of the conversation, his knowledge of horsemanship and breeding already notable, but Marvulf, although usually more into horses than any other subject, had trouble keeping his mind on the conversation or even on the admittedly admirable animals all around him.

He could not wait to see Ahna again, but he didn't believe he would get a warm reception from her, and was far from sure of his own ability to make a better impression today than he had yesterday. He was nearly nervous enough to have forgotten that he was the one who was supposed to be in charge.

It seemed like a very long time before the chief suggested that they head back to camp, yet he realized as they walked over the intervening hill that he had only the haziest idea of what they had been discussing and could not comment on the animals they had seen beyond "They're all beautiful." Jaromir smiled to himself, remembering having been just that distracted by Vladia when he had first met her in her father's tents, himself on a horse-trading mission and not seeking a wife at all.

Chapter 15

Ahna rode back down onto the flats where they were camped
and released Firefly among the other riding horses, after giving her
filly's neck a last fierce hug. There were horses she didn't know in the
field, but there often were, and she did not see Golden Boy. Perhaps
he would not have been released with the riding mares and geldings
even if he were here. Prized stallions were frequently kept separate
until the spring, when they were given their own bands of
broodmares. Had Marvulf arrived? She couldn't tell.

Ahna hurried back to their tents, knowing her mother would be
needing her help and feeling a little guilty at being gone so long.
Vladia welcomed her with a smile and directed her to finish
preparing the greens to be mixed with the yogurt. There were a
hindquarter of lamb and a whole rib of beef already browning on a
spit above the fire that burned in the back annex of the main tent,
where they were preparing the food. Fat melted from them, dripping
into the fire, causing sharp hisses and spurts of flame. Every minute or
two Vladia would give the spit handles a turn, exposing a different
side of the roasts to the direct heat of the fire. Ahna took over this task
and that of watching the self-seeded turnips, carrots, and onions that
had been dug from the overgrown gardens of the previous occupants
of this valley, which were dipped in olive oil and herbs and roasting
on shallow footed clay pans set in the coals.

The meal was to be much more elaborate than usual. It seemed
to Ahna that the preparations went beyond what was suitable under
the circumstances; it was more what would have been expected
before formal negotiations between heads of clans on some important

matter. She wondered why Marvulf, coming to collect his blood price, warranted such special treatment.

"Is he here?" she asked her mother. "There are strange horses in the camp pasture."

"Yes, Marvulf arrived some time ago," Vladia answered, not looking up from the cheese and herb mixture she was preparing. "He brought his brother and a friend with him. They are out with your father and brothers, inspecting the broodmares and foals." She was tempted to suggest that her daughter receive the young man with an open mind, but she held her tongue, knowing that her Ahna was as likely to take such advice in aversion as to take it to heart.

"We rode up into the eastern hills," Ahna told her mother. "We saw a lioness."

Vladia looked up in surprise. "You saw a lioness?"

"We did. She was resting in a tree, just watching us. She was beautiful."

"Just watching you," Vladia repeated. "She did not attack, or run away."

Ahna nodded. She looked around, making sure they were alone, and lowered her voice. "I thought she brought a message from the Goddess. I thought She was telling me to be like the great cat, obedient to Her laws and doing what I must, hiding my real feelings when necessary, but staying true in myself no matter what."

"Hush," said her mother, glancing around involuntarily, but she smiled at Ahna, and there was pride in her eyes. "I think you may be right."

When the sun reached its zenith the men returned to the tents for dinner. They were joined by another of Jaromir's foster sons, Tonzyl, who appreciated Vladia's cooking and so usually checked in with his guardian about this time of day. Ahna and her mother had places set for Jaromir and the seven young men on the rugs in the main tent, with starters consisting of bowls of fruit - grapes and figs and orange sea berries, a wooden trencher of the wild greens mixed with ewe's milk yogurt, honey and herbs, and the large bowl of crumbled goat cheese and herbs. Next to them rested a flat woven basket piled with another treat - round loaves of fresh bread leavened with soured milk and flour paste from the tent village's only baker and a pottery dish of butter.

Vladia presented the pan of warm water for the men to wash their hands as they came in, and Ahna held the towels for drying. There were also bowls of water and small towels in the eating area. They ate with fingers only, or if the food was mostly liquid, drank it from plain pottery or tightly woven reed cups. They cut their meat when necessary with the knives they wore sheathed at their waists. Finger bowls were only found at formal meals like this one, except in a few families where the men demanded an extra effort of their women all the time.

Ahna smiled at her father and brothers as they wiped their hands and thanked her, but when Marvulf and the strange young men stood in front of her she kept her eyes firmly lowered. Marvulf thanked her by name, adding,

"I have something for you. I will give it to you after dinner." Even then she did not look at him, but she couldn't help wondering what he might have brought her.

The men sat and ate, talking of horses and breeding, of cattle, and of some of the more interesting places they had camped or visited in the last couple of years. Her younger brothers, used to less formal meals at home, tried once or twice to include Ahna in the conversation about horses, but although she smiled at them she shook her head slightly and kept to her tasks. She and her mother served the main course when the men were ready: the roasts, broiled tongue and liver of beef, a platter of tender stewed chunks of dog, a pair of wild partridges that Moshel had brought in early that morning, steamed with herbs in a covered pot, and the fire-browned vegetables. They kept the clay cups filled from jugs and pitchers of beer or fermented milk or wine as each drinker desired. Even Ahndru had wine, well watered, and was given a small cup of the beer from Marvulf's clan.

The food was delicious, the meat brown and crispy on the outside, pink and tender and juicy on the inside, the vegetables evenly roasted, the fruits sweet and ripe, and everything seasoned to perfection. Ahna's family praised it all lavishly, and Marvulf followed their lead. While men had no obligation to thank their women for doing their duty, Jaromir had taught his sons that letting women know their extra efforts were appreciated resulted in more treats in the future.

When the men's eating tapered off to picking at the fruit and cheese, the women brought hot drinks and took the uneaten food back to the cooking annex, where they made their own meal of leftovers while they were clearing up. Ahndru's herd dog, Essie, a mannerly brown and white bitch with half-pricked ears and a single black patch covering one eye, also had leftovers. Jaromir preferred that the family dogs not share family meals, although in some tents the herd dogs were allowed to seize choice tidbits right along with the men, even before the women and smaller children.

When the women had left them to their own devices, the chief sent his sons and foster sons to the practice fields with Marvulf's brother and friend, saying he and Marvulf had business to discuss. The younger men went, elbowing each other and laughing; if they did not know what business was to be discussed, they could make a shrewd guess.

"Do you still wish to marry my daughter?" Ahna's father asked the tall easterner when they had gone.

"After that meal, even more than before," affirmed Marvulf. "You are blessed to have such a fine cook in your wife, and I would be lucky indeed to have one trained by her preparing my food."

"Indeed, they are both excellent cooks." Jaromir agreed. "Ahna is also a fine seamstress and basket-maker, and her pots and the other household utensils she makes are always adequate. She has helped with birthing ewes, mares, and pups, and has aided her mother at the birth of babies as well. She promises to become an excellent midwife. She has a good disposition, is soft-spoken and kind, and she has always been very helpful with her little brothers. She is a hard worker and has learned all her lessons well, including, I believe the lesson she learned yesterday," he added with a smile.

"I do have one concern, as I told you yesterday. Ahna can be independent and willful and sometimes even stubborn to the point of argument. I believe she is capable of great loyalty, and could keep her husband as happy and contented as her mother has made me, but she will need to be held on a light rein, at least until she gets to know your ways and accepts your wishes and requirements as her own. Do you think you have that much patience?"

"I believe so," answered Marvulf seriously. He took a swallow of wine. "The most useful... the smartest horses and dogs often require a lighter touch and more consideration in their training than the average, and are easily ruined by rough or impatient handling. I thought about what you said yesterday. I know both horses and dogs that have been made mean and unpredictable, even though usually obedient, by cruelty or thoughtlessness. How much more true that must be of a spirited woman! If you give Ahna to me, I will do my best to manage her with the care that her courage and quality deserve."

Jaromir thought about that for a moment, studying the young man before him. Finally he said, "I know it isn't fashionable, but you might get on better if you thought of yourself as partnering with Ahna, rather than as 'managing' her."

Marvulf nodded, but privately he thought that sounded a little too much like letting the girl have her own way. He believed as he had been taught that animals and women alike needed to be schooled to unquestioning obedience, both for their usefulness and for their safety as well as the safety and comfort of their owners or riders or husbands. The surest way to do that was indeed to train them with kindness and understanding, but firm mastery must also be established and maintained.

The two men discussed bride gifts and Ahna's dowery. There would be an exchange of their best livestock, both horses and cattle; such transactions were the primary way in which the clans kept their herds as well as their own offspring from becoming inbred. As well as the pick of her father's horses and cattle, Ahna would bring household goods, pots and baskets, clothes and furs and rugs and a pair of fine new double-walled felt tents, most of which she had made or helped make herself. Marvulf told Jaromir that in his clan a woman did not own anything except her personal clothing; even her jewelry and household goods were ultimately the property of her spouse. He was willing to concede privately that Ahna's household and her horses should be hers rather than his, but he had to point out that in the eyes of the rest of his clan he alone would have the disposal of all such property. For his part he would bring some of his finest horses and cattle as bride gifts for the men of her family, and jewelry from their accumulated treasures for her mother. He offered to give the chief a hardworking young concubine, knowing that losing Ahna would mean he had only Vladia to do all the women's work of their household, but Jaromir refused.

"I have had peace and contentment for twenty years with only one woman," he said again. "I would be a fool to change that now. Our three older boys are all fostered out, and will be setting up their own tents and families when they return to us. Vladia will have only myself and the two younger ones to look after, and other women of our clan have always helped her when she had need. We will miss Ahna very much, of course, but it is time she made her own life and family, and we will get along fine as we are."

They sat in silence for a little while, each thinking his own thoughts. Jaromir shifted his weight on the rugs; he was getting old if sitting in one position for an extended period could become this uncomfortable. Finally Marvulf spoke.

"Do we have an agreement, then? Will you formally accept my suit?"

"Yes," said Jaromir. "There is no one of close to our status in our own clan who is suitable for Ahna, much as I would like to have kept her near by. If she is your wife her social position will remain the same as it is here, and I believe, I hope, that you will also allow her to be herself, within reason. She will make you an excellent wife. She could have a good life with you."

Marvulf reached out his hand, and their palms met. "She is a treasure, and I will treat her as one. She'll give me strong sons; we will have a fine life together." He stood up, and stretched his own legs and back. As Jaromir got to his feet, he said,

"Do you wish to be married during the traditional rites in the spring?"

"Would the full of hunter's moon this fall be too soon?" asked Marvulf. "Father really is eager to see me wed. I would not want to wait until winter moon, and interrupt the solstice celebrations. The area where we are now camped is a little too limited in its resources for our herds, so we will be moving on in the spring. I think Father wants me established in my own household and in the clan councils before our next campaign."

Jaromir thought about it.

"That is only a ten-day more than two moons away. It may seem hasty to some people, but it can be done. I will speak to the priests about a special ceremony. I don't think they will object; the high priest has been after me to curb Ahna's freedoms and get her wed. Just between us, he had his eye on her for his son Srogaraad, and there is a man who would not treat her with any consideration beyond the barest expedience!" Jaromir glanced around the tent, then confided, "He is short-tempered, mean and as jealous of his own prerogatives as his father. It is not a match that would prosper."

"Then it is well we came to your horse fair, and, unusual as it was, well that you allowed Ahna to race, or I would never have met her," commented Marvulf. "May I go and find her now? I would like to make my peace with her, if I can, after that farce yesterday."

"Yes, go ahead," said his future father-in-law. "Do you mean to tell her that you have asked for her, and that we have a contract?"

"I will see how it goes," said Marvulf. "If it feels like she may be agreeable I will, but if she shows any aversion to me I would like some time to let her get to know me better. You have said that she is not yet anticipating marriage to anyone. I don't want to trigger the stubborn resistance you have spoken of by surprising her with knowledge of an imminent marriage to someone she thinks she fears or dislikes."

"That is wise," agreed Jaromir. "I won't speak to her of this until you are ready. I think you'll find her with her mother in the cooking annex, or perhaps at the brook washing up. Tell Vladia I said she was free to go with you. It might not be a bad idea to ask her to go for a ride, especially if you mean to take her mare with you today."

"I think I should, don't you?" asked Marvulf.

"Yes, I do. That is what she believes you came for. Oh, Ahna also wants you to have the saddle and trophy that Firefly won. She said she does not want them, since she will not have the mare. The saddle is a work of art, too fancy to be practical, but it is beautiful!"

"I will take them with me and keep them for her," said Marvulf.

Jaromir nodded as if that is what he had come to expect. He turned to leave the tent by the main entrance, getting back to the business of a clan leader, and Marvulf went out the other way in search of Ahna. Vladia was alone in the kitchen workspace. She gave him a smile and approved of his plan to go riding with her daughter.

*   *   *

Marvulf, following her mother's directions, found Ahna by the stream that the women of the camp used for bathing, washing clothes, and scrubbing cooking utensils. She had just finished with the cooking and serving pots. She greeted him quietly, gathered up the clean housewares, and started back to the tents. He walked beside her in silence.

They went into the annex and Ahna put away the pots, bowls and platters. Then she turned to her mother.

"What's next?" she asked.

"Everything is under control here," answered Vladia, smiling to herself at the picture of this proud young man tagging along after her daughter like a puppy. "I think you should take Marvulf out and introduce him to Firefly. I understand they didn't have a very positive first meeting yesterday." Vladia indicated Ahna's saddle-bags, closed and sitting by the smallest hearth. "Take as much time as you need."

Ahna frowned and started to object, but her mother looked at her steadily, and she sighed, gave Marvulf a brief hooded glare that morphed into a slight smile, and said, "Come on." Without asking if that was his wish, and without checking to see whether he was coming, she picked up the saddle bags and went out to the equipment tent.

He followed her, annoyance surfacing at her abruptness, but when he entered the storage area she was waiting for him.

"I'm sorry, I did not mean to be rude," she apologized. "I am too used to dealing with my brothers, but I owe you proper formality. Do you want to make friends with Firefly?"

His pique evaporated. "Of course I do! She is the most amazing mare, and we need to be friends. I did not get off on the right foot yesterday, with her or with you. I acted in disappointment and anger, which I usually make a point of not doing. I did not mean to frighten you."

Ahna started to deny having been frightened, but realized that that would not be entirely true. He was not looking at her, was fishing around in his knife case, and while she watched he pulled out her silver-hilted bronze gathering knife. Then he looked up.

"I brought this back to you," he said, taking it by the blade and holding it out to her. "It's too pretty and too useful to lose."

She looked at him in shock and put her hands behind her back.

"But... but I... I *stabbed* you with it! You want to give it back to me?"

He grinned. "Not for stabbing, except maybe vegetables. I think you acted in haste and anger, too. I don't think you will do it again, and I won't pull you off any more horses unless you want me to." He continued to hold out the knife, hilt foremost.

Reluctantly the corners of her mouth turned up. "I don't think I want you to," she said. She took the knife and put it back in its place at her waist, and then she did smile at him. "Thank you."

Marvulf found himself trying to catch his breath. He'd been too preoccupied with his own emotions to notice her smile after the race the previous day, and she had had no occasion to let him have one since, until now. He was already enthralled by her beauty. He thought he might die for that smile.

She watched him for a moment, but when he just gazed at her and said nothing further she turned back to the equipment on the floor of the tent. "Do you want to try Firefly?" she asked. "No one has ever ridden her except me, but I think she will be all right if you make friends with her first."

"She is too small for me," he said. He picked up his own saddle and bridle. "We could go for a ride, though. This is interesting

country. You might show me some of it." He watched her, and seeing
a hint of a nod, continued. "I will ride Dusky Lady, my war mare, and
you may ride Firefly."

She was happy at the prospect of another ride on her mare, but it
felt odd, having him give her permission. Firefly was his horse now,
she realized, and that was the way it had to be. The smile vanished.
She picked up her plain saddle and Firefly's hackamore. Her eyes fell
on the gaudy silver-mounted prize saddle that sat beside hers at the
end of the row, and she looked away, wishing briefly that they had
never raced at all.

"That's the saddle your father was speaking of, that you won
yesterday," Marvulf commented, examining it more closely. "It is
magnificent."

"Yes," she answered shortly, adding a saddle cloth to her burden
and heading for the tent flap. "Firefly won it. It belongs with her. Take
it, too, when you go."

"I will," he said, and followed her from the tent.

They walked to the home pasture and called the horses to them.
Marvulf's mare came right up to him, but Firefly hesitated when she
got close, blowing out her nostrils at Marvulf, then circling around to
come to Ahna on the side away from him, her ears slightly back. He
was glad; she might as easily have decided to drive him away. He
watched her out of the corner of his eye, busying himself with his
own mare while Ahna soothed the filly and tacked her up. When the
horses were ready Marvulf mounted without approaching Ahna or her
mare.

"Let her get used to my being nearby," he said. "She needs to see
me acting normally, see that I am not going to harm her or you, and
see how my horse accepts me. She must have thought I was crazy
yesterday. It isn't usual for a horse to bite someone if it is not war-
trained, especially not one with as kind a disposition as she seems to
have."

"She is not war-trained," said Ahna, swinging up onto the filly.
"She was protecting me. It may take her a little while to get over that
first impression. She doesn't trust you. Usually she is very kind. I was
wrong to say that no one else has ridden her; my youngest brother

and his friends ride her sometimes, bareback in the pasture. She is especially careful with the littlest ones that are just learning to ride." They trotted away from the meadow, crossing the river and starting up the same unmarked path that Ahna had ridden on that morning. At the crest of the hills, six or seven miles away, there was a great view of all the surrounding country.

Marvulf had an idea. "I have twin sisters at home, just four summers old. Perhaps Firefly can teach them to ride."

Ahna smiled. "She would be perfect with them. Twins. Isn't that unusual in your clan? It is in ours."

"Yes, it is unusual for them both to live, but all the rest of my mother's children are boys. She was not well for several months before Liviia and Laaria were born, and died only a few days afterward. My father decided that, since the babies were equally strong, they should both be given a chance to grow up. Vyarhe, my foster mother, nursed them. She is a kind, jolly woman, and almost as good a cook as your mother. You would like her."

They rode side by side; the steep hillside, having been stripped of trees and the larger brush for firewood, was open enough that they did not have to follow the track exactly. The sound of late summer insects filled the warm afternoon air. The sky, so clear that morning, was now obscured by a light haze, and there was no wind at all. The horses' tails slapped back and forth constantly, they frequently shook their heads to get bugs out of their ears, and both Ahna and Marvulf were forced to ward off attacking insects.

"I see no signs of rain," Marvulf commented, slapping vigorously around his ears "but my Uncle Rampat would say that all these biting flies portended a storm." Ahna reached into her saddlebags and got out a little pot of salve; skimmed beef fat mixed with crushed pennyroyal, tansy and sage. She handed it to Marvulf, saying, "They're common garden herbs in fat; they help keep the bugs away."

He rubbed some on his face, neck, and hands, then handed it back to her.

"Thank you," he said. "Vyarhe makes an insect repellant, too, but I often forget to pack it. I usually only remember it when it's needed, and that's too late. I need someone to remind me when I'm packing, I guess." A little smile creased her cheeks as she rubbed some on herself.

"How many brothers do you have?" Ahna asked after they had ridden for a space in silence.

"I have five younger brothers, four half-brothers and three half-sisters. My father has a second wife and two concubines. My foster-mother is first-wife. Her own children stayed in the tents of her former father-in-law; my cousins are all beyond needing her personal care. Her husband, my Uncle Nyedd, was gored by a bull a few months before my mother died. My father took Vyarhe as his new first-wife. She was pregnant when my uncle died, gave birth to a stillborn baby on the day my mother died. It seemed meant that she should raise the twins."

"You have a very large family," Ahna commented. "Your tent must be quite crowded."

"Our family really isn't much larger than others in our clan," he answered. "We have three living tents. Each of the women has her own. They all share a kitchen and work tent, of course. Your folk have large families, too. Your mother has six children. All women want many children, just as we want many sons. Some of the men have several concubines as well as two or three wives, though personally I don't know how they manage so many!"

Ahna held her tongue, though she knew that despite his certainty, all women did not want many children. The Goddess taught that there could easily be too many children, that smaller families were healthier in themselves as well as better for the long-term health of the culture and the environment. Nor did most women wish to share their husbands. She knew that her own home was more peaceful than most of the multiple-female households that were also common in her clan. In such households bickering and rivalry among the women was only equaled in its frequency by squabbling and even fighting among the children. She also knew her father had turned down several opportunities to add another woman to their home.

As if he had some idea what she was thinking, Marvulf spoke again, a little defensively.

"My father's wives and concubines get along very well. They like each other. They work together without conflict and the work is well and quickly done. I know that is not always the case. I think our family is peaceful because my father is careful to treat them all with equal consideration, taking into account their respective positions. He does not show favoritism."

"Tell me about Firefly's breeding," Marvulf began again after another silence. "Your brother said she has the same sire as that black colt of his. Who is her dam?"

"Summer Storm, who was my father's race mare when he was Moshel's age, and then his first war mare. She had many foals, and they are all wonderful animals; her blood is in great demand among our clans. She had been two years barren when Father brought home the southern stallion, and I think he meant to cull her, but he gave her one more spring, and she got with foal. Firefly was her last baby."

"Where did the stallion come from?"

"We don't really know," Ahna answered. "My father got him when the men raided the same town where he found my knife. It was beside a great river, and there were many unusual animals. As well as the stallion, he brought home a red and white bull, much larger than our cattle. The bull was too quiet and gentle, though. He lost weight turned out with our herds and could not compete with our bulls for cows, so we do not have any like him now.

"The stallion did very well among the other horses, but my father thought his foals were weedy, and had him gelded for war use after the first ones were born." She patted Firefly on her neck. "I think he wishes he had kept him whole now." She paused, a faraway look coming into her eyes. "Father brought me a kitten from that place, too."

"A ... kitten?" asked Marvulf.

"A baby cat, small enough to sit in my hands, with large triangular ears and a long wedge-shaped face and soft brown and cream fur and big green eyes. It grew in a few months to be about a quarter the size of a dog, long-legged and long-tailed and lean. It never got any bigger than that. It would make a contented rumbling noise in its throat when I stroked it. It slept curled in my furs, and caught many small rodents around the camp."

"What happened to it."

"I don't know. We moved camp when we had had it about two summers, the first time we'd done so since Father brought it home. It disappeared. I suppose it did not come with us when we moved. It was a pleasant animal to have around."

"I have occasionally seen small wild cats, especially around the grain storage places of the others, but they don't look much like what you just described. They are usually orange or grey-striped, and they certainly don't seem friendly!" he commented. "Your cat sounds more like a dog, at least in its disposition. Maybe it came from as far away as the stallion and the bull."

"I thought so, too," said Ahna. "Your Golden Boy must be from a distant land, as well. I have never seen a horse of such an unusual color, and he is so much taller than the rest of our horses, and rangier, too!

"He is from the steppes on the other side of a wide mountainous region a long, long way to the East," confirmed Marvulf. "My mother's brother made a journey to that area because he heard tales of these horses. He was gone two years. He came back with Golden Boy, who was a rather plain, gangly yellow yearling at the time, and two mares. The mares are bays, but they are obviously of the same breeding, taller and leggier than our stock, and with that polished sheen to their coats, which are unusually short and fine even in the winter. That was four years ago. We don't know yet whether Golden Boy will pass on his coloring, but he has proven himself strong, fast and enduring in many races. I am not war-training him; we will start using him for breeding in the spring. I hope his characteristics prove more preponderant than have those of the mares; so far their foals take almost entirely after their sires. It is hard to tell them from any other of our horses. My uncle is very disappointed in them."

"That's too bad, but Golden Boy may be different. He is certainly not plain now." Ahna said. "He is a magnificent horse. I don't think we could have won yesterday if I were not so much lighter than you; Firefly had a real advantage. I wish you luck breeding him. He would surely get foals like himself if you bred him to the mares your uncle brought home."

"He is a great horse," agreed Marvulf, "and Firefly is a wonderful mare. I mean to breed her to him. I cannot wait to see the foal."

"She will be a good mother," said Ahna, subdued. She'd been reminded that Firefly was no longer hers, and that she would never know her babies.

Just then Firefly shied sideways, one quick step, tossing her head and staring to the right. Ahna looked that way to see that they were passing the tree where the lioness had been resting only that morning. There was no sign of the great cat now, though. She patted Firefly's neck, soothing her.

"What got into her?" asked her companion, looking around to see what might have spooked the filly.

"Perhaps she caught a whiff of something on the air," Ahna answered. She said nothing of their earlier sighting of the lioness.

They topped the rise. From this vantage they could see the clan's sprawling camp in the wide valley behind them, and the ruins of the town a few miles downstream to the south. Except for the storehouse, it was now little more than flattened rubble that would soon be just a patch of weedy stones. They looked out over far-flung fields and pastures where the clan's livestock grazed. They could even see part of the long meadow with the little tributary where the racing had been held. In the other direction there were more scrubby ridges, the nearer ones stripped of their trees by the clan's endless need for fuel. A somewhat taller hill stuck up rounded and rocky against the horizon. Northward lay a range of ridges, almost mountains, still covered with real trees, a forest of mostly evergreens with many tall cypress, dark and brooding under the hazy sky.

"If we go up there, we will be able to see all the way to the big water ... the sea," Ahna said, pointing to the rounded height to the east.

"I've only seen the bay we had to come around to get here," commented Marvulf. "Let's go take a look." He had an idea. "This isn't a level race course. I'm thinking Dusky Lady and I can get there before you can."

Ahna almost laughed. She and Firefly knew every inch of these hills. "You're on," she agreed.

"Go!" he said, and she turned her filly to the south, starting down that side of the hill at a trot.

Marvulf's brows furrowed in thought as he started down the hill to the east, directly toward his destination. Why had she gone off in the wrong direction? Suddenly Ahna and Firefly appeared around the side of the hill and pulled up abruptly.

"Watch out for the canyon!" she called over the intervening low bushes. Then she turned the mare around and trotted back out of sight.

Oh-ho, so she thought he needed warning about the terrain. He continued down the hill, contemplating the lay of the land. If there was a canyon ahead of him, and if it drained to the south, as all waters in this area appeared to do, then he should be able to get around it to the north. He turned Dusky Lady at an angle down the hill and toward the northeast. In a couple of minutes he came on a well-used game trail heading in that direction, which confirmed his thoughts; the wild animals that made the trail were probably avoiding the canyon as well. He let his mare step out into a brisk trot, and they made good time toward the wooded slopes to the north.

Well over a hand's time later Marvulf finally reached the hilltop he had been aiming for. His chosen path ended up taking him right along the rim of that infamous canyon, narrow and not deep, but too wide to jump and with rocky sides far too steep to be negotiated by a horse, with or without a rider. It went on back toward the northern hills much further than he thought it should. When he finally reached its head, where a waterfall could be heard draining into it, he found a little valley with more gradually sloped sides. The track he was following turned across that, dwindling to a faint path hemmed in by the undersides of tall, closely spaced evergreens and sparse underbrush, spiky with dead twigs and branches that he and his horse had to push through. True, when they had attained the other side of the valley, their chosen route was again open and easy, but it took an inordinate amount of time and effort to get that far.

Ahna sat on a large square stone in the middle of the reasonably flat open area on top of the hill, munching on some dried beef from her saddle bags. Firefly was picking the sparse grass that grew between stones a little way away. Her saddle and hackamore lay on the ground beside her.

The girl stood up, smiled at Marvulf, and held out her water skin. "I have food, too," she offered. "Please get down and get something to eat and drink, and give that poor mare a rest."

"Next time I'll follow you!" he said ruefully, dismounting, undoing his girth and lifting the saddle off Dusky Lady. He used the damp saddle cloth to rub away the sweat marks on her back and belly, then shook the wrinkles out of it and spread it on a rock to dry. He pulled some spiky twigs out of the mare's tail, and others out of her mane, summarily straightening the tangled hairs. Then he took off her bridle, replacing it with a halter and ground tie. All their riding horses were trained not to wander more than a few steps when the short rope was dangling down in front of them.

"How long have you been here?" he asked, as he sat down on the rock and accepted the water skin. He took a swig and grinned in delight when he found it held beer rather than water.

She shrugged. "Not long." She had been there for nearly a half hand, but she did not want to emphasize the extent of his failure to make good on his challenge. She changed the subject, turning his attention to the view in front of them. Across the intervening hills they looked at the sea; they only knew what it was because of its unusual flatness. Even then they might have thought it was just more pale, hazy sky, it was so nearly the same color, except for the handful of misty grey-green islands pushing up out of it on the horizon.

While they were admiring the view a long low growl interrupted them. They both snapped around in alarm to see, not an animal, but immense grey and white anvil clouds climbing the sky in the south, their undersides an ominous black. As they watched, lightning lit up the darkness beneath the clouds, followed after several seconds by another threatening growl. Now a southerly breeze was blowing, straight into them.

"I think we'd better go," Marvulf said, standing up and grabbing his gear. Ahna obeyed him without a word, snatching up her tack and calling to Firefly. Both horses came promptly. Within moments they were mounted and headed back to camp at a brisk trot. This time Marvulf did follow Ahna, glancing to the south each time they topped a ridge or crossed an open area that afforded a view of the oncoming storm.

It wasn't wasting any time. Every glimpse he got it seemed to leap closer. The thunder rumbled louder and louder. Soon the sunshine they had enjoyed all day began to be obscured by scudding clouds, forerunners of what was coming. The breeze morphed into a contrary wind, picking up dust and twigs and throwing them in the horses' faces and their own when they were out in the open, slapping branches around them when they were among the trees. The horses tried to turn their tails to it, but the way home was generally across the wind; their riders kept them headed straight. They topped the last hill. They could see people around the tents in the camp below, checking and reinforcing the fastenings of the heavy felt, some of which was already flapping hard enough to be seen even from this distance. They saw the herders and their dogs gathering their charges and moving them to sheltered locations on the north side of slopes or banks. They kept going as quickly as they could, for fat cold raindrops were striking here and there; the storm was almost upon them.

It broke over their heads partway down the last rocky slope, rain in torrents, like standing in a waterfall, except that the wind was now so strong that the water came at them sideways. Some of it appeared to fall up! The light failed, eliminating any hope of seeing where they were going, and within moments the steep almost barren ground was slick and running with water. They could not even see each other except as shadows, although they were riding side by side. They slowed to a walk. Firefly and Dusky Lady picked their way down the trail without guidance from their riders; Ahna and Marvulf trusted the horses' eyes and instincts in situations like this more than their own. But Marvulf urged his mare on when she again tried to turn her tail to the storm.

"We'd best keep going," he shouted over the racket of wind and rain. "We are too exposed to lightning here, and we're nearly down." Ahna didn't answer, only edging the filly a little closer to Dusky Lady. Thus it was that Marvulf saw what happened when a blinding flash of lightning and its attendant ground-shaking clap of thunder startled Firefly into shying off the trail and onto a loose patch of water-logged gravel that gave under her feet. She scrambled for balance, only to stumble onto an even steeper and greasier slope. She started sliding, her hooves scrabbling among the stones, and nearly went down. With a violent wrench she saved herself from a fall, but Ahna went off over her shoulder, tucking her body into a roll that was meant to keep her out from under the horse's feet and safe from injury.

Firefly stopped, digging her hooves into the slippery slope, and gingerly turned back toward the shadow on the ground that was her mistress. She scrambled a few steps up the hill, slitting her eyes and shaking her head against the storm in her face. When she reached Ahna she stood over her, trying to shelter her from the rain, nuzzling her still form.

Marvulf leaped off his mare and, dropping her reins on the relatively secure footing of the trail, hunched at the top of the treacherous bank, calling Ahna's name. He could make out the dark bulk of Firefly standing motionless on the side of the hill a few paces away, but could find no sign of her rider in the rioting gloom, and his calls received no answer. He started slipping and sliding down the bank toward the horse. He got close enough to see Ahna, inert on the ground just as she had fallen, and Firefly standing over her. But when he tried to get closer, the mare pinned her ears flat to her head, stretched her neck toward him and bared her teeth. He stood still, afraid she might lunge at him and inadvertently step on Ahna.

"Come on Firefly," he spoke soothingly. "You've got to let me help her."

The filly snaked her head slowly back and forth, her ears still pinned, for all the world as if she were saying, 'no way!' The wind had dropped, and the sky began slowly to lighten, though the rain still fell heavily and water still poured over the ground in rivers; they were all as wet as if they had been swimming in a lake. Marvulf balanced awkwardly on the steep, stony slope, wondering how he was going to get to the girl without being attacked by her overprotective horse.

"Ahna," he called again. "Ahna!" Still no answer. He resumed talking to the mare, and after a couple of minutes one ear cocked a little forward. He essayed a step closer, the ear went sharply back, and Firefly thrust her head dangerously toward him, snapping her teeth together. She meant business.

"Ahna," he repeated, knowing that the filly was still going on her impression of him from their first unfortunate meeting, and it might take days to overcome her distrust of him. The still form on the ground stirred, then moaned. Marvulf thought he saw a hand go to her head.

"Ahna, wake up!" Firefly's ears came forward, and she put her head down to nuzzle her mistress. Marvulf saw the hand push the mare's nose away. Then Ahna sat up.

"Are you all right?" Marvulf asked.

"What happened?" the girl asked. "Who are you?"

"I'm Marvulf," he said. "Your horse slipped, and you fell. You must have banged your head. Does anything else hurt? Do you think you can get back on? Firefly won't let me come near."

She said something he couldn't hear, then, a little louder, "Firefly?"

"Your horse," he said. She must really have given herself a knock if she couldn't even remember the mare. "Does anything besides your head hurt?"

"I don't... think so," she replied after a moment. It was still raining, but the fireworks and wind at the front of the storm had moved on.

"When you're ready, try to get back on," he said. "We need to get you home."

"Home?" she mouthed, but after a short rest she used the mare's leg to pull herself to her feet, then stood leaning against her. When Marvulf again suggested she try to get on, she looked around, and then, steadying herself with a hand on the mare, stepped up on the big rock against which she had been lying. Firefly obligingly took a short step closer, and Ahna managed to get into her saddle, clinging to her horse's mane. She had not picked up the reins. Firefly hesitated a moment, then turned and picked her way across the steep slope toward home, holding her head a little to the side to avoid tripping on the reins.

They crossed the swollen stream, and passed the camp field, where the lone herd boy was just creeping out from under his felt lean-to beneath the low branches of a nearby service tree. The brief storm was gone, and the sun was coming out again, shining down on grass and trees and rocks refreshed and sparkling from the rain. Marvulf spoke to the boy, and he walked up to Firefly and handed Ahna the dangling reins. The mare made no objection. Then they rode on through the village to her mother's tents. Just as they arrived Marvulf said, "Look, Ahna, a rainbow!" It was a double rainbow, brilliant against the darkness of the receding storm. The girl smiled.

"Ahna, are you all right?" Vladia had come out of the tent and was staring at her soaked and very disheveled daughter. She reached up to help her down. Ahna looked around at her, cried out "Mama!" and burst into noisy tears.

"Ahna!" repeated Vladia, her shock showing plainly on her face. She hugged her daughter to her as the girl slid off the horse into her arms. "What's the matter? Are you hurt?"

"My head hurts, Mama!" Ahna wailed. "I don't know what happened!" She looked at her father and brothers, flanked by several people who had come out of neighboring tents to see if their help was needed. "I... I don't know who all these people are."

Vladia looked her over carefully, noting a small scalp wound that graced a fairly large lump above her right ear, and traces of the blood that had mostly been washed away by the rain.

"She fell off her horse during the storm," Marvulf said.

"I wasn't riding," Ahna said incongruously. "What storm?"

If she hadn't been so concerned about Ahna's obvious concussion, Vladia would have laughed. As it was she smiled fondly at her daughter. "The storm that soaked you like a muskrat," she said, squeezing water out of Ahna's sleeve. "The storm that is leaving us that rainbow. You banged your head, darling. The blow has made you forget, but you should start remembering again soon. The best thing now is to get you dry, make sure there is nothing else wrong, and then let you rest. Come on." She led Ahna into the tent, with a shake of her head when the entire group wanted to follow her.

Jaromir did follow her. "Will she be all right?" he asked his wife. She didn't recognize any of us!"

"She has a concussion," said Vladia. "Her loss of memory should be only temporary, but she may never remember what happened in the time just before the accident."

"She recognized you," her husband said. He sounded jealous.

I'm her mother, Vladia thought, but she said, "She will probably recognize you, too, after she is rested and the swelling goes down."

He went back out to the young men, and they all went out to the pasture to send Marvulf and his companions on their way back to their camp. He reassured them as to Ahna's health, although thanks to Vladia's qualifier he was not entirely sure of it himself.

"I did not get to ask her," Marvulf confided while the others were tacking up the horses. "Could I come back tomorrow, do you think?"

"Of course, if you want to," said Jaromir, "but she may not remember anything that happened today. She may not even remember you, or any of us, yet. I don't know how long it will take for her memory to come back."

"That's no good," complained Marvulf. "We were getting along all right, and now she may not remember any of it? Well, I am grateful to the Gods that she was not badly hurt." Her father nodded agreement.

"We are leaving," the younger man went on. "We were going tomorrow, but I can probably get a delay of one more day. Then we will have to head back. It will be at least half a moon before I might be able to return. Somehow we have to let her know about the engagement before then."

The other young men came up with Dusky Lady, and he swung into the saddle. "I will not take Firefly today," he said in parting. "It would upset the mare, after everything that has happened, and Ahna may be well enough to want to say goodbye to her tomorrow." They rode out of the camp, and Jaromir and his sons returned to their tents for supper.

Meanwhile Vladia got Ahna into dry clothes, checking her over for other possible injuries, finding nothing more than a couple of bruises. She washed the cut on Ahna's scalp with an infusion of antiseptic herbs, finishing with a clay poultice meant to draw any inflammation out of the truly impressive goose-egg. Then Ahna lay down to rest. Vladia kept checking on her while she was preparing supper. She knew that sometimes the worst effects of head injuries didn't show right away. Ahshela, their most experienced healer, had told them of a man who had gone to sleep some little time after suffering a concussion and never awakened. Vladia told her daughter to rest, but not to go to sleep.

Before she finished preparing supper she took Ahna some meat broth and flatbread. The girl drank the broth and asked for water, but had no interest in the bread. Her mother set Ahndru to watch his sister and talk to her if she wanted to talk, telling him not to let his sister sleep, while she finished preparing the meal. When her husband and sons came in she offered them the bowl for washing, then somewhat hastily served the food. She wanted to know if Jaromir had learned anything about Marvulf's afternoon with Ahna, but the talk was only of the storm and Ahna's accident. She did have to assure her sons and foster son that Ahna would probably be all right.

After the supper cleanup was finished she went in to sit with her daughter, taking her sewing with her. Ahndru had gone out into the evening with his brothers, and Ahna was asleep. With reluctance Vladia decided to wake her. She called her name twice without response, and a third time quite sharply, shaking her shoulder gently.

"What is it?" Ahna asked, a hint of petulance in her voice, when at last she roused. Then her eyes opened wide. "Have I overslept? Is it time to get up?"

"No," her mother assured her. "I'm sorry to wake you, dearest. I just needed to be sure you were OK." She removed the wide head band, and lifted the poultice from her daughter's scalp, breaking the dry edges gently away from her hair. The swelling seemed to have gone down quite a bit. "Does your head still hurt?"

"Yes, but not as much," the girl answered. "I'm really tired. May I go back to sleep?"

"Yes," said her mother, "but I will need to wake you several times during the night, to make sure the bump on your head does not take you away. I'm sorry."

Ahna sighed. "Ahndru was here talking to me for such a long time," she murmured as her eyes closed.

Vladia smiled, both because the complaint in her daughter's tone suggested that she was on the mend, and because the familiar way she spoke of her brother argued that she had recognized him, and taken his presence for granted. The older woman settled to her sewing, anticipating a long night, but reasonably certain that Ahna would be much better in the morning.

Chapter 16

Ahna woke with daylight seeping into her corner of the tent through the vents in the sides and top. She had a slight headache, a very sore spot above her right ear, and a nagging feeling that she had missed something. Something important! She vaguely remembered coming home the evening before, and her mother waking her several times during the night, but she could not remember where she had been before that. She pushed back the covers and started to get up. Vladia smiled at her from the pile of furs beside Ahna's nest where she had spent the night.

"Mother?" asked Ahna. "What happened yesterday?"

"Good morning!" said Vladia. "How much do you remember?"

"Only coming home with... that man, and you waking me up over and over last night. And a wicked headache." She reached up, rubbing gingerly at the tender bump. "I must have hit my head, but I don't remember that. I remember being wet all over. Oh, and there was a rainbow."

Vladia's smile grew wider. "You fell off Firefly during a storm. You did hit your head, probably on a rock. The blow made you forget almost everything: your ride, even who your father and brothers were. Now your memory is coming back. What is the last thing you remember doing before last night?"

Ahna thought a moment.

"I remember serving dinner. That man... Marvulf was there. Then we went out to the pasture so he could make friends with Firefly, but she didn't want to be friends." She looked surprised. "We did go riding, but I don't remember much of that. I certainly don't remember falling off. What a stupid thing to do."

"It was a very bad storm," her mother said. "You know all riders fall. Don't blame yourself. Get dressed and come to the work area. Don't worry about chores; one of the neighbors and her daughter are coming to help me this morning. We do need to talk."

Ahna pulled on her everyday divided skirt of green and tan cotton, her stockings and boots, a bright blue polished cotton blouse, fastened a sash patterned with dark blue and yellow interlocking triangles around her middle with a gold buckle, and tied on the matching gold-embroidered scarf. Then she took it off again and combed out and re-braided her tangled hair, her thoughts churning. Donning the required scarf, she grabbed her toiletries and headed out of the tent to the latrines, passing her father and brothers who were coming in for breakfast.

"Good morning, Father. Good morning, Moshel, Redwolf, Ahndru," she said, giving them a brief smile. She was too wrapped up in her own questing thoughts to notice the grins that blossomed on all four faces, widening as they realized the import of her calling them all by name so casually. She remembered them! They watched her purposeful progress for a moment before turning as one and going into the tent, hurrying straight through the main living area into the kitchen work annex.

They 'good morninged' Vladia in a chorus, and the two women who were helping her. Then Jaromir said, "We just saw Ahna. She remembered us. Does she remember everything?"

"Almost," Vladia answered, crossing the tent toward them. "She doesn't remember the ride, or the fall." She spoke to the young men then.

"There's no room for so many non-workers in this work place. Go back into the living area and in a few minutes we will bring your breakfast!" They looked at each other and left without protest, but Jaromir stood four-square, gazing thoughtfully at his wife.

"She doesn't remember riding with Marvulf yesterday?" he asked.

"No," she answered, "and he is coming back today. Do you know how they got on yesterday?"

"He said he had not found an opportunity to ask her, but that they were getting along well before the accident. He was concerned that she might not remember that."

"He should be! We need to explain it all to her before he gets here. I think maybe we should tell her that Marvulf has offered for her, and that you have a contract with him. There can be such a thing as too many unexpected shocks in one day."

"I promised him we would not tell her until after he had had an opportunity to ask her himself," Jaromir reminded her. "I think the young man still wants it that way."

He went out into the common area to wait with his sons and foster son for his breakfast.

Ahna entered the work annex from the yard, the questions having multiplied in her head while she performed her ablutions until she had no idea where to begin. Leaving the neighbor women to serve the men's breakfast, Vladia brought herb tea, flatbread, curd cheese and sea berries to the second hearth, where two stools awaited them. They welcomed the warmth from the low fire burning there, for even though it was still summer the early morning air was quite brisk.

"Tell me about that man," begged her daughter. "I can't believe I went riding with him and can't remember it! Why would he want to go riding with me after I... stabbed him at the races. Has he taken Firefly?"

A little smile touched the corners of her mother's lips. "His full name is Marvulf Storm. He is the eldest son of the chief of the Red Wolf clan, a mountain clan that is part of that horde to the east. Between you and me, I think the whole incident at the races happened not because Firefly beat his horse, but because he was fascinated by you. Going riding is not a common way for a young man to court a girl, but Marvulf may just be smart enough to know that it would please you more than any other activity."

"*Court* me? After I stabbed him? He must be *insane*!"

Vladia laughed out loud. "Oh, I don't think so," she said. "You are a very beautiful and accomplished girl. From what your father said of his words after the incident, Marvulf particularly admires your courage."

"Foolhardiness, more like," said Ahna, thinking that her 'courage' had lost her Firefly. She summarily dismissed the idea that this strange man from a distant clan could be interested in her becoming his wife. She finished her tea, her face and thoughts somber. "If he is coming back, Firefly must still be here. May I go and say goodbye to her now?" she asked. "I don't want to do it in front of him."

"Yes, of course you may," her mother said. "Go along." She indicated a pile of carrot trimmings and feathery tops next to the young neighbor girl who was preparing vegetables for dinner. "Take her those, why don't you."

Ahna rinsed her cup in the wash bucket and put it away, tied the carrot ends and tops into an old scrap of linen, and left the tent by the back door. Firefly nickered in greeting, running to her when she entered the camp pasture. Ahna gave her the carrots, then buried her face in Firefly's mane while the filly searched the ground for any bits she had dropped. There were no tears today. After a few minutes she sent the mare out with the rest of the riding horses on the grass, green and sweet after yesterday's rain, and turned back toward the tents on leaden feet. Coming toward her on the track from the north was an incredible horse, taller than any of their horses and of a bright yellow color that gleamed like polished gold in the sun. She stared, remembering Golden Boy, only gradually registering Marvulf on his back. He sat his saddle as if he had been created there, his long legs molded against the horse's sides, his well-muscled torso moving imperceptibly with the motion of his mount. He was dressed in dark green pants, shot with gold and tucked into tall polished leather war boots, a red and grey shirt of some tightly woven material, a heavy gold chain around his neck and an incised gold armband below his right shoulder. He was so blonde his hair was almost white, and as beautiful in his own way as his horse. And he was smiling at her.

Ahna closed her mouth and put her hands, with the soiled piece of ragged linen, behind her back as he rode up and slid to the ground. "Good morning, Ahna," he said. "I hope you are feeling better. How is your head?" He was still smiling.

"B..b..better," stammered Ahna, feeling uncouth. The young man turned to his horse, preparing to unsaddle him.

"There are no mares in heat in the field, are there?" he asked, glancing at her. She shook her head. He turned back to his horse, wanting to give her time to compose herself, needing time to gather his own thoughts. The effect she had on him was... unsettling. "Golden Boy has never had any mares. He will be all right out with the others as long as there are no other breeding stallions or mares in heat."

Ahna shook herself mentally and answered him. "No. None of the riding mares are in season, and the stallions are kept separate at this time of year. I... I have been saying goodbye to Firefly." The profound sadness that appeared in her eyes was almost more than he could stand. He nearly told her right then that he meant to give her back her horse, but his original reason for not doing so still held, so he didn't. He removed the saddle from Golden Boy, giving the slight sweat marks on his back and belly a cursory swipe with the saddle cloth before he took the bridle off and sent him out into the field.

The golden stallion immediately began prancing through the herd, his ears pricked and active, his tail flagged and his action high and long, a floating hesitation in each step: introducing himself to the clan's riding horses, showing off, making friends. The other horses responded, some squealing and even kicking, although not in serious defense, others trying to get close, to get a good whiff of this stranger. Firefly watched him a moment, then went back to grazing.

Marvulf picked up his tack and fell into step beside her. "That fabulous mare thinks she is better than he is. No other horse has ever beaten Golden Boy in a race!"

"Of course your horse was carrying a great deal more weight than mine," the girl said. "It must have been almost an unfair advantage."

"Oh, it was," he capitulated, grinning at her. She laughed again.

"You're a good sport. Except for my brothers, I don't know many men who are." Then she winced, giving herself a mental kick. What was the matter with her, that she could not watch her tongue better with him? She would get herself in trouble for sure.

He just smiled. At least for the moment he was willing to give her far more leeway than he would have allowed any other woman. He was mostly concerned with finding a way to get her off by herself, to make an opportunity to bring up the subject of marriage. But he couldn't think of anything that didn't seem obviously contrived. They approached the tents, taking the tack into the equipment area. He left his saddle and bridle in the visitor's space near the tent flap, shook out his saddle cloth and hung it on a drying rack. Then he opted for the direct approach.

"Do you think we could go for a walk and find some place to talk? You might like to know what happened yesterday."

She considered him, remembering what her mother had said. She was used to her brothers doing things with her, but even that seldom included "talk." It would have been much more usual for him to seek out her father and brothers, to spend what time he had here with the men.

"I don't see why not," she answered finally. "I've been let off chores for today," she smiled, "probably because of the knock on my noggin, and I would like to hear why I was hurt; I've fallen dozens of times without injury. Just let me tell my mother we are going."

They went into the work tent and found Vladia and the neighbor women preparing dinner. Marvulf greeted Ahna's mother with respect, and she gave them not only her blessing for their walk, but a cloth bag containing flatbread, cheese, a few olives, salty dried beef and ripe pears, and a small bladder of beer.

"Now you will not have to worry about getting back for dinner," she said, smiling. The young couple thanked her and went back out into the camp, moving between the tents along the main thoroughfare, discussing the meaning of the various yard sticks, and the designs embossed or painted on the tents.

They nodded to the folk they met, exchanging greetings, but no one stopped to talk. When they were passing the enclave of the priesthood, fronted with a forest of bronze and black and gold yard sticks that indicated the High Priest and his underlings were all present, a slender but fairly tall young man in priestly robes came out of one of the tents, stopping to stare when he saw them in the lane.

He had thin, lank dark hair, slightly lopsided features that somehow made him look dangerous rather than comic, and an expression of permanent petulance. Ahna tensed.

"What is it?" Marvulf asked quietly.

"Srogaraad," she said, without looking at the priest. "He is the only son of the High Priest. I've been avoiding him since, well, since I became a woman. He wants to marry me." She shuddered.

Marvulf was reminded of Jaromir's comments about the priest. Srogaraad moved toward the path as if to intercept them. As they came level with him they nodded and tried to walk on, but Srogaraad had other ideas. He fairly leapt to plant himself squarely in front of them, his attitude hostile.

"Where do you think you are going, an unmarried woman and a stranger to our clan, with no sign of even a chaperone?" he demanded.

Marvulf said quietly but firmly, "We are going for a walk. We have Vladia's permission."

That was the wrong answer. The priest turned red, his ire palpably increasing.

"You throw a woman's 'permission' in my face? That is no 'permission' at all!" He rounded on Ahna. "You should be dead, or at least severely punished. The law is clear and not to be ignored. Be sure that the Gods will chastise you for your transgressions, and your father for protecting you, and you," to Marvulf, "for not insisting that the law be enforced, especially as it is the same in your clan as in ours."

They gave him no answer. He continued to glare at Marvulf, getting angrier as the silence lengthened. Marvulf touched Ahna's arm and moved as if to go around the priest, but he only stepped closer to the tall young easterner.

"You are a stranger here. Your clan is not one of our allies. Who is your sponsor? You should not be in our camp without an escort. You definitely should not be in the company of one of our women without a chaperone! It is against our customs for you to be in her company at all outside of the tents and presence of her father." He took a tight hold on Marvulf's sleeve, and with his free hand grabbed

Ahna by the front of her shirt, then started marching them toward the priest's tents. "You're both coming with me to my father. He'll sort this out, and you won't like the consequences."

Several people were looking their way now, attracted by Srogaraad's loud, belligerent tone, but no one interfered. "You are making a fool of yourself," said Marvulf quietly. "Jaromir is my sponsor, and we have every right to be going for a walk together."

The young priest continued to tug them along. "You lie," he spat. "You have no rights in this camp because you are an unsanctioned stranger, and she has no rights because she is an unattached woman, and one who flouts the authority of the Gods at that. You are both in violation of the laws and you will both pay accordingly."

Marvulf looked at Ahna, shrugged, and then planted his feet, causing the slighter man to stop abruptly. "I do not lie, and no jumped-up priest will say I do," he growled low. "I came here on an entirely peaceful mission, but your actions come close to forcing me to challenge you. If I do, you will die!"

Srogaraad looked momentarily taken aback, then rallied, more belligerent than ever. "You cannot challenge a priest," he sneered. "It is against the law."

"In my clan there is no such law, and I don't believe it is a law that would hold between clans," snapped Marvulf. "But listen, Srogaraad," he went on, adopting a more conciliatory tone, "you are making a mistake. There is no reason why you should be told this, except that it would be to your disadvantage if this disagreement went any further; you would end up looking the fool. Ahna's father and I have a contract. She is going to be my wife. That makes me a veritable member of your clan and gives me the right to go anywhere with Ahna that I please, with or without a chaperone. Now release my sleeve and my future bride, and we will be on our way."

Srogaraad did release them, but he looked both perturbed and angrier than ever, as if he might have attacked Marvulf without ceremony if he had had a weapon. He glared at the tall blond man, then turned to Ahna. She was staring at Marvulf, a look of surprise on her face. The priest began to grin evilly.

"That *is* a lie, isn't it," he said to the girl. "There is no such contract."

She looked at him, shook herself slightly, then looked back at Marvulf. She smiled.

"Of course there is a contract," she said. "but it is supposed to be kept secret until Marvulf's father can be informed of it." She regarded Srogaraad blandly. "You won't tell anyone, will you?"

The priest raised a hand as if to hit her.

"I wouldn't if I were you," warned Marvulf in a low, dangerous tone. "Many people are watching you. If you strike Jaromir's daughter, you will owe him blood price, and you will pay it at the tip of my sword."

Srogaraad glared around, to find that Marvulf again spoke only the truth. He used some very unpriestly language under his breath, then, only a little louder, said through gritted teeth,

"She was promised to me. If I cannot have her, you certainly will not. Your marriage will never take place. I will see to it!" He turned and stalked back into the tent.

"I was never promised to him!" Ahna said indignantly.

"I know you weren't," Marvulf said soothingly, touching her arm and walking on. He wanted to avoid an argument between them. He could not be seen arguing with a woman on the village lane in plain view of everyone. He feared an argument was inevitable eventually; this seemed to him to have been the worst possible way for her to find out.

"Your father told me a little about Srogaraad," he went on. "I think he understated the danger. That man would positively enjoy beating his wife."

Ahna was not to be distracted. "Am I promised to you?" When he didn't answer immediately, she went on, "...or did you make that up to get him to leave us alone."

Marvulf looked at her. "I did not make it up. I really will not lie if it can possibly be avoided. That situation did not begin to approach the seriousness of one that would cause me to lie. Your father and I have a contract."

Ahna looked at her feet, scuffing the dirt path as she walked. "I didn't know," she said softly. He shook his head.

"You didn't know," he agreed. He would have gone on, but she was not paying attention.

"Father did not tell me. He did not ask me." She was clearly upset. "I did not think he would arrange a marriage without my knowledge."

"I don't think he would have, either, if he had any choice," Marvulf explained. "He told me that *I* needed to obtain your consent to the match, Ahna. The contract is contingent upon your agreement."

She looked at him. "Then why did he make it before asking me?"

"I think there were several reasons. We just met perhaps the most urgent one. Apparently the High Priest has been hounding your father to betroth you to his son for some time. Jaromir was afraid that your flouting of the law by sticking a knife in me would give the priests leverage to force him to comply. He may be the chief, but that position is completely dependent upon the consent of your people. Your actions, misinterpreted and reinterpreted and kept in everyone's view by the priests, might be enough to threaten his position, and even your family's place in the clan, if the priests don't get what they want. Your father believes the only way to save you from a marriage with Srogaraad, or alternatively your family from demotion and perhaps even exile, is to get you betrothed to someone else, someone whose own social position is unassailable, someone who preferably does not live within reach of the priests' anger, without delay." Marvulf chuckled. "I think your father may see me as something of a golden opportunity."

"That seems like a good reason," mused Ahna, "but I still don't understand why he did not tell me. Does he believe I would not see the necessity? I am *afraid* of Srogaraad!"

"You should be! The woman that isn't afraid of that bully must be foolish indeed. Your father didn't tell you of my offer because I asked him not to," Marvulf admitted. "I was really worried that your unfortunate first impression of me would cause you to refuse to even consider me as a husband. Then when I realized how much Firefly meant to you, that she was not just the best of a family herd, but your only horse and very special, and I had named her as my blood price, I thought you would have even more reason to reject me out of hand. I begged your father for a chance to change your opinion of me before you became aware that I had offered for you. That was why I wanted to go riding with you yesterday."

Ahna looked thoughtful, but said nothing. After a moment Marvulf went on.

"Your father truly values your mother. He says they are happy together, that it has always been that way. Your tents are peaceful and welcoming, not to mention that eating your mother's cooking every day must be like living in paradise. When I saw you at the races, when I saw your beauty and courage, I wanted you. My father has been after me for two years to choose a wife, but I resisted because I had never met a girl I wanted to marry. I wanted to marry you the moment I first saw you, even before I met you. Then when I came here and met your family and recognized the harmony in your home, I wanted that for myself, for my own future family, as well. I did not want to jeopardize my chances by forcing you into marriage.

"Ahna, you are desirable to me on all counts. Nothing that I have seen says any different. I feared losing you before I had begun to try to win you. I would not cause you distress, yet it seems that most of my decisions regarding you have been poor ones. Is there any chance... will you at least consider my offer?"

She glanced at him again. "Yes, I will consider it," she said quietly. "Come on. I'll show you one of my favorite places." They had left the clustered tents and were now walking across open, rolling country where some of the sheep were grazing, watched by boys and dogs. They passed a small barrow where the men killed in the raid last fall and the few elders who had died last winter were buried.

She led him around the side of a low, stoney hill to where a little brook, edged by a few tall trees, tumbled down a rocky cut from a higher dell and burbled away into the meadows. Though only a few minutes' walk away, the spot was out of sight of the camp. There were some outlying rocks in the shade of the last trees, smoothed by the passage of many years of water. Ferns and late summer wildflowers flourished there. Butterflies and dragonflies, grasshoppers and bees and crickets filled the sheltered spot with motion and sound. There was just room on one large, flat, shaded rock for them both to sit and spread out their dinner. She meant to remain on her feet, waiting on him, as was proper, but,

"Ahna, sit down," he commanded. "I want to talk to you, not up at you." She joined him on the rock, grateful to be out of the sun, which was nearly to its summer-heat-generating zenith.

She got the food and the bladder of beer out of the bag, spread the bag on the rock and put the food on top of it, then broke the generous chunk of hard ewes' milk cheese into two and handed the larger piece to Marvulf. "Tell me about our ride yesterday," she requested. "I still don't know how I came to fall."

"That was an accident, neither your fault nor Firefly's," he said. "The storm was intense; lightning flashed right above our heads when we were on that narrow stretch near the bottom of the hill. The thunder came at the same moment, sudden and deafening. Your mare shied, lost her footing, started sliding down that steep bank, and nearly fell. She righted herself, but dumped you in the process. Yes, I know you know how to fall off without getting hurt, but a misplaced rock can interfere with the most well-planned tumble. It was quite a large rock that you were lying against when I finally got down to where I could see you."

"How did you get me out of there?" she asked.

"I'm sorry to say that I didn't," he admitted. "Your fierce little mare wouldn't let me near you!"

"Firefly?"

"Yes, Firefly!" He grinned. "She has good reason to mistrust me."

"How did I get off that hillside, then?" she asked.

"You got yourself off," he answered. "You woke up, and you didn't know who I was, or even recognize Firefly, but after a little while you were able to get back on. The storm had let up by then, and you rode home with me. That's the whole story."

"Thank you," she said. She sat thinking, watching the little brook flowing in and out of dappled patches of light. They finished their dinner. He was mesmerized by the water, too, lulled nearly to somnolence by the ambience and the beer, when she spoke again. "Tell me about your family."

With a profound sense of having been here already, Marvulf told Ahna everything he had told her the day before, with nearly identical responses from her. He also told her what he had told her father concerning her property rights, if she married him.

"In the eyes of my clan, all the property you bring to the marriage becomes mine exclusively," he summarized, "and I alone would be legally able to decide its disposition. I swear to you that in my eyes all such property would remain yours, as it is here, and that you would have the sole disposal of it, subject in only the most major cases to my approval." He laughed. "I guess I would want some say in the matter if you decided to dispose of the roof over my head." She had begun frowning at "subject to," but relaxed and laughed as well at the picture of them tentless. Then she stopped him cold with a question which he could not answer as he knew she wanted.

"If I married you, would I be the only woman in our tents, unless, of course, we had daughters?"

"I... don't know," he responded honestly after a minute for thought. He hoped it was not a deal-breaker, but he would not lie to her. "I know that arrangement works very well for your father. I do not know if it will work for me. In our clan every man has at least a concubine or two, many have second wives and some have three, though that seems to me excessive. I am willing to try it your way, but I cannot promise that it will always be so. I can only promise, and this I do promise, that as long as you are my wife you will be my number one wife, with authority over all other women in our tents."

She sighed softly, but made no other comment. She did, however, have more questions.

"Would I have authority over the feeding and raising of our children?"

He hardly knew what to make of that. "Over their feeding, certainly. What do men know of the feeding of children? As for the way they are raised, the training of boys is a man's job. They need to learn many things that women cannot teach them. When they are small they learn what they need to know from their mothers, but well before they approach puberty they need the companionship and training of men. The girls, of course, would be entirely in your purview." She made no comment, glad that he had overlooked one vital aspect of the feeding of babies in which many men did intervene. She meant to hold him to his words today, as a promise if necessary. She had one more question.

"Is there a women's society in your clan, and would you permit me to join it?"

"There is a women's society, and of course you may join it! My foster-mother is, I believe, one of the leaders. They have their own observances and celebrations, and I believe even competitions. They companion and help and learn from one another just as the men do with other men. Do you know of clans in which there are not such societies?"

"No," she answered, "but the High Priest in our clan is trying to have our women's society disbanded. He would turn our women into concubines in all but name, and mute, ignorant concubines at that."

"Having met his son and heard his own foolish rantings at the race meeting, I'm not surprised. I am amazed, however, that your council tolerates such behavior. Certainly any priest who carried on in that fashion would be laughed out of our camp." He shook his head in wonder.

"Then your folk must have more sense than mine," she retorted. "Zynjaar Is very clever with words, and quick to turn circumstances to his advantage. People fear him, though they, and he, claim it is the Gods they fear, or should fear."

"Well," Marvulf laughed, getting up and helping her gather up the remains of their dinner, which she packed into the basket, "he is not a dog. He will not follow you. Marry me and you will be rid of his kind for good."

"That is a pleasant thought," she said, as they started back toward the tents.

Marvulf kept waiting, but she said nothing further. Finally as they approached her mother's tents he broke the silence.

"I have to be getting back soon," he said, "and tomorrow we are leaving for home. When do you think you might be able to give me an answer?"

She glanced at him sideways, shrugged, and ducked through the open flap into her mother's work tent. He followed her, frustrated, even annoyed.

Vladia looked up from the piece of mutton she was basting. She studied first Ahna, then Marvulf.

"Well?" she asked her daughter.

"Yes, I will marry him," Ahna answered her, causing Marvulf to let out a whoof of relief, mixed with not a little exasperation. Ahna looked at him and smiled, then turned back to her mother. "I don't suppose I really have a choice; at least the other options are rather unpleasant. But he" Ahna indicated Marvulf "is trying very hard to make believe that I do have a choice, and that is kind of him. In fact," she confided in a lowered but still clearly audible voice, "I think I might *like* to marry him!"

Vladia burst out laughing and set down her baster to hug her daughter. Marvulf stepped closer as her mother released Ahna, then put his own hands on the girl's trim shoulders and looked down into her mischief-lit eyes.

"You… You…" he couldn't think of a fittingly descriptive word. "You were teasing me! Now you've told me here, in public, where I can't kiss you." Ahna laughed up at him.

"We aren't 'in public,' and perhaps we're not as strict about things like that in this clan," said Vladia. "Go ahead and kiss her. I won't look." Suiting her actions to her words, she returned her attention to the meat, and if she glanced toward the couple a few seconds later neither of them noticed, nor would they have cared.

They broke apart when Jaromir, coming through the curtain from the main tent, exclaimed in pleasure. He, too, was much relieved, but he did not show it.

"Good," he said. "That's settled. Are you staying for supper, Marvulf, or do you have to get back?"

"I really do have to go," the young man said, "right now." To Ahna he said, "I'm sorry, but I must. I wish I could take you with me.

Still, two moons is not such a long time. I will be back before you know it." He pulled off his gold seal ring with the two wolves carved in it and held it out to her. "Keep this for me until I come back. I'll bring you a more suitable one then. Keep out of the way of that priest!"

"I will," she said," taking the ring and clutching it tightly.

"You take good care of Firefly!"

"Be sure I will," he promised. "I'll make friends with her, too. Bet she won't be any easier than her mistress."

They all laughed, and he turned to go. Jaromir, whose brows had snapped into a frown at mention of the priest, said, "I'll come help you catch her up," and followed his future son-in-law out the door.

Chapter 17

After breakfast the next morning Jaromir went to arrange with the High Priest for the marriage celebration. He was taken aback, but not really surprised, when Zynjaar summarily turned him down.

"You know…" began the thin, scant-haired, beak-nosed priest when the chief made his request. Zynjaar paused, then started again, drawing himself up to his full, bronze-robed height (he was a whole hand shorter than Jaromir) and putting all his authority as the clan's religious leader into his voice, "You know very well that I have honored you and your daughter by choosing Ahna to be my son's wife. You had no right to betroth her to this stranger from another clan instead. I might have understood, though it would still have been an insult unless you had consulted me first, if you had made a contract that cemented relations between our clan and one of our allies. The Red Wolf clan is not one of our allies, and geography dictates that they never will be. You know perfectly well that we are the easternmost clan of our horde, and that we are now moving down the west side of a large body of water, an arm of a vast sea which our forward scouts tell us will only get wider. The horde to which the Red Wolf clan belongs will have to move down the east side of that sea, or they will soon be fighting with us for territory. If Ahna marries this... this foreigner, one of our most accomplished and desirable young females will be lost to our clan forever, without even any political gain to show for it.

"I find your ill-considered contract even more unacceptable because, as I have heard, the clans of that horde still worship goddesses and follow false gods. They are doomed to a fate I would not want to see for our folk. I realize that is probably of less importance to you than it is to me, but I still find it hard to believe that you, of all men, have sanctioned such a match when it means you will never see your daughter again.

"But all that is beside the point. Your treatment of myself and my son, your lack of concern for our interests in this matter is beyond being an insult. If priests were allowed to make challenges, if it weren't against the commands of our Gods for me to fight, I would challenge you. As it is, I can only turn down your request to perform this marriage. The Gods will not look on it with approbation, and neither do I."

Jaromir curbed his inclination to sneer. He knew as well as the priest did that there would never have been a challenge under any circumstances; the chief was a renowned fighter. There had been no challenges in years; all the early challengers had died.

"I have never told you," said the chief mildly, "that I was willing to betroth my daughter to your son. I have many times told you I was not."

The priest's face swelled in anger. "I have asked often enough," he snarled, "and you have made excuses. You have not said the answer would always be 'no'! Srogaraad is the most eligible man of the right age in our clan. It is a highly suitable match. You had no reason to say no. My son and I have believed all along that when you thought your daughter was ready you would agree."

"What would you have me do, then?" said Jaromir, reining in his anger at what he knew was merely a political and personal power play, having nothing to do with either the Gods or the welfare of the clan, and not much to do with Srogaraad and Ahna. "I cannot rescind the contract. Marvulf would almost be forced to challenge me, and then we would be risking blood feud!"

"He is from an out-clan." Zynjaar repeated. "You could ignore his challenge with impunity and send him on his way. Even if you killed him, and his clan declared blood feud, they would have no opportunity to pursue it. We will be moving in different directions in the spring, with an impassable body of water between us." The priest lowered his voice to a more conciliatory and persuasive tone. "If you offered him a fair breach-of-contract price, perhaps half of Ahna's dowery, he probably wouldn't even challenge you. You are the clan chief. You owe it to the clan to keep your daughter at home."

"You would have me do that, although you know it is dishonorable?" asked Jaromir. "It would bring dishonor on our clan as well as on me!"

The High Priest could hardly say that that was just what he wanted, although he suspected the chief already knew it. Instead he said, "It is not as dishonorable as breaching your contract with me, or even as giving one of our best women, and some of our best livestock as well, to an out-clan!"

"There was never a contract between us," declared Jaromir, "and there never would have been."

"Well, pending contract, then," said the priest, ignoring the second phrase, "but that is of no moment. No priest of this clan will sanctify the contract you have made. We don't want the Gods angry at us!"

"I suspect they already are, for your misuse of their authority," snapped the clan chief, his patience at an end. Zynjaar started to turn red; that really was an insult. Jaromir spun on his heel and walked out.

*   *   *

When Jaromir arrived back at their tents he found Ahna, who had finished her regular morning chores, pounding wool into felt in the sunny work area outside the annex. A whole row of hemp sacks, recycled grain bags from the Others' storehouse that now held wool from their own sheep, stood against the tent wall near her. He had given her enough from the spring sheering to make both of her new tents. Later in the day her mother and some of the neighbor women would come to help her. Two moons was not enough time for one girl to make two tents, say nothing of the other preparations that were necessary. Indeed, Ahna had been working on her trousseau for years and had all of her clothing finished, folded neatly into the soft, rich new furs that would make up her marriage bed. No girl made the bulkier items, such as tents or pots or baskets, until she was engaged. It was too much trouble to move such things between camps if they were not in daily use. Many marriage contracts were made in the summer or fall, but very few marriages took place until the following spring, affording most of eight moons in a sedentary winter camp for a girl and her family to finish her preparations. Two moons was a very short engagement. It presented some logistical problems which Vladia had promptly set about solving.

Jaromir watched Ahna for a moment, then sat down cross-legged on the ground near her.

His daughter had greeted him when he walked up, but continued to concentrate on her work. Now she paused and stared at him, puzzled. It was very unusual for any man to pay even passing attention to a woman working.

"Father?" she asked.

"I need to talk to you," he said. "What exactly did Srogaraad say to you yesterday when you were out walking with Marvulf?"

Ahna thought a moment. "He said I had been promised to him, which was entirely untrue, wasn't it?"

"Of course it was," her father reassured her. "His father kept trying to get me to discuss a contract, but there are no circumstances under which I would ever give you to him."

"I knew you wouldn't," she said. "I knew he was lying, and so did Marvulf."

"Why did the subject come up?" Jaromir asked. "I asked Marvulf, but he only said that Srogaraad had threatened to stop the marriage. He was in a hurry. He said to get the details from you."

"Srogaraad stood in front of us and accused Marvulf of being a stranger without a sponsor, and of breaking the law by being out with me without your permission and without a chaperone. He said by law I should be dead. He began dragging us into his tent, supposedly to his father for judgment. Marvulf had to tell him of his contract with you to get him to leave us alone."

Jaromir looked at his daughter curiously. "Didn't that... bother you, learning of it like that?"

Ahna's lips curved up a fraction. "It did, a little," she admitted "I'm afraid I got back at him."

Her father laughed. Vladia had already told him about that. "What did Srogaraad say when you convinced him you were engaged?" her father continued.

"First he said we were lying. Then he said that if I was not to marry him I certainly wouldn't marry Marvulf. He said, 'The marriage will never take place. I will see to it!' He sounded... vicious... frightening. Father, I don't know what he can do to prevent it, but I think he meant it."

"Unfortunately there are many things he might do to try to prevent it," said the chief. "Let's hope that some of them are things even he wouldn't do." Ahna shivered, but said nothing. "He did do one thing this morning," Jaromir went on, "or at least his father did. Zynjaar refused to perform the ceremony or allow any other priest in our clan to do it. He refused to sanction the contract in any way. He talked just as Moshel says he did at the races, when he tried to prevent you and Firefly from running.

"Zynjaar's refusal to conduct the ceremony is little more than a nuisance," he went on. "We will get a priest from another clan. If worst comes to worst and we cannot do so, we will send you and a chaperone home with Marvulf, perhaps one of your brothers, and then he can serve as witness to your marriage before one of their priests."

"I want to have a proper wedding here, in front of my family and friends," Ahna said.

"So it should be," her father agreed, "and we will do everything we can to see it happens that way. Meanwhile, I don't know what else Srogaraad and his father may try. We can hope it will be no more effective than this ploy. Meanwhile, it's important that you do as Marvulf said and stay away from Srogaraad." He looked around, ascertaining that there was no one close enough to overhear.

"In particular you must avoid being alone with him. Indeed, I think you should not be alone at all. I would not put it past him to take your maidenhood, were he to catch you by yourself, and then of course Marvulf could not receive you as his wife. If there were no witnesses, and perhaps even if there were and you were seen to be fighting him, the rape would be determined to have been your fault, not his. You would have to marry him. That may not be right, but that is the way it is."

Ahna nodded. "Mother told me. I will not leave our tents without asking one of my brothers to accompany me, except just to do chores, and I will be sure to do those only when there are friends of ours around. I have so much to do before Marvulf comes back that I will not have time to go off anywhere, anyway. Mother is sending to Tzyoner for a concubine to do most of my work, so I can concentrate on this." She did not say so, but she had little interest in riding without Firefly.

*   *   *

During the next half-moon Ahna stuck very closely to their plan, only going out for personal reasons or to do chores, and then only when there were friends present, or she could get one of her brothers to go with her. Jaromir had to explain the necessity to Ahndru when he got tired of being asked to accompany her to the latrines, or to wash the clothes, or to stay by her if she was working outside alone. His enlightenment was enough to cause her little brother to threaten to challenge Srogaraad; the impracticality, not to say the illegality, of that course of action also had to be explained. At least he no longer objected if asked to stay near her. Often he could hardly be persuaded to leave her even when she was inside the family tents or with friends.

The concubine, a short dark girl about Ahna's age named Sara, came and took over most of her regular chores, returning to her tent in Tzyoner's compound at night, because there was no place for her in their tents, and Vladia would not make her sleep in the work tent hearth, as some were required to do. Ahna spent most of her waking time working on her trousseau, spending fine days in the outside work area making felt for her tents, stitching the pieces together with deer or cattle tendon fibers pounded into workability, or embossing designs in the felt. Many of her friends and their mothers came to

spend two or three hands' time helping her. Some worked on the
tents, some made baskets or leather for riding clothes and boots.

No pottery was made. It was simply too heavy and too breakable
to be hauled all that distance to her new home. She would make
what she needed once their tents were established. She knew how to
choose and gather clay that would make usable pots from the stream
banks, how to shape it and dry it and bake it in the outdoor fires;
those lit by the livestock guards were good for this purpose because
they burned all night and were not allowed to die down. Often the
women of the clans left all but their best pots behind because of the
weight when they moved camp, making new ones as needed. They
had a few bronze cooking utensils found in the settlements of the
Others, although most of the available metal was used for weapons,
but they also used skins or even tightly woven baskets for cooking
and serving food. They could do entirely without pottery if necessary.

On less fine days Ahna worked inside, putting the finishing
touches on her wedding outfit. It was a dress of fine linen, a soft
tightly woven material taken from one of the towns her clan had
overrun, short-sleeved, as her arms needed to be bare to display her
bracelets, and cut just low enough to properly show off her
necklaces. A bride traditionally wore all her jewelry. The dress was a
natural cream color that was nearly obscured by beautiful many-
colored embroidery around the bodice, supplemented with appliqué
on the long full skirt. The designs were mostly of traditional abstract
patterns with their own complex meanings: spirals, stylized bull's
horns, fish, symbols handed down from mother to daughter for
millennia. They depicted the holy cycle of life and death and rebirth,
and the connections between all things living and not in their world:
the teachings of the Goddess. The men thought they were fertility
symbols, and as such they were acceptable, especially at a wedding.
The same symbols were embroidered on the skirt, but here they
wended their way among stitched-on painted cutouts of animals, both
domestic and wild, many with babies, some in mating postures. These
really did represent fertility and the expectation of children, as well as
a desire to ensure the continued health of the natural world on which
the nomads had always been dependent.

Ahna made matching low shoes of soft, cream-colored leather, similar to those worn by women and men inside the tents in the winter time, except that the latter had the fur still on to line the slippers with warmth. With the help of the older women she made an elaborate headdress of a gauzy pale golden material pleated and gathered in layer upon layer, with polished stones and tiny gold and silver charms catching the light all over it, that would sit like a crown above her brow and flow down her back nearly to the ground. She wore the ring that Marvulf had given her on a thin piece of braided hemp around her neck. The only ring she would wear during the ceremony was the one he would put on her finger at the end to signify that she now belonged to him.

Several times she saw Srogaraad watching her. Sometimes he would glare at her, sometimes look right past her as if he didn't see her, but always he went away once she was aware of his presence.

Jaromir heard from his friends and contacts that Zynjaar and his subordinate priests were talking to most of the men, spreading the idea that it was not fitting for the chief to marry his only daughter off to a man from another horde altogether. The priests said that the marriage contract dishonored the clan and angered the Gods because the Red Wolf clan worshiped false gods, and even goddesses. They also said the marriage was against the Lion clan's best interests.

Jaromir also was told that for the most part the arguments of the priests were met with polite inattention, and in a few cases not so polite disbelief. More than one man had apparently said something like 'Why are you so insistent about this? It is Jaromir's business, not ours, and not yours. What's in it for you?' There were a few hangers-on like Jumri who tried repeating the high priest's arguments to their peers, as did his son Stepan, initiated into the warrior caste the previous spring and so able to speak on such matters. As the days passed it became clear that most of the men thought Ahna's father had done the right thing. Nearly everyone loved, or at least admired, Ahna as the daughter of their chief and an accomplished, properly modest young beauty of whom they could be proud. Almost no one liked Srogaraad, or would have wanted a daughter or sister married to him, even though most honored his father as their spiritual leader, their contact with the Gods, whom they should heed.

One afternoon Ahna was working out in the sunshine when Redwolf and a couple of his friends rode their horses right up to the tent. She looked up from her work to see Ahruset lifting Ahndru carefully down from in front of his brother, who was uncharacteristically naked from the waist up. Her little brother's left leg was held in a fixed position by three or four sticks, the whole wrapped in Redwolf's tan shirt, and Ahndru was trying very hard not to cry. Ahna scrambled to her feet, thrust her head into the tent and called "Mother, Ahndru's been hurt!", then hurried to her brother's side. Redwolf dismounted and took his little brother from his friend, being very careful not to jar the bandaged leg any more than he could help. Ahna took Ahndru's hand and walked beside them toward the open tent flap where Vladia now stood waiting.

"He fell between his horse's legs when he was trying to recover his mock saber from the ground," explained Redwolf to his mother and sister. "There's a bleeding bruise and I think the leg may be broken."

Ahndru had a painful grip on Ahna's hand. "It hurts… it hurts really bad!" he told her in an intense whisper. She squeezed his hand. "Mother will fix it," she assured him.

Vladia led the way to Ahndru's sleeping furs, sending Ahna to her own private quarters for her medical supplies while she helped Redwolf ease his brother down onto the bed.

"Now get a bowl of hot water from the big pot on the hearth," she said when Ahna handed her the rabbit-skin pouch. "Bring a cup and scoop, too" she added as her daughter headed toward the work annex. When Ahna returned her mother had removed the shirt-bandage and was gently examining Ahndru's leg. A shallow, oozing gash, curved like the edge of a hoof, on the inside of the shin about a third of the way down from the knee to the ankle exposed a short stretch of white bone, but that portion at least seemed to be intact. Still, something about the leg didn't look right to Ahna. "Is it broken?" she asked.

"I'm afraid so," the older woman answered. "See the slight bend to the inside? I think the blow cracked the bone just below the knee. There is some swelling there, but not, thank… all the Gods, in the knee itself. The bone is not very far out of line. We can straighten it and put a better splint on it. If you do not put weight on it, youngest son, until Ahna's wedding, it should heal very well. Did the hooves hit you anywhere else?" Ahndru shook his head no.

"Stir a quarter scoop of the willow bark powder and a large pinch of the crushed valerian leaf into a cup of hot water," she instructed Ahna. "Put a scoop of the dried blackberries and a quarter scoop of the powdered sweet leaf in as well; they will help the taste." She watched closely while Ahna found the correct herbs and fruit, each packet marked with multicolored ties that identified their contents, and measured them into the cup, then poured in some of the still-steaming water. When Ahna gave her the handleless baked clay cup she set it aside to cool, smiling her approval, then turned back to her son.

"When the tea is cool enough, you can drink it. It will take away some of the pain," she promised. "I am going to wash the blood off your leg now, but we will not try to straighten it or put the splint on until the medicine is working."

Just lying still with the leg supported had eased Ahndru's agony enough that he was able to pick up on something else his mother had said.

"Do I really have to stay in bed until Ahna's wedding?" he asked, not hiding his dismay at the prospect of such an endless period of inactivity.

"No indeed," said his mother, laughing. "I think it might be close to impossible to keep you confined that long. I said you would have to keep your weight off that leg until then." Her youngest son opened his mouth, but she held up a hand. "You will be able to go out with crutches. They are two sticks that you lean on, so that you don't have to use your injured leg. I will show Ahna how to make them for you, when we are done here."

"I can make them," offered Redwolf. "Ahruset had to have them when he sprained his ankle last year. He was so hard on them that they fell apart, and I helped him mend them. I remember how to make them, I think."

"Show me," said his mother, handing him a short whittled stick and pulling a corner of felt rug away from the hard-packed dirt floor. Red Wolf quickly drew two long lines that were separated by a perpendicular line at the top, had a second shorter cross line about halfway down, and came together in a point at the bottom.

"The top bar was about a handspan long, and the crutches were just long enough to fit under my friend's arms when he stood upright. They were fastened together with hemp string and hoof glue, and the top bar was padded with a scrap of sheep's pelt," he said.

Vladia smiled at her son. "That's exactly right," she said, "but are you sure you want to make them? It is usually considered women's work, and you will be inducted into the warrior society in a few moons. You are nearly a man."

"I like making things," said Redwolf, "and besides I want to do it for Ahndru. I should have checked the saddle before I gave it to him. I had no reason to think it would not be safe; it's been less than a moon since it was in regular use."

"What saddle?" said Ahna and her mother at the same time. "Wasn't Ahndru using his own saddle?" asked Vladia. "What did the saddle have to do with his accident?" asked his sister.

"Your saddle," said Redwolf to Ahna. He looked at Vladia. "Ahndru's saddle is too small for him now and I thought Ahna's might be perfect, and it was." He looked back at his sister. "I knew you would not mind if he used it."

"Of course not," she said. "You can have it, Ahndru. It will do until you are big enough for a man's saddle. What happened?"

"The girth was apparently frayed," her brother answered, "up under the flap on the far side. I guess Ahndru didn't check it, either."

"I did too check it!" interrupted his brother. "I yanked the girth and all the attachment leathers to make sure everything was OK before I put it on Digger. We always do that before we ride."

"You're right, we do," soothed Redwolf. "I should have known you would."

"Anyway," he continued, "the girth was tight when he got on, but it began to loosen up when we were doing our exercises. I saw him tighten it just before the accident. When he swung down at the gallop to pick up his practice weapon, the saddle slipped around under Digger's belly. Ahndru clung to it, and hollered at his pony to stop, but before Digger could respond the girth broke, dumping Ahndru right under the his feet. Poor Digger. When the saddle came off he wrenched himself into the air sideways. He froze the instant his hooves touched the ground again, he was trying so hard not to step on his rider, but one of his hooves had already hit Ahndru's leg when he jumped. It could have been much worse. That's a good pony!"

"He's a great pony," Ahndru put in, "but I am getting too big for him, too."

"Yes, you are," agreed his brother. "When your leg is healed, when you are able to ride again, we'll have to ask Father for a horse for you." Pain or no pain, a grin spread across the boy's face. "Next spring I will be ten summers old. Do you think I will get a foal to raise, like you and Ahna did?"

Redwolf leaned over to pat his brother on the shoulder. "I bet you will, if you take care of that leg so it heals straight and strong. You need two good legs to train a foal, you know."

"I'll take extra special care of it," promised Ahndru.

Both Ahna and her mother were looking thoughtful. Jaromir was very particular about the soundness and safety of their horse gear, and was always checking it.

"You'd better have your father look at that girth," said Vladia to Redwolf. A worried little frown knitted his forehead.

"I'm sure he will not blame you," his mother continued, "but I know he will want to determine what did go wrong."

"I'll tell him about it when he comes in," Redwolf agreed.

Vladia handed the cooled tea to Ahndru. "It doesn't taste very good," she warned him, "but it will make you feel better and help you sleep. Drink it all." The boy took a taste, screwed up his face, and drank it down fast. His mother went back to work cleaning up the cut and putting an antiseptic poultice of yarrow leaves and yellow balm on it. She would set the leg and splint it with straight sticks wrapped in soft rags once Ahndru was relaxed and sleepy from the medication.

When Jaromir came in Redwolf told him of the accident, and the broken girth. His father had washed his hands for supper, but it had not yet been served.

"Show me," he said to his number four son, and they both went back out to the equipment tent, where Redwolf's friends had left both boys' riding gear. When they came back in the chief looked grim.

"What is it?" said Vladia as she again held the washbowl for him. He appeared so concerned that she knew he had found something, and she could not resist asking. He did not seem to notice her unsolicited question.

"How is Ahndru?" he asked.

"He is sleeping," she answered. "The bone was only a little out of place, and was easily set. The leg should heal as strong as it was before. He was very brave. What did you find out?"

"The girth had been cut, most of the strands severed half way through from the underside," he answered. "You can clearly see the clean edges where they were cut. It is very different from the other half of each strand, which is pulled and frayed. A normal inspection would have shown nothing wrong, because you could not see the cut part unless you unlaced that end of the girth from the saddle. Even a good hard pull would not have warned the boys; it needed the repeated stresses of an energetic ride to fray the strands to breaking. Probably a few broke, causing the girth to become loose. Ahndru tightened it, putting more stress on the remaining strands. When he leaned down sideways, the extra pull broke more and stretched the remaining bits, loosening the saddle enough that it slipped. He clung to it, and his weight caused the rest to snap."

"The damage was meant to remain undetected," Jaromir repeated. "Someone wanted a member of our family, probably Ahna herself, to take a dangerous fall."

"Zynjaar's son?" asked Vladia in a near whisper.

"I can think of no one else. I can't imagine that it could be anyone else!" said her husband almost as quietly. "I am going to take this to the council, although I cannot name him because I have no proof." He took his place on the rugs and waited for his meal to be served. Ahna came in with flatbread and bowls; supper that night was a savory stew of leftover chunks of mutton in a lemon sauce with wild onions and herbs which her mother had collected and other vegetables that she had bartered with a neighbor to obtain. Jaromir broke with normal clan etiquette and told his daughter, along with Moshel, what they had found in the equipment shed.

"Thank you for telling me, Father," Ahna said, then went to get the drinks from the pantry while her mother brought in the food. The men answered Moshel's many questions; he had been out hunting with some friends and knew nothing of the incident. Then they discussed what was to be done.

"I want one of you near her all the time from now on," said Jaromir. "Srogaraad intended that she be hurt, or even killed. Or perhaps he hoped to follow her when she went riding alone, which she used to do so often, and have her right where he wanted her when she fell off. I don't think he can have done it only for a warning. She rides hard, and often on hills and along trails that can be hazardous. Certainly he had no way of knowing that she was not going to ride any more, or that Ahndru would use her saddle.

"Whatever he wanted, it didn't work, and he will know why it didn't work soon after I take the saddle to the council and tell them what did happen. The story will be all over camp by tomorrow night!"

"Why tell the council, if you can't accuse him?" asked Redwolf. "Won't you just be letting him know we know?"

"That is why," answered his father. "The men on the council aren't stupid. Most of them will realize immediately that he is probably the culprit. They will start watching him. He will know that if he does anything else which can be proven to be human-caused, he will be the obvious suspect in everyone's mind. I hope that will prevent him from trying any other tricks."

It all played out exactly as Jaromir had said it would, up to the part about prevention. He took the saddle to the council meeting the next morning, showing the other councilors the evidence and telling them what had happened to his son. The senior councilor ventured to suggest that perhaps it would have been better for the peace and honor of the clan if the chief had listened to the High Priest to begin with, but Yashihar spoke firmly to him.

"Our Chief is not responsible for this breach of the peace of our clan. The person who sabotaged that saddle is. Such an underhanded, clandestine attack is not fitting or honorable! How can you say that giving in to such egregious bullying is better than standing up for ourselves? That in itself is not honorable. It's a good way to become a slave. I know he is your son-in-law, but would you really have us all bow to the personal whims of the High Priest? He may represent the Gods, but he is only a man, after all." There were some nods around the circle. The eldest councilor took a drink from his cup and said nothing more. Even Jumri, so often Zynjaar's champion, held his peace. Yashihar turned to Jaromir.

"You will need to keep a close watch on Ahna," he said.

"I intend to," agreed her father.

"We will speak to Zynjaar," the horse master went on. Jaromir started to object, but Yashihar overruled him. "Don't worry, we will not make any accusations. We will simply tell him what happened, and suggest that the guilty person is breaking our laws and dishonoring our clan and needs to be stopped. We will ask him in all innocence to help us. I cannot believe he knows this sort of thing is happening and I think he needs to know." Again nearly everyone nodded, including the chief.

The meeting with the high priest did not, however, go well, as Yashihar later reported to his friend, who diplomatically had not attended. Zynjaar blamed the whole thing on Ahna, saying that her actions had angered the Gods and disrupted the peace of the clan so greatly that it was not surprising that some of the men wanted to teach her a lesson. He made it clear that although he did not perhaps go so far as to applaud the activities of the vandal, he was certainly willing to condone them, and not at all willing to help find the culprit with an eye to chastising him.

"That female needs a lesson in what is right and proper, and her father, too," he insisted. "The Gods have already punished her with one fall. Now They have caused her brother to be hurt. They will continue to punish her, and her family, until Jaromir mends his ways, and puts her firmly back in her place. What's more, the Gods will punish you and the rest of the clan for permitting such behavior. It is beyond what They will tolerate. Whatever calamity befalls, it will be your own fault. I have warned you!"

"The whole argument is absurd and self-serving," commented Yashihar to Jaromir, "but he was so forceful, is so persuasive, that half the councilors were close to apologizing to him by the time we left."

"He is all too good at twisting circumstance to bolster his arguments," observed the clan leader.

Chapter 18

A few nights later Ahna was finishing up her chores in the work area when she heard a strange noise, almost like a small child crying intermittently. It sounded like it was just outside their tents. Her parents had gone to Vladia's quarters and her brothers were playing a complicated game that used different colored stones as pieces in the main living area. There was much badinage and laughter; apparently Ahndru was beating his older brother and foster-brother all hollow. The noise from outside came again and, a few moments later, yet a third time: a drawn-out wail with pain in it, although sounding less like a child now. Ahna remembered she was not to go outside without a companion, but she wanted to investigate. Something or someone was in trouble.

She looked toward the passage into the main living area, to see Moshel looking back at her. The pained wail came again. "What is that?" asked her foster-brother in a low voice. Ahna shrugged.

"I don't know: some kind of animal," she answered, moving quickly toward the outside door as another cry, louder and more desperate, split the air.

"Let's check it out. I'm right behind you," he said, crossing the tent toward her.

Ahna reached the outer tent flaps, tossed one back to let some light out into the yard, and stepped outside. She paused while her eyes adjusted to the night. A waning three-quarter moon shown fitfully between scudding clouds, reminding her that the next full moon but one would bring Marvulf and her wedding. The wail recurred, this time rising to a shriek of agony. It seemed to come from just around the work tent toward the back of the complex. The panic in that last cry caused Ahna to hurry. The area behind the kitchen was in deep shadow, the tent itself cutting off the moonlight. A jerky, uncoordinated movement of something lying in the shadow, something pale colored and not as big as a dog, impelled Ahna forward, fearing that after all the sounds had been made by a baby. She entered the darker area, and found herself looking down at a large rabbit, now mute, that twitched and struggled to run, although the unnatural angle of its legs made it clear that it would never run again. Realizing with horror that someone had mutilated the poor animal, she started to kneel, turning her head to speak to Moshel. She caught just a glimpse of the man who bent to grab her, clamping her arms to her sides and lifting her off the ground with one arm, while he slapped a hand full across her mouth and began to run with her held against his chest, keeping to the shadows. Somewhere behind them Moshel called "Ahna?", and again, much louder, "Ahna! Where are you?"

Moshel took one look at the poor rabbit, whose struggles were becoming weaker, and knew what had happened. She had been standing here just a moment before. He had turned, thinking to fetch Redwolf, then thinking better of it had turned back, and in that few seconds she had disappeared. The moon went behind a cloud; suddenly everywhere was deep dark shadow. "Redwolf," he bellowed, "someone has Ahna!" He moved forward, groping in the dark but determined to find his foster-sister. He was still looking in the deepest shadows of the tent when his eye caught a movement to the side. He whipped around, seeing only a large ungainly mass that was moving rapidly away from him, deeper into the tent village on a path he could not see but knew was there. Moshel plunged after it, hoping against hope it was the person who had Ahna. "Stop! Thief! Kidnapper!" he shouted as loud as he could, praying his shouts would bring help. Then he stopped yelling and concentrated on speed. If his quarry managed to get out of sight around the dark tents, Moshel might lose him altogether. Just as it appeared that would happen, the figure ahead seemed to stumble, almost to fall. In a flash Moshel had caught up. "Stop, Srogaraad!" he commanded, grabbing the figure by the back of his shirt. He was rewarded with a grunt as the man turned and drove a fist into his face, knocking him back.

"Moshel! Help me!" he heard Ahna cry as he hit the ground. The shadowy figure ran on down the path, but now he seemed to be hampered by something. Moshel scrambled back to his feet and took off after them again. Ahna kept making noises, although they were muffled and indistinct, as if her face was being pushed into some soft surface. This time when Moshel caught up he did not warn his target. Instead he gripped the kidnapper's arm and leaped to the side, using the weight and momentum of his own body to swing the man around, trying to throw him on his back, so that neither of them would land on Ahna. He succeeded only partially; the assailant managed to shake Moshel off and keep his feet, but he dropped the girl. She scooted along the ground to get away from him and he dived after her, only to find Moshel clinging to his leg. He kicked out viciously, hitting Moshel's shoulder and again breaking his grip, but a light shown out suddenly from the entrance to a nearby tent and a man emerged, dressed only in a loincloth but with a sword in his hand, and called out, "Who's there? What's going on?" Ahna's attacker turned and fled.

Moshel reached Ahna just as Redwolf and the man from the nearby tent, who turned out to be Glygan, one of the council members, converged on them. She was huddled on the ground, hyperventilating now that the danger was past. She managed a nod when Moshel asked her if she was all right. Redwolf dropped down beside her to help her calm herself, and Moshel turned to explain to the puzzled councilor. When he told Glygan of the cries in the night and the mutilated rabbit, and the chase and ultimate rescue of the girl, their benefactor had only one question.

"Did you see who it was?" he asked, his voice grim.

"No, it was too dark," said Moshel unhappily.

"I just got here; I didn't see him at all," said Redwolf. He turned to his sister, whose breathing had calmed. He stood and helped her to her feet, then asked "Do you know who it was?"

"I know who it was," she said, "but in the dark I did not get a good look at his face. I cannot say for sure."

Jaromir arrived then wearing only his pants and, after a brief explanation from Moshel, sent his children home without speaking to Ahna. Thanking Glygan sincerely for his timely intervention, the clan chief then escorted the councilor back to his tent.

When he got home a little while later, the chief found the three siblings and his somewhat disheveled wife - they had sent Ahndru to bed - standing around waiting for him, sipping hot drinks that Vladia had prepared. He praised Moshel, whose right eye was beginning to show a bruise, for his diligence and his success in rescuing Ahna.

"I know you would not have gone out there without either Moshel or Redwolf, so I will not scold you," he said to his daughter. "In future, though, let one of them investigate any strange noise or other distraction you may hear or see. Do you believe it was Srogaraad?"

"I do," she said. "He was not heavy, but tall and very strong. I kicked and fought, but it was like fighting with a rock. Once or twice I managed to get one leg between his, and almost tripped him. I wish I'd gotten a good look at him!"

"That probably wouldn't have helped," her father said, "because a woman may not testify against a man. I wish one of your brothers had gotten a good look at him. If we could identify him for sure before the council we could get him banished for grabbing you like that. As it is, I fear his near success tonight will just make him more determined and bolder in his efforts to get to you. The man is obsessed. He has lost all sense, and that makes him very, very dangerous. You must be even more careful. Taking Ahndru with you to wash or do your morning chores is no longer enough. I doubt that Srogaraad would care that your brother was a witness if he could be assured of getting away with you, if only for a little while. He might even be willing to hurt Ahndru to accomplish it, although that would mean he owed blood price to me, or risked blood feud." He looked at his wife, then turned to his son and foster-son.

"I am going to excuse you both from many of your usual chores for the next two moons, including any night duty you may have,

Moshel. During the day I don't want you to let Ahna out of your sight."

"Father!", she protested. "Does that mean they are to watch me bathe, or use the rails?"

"Not if there are several other women nearby, and you take great care to stay away from any place where an attacker might hide and grab you," said Jaromir. "Then they can look the other way, but they are to accompany you to and from anywhere you need to go, and stay within calling distance no matter how many companions you may have! If you *must* go somewhere without numerous other companions, then your brothers must go with you, and keep you in sight. Even your mother will not be enough unless there are several others as well. I regret the necessity, but your safety is more important than your modesty." He looked at the young men, who looked nearly as dubious as their sister. "Any of your modesties!" he emphasized, causing them all to laugh.

Ahna looked appealingly at her mother, but only got a shaken head in response. "I will keep them with me," she said to her father at last. "I really was terrified tonight. That man is crazy!"

"We will stay with her," said Moshel, and Redwolf nodded agreement. "What about at night?" he asked. "Srogaraad might just be nutty enough to sneak in and steal her right out of her furs."

"I was coming to that next," said Jaromir. Privately he did not think that if the priest had the guts to come into their very home and into Ahna's sleeping quarters, he would bother to try to sneak her out. It was more likely that he would attempt to accomplish his objective right there, but the chief did not voice that concern. Instead he said, "We will take turns guarding her at night. Each of us will take one half of each night, so that you will have two nights in a row when you must watch. On the third night you can just sleep." He smiled. "You may bring your bedding and put it out here where you can watch the entrance and Ahna's sleeping place, but you are not to go to sleep during your watch! The furs are only to provide a comfortable seat. We should not have a lamp lit, either. If he does come, the lack of light in here and our familiarity with the layout of the tent will give us an advantage. When he comes, stay quiet until he tries to enter Ahna's cubby. If we are to accuse him before the council we have to have evidence that he was really after her, but be sure not to let him too near her. I don't think he means to kill her, since he did not do so when he had the opportunity tonight, but he might anyway if he thought he was going to be stopped. When he is obviously going in to her, call for help, and move to capture him. Once we have him, we will make a light and identify him for sure. I will take the first watch tonight, and then I will wake you, Redwolf, for the second watch. Moshel, you have already had enough excitement; you did an excellent job. You have earned your sleep."

"You sound as if you think he really will come, Foster-Father," said Moshel.

"Unfortunately I do," confirmed Jaromir.

*   *   *

For six days they had peace. With both young men around the tents most of the time, Ahna was never alone. She started to notice that Redwolf was visiting the work annex with increasing frequency, especially when meals were being prepared. Since he always came away with food, she and her mother both thought he was going through another growth spurt. Then one day when Ahna was helping prepare an unusually elaborate meal for guests from another clan, Redwolf came in no less than three times. The first time she and her mother were the only ones there. For some reason her brother looked disappointed, but he asked for some fruit and went away again. The second time she was looking right at the doorway when he came through it. His eyes fixed on Sara, enveloped in a brightly patterned apron too large for her and with strands of dark hair that had escaped their restraint falling about her face, at the second hearth collecting the baked flatbread and putting some more dough on the hot stones to cook. The boy's face lit up.

"Yes, Redwolf?" said his mother, who was preparing a tray of sweets and barely glanced at him.

"Could I have some flatbread and meat, please?" he asked, but his gaze remained on the concubine. Even before Vladia indicated her assent Sara had put a piece of hot flatbread onto a woven plate and, taking a knife from the work table, headed over to the main hearth to cut a slab of meat from an inconspicuous spot on the whole rib of beef roasting there. She brought the food to Redwolf with a smile. He took it, but kept looking at her. Her smile faded, and she turned back to her task. After a moment he called, "Thank you," and left the workspace.

The third time Moshel had just come in for a cup, and when Redwolf entered Ahna indicated his presence to her foster brother. Sara was scraping vegetables, and Redwolf asked for a carrot. Moshel's eyebrows went up, and he mouthed 'a carrot?' Then, as the concubine took one of the scrubbed vegetables to the freckled young man, and he accepted it without even glancing at it, Moshel started to grin. When Redwolf left Moshel went with him.

"Do raw carrots make a good appetizer?" he asked. There was no answer.

What do you think, Redwolf?" No response. "Redwolf?"

Ahna's brother shook himself out of his reverie.

"What? Oh, I'm sure you're right." He didn't see Moshel's widening smile.

"She is very pretty, for one of the Others," his foster-brother said. "Don't you think so, Redwolf?"

The boy nodded several times, as if his head had forgotten to stop bobbing, then twitched and said, "Pretty enough, I guess."

Both Ahna and Moshel teased him relentlessly for the next couple of days, but he could not stay away from the work tent, not if Sara was there. Then one day when the women were serving dinner, and Redwolf glanced toward the entrance to the work tent for the umpteenth time, Moshel and Ahndru started to laugh.

"What's so funny?" asked Jaromir.

"Redwolf's been smitten by a girl," said Moshel.

"I have not!" his foster-brother insisted.

"What girl?" asked Jaromir, smiling too, but when Ahndru told him his smile disappeared. He glanced at Vladia, who was setting down a woven platter of fruit and honey cakes. She met his eyes and nodded.

When Sara returned with the wood that afternoon, Vladia called to her, and invited her to sit down with a cup of tea, knowing by the alarm on the girl's face that she was aware this couldn't be a pleasant conversation.

"I'm terribly sorry, Sara," Redwolf's mother began, "but we will need to get another, older concubine from Tzyoner. You are a very good worker, and a lovely person, but we cannot have you here any longer. I believe you know that Redwolf is falling in love with you, or thinks he is. Since you have only been with the clan a year, and are still learning our language, you probably don't know what the consequences of that would be for him if we let it happen."

"I know he never... marry me," the girl said. "I... I could be... concubine?"

"Not for years yet," Vladia said. "Young men who have not been initiated cannot have concubines, and it is firmly discouraged for any man who does not already have a wife, unless he is a widower. Besides, if he does fall in love with you Redwolf would not, I believe, be content with your remaining a concubine. He would want to marry you, and that would ruin him, and probably the rest of the family, too. It is just not acceptable for clan men to marry your people."

Sara looked down at the floor, and surreptitiously wiped tears from the corners of her eyes. "I... I not want to hurt your family," she whispered. "You... you nicest people in clan." Vladia stood up and hugged the unhappy girl.

"I'm sorry," she said again. "Please ask Tzyoner to send an older woman tomorrow."

The next night Ahna went to sleep secure in the knowledge that her brother was on watch outside her curtain. Some time later she came suddenly awake, her eyes snapping open on a looming shadow that blocked the moonlight filtering in through the overhead vents, a hand clamped hard across her mouth, and a heavy weight pinning her to her furs.

"Be quiet, now," her assailant whispered. For answer she twisted her head a little to the side and clamped her teeth down on the ball of his thumb.

The man snarled and started swearing softly, but he did not snatch his hand away. Instead he wadded up some of her bedding with his other hand, then stuffed it into her mouth under the one she was biting, and pressed harder. Then he shifted his knee, for that was what was pushing into her stomach, enough to strip her covers away. With his right hand he took hold of her night shift at the throat. One swift jerk tore it from neck to hem, and he looked down at her, sucking in his breath admiringly. She struck out at him with both hands and kicked at him, too. He replaced his knee, pinning one arm and her waist beneath it, and slapped her offhandedly. Then he started fondling her breasts.

"Lie still," he commanded in a hoarse whisper, leaning more of his weight on her. "This will only take a minute." His left hand shoved the wad of fur further into her mouth. His right was now busy untying his sash and pulling off his own pants. "I wish we could make it longer," he said conversationally, "but the important thing now is to get it done. Once I have your maidenhead, you can scream as much as you want. By all our laws and customs, you will be mine." He giggled. "That foreigner won't even want you anymore!"

She tried to hit him, her free arm flailing wildly, but the fur crammed into her mouth and across her nose was cutting off her air and stealing her strength. She crossed her legs, determined not to make it easy for him, and he snorted in disdain.

Just as her attacker got his pants completely off and his male tool, all too ready to go to work, freed of its restraints, Ahna heard someone in the main tent say, "Redwolf? Redwolf!" Though she was close to blacking out, she struggled harder, kicking and hitting at him, trying to get his hand off her face, trying to make a noise, or make him make one. Then he did. With an exasperated grunt as her fist connected, he clenched a fist of his own and clouted her above her ear, right on the old lump where she had fallen against the rock. Pain shot through her head, accompanied by a flash of white light, and she slid down into darkness.

Chapter 19

Ahna could not have been out very long, but when she came to everything had changed. Her mother was sitting beside her on her sleeping furs, bathing her forehead and the abused bump with cool water. Her head hurt, but not enough to keep her from looking around in wonder. The tent was full of light. Numerous mutton-fat lamps, and even some of the others' candles, burned both in her cubby and in the main living space beyond. The drape had been pulled back from in front of her bed and she could see Moshel standing outside her quarters, barefoot and bare chested, looking toward her. Redwolf was there, too, leaning on his foster brother. He was fully clothed and had a bandage tied around his head. Beyond them she could see right into her little brother's cubby on the other side of the tent, for that curtain, too had been pulled back, and Ahndru was sitting up in his furs looking across at her. He gave her a grin and a fist pump when he realized she was awake and looking at him.

At least three of the men from neighboring families were also standing in the living area. On the floor between them, as far from Ahna as her brothers could get him, sat Srogaraad, trussed like a sheep for slaughter, and gagged. They had not even let him put his pants back on! Ahna shuddered when she saw him.

"Did he... did he succeed?" she asked her mother in a breathy whisper.

"No, he did not," Vladia assured her. "Moshel stopped him in time. Moshel thought you were OK, but I checked to be sure. It's a good thing, in many ways, that he didn't succeed. I think your father and brothers would have killed him out of hand if he had, and then we would all have been banished. It's not right that a priest should be exempt from violence if he is willing to use it himself, but that is the law."

Ahna was just about to ask where her father was when he came into the tent, followed by several members of the clan council. They looked at Srogaraad and at the two young men.

"Was it really necessary to tie him up like that?" asked the oldest, the priest's maternal grandfather. "I'm afraid it was," answered Jaromir. "Once my foster son pulled him off of my daughter, his one thought was to get away." He indicated the bruises on Moshel's face and his cut lip. "He would have, too, if I had not been awakened by the ruckus and come to help. We had to restrain him. We will release him when his father gets here if Zynjaar gives his word that Srogaraad will not flee. We need to settle this here and now."

After a moment the councilor nodded. Then Glygan spoke up. "You found it necessary to gag him, too?"

"We did that because of the unending stream of invective that he was spewing. It even woke people beyond our tents," Jaromir's neighbor Lwenli said, indicating the men who now stood silent but observant against the wall behind the priest.

"I think we might be able to remove the gag now," the clan chief commented, reaching down and doing so, only to have Srogaraad attempt to spit in his face. He jumped back, as the rest of the men in the room also took a step back in disgust.

"Trust him to make the most deadly of all insults when he knows he cannot, by law, be challenged," said Jaromir without rancor.

"What could you have been thinking, Srogaraad?" asked his maternal relative. Although the old man was some steps away in the middle of the tent, his grandson spat at him, too, eliciting a gasp from the councilors and a "tsk" from Yashihar, who was coming through the main tent flaps, accompanied by the rest of the councilors and Zynjaar.

The High Priest ignored his son's behavior, unacceptable as it was. Instead he addressed Jaromir.

"You have no right to hold my son here," he blustered, his deep voice full of righteous outrage. "You have gone too far. Let him go at once!"

Moshel stepped forward. "He would have fled if we had not tied him. I caught him in the act of raping the chief's daughter, a maiden of the clan. That is against all our laws and customs. We wished to bring him before the council for judgment. He obviously had no such wish."

"That is absurd, an unacceptable insult," snarled the high priest, ignoring Moshel and addressing Jaromir. "You only had to bring the charge against him in council meeting tomorrow, as would be right and proper. He would have come and answered your charges then, and he will do so. Now untie him, give him back his pants, and we will go home to bed."

"He might have come to answer the charges," said the chief, "but if you all had not seen him here what then would keep him from merely saying we were liars, that he had been in his bed all night. If he could produce a couple of 'witnesses' to his claim, it would be our word against yours, and you probably could have gotten him off with no more than a scolding, if that. His attack on my sons alone, unprovoked and here in their own home, warrants a high blood price, the more so because he himself is immune from violence. His worst offense carries a mandatory sentence of banishment. Ahna is my daughter, so the offense is against me, and I demand that he be permanently banished!"

Zynjaar changed his tactics. "You say you caught him in the act of raping your daughter. Has he raped her? Is she no longer a maiden? If that is so then she must marry him, and if you banish him you banish her as well."

"No," said Moshel, "he did not succeed in raping her. I stopped him in time."

"Oh-ho," crowed the High Priest, "then he is not guilty of rape, and is not subject to banishment at all! You have no proof that he meant to rape her if he didn't actually do so."

"Enough!" snapped Yashihar. Zynjaar tried to interrupt, but the horse master kept on in a commanding voice that nearly matched the

High Priest's own. "You're trying to twist the facts before we even
know what they are. This is a matter of civil law, a matter for the
council, not the priesthood. *We* will hear the evidence and *we* will
decide. He looked around at the other councilors, received nods from
several of them. "And we'll do it here and now while the evidence is
fresh."

Again receiving nods of agreement, this time from all the
councilors except Jumri, Yashihar turned to Zynjaar. "Will you assure
us that your son will not leave without our permission if we untie him
and allow him to resume a more seemly attire?" he asked. The priest
nodded curtly. "In that case, please instruct him accordingly. I would
not want him to run off and then claim that he had not seen your
nod."

Zynjaar gave an exaggerated sigh, turned to Srogaraad and said,
"Do you promise me and the council that you will not leave here
until you have permission, if they release your bonds, son?"

"Yes, Father," said Srogaraad. "They wrong me. The female is a
witch. She made me do it. She has put a spell on me. I demand that
she be killed and burned as..."

"You will get your chance to testify," Yashihar interrupted him. "If
I were you, I would consider carefully what defense you mean to
use." He didn't think the 'witch' argument, new on the scene as it was
and apparently requiring that for some unfathomable reason Ahna
wanted to be raped by a man she feared, would sway very many of
the councilors. "Until then please be quiet," he finished.

He signed to one of the men standing against the wall to untie
the young priest, and himself went into Ahna's space to retrieve his
pants and belt from the edge of her sleeping furs where Srogaraad had
discarded them. Finding the accused free of his bonds and standing
self-consciously in the middle of the main tent, Yashihar handed the
clothing over without comment, then set about getting the councilors
seated in a semicircle facing the center. Srogaraad turned his back
and pulled his pants on, tying the sash belt and noting with
satisfaction that the horse master had not bothered to remove his
knife.

"We need a moderator, a neutral party," Yashihar was saying, "to call witnesses and to keep order. I cannot do it. I am a member of the council and one of the judges." He looked around. The neighbor who had spoken before stepped forward. "Will I do?" he asked. Yashihar looked around the circle again, and receiving nods from the councilors, looked at the High Priest, who after a moment or two also gave a grudging nod.

"You will do very well, Lwenli," the horse master said. "Thank you." He sat down in his place in the circle of councilors, and the newly appointed moderator, a solid sandy-haired warrior of middle years and erect carriage, said, "Jaromir, since you are bringing this charge against Srogaraad, I think you should be the first witness."

The chief stepped forward. "I am not a witness to the attempted rape," he began, "only to events afterward, but I do have one piece of relevant information. Srogaraad, when my daughter and Marvulf Storm told him they were engaged to be married, threatened them. He said he would prevent the marriage. He said he promised it."

"Did you hear him say that?" asked the High Priest belligerently. "No," answered Jaromir.

"Than you have no evidence that it happened beyond the word of a woman," sneered Zynjaar.

"On the contrary," said Jaromir quietly, "it was Marvulf who told me of it."

"A foreigner," his interlocutor answered, the sneer becoming more pronounced, "is no better than a woman!"

"Please do not comment on the quality of the testimony," Lwenli admonished the priest. "That is for the councilors to decide. Go on, Jaromir. What do you know of what happened here tonight?"

"Because of the threat I have mentioned," the chief began again, "and because of the untoward things that have been happening recently of which you are all aware, including the attempted kidnapping of my daughter six nights ago, my sons and I have been keeping a guard on my daughter at all times. It was Redwolf's turn to watch for the first part of tonight. He was to have awakened me when the moon set; I was on duty for the rest of the night. He brought his sleeping furs and piled them near the work annex door where he could watch both her closed curtain and the main entrance. Then we all went to bed. He did not intend to sleep, though."

"My sleeping space is right over there," he continued, indicating the closed drape next to Ahndru's open one. "About a hand before moonset I was awakened by yelling and the sounds of a struggle. I came out immediately, to find my son Redwolf lying on the floor and my foster son Moshel struggling with Srogaraad, who appeared to be trying to leave even though he was naked from the waist down. Just as I arrived he hit my foster son in the face, knocking him down, and turned and ran for the door, but I was closer and got there first. He tried to push past me. I took hold of his arm to prevent it and told him he had to stay here. He reached to his waist as if looking for something, which of course was not there, and then he started to hit me. Moshel came up and grabbed his other arm, at which point he tried to kick us, and also began yelling again, mostly to the effect that we should let him go, that we had no right to hold him, that we were breaking the law by 'attacking' him, interspersed with a great deal of vicious invective unbecoming, to put it mildly, on the lips of a priest. We were trying to figure out how to restrain him without hitting or otherwise hurting him, given his continued efforts to escape, when some of our neighbors arrived. With their help we tied him up, still struggling and swearing. Then I went to my son, and my wife, who had come out of her quarters, went to check on my daughter. Redwolf woke up as I was examining him. He had blood on the side of his face. It appeared that he had been hit with something hard and knocked out."

"We will let Redwolf tell his own story," said Lwenli. "Is there anything else?"

"I did find a billet of firewood on the floor next to Redwolf," Jaromir said. "It had a little hair and blood on one end." He showed them the two-foot stick of split wood, handing it to Gylgan when he indicated a desire to examine it. The councilors passed it around while the chief continued speaking. "As soon as I was sure Redwolf was all right, and my wife assured me that my daughter was also well, although she was not yet conscious, I left my family in the care of my neighbors and went to rouse the council, starting with Horse Master Yashihar." He looked around. "The rest you know."

"Are there any questions?" the moderator asked. The councilors looked at one another.

"You did not see Srogaraad attempting to rape your daughter?" asked the eldest.

"No, I did not see him near her at all," Jaromir answered. "I only came in at the end of the action, as I told you." After a moment's silence Lwenli said to the chief, "There do not appear to be any more questions. Thank you, Jaromir."

"Will you tell us what you saw and heard tonight, Redwolf?" he asked next, turning to the young man.

"He is not yet a man! He cannot testify," objected Zynjaar.

"It is up to the councilors to make that decision!" repeated Lwenli a little testily. "Everyone knows the boy's age. Please stop interrupting. Go ahead, Redwolf."

"It's a very short story," Redwolf admitted. He was mortified that Srogaraad had been able to get past his guard. "I brought my furs here to sit on for my watch, as my father said. I stayed awake, keeping an eye on the door, listening to the crickets and watching the light of the moon move across the floor. I thought I heard a step behind me, and started to turn around. Something hard hit my head, and the next thing I knew I was laying on the floor with my father kneeling beside me and my mother crossing the tent toward me carrying a lamp. Srogaraad must have come in through the work annex and snuck up behind me."

"Only tell us what you actually saw or heard, son," admonished Lwenli kindly before Zynjaar could object.

"I beg your pardon," said Redwolf. "When I woke up Srogaraad was tied up over there, swearing worse than I ever heard even the Dedicated swear and demanding to be let go, with Moshel and our neighbors standing over him and no pants on. They asked him to stop swearing. When he would not you sent Moshel for a dish rag from the kitchen and they gagged him. My father went out then, saying he was going to bring the council. That is all I know."

There were no questions. Lwenli excused Redwolf and turned to Moshel. "I think you may know more of this incident than anyone else," he said. "Please tell us what you saw and heard, Moshel."

"The person who knows the most about it, besides Srogaraad himself, is Ahna," Moshel pointed out. "That may be so," said Lwenli, "but she is a girl and cannot testify. You will have to tell us what you saw and heard."

"I don't know what woke me," began Moshel. "I was not on guard duty tonight, and was looking forward to a good night's sleep. I sleep is the secondary tent, so I don't think I was close enough to hear anything, but I woke with the moon shining in my face, and for some reason I felt very uneasy. I decided to check on Redwolf and Ahna, pulled on my pants, and came here. I found Redwolf on the floor, out cold with that bloody piece of wood beside him. I called his name, but he didn't respond. Then I pulled the curtain in front of Ahna's cubby aside and saw Srogaraad trying to get her legs separated and get on top of her. She was limp, inert, with her head angled a little oddly to the side and her eyes closed. He must have knocked her out."

"Did you see him hit her?" demanded Zynjaar.

Lwenli held up his hand at the priest. "Just what you actually saw, heard, or did, son," he reminded Moshel.

Moshel pointed at Srogaraad. "I saw him, naked from the waist down, his penis erect and fully engorged, forcing Ahna's legs apart and starting to get between them."

"Wasn't it dark in there?" the High Priest interrupted again, his tone aggressively disbelieving. "You couldn't have seen all that!"

"You are not a witness here!" snapped Lwenli. "If you don't stop interrupting I will have to ask our neighbors to gag *you*! For the last time, it is up to the council members to ask questions and decide upon the value of the evidence. Go on, Moshel."

"There was moonlight coming down through the open vents, and my eyes were adjusted to the dark. I'd come over without a lamp and there was no light in the main tent except that of the moon. I could see Srogaraad and Ahna well enough. I yelled "Stop, Srogaraad!" He did not even look at me, and did not stop. Instead he tried to get himself into position to penetrate her. I took two quick steps across the small space and grabbed his shirt, dragging him off of her. He swung his fist at my head, but I blocked his arm, got a fresh grip on the back of his shirt and dragged him out into the main tent. He yelled 'Let me go, you pigturd, you cannot attack a priest!' Since I was now between him and Ahna's sleeping cubby I did let go of him. I did not think he would run off without his pants, but he spun around and ran for the tent flaps. He tripped over something and half fell. I did not want him to leave, so I grabbed him again. He renewed his demands for me to let him go, including accusations and swear words. I was trying to pin him with a wrestling move when he hit me in the face with his fist, knocking me back. He got up and ran again. Jaromir was there; he stepped in front of the priest and grabbed his arm. Srogaraad was still swearing and trying to hit my foster-father with his free hand. I jumped up and secured that arm. He started kicking at us, anything to make us let go of him. Then you and some other neighbors appeared, dressed as I am only in their pants, and between us all we got him tied up, though he never stopped trying to escape until he was securely trussed, and he never stopped yelling and swearing until you sent me for a towel, Lwenli, and gagged him.

"Jaromir was helping Redwolf. I went to check on Ahna. Her mother was already there. She said that Ahna was unconscious, that she could not wake her, and that there was renewed swelling around the old bump on the side of her head."

Zynjaar started to speak again, but Lwenli, who was watching him, took a step forward with his hand held up and the priest closed his mouth.

"I told Vladia I did not think he had penetrated Ahna, that he was trying to when I dragged him off her," Moshel went on, "and Vladia said she had checked and he definitely did not succeed in raping her daughter. Redwolf woke up then, and the chief told us he was going to get the council members. He thanked the neighbors for their help and asked them to stay and look after us while he was gone. They took turns going back to their own tents for the rest of their clothes, but I decided not to leave. Ahndru was calling to know what was going on; he has that broken leg and has orders not to get up without help. I pulled back his curtain and told him briefly what had happened. Lwenli's son went around lighting all the lamps with a taper from the banked fire in the kitchen, and Lwenli bandaged Redwolf's head. My foster brother wanted to get up, so we helped him to his feet, and he and I were standing at the open curtain to Ahna's cubby when she woke up, too. Her mother assured her that she was all right and then Jaromir came back with the rest of you, and here we are."

Lwenli then asked his second son and the other two neighbors to tell what they had seen. All three corroborated Jaromir and Moshel's stories about Srogaraad's actions and appearance when they came in, and the things that happened after that. They added that they had seen Srogaraad hanging around where he could watch Ahna numerous times in the last ten-day. The eldest asked if he was not simply pursuing his priestly duties in their neighborhood, but none of them had seen him visiting the sick or doing anything else that could be construed as priestly duties.

With so many in agreement about what they had seen and heard, Lwenli excused himself from testifying, saying he was not needed and it was important that he maintain the role of moderator.

Finally he turned to Srogaraad and asked him if he wanted to explain himself. "You do not have to testify," he told the priest. "No man is required to testify against himself, probably because such a requirement would only lead to lying."

"Yes, I want to testify," said Srogaraad. "She made me do it."

Lwenli sighed and glanced at Yashihar, who shrugged. "Go ahead," the moderator said to the young priest. "Start at the beginning. Tell us how Ahna made you do it."

"I think the beginning was about two years ago," Srogaraad said pensively, using a priestly storytelling mode, mesmerizing and persuasive, "when she became a woman. It seemed she was always around, riding that horse, racing immodestly with her brothers, wandering through the village and over the hills with the women, always watching me, flirting with me from a distance, doing so much that was improper for a girl. She would not let me stop thinking about her. I don't know how she did it. Do any of you know how witches do what they do? No one knows except the witches. If you do know, then you are a witch."

"The truth is she made me desire her, and since the only honorable way to have a maiden of the clan is to marry her, I wanted her for my wife. She wasn't ideal. Left to myself I never would have chosen a woman as spoiled and impertinent and unwomanly in her behavior as she is, but she has bewitched me. My father approached her father about a contract, but he refused to make one. Over and over he refused. We thought probably he believed her still too young, so we waited, only occasionally reminding him that we expected a contract when the time was right. Meanwhile she kept teasing me, kept tying her spells tighter around me, until I couldn't wait to make her mine."

He paused a moment, as if contemplating what might have been. A note of petulance and frustration crept into his voice. "Then her father gave her permission to ride in the races," he went on, "against all our laws and customs. She flaunted herself in front of the men. Her behavior, and the clan's acceptance of it, angered the Gods. She was disciplined by that stranger from an out-clan, and she pulled a knife and stabbed him. For that she should have died, or at least been severely beaten, but she has bewitched him, too, I guess. He would not invoke the penalty, although it is the same in his clan as in ours."

"Her spell by then had such a hold on me that I did not want to see her die. Despite her transgressions, we meant to offer for her one more time. She is well trained; her domestic skills are acceptable, and I believed that her social misbehavior could be trained out of her. Then I saw her walking, alone and unchaperoned, with that unsanctioned stranger, Marvulf, and they said her father had made a marriage contract for them, in spite of her having been promised to me for so long. That our own chief would give his only daughter to another horde altogether, give away her fine breeding qualities. It is not fitting. It made me very angry. She must have increased her spell; I could not let her go despite her unsuitable behavior, her blasphemy. That alone proves she bewitched me, otherwise how could I even consider tying myself to such an evil creature? I told them I would not allow the marriage and she smirked, as if I had done what she wanted."

"We tried to show the way to the members of the council and indeed to all the men of our clan, but she must have bewitched nearly everyone, for few could see the light. I could not stay away from her, was forced by her spells to be near her, no matter how much I did not want to be. Finally, tonight, I found myself coming here against my will. She drew me to her. She wanted me to take her. I don't know how or why, but she did." He stopped talking. There was a short silence, broken only by someone in the back of the tent turning and expectorating out the door.

"Do the councilors have any questions?" asked Lwenli.

They looked at one another. "Several," answered Yashihar dryly. He bowed to the eldest first.

"Why did you cut the girl's saddle girths and make those other clandestine attacks on her and her family in the last half-moon?" his mother's father asked.

"I... didn't," the young priest denied. "I had nothing to do with any of that! She and her family are feeling the disfavor of the Gods, just as my father has said."

"The Gods did not cut that girth!" stated Yashihar. "That required the hand and knife of a man." He looked pointedly at the long knife in its sheath on Srogaraad's belt.

"Others are unhappy with the ongoing blasphemy from Jaromir's family. The Gods are using someone to punish them. No man caused Ahna to fall off her horse and hit her head. That was a storm sent directly from the Gods!"

Another of the councilors spoke up. "Are Srogaraad's boots in Ahna's sleeping area?" he asked generally. Jaromir glanced at his wife, still sitting beside Ahna beyond the open curtain. She shook her head no, and the clan chief answered "No, they are not."

"Do you usually go out barefoot at night, Srogaraad?" he then asked, looking pointedly at the priest's bare toes sticking out of his pant legs.

"No, I don't" he answered, glancing involuntarily at the door into the work annex, then quickly down at his feet as if surprised. "I told you she has bewitched me. I didn't even know I had come out without my boots." Moshel had seen that quick look at the back door. While he was considering it, he saw the High Priest duck out the front. He turned and pushed through the flaps into the work annex, ran across it, and stepped outside. He looked around quickly but carefully; in just a few moments he found a pair of boots partially hidden under a pile of empty fleece bags in the area where Ahna had been working on her tents. He picked them up, and looked up as Zynjaar came hastily around the corner of the tent. The priest winced when he saw Moshel with the boots, then looked around as if he was lost. "I need to go to the rails," he said lamely. "I'm not used to this part of the camp in the dark."

"It's back that way and down the path to the left," said Moshel, accepting the ruse. He took the boots back into the annex.

When he stepped into the main tent Srogaraad was apparently answering another question with the same line about Ahna's bewitching of him and angering of the Gods. The sudden stillness as everyone realized what was in Moshel's hand got his attention. He broke off as Moshel approached him.

"I found these under some hemp bags out back," said the young warrior, holding up the boots. "I do not think they belong to any member of this family."

"Are they yours, Srogaraad?" asked Yashihar bluntly.

The priest started to shake his head, then thought better of it. Anyone's boots could be identified by the person who made them, and the fit. His mother had made his boots, and always put the sigil of the owner under the cuff. "Let me see them," he said, and Moshel handed them to him. He made a show of examining them, then said, "Yes, they are my boots."

"If you came out without boots, as you said, how did your boots get out by the back door, and why were they concealed?" asked Yashihar.

"I have no idea," the priest claimed, "I don't remember leaving them there. It must have been part of her spell." Even he seemed to feel this excuse limped. He looked angrily at his father, who had just come back in and would not meet his son's eyes.

There were no further questions for the accused.

"It is true that Ahna cannot testify," said Yashihar then, "but Moshel has said that she appeared to be unconscious when he pulled Srogaraad off of her, which, if true, is not consistent with Srogaraad's claim that she wanted him to rape her. I, for one, would like to examine her, if Jaromir will give his permission, to see if there is evidence of her fighting him."

"I do give my permission," the chief said, "but I think there should be at least two to examine her." Everyone knew Yashihar was his friend; he thought it essential that there be more than one person to testify to what the Horse Master found.

"I, too, would like to examine her," said Srogaraad's grandfather. Jaromir gave him a nod of respect and approbation. The two men went into Ahna's sleeping space, but they did not close the curtain behind them. The entire assembly watched while, without touching her, they examined Ahna. She blushed ferociously as they looked first at her arms and legs, her mother saying nothing but moving the coverlet to show them something on her thighs, and then at the elder's request holding a lamp close to her face while they looked at something there. When they came back out the old man appeared shaken. He gave Srogaraad a look in which disgust and sorrow were equally mingled and silently resumed his place in the circle. To Lwenli's raised-eyebrow inquiry he responded only with a wave toward Yashihar, then dropped his eyes and contemplated his hands in his lap.

"Please tell the council what you found, Yashihar," said the moderator, but the Horse Master turned to Srogaraad, and in his eyes and voice there was not only contempt but an intense anger.

"If, as you say, Ahna brought you here with a spell because she wanted to be raped," he demanded of the priest, "how came she to be out cold when you were pulled away from her, and why are there great dark bruises on her arms and legs and especially high on her thighs and around her mouth, as if she had been fighting. She was clearly held down, silenced, and battered with force because she fought you. Finally, how came there to be a fresh bruise and swelling on the side of her head where the old injury was quite healed, a bruise which must have come from a blow that knocked her unconscious? Can you explain that?"

"I've been told Women always pretend they don't want it, especially after they have been asking for it," answered the young priest. "Perhaps it gives them more pleasure to fight. I don't know. I haven't much experience with them. If she had not wanted to be raped, she would not have bewitched me into wanting her, and I wouldn't be here now. Her struggles were just for show. Besides, no man has the right to question any other man's treatment of his woman."

"She is not your woman!" Yashihar snapped. He turned to the rest of the council. "I for one have seen and heard enough." There were nods all around the circle, even from the eldest, although he did not look up.

"Then the council will deliberate among themselves," said Lwenli. "Jaromir will of course abstain, as he is the injured party. Do the rest of you wish to retire to a different location for your discussion?" The councilors looked at one another, most shaking their heads. Stepan's father looked at Zynjaar, then said tentatively that he thought they should wait the deliberations until tomorrow. No one agreed with him; Gylgan voiced the general opinion when he said they should get it done now.

"No," Yashihar answered Lwenli. "A corner of this tent, perhaps Jaromir's sleeping quarters, will do fine." The clan chief showed them his private space, and they took a lamp and crowded into it, dropping the curtain behind them. They were gone perhaps a hand's time, and the murmur of their voices seldom rose enough for the words to be understood, although there was little talk in the main living area. One phrase they did hear. Into a momentary silence among the waiting men someone behind the curtain protested, "No woman is that important; this is the High Priest's son!" They did not hear the response. Srogaraad took a minute to pull on his boots, then sat down and spoke quietly to his father, who answered him as quietly. When the councilors came back out they looked grim.

"The council has asked me to be their spokesman," said Yashihar when all were again seated, and Srogaraad stood before them with

his father on one side and Jaromir a couple of steps away on the
other. "We have made our decision, and it is unanimous." Zynjaar
glared at Stepan's father, who stared right back at him. "We do not
find any evidence that Ahna is a witch," the horse master continued,
"nor that she has encouraged Srogaraad in his pursuit of her. Although
some of her actions are unconventional, her manners, her skills, and
her attention to the duties of a young woman of our clan have always
been unexceptionable. What's more, far from encouraging attentions
from you, Srogaraad, most of us have observed on more than one
occasion that she has avoided your company, and even appeared to
fear you.

"All the evidence we have heard and seen says that you came
here tonight with the intent of taking Jaromir Winter's daughter Ahna's
maidenhood, and thereby forcing him to marry her to you, as is the
law in our clan once a woman has been raped. You have by your own
words admitted that you did come here tonight to rape her. We
believe that you knew there would be a guard meant to prevent just
that, so you removed your boots outside and approached Redwolf
with stealth, striking him from behind with a weapon and knocking
him out, which by law is a second offense for which Jaromir is
entitled to blood price, as he cannot challenge you to redress the
wrong upon your body because of your caste. The blood price is
increased three times because your dishonorable action against his
son took place in his own home, because Redwolf is still a boy, and
because he was unarmed.

"The charges have been proven beyond any doubt that we can
see. Therefore we find you guilty. For the attempted rape of Jaromir's
daughter we sentence you to permanent banishment from this clan.
Your actions have shown you to be unworthy to be a representative of
the Gods, so you are also stripped of your priesthood and its
protections."

"Only the priesthood can take away a man's robes," objected
Zynjaar, but even he seemed subdued by his son's behavior and the
extent of the evidence against him.

"That is another of your newly invented rules with which we
simply do not agree, Zynjaar," said Yashihar. "No one can be above

the law, or the law is meaningless. Nor can anyone make their own laws to suit their convenience." He looked directly at the High Priest.

"We understand how hard these proceedings must be for you. Look into your heart. If this were not your only son standing here, but were instead one of our sons that had done what he has done, would you not be siding with us instead trying to defend him? I don't require an answer to that question, just that you consider it." He turned back to the accused.

"If, Srogaraad, you are found by any member of this clan after tomorrow at dusk, you may be killed, with no more consequences to the one who kills you than if you were a badger or a fox. If you are found within five miles of our camp, it will be the duty of those who find you to kill you. For the blood price owed we also order that all your personal livestock and property is forfeit, except two horses, your clothes, and your personal weapons. Jaromir may take his pick of your property for himself, Redwolf, and Moshel before whatever is left is distributed among the families of men who have been killed while fighting for the clan."

Srogaraad had been listening in growing disbelief and anger while the verdict and sentence were specified. As Yashihar finished the ex-priest yanked out his knife, raised it high and struck at Jaromir, yelling *"You* will never..." He was brought up short with the point of his weapon scant fingers from his surprised target by two young warriors who had been standing against the wall behind him during the entire proceedings, on their toes watching him, knowing he was potentially worse than one of the Dedicated because more unpredictable. He tried to struggle, but Lwenli stepped forward and wrenched the knife from his hand, and his captors twisted his arms behind his back, forcing him to his knees. Yashihar consulted with the other councilors for a short time, then turned back to him.

"I don't know why we continue to be surprised at the depths of dishonor to which you are willing to stoop, Srogaraad. Had you killed, or even seriously injured, our chief, your life would be instantly forfeit. By law, since you did not draw blood, we cannot put you to death, but we are agreed that in view of this attempted murder you will be banished without honor, and without either a horse or a weapon of any kind."

"He will die!" exclaimed his father.

"I fear that is unlikely," answered the Horse Master. "He is too mean to die. The sentence stands." He glanced at Jaromir, who had gone to speak to his foster son, and pointedly had his back turned to the priests.

"Come, Zynjaar. We will see you home, where you can get your son a traveling pack, which we will inspect to be sure the terms of the sentence are followed, and send him on his way in good time to avoid his being hunted like a sheep-stealing wolf." Yashihar nodded to the two young men, who pulled Srogaraad to his feet but showed no disposition to let go of his arms, and preceded them out of the tent.

Chapter 20

Yashihar and the two warriors escorted Zynjaar and Srogaraad back to their complex of tents. It was some time after moonset, but the stars had not yet begun to fade. When they reached the tent of Nuzeani, Srogaraad's mother, Zynjaar tried to dismiss them, but Yashihar stood his ground and looked the high priest in the eye.

"We are not leaving," he stated, "until we have checked Srogaraad's pack to make sure that the terms of the sentence are being obeyed, and seen him to the five-mile limit. You may have forgotten, Zynjaar, that he just tried to kill our chief, but we have not. Because he knows the law, and still tried to kill an unarmed man in front of many witnesses, we are convinced that, at least at this moment, he is not concerned with preserving his own life. We are charged to be certain that he has no opportunity to return and take someone else's life before the amnesty period expires."

"You will simply kill me the moment it is legal," said Srogaraad bitterly.

"That is what *you* would do," said one of the young warriors. "We are men of honor. When we have passed the five-mile limit we will let you go. We will not kill you unless we catch you within that area on some future occasion, after the amnesty period has passed. You will have time to thoroughly remove yourself from our vicinity, even on foot. We advise you to do so without delay. Please get the things you plan to take with you now."

"We will wait for you," said Yashihar. "You'd best hurry; we're all tired."

The high priest and his son went into Srogaraad's sleeping quarters and dropped the curtain. Yashihar signed to one of the young men to go outside and watch to make sure Srogaraad did not try to escape their supervision by creating a new entrance. They had taken his knife, but not his father's. The second warrior took up a post at the back of the tent, while Yashihar waited by the main entrance. They could hear murmuring between the priest and his son; they made no effort to hear the words.

Zynjaar was pleading with Srogaraad not to double back and seek his revenge at the cost of his own life the moment his escort left him alone.

"Wait," begged his father. "I will bring you what you need. You don't have to throw your life away. I promise you I will get back at Jaromir and that wicked girl."

"What good is my life now, without wealth or power, without even a home or a people," whined Srogaraad, but he did not want to die.

"You are young and strong and savvy. You will find a place, and earn back your wealth and power," his father assured him. He did not berate his son for his actions; he knew why Srogaraad had gone to rape Ahna. He only wished the boy had succeeded. The only consequence then would have been a relatively moderate wergild, such as that which might be paid for the death of a prized stallion, to compensate Jaromir for the loss of his daughter as a marriageable commodity. He did not for a moment believe that Jaromir would have exiled his own daughter just to punish Srogaraad for taking her.

"Where will we meet?" Srogaraad asked in a lower tone.

"Remember that cave in the cliff above the river a couple of miles south of the old town," asked the high priest, "the one where the Dedicated found all those children and elders of the others hiding among the bones of their ancestors? The one where we rededicated their own altar to our Gods by sacrificing *her* on it?" His son nodded. He was not likely to forget.

"Wait there. It is outside the five mile limit and our own people avoid the place. I will come when I'm sure these fools have stopped watching me. It should only be a couple of days, but take enough food for a week, just in case. I'll bring horses and weapons."

"Be sure you bring Sundancer," Srogaraad said. His father prudently did not remind him that his favorite horse, all his horses, were forfeit to the chief. His son would have to make do with horses from his own stock and Zynjaar couldn't see giving him the finest of them, either. He avoided the subject for now.

They finished putting clothes and an extra pair of boots in a pack and tying Srogaraad's sleeping furs into a roll. Then they went out into the main living area where Nuzeani met them, having dressed and come out of her sleeping quarters to see if her men or the visitors needed anything. Her husband ordered her back to her furs without explanation and her son didn't even glance in her direction, heading instead for the pantry. Yashihar accompanied him, watching while he gathered as much dried meat and fruit as he could get into the pack, a skin of beer and a couple of extras for water, a flint, some fish hooks and line, and a large ball of hemp cord for snares, since Srogaraad would have no weapons for hunting.

When the pack could hold no more, Yashihar inspected it to make sure nothing that could be used as a weapon had been included. Then he sent one of the young men after three horses from the night pasture.

"I will get horses for myself and my son," said Zynjaar.

"Srogaraad walks as ordered," contradicted the horse master, "and there was nothing in the judgment about anyone accompanying him." Zynjaar started to protest, but Yashihar kept speaking.

"The council gave me the duty of seeing your son into exile and we will do it my way."

When they finally started out it was still full dark, but something in the texture of the night sky said dawn was not far away. Before long the stars disappeared, the sky lightened from indigo to ultramarine, and soon a few high clouds were picking up streaky red hints of early sun. They were walking southeast toward the coast of the inland sea. There were no other clans or towns among the rugged hills in that direction, so Yashihar thought it the best way to send Srogaraad. Each time they topped a rise the sky was lighter; a spectacular rose and gold and blue sunrise greeted them as they crested the second line of hills. From here they could see the distant flatness of the sea, still nearly thirty miles away. They could also see an open route in that direction, down the side of the scrubby, nearly treeless ridge, open for well over two miles ahead, with only a band of shelter from real trees left standing along a water course in the valley between the hills.

"We are almost to the five mile limit here," said Yashihar. "If you stay to the east of this line of hills, Srogaraad, you will not be in danger of entering the restricted area by mistake. Still, I would keep moving if I were you. The warriors often hunt in this area, and as of dusk today you, too, are fair game. There are not many that would hunt an unarmed man no matter what he has done, but some would, and your deeds have angered more than a few. Now get on with you. We will watch you go."

Srogaraad, saying nothing, turned away and plodded on down the far side of the steep, rocky ridge, his eyes on his footing. When he had gone a couple of hundred paces Yashihar dismounted and stretched his muscles. He signed to his companions to dismount as well. They got food and drink out of their saddle bags, then, hanging their bridles around the horses necks so they could pick at the scanty grass, the men sat down on a convenient outcrop to watch the sunrise and the receding back of their charge, and ate their breakfast.

The sun climbed higher until it was no longer shining directly in their eyes. Srogaraad disappeared into the trees along the little river below. His escort caught up their horses and packed up their things. After a short while they saw him beyond the copse, crossing the grassy valley floor between scattered trees. He did not look back. They mounted up and watched a little while longer. When he was just a tiny figure clambering up the next steep slope, still going in the same direction at the same steady pace, they turned their horses and started back down the other side of the ridge, their task complete.

They let their horses pick their own way, tired from the long night and in no hurry to get home to other duties. Presently one of the young warriors addressed the horse master. "Will you tell Jaromir in which direction he has gone?"

"Why shouldn't I?" asked Yashihar. "If you are thinking that the chief will go after Srogaraad, or that he will allow his sons to hunt him, an unarmed man on foot, you are very wrong. They have far more honor than that. Jaromir has never been one to hold a grudge or seek revenge for wrongs done to him; he lets the law deliver justice. I'm certain that he will think Srogaraad has been adequately punished given the fact that he didn't succeed in doing any real harm. The chief just wants to be sure that this mad dog will not come back, that his daughter and family are safe."

"It's too bad he made that contract for Ahna with the outclanner. Now that the problem here is gone he could have kept her at home," said the second warrior.

"Since it was that contract that triggered the behavior that got Srogaraad banished," said Yashihar, "if he had not made it the problem would still exist. It's unlikely that Ahna could have lived here in peace under any circumstances with her tormentor in the same camp, and Marvulf will make her a good husband. Jaromir has done the best he could for his daughter, although he will miss her."

The conversation turned to horses. The young men took advantage of their opportunity; they delved the famed horse master's experience for gems of wisdom as they made their leisurely way home through the early fall morning.

*   *   *

Srogaraad's throat was dry and he was hungry, but he refused to let his guards see his distress and he did not want them to know where he was really going. When he entered the copse of trees along the river after they had let him go on alone, he continued until he was sure they could not see him, then he turned and looked back through the leaves and brush to check on them. They were off their horses and seated on a rock. They seemed to be eating, and he saw one of them tip up a skin of some liquid for a drink. He called them a rude name, dug in a side pocket for a piece of jerky, and kept walking, chewing on the tough, salty dried meat as he went. He stopped at the little river just long enough to scoop up some water and drink it out of the palms of his hands. Then he continued through the copse, across the meadow beyond it and started up the next hill without looking back, determined that the watchers would think him resigned to his fate.

He crossed the next rise still without looking back, but once he was out of sight on the other side he stopped, shed his pack, and keeping low he crept back to the top of the hill and looked at the opposite ridge from behind a convenient rock. He could clearly see the outcrop where his 'escort' had been seated, but there was no sign of them or their horses. He dropped back down the hill to his pack, sat down and pulled out some more dried meat and fruit and the skin of beer. He ate and drank and rested, trying to think of ways in which he might get his revenge. Finally he donned his pack and went carefully back to the top of the hill to check again. Puffy clouds had begun to appear in the blue above, but they were the only thing moving that he could see. The crest of the other ridge remained empty of human or horse, neither was there any sign of life in the meadows below. With a faintly nasty grin he strolled back over the ridge and down into the valley he had just left.

When he reached the level going near the river he turned to follow it south, making for the cave where his father had promised to meet him. He would be bringing horses and supplies, but most of all he would be bringing weapons. Srogaraad had the beginnings of a plan. When Jaromir and his sons came after him, he would be ready. He took it for granted that they would come; it was what he would have done. They were excellent hunters as well as warriors, but he would have a huge advantage because they would believe him to be afoot, unarmored and unarmed. Their precautions would be those of hunters, not fighters. He would take out the boy Redwolf first. He knew that would give Jaromir great pain.

Srogaraad was watching outside the cave two days later when his father rode up. He ran to meet Zynjaar, looking with disfavor on the three nondescript brown horses he was leading.

"Where is Sundancer?" He demanded. "Those are not my horses!"

His father dismounted and ground-tied all four horses. Then he dug in his saddle bags and produced a skin of wine, a small handleless basket of pears, and a packet of fresh flatbread.

"I'm sorry, son," he said, holding out the food placatingly. "I could not bring your horses. They were forfeit as the blood price ordered, and were gone before the day you left had ended. You will have to settle for some of mine."

"I'll settle for nothing! *You* could have bought Sundancer back." Srogaraad snarled. "Those … those thieves will not have my horses, I will get them back if *I* have to steal them!" Zynjaar almost laughed, but stopped himself in time. Srogaraad was looking the horses over more closely.

"You didn't even bring me your best," he accused.

"I was afraid you would be the target of brigands if your horses were too obviously fine, and you alone," his father explained. "These are sturdy, sound young animals, and the mare wearing your saddle, Quickstep, is war trained. She will serve you well without tempting someone to stick a knife in your back for her."

"I guess they'll do," Srogaraad conceded grudgingly. "I'll need to be inconspicuous to turn the tables on Jaromir when they come hunting me. You brought me weapons?" The high priest indicated the fine sword strapped to the high-cantled war saddle Quickstep wore, and two short javelins in their own loops on the other side. He handed his son the food, then reached down to his own belt and unfastened a sheath with a long, wicked bronze knife, its deer antler hilt carved with religious symbols, from beside his own. It was the one Srogaraad had used to perform the sacrifice in this very cave. He handed that over, too, and indicated the first pack horse.

"Your bow and arrows are there, on the pack horse with a winter traveling tent and some extra furs. The other pack horse has mostly food and cooking supplies. One horse can carry everything in a pinch. I didn't know whether you would want two or three horses."

"Two will do," said Srogaraad. "The more horses one has, the harder it is to stay hidden."

"True," agreed Zynjaar, "but I don't think you will need to hide. You should head out further south and east where I don't think the clan will be going. Scouts say there is no good grazing for cattle or horses in that direction, nothing but tiny villages that wouldn't support us, as much as we have grown."

His son opened his mouth, his brows drawing down in a frown, but the priest forestalled him. "You *would* have an advantage, with weapons and horses they did not know you had, when Jaromir and his sons came out here hunting you, but if that is your plan you will have a long and fruitless wait. They will not come."

"Of course they'll come!" the younger man argued. "Would you let an attack on me go unavenged, especially if there were no attendant consequences?"

"No, but the chief is not like us. He has told his sons and his friends that you are to be left alone as long as you come no closer to the tents than five miles. He said that blood price has been paid and justice already meted out to you. He has made them all promise that they will not hunt you outside the limit. It's just as well. If they had come hunting you, it would not have been just Jaromir and his sons; it would have been half the warriors in the camp. You might take some of them by surprise, but they would get you for sure." His son looked thoughtful as that image penetrated.

"It's strange," Zynjaar continued. "The chief did not keep any of your livestock, and neither did his sons. Your animals were all distributed among the families whose warriors were killed last fall and who do not yet have an adult male to look after them."

"That doesn't make any difference," growled Srogaraad. "Jaromir is still responsible for my losses!" His father thought the younger man's actions had had quite a bit to do with it, but he himself still wanted very badly to get back at the clan leader, who not only had caused the loss of his son, but too often succeeded in thwarting his own ambitions.

"I will find a way to get back at Jaromir," he repeated, "and punish that uppity girl as well. You should put all this behind you and seek a new life! There are two sets of priest's robes, well made and richly decorated, but in black instead of our clan colors, in your packs. I'm sure you can find a village where you can make yourself their spiritual leader with the help of our Gods.

"A village," sneered Srogaraad. "A village of the *others*! A hundred people, or two hundred at most. Goddess worshipers!"

"You can show them the light," suggested his sire. "With your talents it will only be a stepping stone to greater things." He started to unsaddle his horse. "Let's unpack and have a real meal together before I have to go back." Together they unloaded the horses, taking everything into the cave. When the horses were wiped off and grazing on the grass that still grew thick on the southern slope in front of the opening, they sat down to do justice to the wine and bread and fruit, augmented by some fresh roast beef that had also been in Zynjaar's pack.

"How do you mean to get Jaromir?" Srogaraad asked when he had taken the edge off his hunger.

"I don't know, yet," admitted his father. "Be sure I will think of something."

"I may know a way," his son said. "The consequences might be kind of extreme," he warned, "but if you could saddle the chief with them, you would bring him down for sure. We have been saying for a moon that Ahna's actions have angered the Gods so much that something terrible is going to happen. What would you say to a nice little plague?"

"What are you talking about?" asked Zynjaar. "How could you guarantee a 'little' plague?"

"I guess you couldn't *guarantee* it, but you could fairly effectively limit fatal exposure to those you would least mind losing if you went about it carefully. I got here the day I left home, and since then there has been nothing to do but wait. I've been out exploring the area. Yesterday I saw something that may answer. Some of the Others managed to hide from our warriors last year. Several of them have been living with a few animals that also survived, some of those flightless birds they call chickens, and some of those disgusting unclean pigs, in a partially burned barn just outside the wreck of the town. I did not go close, and I don't think I was seen."

"How will a few stray Others answer our need?" asked the priest.

"Most of them will serve only by their absence. I counted 6 bodies, just lying around and some beginning to reek even from a distance, but there was one I saw still alive, a young girl. She came out of the barn while I was studying the scene and, calling out, ran over to one of the others, a woman, knelt down and tried to rouse her. The woman may not have been dead yet. I thought I saw a faint response. The child appeared fairly healthy. At least she moved and cried out with strength. The others did not die of starvation. I saw several animals of both kinds alive and apparently well, although there was one dead pig among the humans. There are still vegetables in the overgrown gardens that they were probably eating, too." His father said nothing. He was paying close attention, and looked very thoughtful.

"I have been thinking on this all night," Srogaraad continued. "You could take the child to Jaromir. If he did not want her I bet that wife of his would. The child has to be a carrier of whatever disease killed the others, if she does not get sick herself. Vladia is one of the leaders of the women's society. She would probably be one of the first to take the disease, and Ahna as well. They are interacting with the other women on a daily basis, and the chief of course is constantly in close contact with the men, his sons with the young men and boys. The pestilence would spread rapidly. The women of the society would insist on nursing the sick even if they tried to isolate their families. The healers would get sick. You might rid yourself of all your greatest rivals with one stroke!" Srogaraad was grinning nastily.

"Diabolical," commented his father. "How would we avoid coming down with the disease ourselves?" He had another thought. "What if so many died that we were too weak to take another town? We are using up the resources in this area; we'll have to move on next year."

"The sickness looked like winter fever to me," his son explained. "At least from what I could see there was no sign of bloating or sores on the victim's faces and arms. If you see something that suggests a more dangerous disease when you get closer, you can simply turn and ride away. It is a little early for the winter fever and it has to be quite virulent to have killed so many, but generally the winter fever only kills the weak. Nearly everyone gets it, but for the most part it is the very young, those who are already sick or injured, the elderly, and those who do not take the time to rest and recover when they come down with it who die. The important people in the clan, the warriors and the strong young women, should survive. It is likely that all of those Others were physically weakened, given a year of hiding and living hand to mouth."

"If you and the other priests and their families shut yourselves in your compound to 'fast' and pray to the Gods to free the camp of the disease, refusing all interruptions, you could avoid being exposed during the first bad outbreak, and almost guarantee yourselves mild cases if any when you do emerge. Best of all, Jaromir will take the blame for keeping the child in the camp. If he survives it will need but a little push to rouse the men against him and force the council to appoint a new chief. You might even get a whole new council for your efforts. Every man of the clan will have lost someone dear to him, or fear doing so. You need only convince them that the Gods will answer their prayers if they get rid of the one who has angered Them, and you should have them."

"If it really is just winter fever, I'll do it!" the high priest decided. To accomplish even some of these ends Zynjaar would gladly gamble his own life, especially as it appeared he might manipulate the odds in his favor with impunity. He refused to consider his sworn duty to serve and protect his people as spiritual leader of the clan. After all, they had ignored his warnings and sided with Jaromir, his enemy and an enemy of the Gods.

"You'd best get going, then," said his son. "You will need some time to coax the child out of hiding and earn her trust enough to get her to come with you, and you don't want to be taking her into camp after dark. I don't need to warn you that you should not get close to, let alone touch, either her or any of the Others. Not even if one of them is wearing a fortune in gold! Take the second pack horse for the girl to ride."

"I will take her straight to Jaromir. I can say I was out hunting and found her near a pigsty in the woods," Zynjaar said. "It will account for the empty packframe; I might have needed the horse to bring back game."

"Since you are going through with this," said Srogaraad, "I will take your advice, Father. Tomorrow I will go looking for a new life. I know Jaromir and Ahna will get what's coming to them now."

Without further discussion they caught up the high priest's two horses and replaced their tack. Then they wished each other luck, and Zynjaar blessed his son, mounted up, and trotted away. He looked back once, but the younger man had already disappeared, probably back into the cave.

Chapter 21

About a hand later by the sun the priest was searching around the destroyed town for the half-burned barn Srogaraad had described. He found it with little trouble. There were vultures flying reconnaissance overhead and, as he discovered when he got closer, several on the ground where the six others were lying, now all obviously dead. The vultures flapped reluctantly back into the sky at his approach, but they did not go away. They joined their fellows, circling, expectant.

There were chickens pecking at the ground in the yard, particularly around the bodies. In at least one case they seemed to be taking advantage of their erstwhile owners' misfortune, although it may have been that they were only after the myriad insects buzzing around the corpses. They paid absolutely no attention to his arrival, although his horses danced in mild alarm when one ran flapping away from the approaching hooves. He soothed his mount and looked around some more, muttering a term of disgust at the sight of two dead pigs, also attended by flies and flightless birds, and the two or three live ones rooting among the trees beyond the barn yard.

The dead were two women, two men, and two half-grown children. One woman, the children, and one man had been laid out in a row about a hundred paces from the structure, all naked. The second man, barefoot and wearing only a ragged loincloth and some sort of necklace, lay near them, crumpled up at an awkward angle, as if he had collapsed after arranging the other bodies. The woman Srogaraad had spoken of lay nearer to the barn. Someone had made an effort to straighten her tattered white dress, full-skirted and shamelessly open at the chest as it was. The girl, probably, had also folded her arms across her breasts and, as he could see when he got closer, closed her eyes. The dead priestess' dusky skin was completely clear, if paler than he thought normal. All the most dreaded diseases he knew left obvious marks on their victims. He concluded that his son was most likely right in his diagnosis, so he carried out their plan.

Dismounting from his horse, he pulled from his saddle bags two pears, a loaf of flatbread and, with some reluctance, a stick of hard honey candy, the last of that they had found in the town's stores. Zynjaar had not given any to his son. The High Priest had a decided sweet tooth. Walking toward the intact end of the barn, he called out.

"Hello. Anyone there?"

There was no answer, but he caught a hint of movement in the shadow inside a partially open wooden door that sagged on leather hinges. He smiled, checked that he was well away from all the bodies, and sat down cross-legged on the ground. He held out the food, making sure the candy was clearly visible. "Come out," he called again in his most persuasive tones. "You must be hungry. Here is food." He knew the child could not speak his tongue, but the language of food and kindness was universal. After a minute or two, when there was still no further sign of movement from the barn, he got up, took several steps forward, dusted off the top of a sizable rock not far from the door with the hem of his robe, and placed the bread on it. Then he moved back to the same spot and resumed his seat.

"I'm sorry your folk have died," he said softly but clearly, putting the rest of the food in his lap, pointing to the bodies and then placing his face in his hands and bowing his head to convey sorrow. "They would not want you to be alone. Come with me and I will find you a new home." She would not understand the words, but the tone would reassure her. He wore his plain traveling robes; he hoped they would reassure her, too. He knew the others had priests as well as priestesses. He kept talking, intoning a sonorous prayer for the dead, bowing his head and keeping his rich voice low and soothing. The words were hardly appropriate, but she would not know that, and he carefully avoided addressing the prayer to his own Gods, who would surely have laughed at him if They were not insulted.

After a few minutes a dark-haired, dark-eyed child appeared in the doorway, wearing a torn, dirty, sky-blue shift too small for her and nothing else. She gave him a frightened look, then stepped forward warily, snatched the bread and ran back into the barn.

"Very good," he applauded, still in that soothing tone. "Bread will help your hunger. He remained where he was for a few minutes, then got up and placed the pears, small and a little hard but quite sweet, on the rock. He retreated, sat back down and resumed his monologue. He did not have so long to wait this time. She came out, went straight to the rock and picked up the pears, then retreated in her turn and stood in the doorway eating them, watching him. He kept talking.

When the pears were gone he took his personal water skin from his belt, filled as it was with clear water from the last shady brook he had crossed, and looked at it regretfully. It was a good one; he hated to lose it. But he got up again and placed the water skin and the stick of candy on the rock. She ducked back into the barn when he stood up, but came out at once when he was again seated in his place. With youthful dignity she walked forward and took the water skin and candy. She stood watching him a moment more, then sat down on the rock, drank the water, and chewed on the sweet.

When the hard candy was about gone, Zynjaar stood slowly and turned toward his horses. The child also stood, but did not flee. "I'm going home now," the priest said over his shoulder as he tightened his horse's girth. "Will you come with me?" He exaggerated the questioning note, waving his hand toward the horses. He went to check the pack saddle as well, then turned to look at the child. He made a beckoning motion with his hand and pointed to the pack horse. "You can ride this one," he said. When the child did not move, he first pointed at her, then turned and pointed at the horse, and finally pointed toward the Lion camp, away from the barn and the town. "Come on," he coaxed. "You will be much happier there. For one thing there is more food." He mimed eating, then pointed to the north again.

When she still did not move, he mounted his good brown gelding and turned its head toward home. He put as much finality and sadness into his voice as he could: "I'm sorry you won't come. Goodbye." He allowed the horse to move out, but kept him to a slow walk. He had only gone a few steps when a cry that might have meant "wait" sounded behind him. He tightened his reins and turned to looked back. The girl, still carrying his water skin, was hurrying over to the dead priestess. The child knelt and kissed a cold cheek, then pressed herself against the bare bosom for a moment, causing the priest to wince. Then she stood up and walked toward him. "Good," he said, smiling as kindly as he could. When she made to approach his horse, however, he pointed to the pack horse. "You ride that one," he said, pointing again, first at her and then at the pack saddle. She looked at the horse, then back at him. She stepped toward the pack animal, looking at him inquiringly.

"Yes," he confirmed, nodding vigorously. "You ride that one." He made an upward motion with his hand that he hoped would convey the idea of mounting. She smiled, patted the horse on the neck and said something to it, then, using the coiled pack straps for hand grips and then steps, scrambled easily up its side and sat astride the empty pack saddle, pulling down her soiled blue skirt as best she could. She tied the water skin to one of the pack straps, gripped the front bar of the pack saddle with one hand and the horse's mane with the other, then nodded to him gravely. He smiled again, this time in amusement tinged with a little admiration. She was rapidly proving herself capable as well as courageous. It was a shame she would never grow up. He put his horse to a walk, then to a slow trot, glancing back to be sure the child was secure. She was jouncing a little on her awkward seat, but showed no signs of losing her balance. She grinned reassuringly at him.

The westering sun was still more than a hand above the horizon when Zynjaar rode in among the tents with the girl on his pack horse trailing behind and went directly to Vladia's compound, calling for the clan leader. He did not dismount.

When Jaromir came out to inquire his need, the High Priest said, "I was out hunting this morning. I killed no deer, but I did find this girl of the others in the forest, the only one living with some animals that must have escaped your warriors when you took the town. She was wary of me, but hungry enough to be coaxed with food. Winter is coming. I'm not allowed to kill, of course, and I did not want to leave her there, since the Gods must have helped her to survive this long. She's a fetching little thing. I brought her here first because I thought you and your wife might like to keep her. You will be losing your only daughter very soon, and your wife will need help. The girl does not speak our language, but I don't doubt she will learn it soon enough. All the concubines do."

Jaromir looked at the child, who was attractive even if her shift was ragged and dirty and herself a little unkempt. She appeared to be about the same age as Ahndru. His inclination was to refuse because she was with the priest, but he knew what her fate would be if she was sent to the tents where the unattached concubines lived. She would join their ranks; some men liked their women very young.

As if he could read the clan leader's mind, Zynjaar said, "If you do not want her I will take her to Tzyoner. He will feed and clothe her and treat her well."

The chief snorted at that last and turned to his son, who had appeared beside him from within the tent. "Redwolf, would you go ask Tzyoner if we can borrow that girl Sara for a little while? I believe she might be able to translate for us, and we can question this child." Redwolf nodded and hurried away.

"What could a girl child who has been living with animals tell us?" demanded the priest, hiding his alarm. "This seems a waste of time at the least!"

"If I am going to give her a home I want to know something about her," Jaromir said patiently. He distrusted the high priest. He did not know what Zynjaar was up to, but he feared there was something more to this than was apparent on the surface. Briefly the thought of plague crossed his mind, but he dismissed it at once. The girl was dirty and a little thin, but she looked healthy, her eyes clear with no signs of discharge from her nose or sores on her face or limbs. Besides, while he was quite sure that the high priest would bring a pestilence down on Ahna and her family if he could safely do so without exposing himself or the rest of the camp, he was equally sure that no sworn priest would or could deliberately bring sickness on his entire clan. That was too dishonorable even to contemplate. Vladia's tents were right in the middle of the village and people were always coming and going. Any disease in their home would be spread through the entire population before it was even recognized for what it was. That could not possibly be Zynjaar's purpose.

"What do we ever know about concubines?" the high priest was demanding. He feared that the chief might ask the wrong questions. "She is one of the Others, she is female, well made, and smart and brave enough to come with me. She is too young to have contracted any venereal disease. What else do you need to know?"

Jaromir saw no point in explaining that he wanted to know where her folks were and how one so young had survived for a year alone, if she had been alone. "We will wait," he said.

"Redwolf came back in a very few minutes with Sara. When the older girl saw the child on the horse she cried out "Ester!" She started forward, then hesitated and looked at Redwolf, then at the chief and the priest. "You may go to her," said Jaromir. Sara ran to the horse and helped the girl slide down from her perch, taking her into her arms and hugging her fiercely. Ester was in tears, and when they turned back toward their observers, it was clear that Sara's eyes were not dry, either.

"You know her, Sara," said the clan chief. "Who is she? How old is she?"

"She is my... my second sister... my mother's sister daughter," the young concubine answered haltingly. "This her... ninth summer."

"Where are her parents?" he asked next.

Sara asked a brief question in her own tongue, and got a briefer answer. "Dead," she said. "All the others are dead." This was not news to Jaromir. He did not ask how and when they had died. He thought he knew, and was somehow reluctant to remind the child that she was now among the killers of her kin.

"How has she been living?" he persisted. "What has she been eating?"

Sara again questioned her cousin, this time receiving a longer answer.

"She eat eggs from the chickens. She get vegetables from the gardens at night when no fighters around. She hide always in daytime. No fires; she sleep with the pigs to stay warm when it gets cold. When she see him," she indicated Zynjaar with a slight nod, "she sure he kill her, but instead he give her food. He is kind to her. She want to thank him." She looked down, then glanced at the priest with her shy smile. "If it is proper, I thank him, too."

This picture was more than Jaromir could take. He did not realize that the way he had phrased his question and Sara's unfamiliarity with the language had caused her to answer in the singular, making it seem that Ester had been alone, whereas in her own language the child had spoken mostly in the plural. He had heard enough, and so had Vladia, who was now standing with Ahna in the open tent entrance behind him. He glanced at her, received an almost imperceptible nod.

"We will take her," he said to the priest. "Thank you for bringing her to us."

"You're welcome," said Zynjaar, working very hard to keep the smile of triumph from his face. He turned without ceremony and rode away, leading his pack horse. There was nothing for it, he would have to burn the pack saddle.

Vladia and Ahna moved toward the two girls, and Jaromir went back into the tent. Redwolf tried to hang around, his eyes on Sara, but a look from his mother sent him after his father. They were still keeping an eye on Ahna, but it was a much less diligent eye now that Srogaraad had been banished.

"Can you stay, Sara?" asked Vladia. "We would love to have your help assuring Ester that we mean her no harm and that she will have a good home with us. I don't want to get you in trouble if Tzyoner is expecting you back, though."

"Redwolf ask 'till dusk," Sara answered. "Tzyoner agree. I want to stay, help." She still had her arm comfortingly around her cousin.

"Very good," said Vladia. "Are you hungry, Ester?" The girl looked up at her name, and Sara hastily translated the question.

"No, priest gave her food," she told Vladia. She smiled. "She be hungry later!" Vladia laughed.

"Good," she said again, "then I think the next order of business is a bath, and some clean clothes. That shift she has on can be consigned to the rag bag after it has been thoroughly washed. Ahna, go and see what you can find that she might be able to wear, at least temporarily. I will start making a shift for her, and altering a blouse and a divided skirt to fit, after supper. Meanwhile she will have to wear something of yours, and tuck in the excess. Wait here a moment, Sara." She stepped briefly into the tent.

When she returned Vladia gave Sara a ball of strong soap that also smelled of herbs and flowers, and some squares of coarse cotton.

"Take Ester to the river, near the big rocks where the women do the washing. Do you know the place I mean?" she instructed. The concubine nodded. "Good," Vladia said again. "Ahna will be there soon. She will bring clothes for Ester. Get her undressed, show her how to wash her clothes if she does not already know, and then help her take a bath."

"She know," said Sara, sounding if anything a little offended. "She afraid to take bath, 'till now."

Vladia nodded. "I understand. Today she can have a good scrubbing. Try to keep the soap out of her eyes while washing her hair: it burns! "

"We know." Sara said again.

"While you are bathing, teach her our words for things like water and clothes and soap," Vladia concluded.

Sara nodded vigorously. "I do that," she said.

They had washed the tattered shift and laid it out on the rocks to dry and were stepping naked into the river with the ball of soap and one of the smaller rags when Ahna arrived. She quickly stripped down and joined them. It was supper time and there were no other women at the bathing place, but Moshel was lingering out of sight, waiting to escort them back.

They all bathed, sharing the soap and the wash cloth, Ester repeatedly sudsing and rinsing even her hair with vigor and obvious enjoyment. There was much laughter as they tried to converse, and much naming and repeating of objects and actions. When the girl of the Others finally thought herself clean enough they got out and dried off quickly; the sun had set and the evening air was getting quite chilly! Ahna picked up the shift she brought and helped Ester pull it on. It swallowed her slender frame. Then she handed her a prettily patterned gold and brown linen blouse, a nearly new one she had made herself. Ester took it gingerly, staring at it. Suddenly she hugged it to her breast and burst into tears.

"What in the name of the Goddess is the matter?" asked Ahna, aghast at the child's reaction.

"Her mother made that cloth," Sara answered, her look and tone fraught with sorrow. She apparently recognized the material as well. "She was... master... weaver?"

"Oh," was all Ahna could say. "Well, in that case of course Ester must keep it. We will alter it to fit her, but we will not cut off the excess material. She can let it out as she grows, so that she will always have it. She can have any other of my clothes that are made from her mother's weaving, too."

"You are kind," said Sara. "Ester be... will be grateful." She turned to comfort the child and tell her what their new friend was promising.

Ahna looked down in shame, tears in her own eyes. These girls should be reviling her, not thanking her. Her kin had wiped out their kin without a second thought. She promised herself that these two Others, at least, would not continue to suffer bad treatment at the hands of her people.

When they arrived back at the family tents Sara hugged Ester one last time and left, saying only that she did not want to anger Tzyoner. Moshel and Ahna and a transformed Ester went into the main tent to find the rest of the men being served supper by Vladia. Moshel joined the men on the rugs and Ahna hastened to help her mother. Ester looked at first like she might join the men around the food, but she glanced at Ahna, who shook her head vigorously and mouthed a "no." Ester trailed the two women into the kitchen, watching what they were doing, clearly puzzled. When they had finished serving the men Ahna sat Ester down on a stool at one of the work tables. Then she and her mother brought cups of milk and bowls of bread and meat and vegetables, and some of the woven reed mats that served as plates. They sat down on either side of the child and helped themselves to the food, telling Ester, who despite her hunger had not touched anything, to help herself as well. The child kept her eye on the older woman while she hesitantly reached out her hand for some meat. Vladia nodded and smiled. "Yes, that's right," she approved. In a moment Ester was eating ravenously.

After a few bites, Ahna got up to check on the men and fill their drink cups. When she returned she broached the idea of taking Sara in as well, hoping her mother would agree, but Vladia vetoed the idea.

"Have you forgotten how much your brother is attracted to her?" she asked. "I'm really sorry, but it simply wouldn't do. She is a sweetheart, and I hate to think of her lumped in with Tzyoner's other concubines as she is. If she still has not found a better place I promise I will bring her here when Redwolf has gone to his foster clan." That was a whole turn of the seasons away, but Ahna recognized that it was the best that could be done.

After supper Ester helped with the cleanup, obviously familiar with this routine at least. When Ahna took the food scraps out to dump them, she brought in the child's old shift, which had been drying on a rack outside the tent, meaning to put it in their rag bag. Vladia saw how stained it was despite the scrubbing, and told Ahna to put it on the discard pile behind the tents instead. Now that it was as clean as they could get it, there were some patches of an attractive bright blue showing, but as far as Vladia was concerned it wasn't even fit for cleaning rags.

When they were done in the annex, Ester played a few games of stones with Ahndru. He seemed able to communicate with her, at least to the extent of explaining the game, without any mutual language, although Ahna could tell he was modifying the rules to fit the needs of the moment. Ester seemed animated and happy, but before long her energy palpably flagged. Ahna thought she was struggling to keep awake. They put her to bed early in Ahna's sleeping cubby. She meant to continue that arrangement until she was married, after which the space would belong to Ester. It was not common for concubines taken in by clan families to sleep in the main tent. They usually had a nest in a corner of a work or storage tent until they could find the time and earn the materials to make a tent of their own, but Ahna was determined that Ester would not be treated like an outcast. She had offered to share her furs, and Vladia had agreed. The child fell almost instantly asleep.

Ahna started awake toward morning, adrenalin pumping, a picture of Srogaraad leaning over her all too vivid in her mind's eye. But there was no hand on her mouth, obviously no man in her sleeping quarters. Then the child beside her gave a little moan and rolled over, trying to kick off her coverlet, her arms thrashing, too, and one of them flailed against Ahna's shoulder. She sat up, still alarmed, now knowing the reason. She lifted the lid of the hardened clay coal box, managed to coax a tiny flame from the nearly burnt-out coal inside, and lit the bedside lamp, to see that Ester, despite her intermittent, jerky motions, was still asleep. She reached over and put her hand on the child's forehead. Then she leaped out of bed, pulled her blouse and skirt over her night shift, shoved the lamp back out of harm's way, and went to rouse her mother. Ester's skin was hotter than the coal box!

Vladia was already dressed in her house robe, having wakened with a strong feeling of unease for which she had no explanation. She came quickly at Ahna's call, examined the sleeping child briefly, and sent Ahna for hot water and her rabbit-skin pouch of healing herbs. Ahna scooped a pitcher of water from the bronze kettle that always sat in the corner of the hearth, where the heat from the banked fire kept it warm. She ran into her mother's cubby, snatched up the medicine pouch and hurried back to her personal quarters. Vladia had soaked a course cotton wash cloth in the large crock of cool water that sat between the double walls of the main tent, and was holding it against the back of Ester's neck. She was awake now, sitting up against the inner tent wall and very quiet, except for an occasional low moan. She was rubbing at her knees and legs as if they hurt.

"What do you think is wrong?" Vladia asked.

"She's hot, and her legs hurt, and she seems depressed, tired," Ahna answered. "I think it may be winter fever. This is early for it, but the Eldest said it comes at different times in different years. By tomorrow she will probably have a cough and runny nose. It will make her feel lousy for several days, but she is young, but not too young, and strong. She should be fine."

Her mother nodded, agreeing with the diagnosis. "She has been living under terrible conditions for a long time, she is thin, and the fever has hit her fast and hard," Vladia hedged. "We will need to treat the symptoms diligently and beware of complications." She watched while Ahna mixed willow bark tea, using about half of the amount of herb she would have given to an adult, to bring down the fever and combat the aches and pains, putting some chamomile and other soothing herbs and some honey in it as well, although it was very difficult to disguise the bitterness of willow bark. She nodded when her daughter brought the cup of tea and gave it to the child. Ester rejected it after one sip. Ahna put her hand on the child's head, then on her knees, rubbing gently. Then she pointed to the knees, to the cup, and to the knees again, trying to convey the idea that the medicine would make them feel better. Finally she took a sip of the tea herself, then held it out to Ester again. The child screwed up her face, but took the cup and drank it down.

"How often should she be given the tea?" Vladia asked.

"Four times a day," answered her daughter, "and twice during the night if necessary." Her mother nodded again. "What will we do for her if congestion develops?" she continued. Ahna named the herbs and dosages that, served in tea, would relieve congestion of the head and chest, saying she would also rub a salve of beef fat and camphor leaves on the child's chest. The older woman smiled. "Your memory is good," she praised. "You will be a fine healer."

Then Vladia broached the subject they'd both been avoiding. "You know we will probably all come down with it," she said. "We are lucky that she has been here such a short time. Not many people have had contact with her. I did not want Sara here because of Redwolf, but Ester was certainly contagious yesterday, so I think in the interests of limiting the spread of the fever we should have her stay with us after all, at least until this outbreak is past. She will be helpful when we need to communicate with Ester, and she will certainly be coming down with it next. Do you think you could find space for her in here, if I gave you some more bedding? I have a great excess of furs." Ahna nodded. It would be crowded, but neither of the other girls had any possessions to speak of, so they would make do. Ahndru had only inherited his own sleeping space when Pyotrev had been fostered out at the last winter solstice; it would not be fair to either boy to ask him to move back in with Redwolf.

After a while the medications began to take effect. Ester was relieved enough to go back to sleep. Ahna and her mother decided there was no point in themselves returning to bed; it was almost time to get up anyway. They went out to the work area to get a head start on the morning's chores, discussing how best to limit exposure to as few people as possible. They would put yard sticks out both in front and in back immediately with red, black, purple and green ribbons, indicating quarantine, warning people to stay away, but both Jaromir and Vladia had duties they could not assign. Their meetings and consultations would have to be held elsewhere. In most years healthy adults did not get winter fever, or got very mild cases of it, having developed immunity from exposure in prior years, so Vladia did not think it necessary to quarantine herself and her husband, or even Moshel. There had been little winter fever in the camp for several years, though, so she thought it likely that the younger people, especially the babies, and the older folk would be particularly susceptible. They needed to be protected from exposure.

Shortly after breakfast three young girls raced down the path between the rows of tents behind Vladia's complex, on their way to a morning of playing with friends. They had their bone needles and some old rags from their mothers, whose tents were on the far edge of the village. They were going to make dolls of sticks and twine, and dress them up. They had strips and chunks of fur and leather, and tangles of twine collected from the discard piles, as well as the rags. They would get sticks from the piles of fuel brought in for the cooking fires. A delicate blonde child of five summers spotted the fragment of blue cloth that had been Ester's shift, and checked her running steps just long enough to grab it; they didn't have anything that brightly colored. If they cut out the stained places, what was left would really add to the dolls' wardrobes.

Before Vladia and her daughter finished cleaning up after breakfast Ester was awake again, moaning in pain. Ahna went to tend her, while her mother finished detailing the situation to the men. Jaromir said he would go and talk to Tzyoner immediately about Sara temporarily coming to them, before he went to his morning council meeting. He thought probably the concubine caretaker would practically beg him to take the girl once he heard that she had been exposed to the winter fever, and he proved to be right. Sara showed up with her scanty bundle of extra clothes just as they were giving Ester her second dose of medication. The child refused all food, her appetite of the previous day completely gone, and had to be coaxed even to drink water. That worried Ahna and Vladia, because dehydration severely lowered the body's ability to fight off disease. They were glad when Sara arrived; she could talk the child into drinking more.

Sara reported that Ester's throat was very sore, and the cool water irritated it. She also complained of constant aches and sharp pains in her neck, back and knees. "Meat broth," Vladia prescribed, "and more tea with honey, body temperature. We can get a little food into her that way." Ahna went to prepare the broth, and Vladia went to other duties, while Sara stayed to sooth Ester and help her use the pot that had been provided for her personal needs. There would be no trips to the public facilities while she was sick. When the child was back in bed Sara continued talking softly, telling her the best that she knew about her changed circumstances and continuing the cool compresses on her neck, for her temperature had climbed right back up again. When Ahna came in the willow bark was beginning to help, and Sara managed to coax the child to drink an entire cup of the nourishing mutton broth. Then she subsided into another restless sleep. Ahna went to her regular chores, needing to finish them before continuing work on her trousseau, which she meant to do at a friend's tents this morning. She was grateful that Sara was there to watch and help nurse her cousin.

When they gathered at dinner they had much to tell one another, and the custom that required women to serve the meal but not take part in the conversation was dropped. Jaromir said the council members were not unduly worried about the sickness in his house; winter fever came every year. The councilors were more interested in another new development. The High Priest had announced that his followers would begin their moon-long annual retreat, when all the priests went into seclusion, fasted and prayed to the Gods for good luck in battle and a healthy and successful year ahead, right now instead of after the winter solstice celebrations, their usual time. Zynjaar explained that the Gods were agitated and angry with the clan, and it was the priests' duty to placate Them by turning their attention to Them exclusively.

As was usual before the retreat, the priests had already that morning sacrificed two young bulls and a number of sheep and goats, an odd thing to do because the weather was still too warm to keep the fresh meat for any extended period. The clan had now come so far south that it was seldom cold enough to keep meat before the winter solstice moon, and sometimes not even then. There hardly seemed to be any real winter any more. Jaromir said the priests were busy stockpiling a great deal of firewood as well, and appeared to be drying the meat from the sacrifices. They hadn't even offered to share, traditionally an important part of any ritual of sacrifice. Instead they had isolated themselves from the rest of the clan without the usual preparations or ceremonies. It was unsettling.

The council members did agree to avoid Jaromir's tents if possible, and to warn others away, tool. It had been some years since there had been a killing outbreak of disease. No one saw any connection between the priests' actions and Ester's illness, even though Zynjaar was the one who brought her to the camp. The chief told them the High Priest's tale of how he had found the child, and Zynjaar's father-in-law asked, "Did she appear healthy yesterday?"

"Very much so," answered Jaromir. "She looked and acted much better than anyone could have expected given her circumstances."

"Well, there," the oldest councilor said. "Zynjaar couldn't have known she would get sick. Besides, you said he was out hunting when he found her. He undoubtedly meant the game to be added to their supplies for the retreat they were planning." The others all concurred.

Ahna, Moshel and Redwolf reported that none of their friends seemed very concerned either, although they all agreed to avoid visiting Vladia's tents for the time being.

Their mother told a very different story. At a meeting of the women's society Ahshela warned them that Ester's history, added to the fact that she had taken sick so fast and so severely, was cause for serious concern. The Eldest repeated a story her great grandmother, also an Eldest, had told many years earlier, when Ahshela was no older than Ahna and just learning healing techniques. When that former Eldest was a girl, when the clans were just beginning their long march into the southern lands, the clan attacked a town that kept many pigs as well as chickens, sheep, and goats. The nomads did not know anything about pigs, so they left them and the chickens alive in the razed town, with, of course, the corpses of the townsfolk still lying around. Many of the Others did not bury their dead anyway, but exposed them ritually until they were reduced to nothing but bones, so the barbarians at first saw no reason to bury them either. After the time of this story, the clans had begun burning the corpses of the Others along with their buildings to avoid disease.

The clan had come on this settlement in early summer, before the harvest was even begun, not yet having worked out the efficient routine of conquering communities of the Others in the fall, after the harvest. There were no great stores of grain and other foodstuffs to see the growing clan through the winter, which came early and promised to be hard. They began supplementing their food supplies with the pigs and chickens from the ruined town, bringing them into the tent village alive and penning them outside their work tents. The pigs and chickens would eat animal guts, meat scraps, moldy bread, milk or cheese that had gone bad, vegetable trimmings: anything that was thrown to them. The first consequence that they noticed was the fleas. They must have been getting them from the chickens when they killed and plucked them. After that they took to killing the chickens and plucking them away from the tents, using flea repellants, wearing few clothes and washing immediately after if the fleas bothered them. In winter weather some of the folk didn't seem to care. Chicken was a convenient and delicious addition to their diet.

Within a moon, a virulent outbreak of the winter fever struck the camp, hitting first in one of the families that had a large flock of chickens. The disease spread very rapidly and decimated the camp, killing the very young, the elders, and any that had physical weaknesses. It also killed young pregnant women. The deaths were caused by congestion; the affected patients' lungs filled up with fluid much more rapidly than the healers could control it.

In a few weeks the disease disappeared as rapidly as it had come, but it was not the last calamity to visit the camp that season. As the spring approached, more people began inexplicably dying, apparently of heart failure, and age was not a factor. When one of the healers, hunting for an answer, noticed lesions that looked remarkably like coiled worms in some pig meat one of the women was preparing, she realized that the problem might be parasites. The deaths were also more frequent in families that had eaten quantities of pork, evidence enough for her to convince some influential men, who got the priests to blame the pigs for the unexplained deaths.

Since that time no one in the clans would touch pig meat. The priests still had it on their do-not-eat list, although nearly everyone had forgotten why. Nor did they take or eat chickens, although every place they attacked had a good supply of the birds. The priests said these, too, were forbidden by the Gods, and one more proof, if more were needed, that the Others were ungodly animals not worthy of consideration as people.

Ahshela remembered all too clearly her great grandmother's tale of the virulence of the winter fever that year. She thought it likely that Ester got her case of the disease from her close association with the chickens, or perhaps the pigs, and she feared that they were about to see a repeat of that terrible outbreak. If that happened many would have mild cases, she said, but anyone who got really ill would need careful nursing, and many would die in spite of it. Ahna later learned from her mother that the Eldest was urging all the women to stockpile as much of the willow bark, camphor, horse tail and other relevant herbs, especially those that would help the body pass water in a timely fashion and fight fluid buildup, and those that were specific for coughs and congestion. Some of the herbs were, unfortunately, easier to find in the spring and summer, but the Eldest warned her listeners that every plant they could find would probably be needed.

The girls treated Ester twice more during the afternoon and evening, each time having to wait even though her temperature kept spiking dangerously. Sara was invaluable when it came to coaxing Ester to drink her broth and tea and take her medicine. At sunset, as they sat waiting for the latest dose to take effect, Sara began to sing a song in her own language, her voice low and sweet and fervent. Ahna did not understand the words, but the sound was full of meaning, poignant, melancholy at first, then changing gradually to hopeful, and ending on a softly soaring note of joy.

"That is a beautiful song," said Ahna. "What is it about?"

"It is a song to... to our big holy Woman...

"Goddess," said Ahna quietly. "We call the holy Mother of all life the Goddess."

"Goddess," repeated Sara. "I not know you... believe in Goddess."

"Only the women do," said Ahna, "and not all of them. You must not talk about Her around the men; it is very dangerous. You need to be careful even with women."

Sara nodded. Doing almost anything was fraught with danger around these barbarian men. It was safest to do and say absolutely nothing except what they told you.

"This song asks for healing. It is usually sung when... when sick person not... is not getting well."

"The song about... is about death... dying, going to Goddess... the Goddess, and about... new life. Being born."

"Reborn," said Ahna. "Your are asking the Goddess to make Ester better, but if She can't do that, then you are asking Her to safeguard Ester and give her a new life, a new body."

Sara nodded again, smiling this time. "Reborn. Yes. Is more... is more happy... thanking the Goddess, more than asking. Everyone is reborn."

"We are taught that all living things are reborn," corroborated Ahna. "Is it true that your men believe in the Goddess, too, and follow Her laws?"

"Of course is... it is true," Sara said. "All our people know the Goddess, the Mother. Her laws... are for everyone. Her laws... life end without Her laws."

The conversation continued while they took turns holding cool pads against the child's neck and brow and putting warm compresses on her knees and legs. They finally got to bed when the evening dose of willow bark kicked in and Ester fell asleep.

In the middle of the night they were all rudely awakened again. Ester sat up suddenly, coughing uncontrollably, a deep, wet cough that was fearful to hear. Between bouts of coughing she cried weakly, the tears leaking slowly down her cheeks. Her fever now seemed a little less, but her skin was dry and still hot. Vladia came in to check on her and helped Ahna prepare medication to ease the cough and the congestion that caused it. The older woman worked with a grim determination; she knew even the lower fever was not a good sign.

They soon discovered that they had another problem. The half cup of medicated tea that Sara coaxed Ester to drink came back up with the very next coughing bout. They rubbed camphorated grease on her chest. The fumes seemed to ease her breathing a bit, but it did nothing for the choking cough that wracked her frame and left her gasping weakly. Vladia heated wet clay, mixed it with herbs, and packed it on their patient's chest. It dried and cracked with incredible speed, but the next bad coughing bout produced some phlegm as well, and seemed to ease the child a little. She even managed to keep a few sips of broth down. Vladia took to mixing medication into everything they gave her, in the hope that some of it would get into her system.

The fight went on. They repeated the clay compress, and the other medications, but each time they got a positive response their hopes were soon dashed as the disease came roaring back. Toward morning Ester's coughing grew weaker and more infrequent, and her temperature dropped almost to normal, but her breathing was shallow and fast, and she seemed hardly conscious of her surroundings any more. Even Sara could not get her attention. "We're losing her," warned Vladia. She was right. As the first light of the new day began to seep down through the vents in the ceiling Ester suddenly arched her back as if to cough again, gave a last weak cry and stopped breathing. The child's skin, for some time now tinged with blue, darkened briefly, then went pale as milk. Sara wept openly as Vladia laid the child back down on the furs and closed her eyes. The young concubine had lost her last blood relative in the world.

Chapter 22

Five days later Sara, Ahna, and Ahndru all woke with fevers, though none of them, at first, seemed as virulent as Ester's. Vladia was ready, and efficiently treated all three, making sure they stayed hydrated, well nourished, and quiet. The girls did well. Vladia kept their fevers under control with the willow bark, and their aches and pains were relatively minor. Both developed congestion, but it stayed in their upper respiratory passages and camphor relieved it enough that they could sleep. Ahndru's case, however, continued to worsen. His fever kept returning before it was time to give him more medicine. By the third day he was coughing uncontrollably, the growing congestion in his lungs audible to everyone. His broken leg, by keeping him confined, had weakened him that crucial bit; his mother's medications, her attention to every detail of his care, her boundless love were not enough. He died as Ester died, four days after the fever struck. His family were given no time to mourn.

Jaromir, Moshel, Redwolf and Vladia all now had the fever. Ahna first learned they were sick the morning after Ahndru died, when Ahshela herself came into the girls' sleeping space bearing tea with their morning medication. Recognizing her, Ahna sat up abruptly. "Mother?" she asked.

"Yes," the Eldest answered, "Vladia is sick. Your father has a fever, too, but he's been watching her anyway. He came for me at first light, when he found her near delirious. The medication took her temperature down, and she is sleeping."

"Both your brothers also have the fever. Your father wants to help, but if he is to recover he needs to stay quietly in his furs for at least another two or three days, so I hope you two are well enough to get up. I know you still feel rotten, but the fever is gone and most of your congestion, too. No one is willing to come here, not since the child of the Others and Ahndru died. They fear for their families if not for themselves. We cannot blame them."

Her words sparked a flicker of hope in Ahna. "The fever has not spread beyond our tents, then?"

"I'm sorry, I did not mean to give you that impression," said Ahshela. "It has spread. For two or three days now there have been reports of people with fever scattered all over the camp. Some of those that are ill have had recent contact with members of your family, but others have not. No one understands how this is spreading, and even I cannot believe the speed with which it does, or how fast it kills! We had reports of three deaths this morning, all little girls from different families. I'm afraid it's going to get much worse soon.

"The women's circle has organized to nurse everyone, or find people who can. None of the men will help, of course. We are lucky, I think, that the priests chose this time to sequester themselves. It gives us an opportunity to treat the sick openly without facing their opposition, and to teach the other women and girls how to care for their families in this emergency.

"Get dressed now. I've given the rest of your family their morning medication. I am needed elsewhere, if you can manage breakfast for everyone. Be sure you take care of each other, too. Ahna, you know how to administer the medications, and the proper schedule?" The girls assured her that they both did and the Eldest bade them farewell.

Ahna and Sara found that they could keep going if they alternated working and resting in fairly short stints. They carried water, made tea and broth and mixed medicines, cooked and cleaned up, rubbed camphorated fat on chests, emptied slop pots, bathed fevered brows. They spelled each other as well, making sure they each got enough rest. Ahshela checked in on them later that day, praised them for their efforts and assured them that all their patients were doing well. Vladia's fever stayed down with medication. Each time she woke Ahna gave her broth and medicated tea, convincing her that she and Sara could continue to care for everyone and that no one else in the family was seriously ill. Jaromir came in once in the afternoon and backed them up, so Vladia smiled at her daughter and the concubine, told them how proud she was of them, and went back to sleep. They did not tell her that the fever was spreading through the tents like fire on the dry summer steppes.

Ahna wasn't even entirely truthful about their own charges. Jaromir and Moshel would both be back on their feet at least part of the time in a couple of days, but Redwolf's temperature kept spiking alarmingly. Ahshela recommended that they prop him up to sleep, that they give him the expectorants and water-retention preventers even before he began showing signs of congestion, and that they get him up several times a day, if only to take a few steps around his private quarters. She was trying to figure out ways to prevent or at least control the deadly chest congestion, and for some patients her methods worked. By the next morning Redwolf was coughing roughly, his fever still sometimes dangerously high. Sara would not leave him, changing the clay packs on his chest, mixing his medications and coaxing him to drink them, helping him to his feet although he had to lean on her just to stay upright. All that day he got neither better nor worse, but he grew weaker from exhaustion.

Ahna was fixing food for their other patients the next morning when Sara came running into the work tent.

"The congestion is building up again! Redwolf can hardly breathe, and I'm out of clay. Is there more? Where can I get it?"

Ahna looked around vaguely. They had no more clay. The place where they got it was a couple of miles up the river. Someone would have to go for more, but who? When? Her eyes lighted on the pot of onions that Sara had brought from the town's old gardens that morning, still simmering on the hearth, cooked almost to mush because both girls had been busy with other tasks. They were hot, and the odor of onions certainly cleared one's nose; maybe they could be substituted for the heated clay. She told Sara her idea. They drained the mess and mixed camphor leaves with it, increasing its pungency until it made them sneeze.

"You will have to let it cool a little," Ahna warned, "just until you think he can stand it on his skin." Sara nodded her understanding as she left the work area with the onions. Within two fingers' time she was back, and she was laughing.

"It really worked! The onions are much better than the clay. Before they were even cool Redwolf coughed up a whole lot of phlegm. He's breathing easier now, and he has fallen asleep. I'm going for more onions," she finished breathlessly, grabbed a gathering basket and disappeared out between the tent flaps.

The onions continued to work, and Redwolf's breathing improved, but he was still very sick. Late the fourth night his temperature spiked again, so high that he raved weakly in delirium, and both girls worked on him with cool cloths while they waited for the most recent dose of willow bark tea to take effect. Finally he dropped into a fitful sleep, his skin a little cooler. Sara said she would stay with him that night as she had every night; she did not care that it was improper. She fell asleep, of course, curled in her furs beside his, her own exhaustion defeating her best intentions. She woke in the predawn chill to find that her patient, still asleep and much less restless, had sweat beaded all over his head and body. Alarmed, she went running to wake Ahna, and was taken aback when her breathless explanation elicited a happy, if sleepy, grin. "It's all right, Sara" her friend said, "You did it! If he is sweating his fever has broken. He's getting better. Cover him well and let him sleep now. He may even be a little hungry when he wakes up."

That morning, only the fifteenth day after the arrival of Ester, Jaromir and Moshel sat down to breakfast in the main living area. It almost felt strange. When Vladia appeared both men tried to send her back to her furs. She refused to go, saying that she was much better, and that the girls should not have to bear the entire burden of caring for the family.

Ahna came in with the pot of tea, and seeing that her mother would not be swayed, said, "At least sit down and have breakfast with Father and Moshel before you take on anything more." Vladia's eyebrows shot up, but before she could even begin to shake her head her husband said, "Yes, wife, sit down and eat. You have been very ill and need to recover your strength." She looked at him in disbelief, but he nodded and smiled at her, patting the rugs beside him, and finally she sank down cross-legged in the spot he indicated. He smiled again, handing her a piece of flatbread, a few olives and some cheese, and Ahna poured her a cup of hot, sweet tea.

"I don't understand," said Vladia, overwhelmed.

"It's simple," explained her husband. "We are living through a nightmare. We have lost a beloved child and another who might have become as dear to us. For days I have feared for you, and I have learned that life is too short not to live it as I wish. From now on, in this tent at least, you shall have the respect and honor you deserve, no matter that the rest of our people may think it odd, or even unsuitable. The prohibition against interfering in marital relationships has to work both ways. The girls may continue to serve the food, for they are certainly better at it than we men would be, but then they must sit down and eat with us as well. You and they have saved all our lives. I no longer believe our traditional way of treating women is right and I won't do it any more!"

She looked into his eyes for longer than she ever had before, then a little smile curled on to her lips, and she said, "Thank you, Jaromir, for being you." He smiled and offered her more food.

As she started to eat, Sara came in with fresh flatbread and some shredded mutton in a spicy sauce. Vladia told her good morning, then her expression darkened in concern.

"Where is Redwolf?" she demanded, starting to get up. Her husband put his hand on her arm to restrain her, and the concubine said hastily, "He is all right, Vladia. He still... is still in bed. He... was badly congested, and his fever only broke last night, but the cough almost... is almost gone, now, too. He ate breakfast and wants to get up, but we not let him, not yet."

The older woman settled back, turning away briefly as a coughing fit racked her own throat. "I see Ahna has been teaching you, to our benefit," she commented when it subsided. "I am very glad you are here, and very, very proud of you both. You must be beyond tired, but I will be able to help you now. Has Ahshela been here, or did I dream that?"

"Yes, she has been here," confirmed her husband. "She has been overseeing the girls, but she has not had much time, so it is good that Ahna has learned so well." He winced, realizing he'd probably said too much.

"She is that busy?" asked his wife. "Are there many sick?" Jaromir and the girls hesitated before answering, and that was enough. "There are," she accused. "You should have told me. Ahshela must need my help."

"You will be no help to her if you do not get better first yourself!" her husband said, alarmed by her obvious intention to start caring for others immediately. "Ahshela specifically said that you were not to stir from our tents until your fever and cough were completely gone. You will not risk yourself!" He sounded like the old Jaromir, giving orders and expecting to be obeyed, but his wife only smiled at him.

"I will rest until tomorrow," she compromised, "as will the girls, but then, if there is need, we will have to tend to our duties, as you will without doubt tend to yours."

The next morning, true to her word, Vladia was up early, helping the girls serve breakfast, meaning to find the Eldest immediately afterward. Then while they were finishing the cleanup, Ahshela herself walked through the main tent and into their work area. She looked frazzled. Under her dark blue scarf her silver hair was bound around her head as usual, but the numerous stray ends gave evidence that it had been several days since she had braided it. Her blouse, sash, and divided skirts were all wrinkled and a little soiled, as if she had slept in them. Ahna had never before noticed the deep creases in her face or the crisscrossing veins that stood out on her hands, and there were pronounced dark smudges under her eyes.

"Good," the Eldest said without preamble. "You're on your feet again. You can take over here, Vladia, and these very capable girls can come and help us." She smiled at Ahna and Sara.

"They can help, yes," answered Ahna's mother, "but I will come, too. Jaromir and Moshel are not useless. They will look after themselves and Redwolf in this emergency."

Ahshela's eyebrows climbed sharply. "Is that all right with them?"

Vladia's smile was joyful. "Yes, it is. In our tents at least the rules have changed... quite... a lot!" Her comment was interrupted by her coughing, and Ahshela lost her smile.

"I don't think you are ready to come out to work," she said.

"How many people are sick," Ahna's mother asked by way of answer.

The elder dropped her eyes. "Many," she admitted. "Nearly everyone in any given household gets sick once one does. Sometimes an entire family falls ill at the same time. The youngest and the oldest are the worst. Also anyone who was already sick or injured. We are lucky that there are few women far along in pregnancy right now. Anything that weakens a person gives the disease an advantage that our treatments cannot overcome. The congestion comes so suddenly. If it gets down into the chest it usually overwhelms the medications and kills within a couple of days. Too many die. We have saved some who were healthy when they got the fever and who might have died without treatment, but there have already been nearly a hundred that we could not save. There will be more. All we can do is keep trying."

Vladia stood frozen for a moment, mouthing "a hundred," then shook herself. "Ahna, get the medicine bags. Sara, gather as many clean clothes as you can, and bring that bag of onions. You two make an excellent team and should continue to work together, especially as few would take help from Sara alone." She smiled with rueful apology at the concubine, but Sara nodded her head in acceptance and went to get the onions.

"Onions?" asked Ahshela. Ahna, realizing they'd had no chance to tell the Eldest about the onion poultice, explained briefly. She and Sara were both certain the treatment had saved Redwolf's life.

"That's wonderful!" exclaimed Ahshela. She looked at Sara. "I hope there are many onions in those gardens."

"They not... were not dug, last year. They... made seed," explained the concubine. "There are many, but I have to hunt in the... grass... wild plants for them."

"We shall hunt, or rather you young people can. Ahna, your friends have been helping the women's circle. Let's get them together and Sara can take them to the gardens and show them where and how to harvest onions."

"I can show them," said Ahna. "Sara is a better healer than I am. She can start helping the children."

"You are needed with the children, Ahna," said the Eldest. We all know Sara is…" She had to stop to cough, a repetitive hacking which lasted several seconds. When it finally ended she continued. "Sara is an excellent healer, but you must realize the men, maybe even the mothers, will not let her near their children if one of us is not 'directing' her. The two of you can work together after she gets back from gathering the onions."

"You need to go home and rest," Vladia said to the Eldest. "If you don't take care of that cough we will lose you, too, and that would be a tragedy. I know you say that everyone must die, but we need your knowledge."

Jaromir was standing in the door to the work area, listening.

"I will escort her home myself," he said to his wife, "and then I am coming with you. Redwolf is much better. He and Moshel will be fine on their own." Vladia started to object, but her husband overruled her. "I am chief. The people need to see me, to believe that there is still leadership, that things are under control even if they are not." He looked at Ahshela. "Some may be unwilling to have even clan women not of their own families treat their children, because the priests teach that your medicine is witchcraft." She nodded. "I can order them to allow it," he concluded, "if I can't persuade them."

The Eldest stared at him, something akin to amazement showing in her face. He was a good chief, punctilious in his duties, leading the men in war, fairly adjudicating disputes and making decisions about moving, grazing rights, and other such matters, and popular, too, but she had believed him to be a typical male of the clan, thinking mostly of himself. His insistence on becoming directly involved in a health emergency went far beyond the norm.

Jaromir gave her a little bow. "I've realized that we're wrong to deny our women their role as leaders and healers, especially in domestic matters such as this, but it will not be so easy to convince the other men, so I am needed even in this medical crisis." He took the jute sack of onions from Sara, who suppressed her disappointment and went to get gathering baskets. The onions were important, and she knew best how to find them, but she would have preferred to be treating the sick children.

Ahshela gathered her thoughts. "You are especially needed now," she said to the chief. "For reasons known only to themselves the priests have refused to perform their function as spiritual leaders, mentors, comforters. They keep strictly to their compound and won't let anyone in. They claim that they must spend this time in fasting and prayer, to intercede with the Gods. I hope they aren't really fasting. It would be a foolish thing to do, weakening themselves, with the sickness in the camp. But whether or not they are fasting, they are making sure they avoid contact with the rest of us."

Vladia took her rabbit-skin pouch of herbs from her daughter, and started checking its contents. "We will wait for you, husband," she promised. "Where do you want us to go first, Eldest?"

"I don't want to be selfish," said Ahshela, "but please come now and bring the onions to my tents. Both my daughter and granddaughter are very sick. Luliana's baby died this morning."

Vladia looked at her daughter. "You should have told us sooner," she scolded the Eldest. "Of course we will come!"

The next days both dragged and sped by, exhausting, heartbreaking, occasionally triumphant, universally hard on everyone, but especially the women. No one had ever counted the exact numbers, but there were over fifteen hundred people in their clan now, or had been when the fever struck, and among the crowded tents few escaped at least a mild case of the disease. Hundreds of people were sick at once, many at risk of their lives. The caregivers from the inner circle of the women's society, the only ones trained in the use of herbal remedies and in nursing techniques, were too few; most found themselves working all day and deep into the night with little or no rest. There were not enough healers to help everyone who needed help.

For all but the most dire cases they tried to find household members who had not yet become ill or who had recovered enough to get up to do the nursing, but even training them took time, and they had to be watched. Some could not resist using more of the healing herbs than were prescribed, or giving the doses too often; too much willow bark could kill. Some simply got tired and did not treat their patients often enough. Most of the men would not help at all, preferring even the near certainty of losing members of their family to the disgrace of being seen doing 'women's work.' That left the entire burden on the women, which was nothing new. Inevitably, overworked girls and women got sicker than their healthy male counterparts, and took longer to recover, if they did recover. The deaths mounted into the hundreds.

Ahna and Sara seemed to be tireless; they worked as a team, and made each other rest. Ahna's onion poultice was now being used by all the trained caregivers when the congestion moved into a patient's chest. Lives were saved, but if it was not used such patients nearly always died. Some who were given the treatment died anyway; the pneumonia killed with heart-wrenching speed. The poultices had to be started right away and used regularly, and the patients needed to have been strong and healthy when the disease struck. The caregivers found, too, that keeping the sickest ones propped up in their furs, and getting them to their feet frequently, if only for very short periods, also increased their chances of recovery, but all this required intensive and time-consuming nursing care. The one good thing was that few remained in the acute stage of the disease for long. Within three or four days of the onset of the fever, nearly all who got it were either recovering or dead.

Yashihar lost his first wife and a small daughter, but his second wife and two sons and a daughter were recovering, and now he was temporarily heading the council, so many of the elders were confined to their tents with the disease. All the oldest ones had died or would before the epidemic waned. At the first meeting after Jaromir's return the council discussed the needs of the sick. They kept coming back to the fact that it was the priests who were supposed to be providing spiritual and physical comfort and assistance in emergencies of this kind, which they considered the province of the Gods. They were, among other things, charged with burial of any man who had died, a task for which there was now far more than the usual need.

In their absence the council had assigned the job to the unattached warriors, to their dismay. They were the logical candidates, since they had no immediate families who might contract the disease from them, and many had already had the fever and recovered. They were one of the first groups outside of Vladia's compound to become ill, but as they were to a man young, strong, healthy and not under any stress, nearly all recovered rapidly. The unattached concubines, who were also among the first to come down with the fever, were not so lucky. Over half of them died, despite Ahshela's insistence that they get the same care as everyone else. Their caretaker Tzyoner also died.

When the assignment to bury the dead was made some warriors called a meeting to discuss who would do the duty. The question quickly arose whether any of them should do it. Many voices protested that, since the priests weren't doing it, the women should be required to take on the task. It was certainly beneath a warrior's dignity! Then Moshel stood up.

"I know I am only a fosterling here," he began, "and you have no obligation to heed me, but I have to say that this may be a time to show concern for something besides our dignity. Most of you have mothers, and sisters, and many have lost one or both." All the young men nodded.

"Do you really want to give them more to do?" Moshel asked. "You will be putting your mothers and sisters at even greater risk of their lives, those of you who are still lucky enough to have mothers and sisters, just to protect your dignity.

"The priests aren't doing their duty, so I will help bury the men, not for them, but because it will relieve the women's burden a little. Under these circumstances, *not* helping is beneath *my* dignity!"

"You are a fool," snapped Jaromir's fosterling Tonzyl, a tall blond warrior past his sixteenth summer. "You will end just like him, letting his women sit down with him to eat, attending the sick, even emptying privacy pots! No self-respecting warrior would do such things. It is too demeaning. You might as well have become a craftsman, or a priest. The Lion clan should be ashamed. *I* will not make myself less of a man! I would go home today if there were no risk of taking the fever to my own clan, and so would most of the rest of the fosterlings. We're sorry we were ever sent here."

"I hope your clan will never have to deal with an emergency like this," Moshel responded. "You would not be much use to them if they did." At least there were no further protests from Lion clan warriors of the council's orders.

Still, the priests were sorely missed, and many on the council felt they had chosen the wrong time for their retreat. "We should confront Zynjaar," said the Horse Master, "and demand that he send the priests out to us. It may be that, isolated as they are, they are not aware of the seriousness of the disease, or how badly they are needed." That raised brows; few thought anyone in the camp could be unaware of the situation, particularly not the priests, if only because the dead had to be carried right past their compound to the barrow field to be buried. The councilors themselves went to the priests, asking that they end their retreat and do their duty by the people of the clan in this emergency. They excused Jaromir because of the bad feeling between him and the High Priest. He went instead to find and help his wife.

When Yashihar and the five other members of the reduced council approached the priests' compound, a complex of some thirty tents with the largest of them, comprising the biggest gathering tent in the village and the High Priest's household tents, fronting on the main thoroughfare, they found the whole area surrounded by yard sticks with the black, purple, green and red ribbons signifying quarantine - no trespassing: keep out! They stood on the lane and called for Zynjaar, but there was no response. The entire complex seemed extraordinarily lacking in activity. Finally a priest came out of a tent further back and approached them, not closely.

"What must I do for you?" he asked as if he had not heard them calling for the High Priest.

"We need to speak to Zynjaar," said Yashihar, "and to as many of your fellows as we can."

"We are in retreat," the priest answered. "We are to have no contact with the rest of the clan for an entire moon. Only half that time has passed. You know that. What is so important that we must anger the Gods by breaking the holy retreat?"

Zynjaar, flanked by some twenty more priests, now stepped out of the gathering tent and stood listening, but they did not approach the council members either.

"I believe you already know the answer to that question," said Yashihar, raising his voice slightly to make sure that all the priests could hear. There was also quite a crowd of men on the pathway now, drawn by his efforts to get the attention of the High Priest and curious about the outcome of the council's demand.

"There is an epidemic of the winter fever in the camp," the Horse Master continued, "much worse than in most years. Many are sick and dying. It is the duty of the priesthood to care for the folk when they are ill or dying. You are neglecting your duties, which we think is more likely to anger the Gods than any lack of observance of ritual might."

"You are wrong," said Zynjaar, moving a scant two steps closer, then projecting his compelling voice across the uncomfortably wide expanse of bare ground between them. "We are interceding with Them to end the epidemic and to some extent I think it is working." Murmurs of disbelief greeted this statement; everyone knew more people were sick every day.

"Is it not true, as I have heard," he argued, "that it is mostly the women who are dying, while the men and boys are spared?" Some nodded reluctantly, others in dawning comprehension. "The society of priests has been spared as well; no priests have died. The Gods are still angry that the daughter of our leader has been allowed to get away with her unwomanly behavior. Their greatest anger is at Jaromir himself, because he allows her to behave in ungodly ways and thus to set a bad example for the other women. He even invites his women to sit down with him to eat!" Many of the men looked at one another in surprise. Did he really? Even if he did, how did the High Priest know? Why was it Zynjaar's business?

"Look how the Gods sent the sickness first to Jaromir's tents," Zynjaar went on. "I have heard that the chief has lost a son and may yet lose another. The Gods are punishing him. They have brought the sickness on us all, taking the women in particular, because you refused to heed Their warnings and continue to listen to him as your leader."

"The men get sick," called someone in the crowd. "They get better because they are physically stronger and healthier than the women. The priests do not get sick because you are preventing all contact between us. Make them come out and do their duty for the people; see if they avoid getting the fever then!"

"We do our duty now!" the High Priest declared. "Our greatest duty is to fast and pray, to sacrifice to the Gods and try to curb Their anger. We ask that They tell us what we must do to end the epidemic. What I have told you is what They have told us. They will tell us more. To break the retreat now would be to break our line of communication with Them, angering Them anew, and assuring that we will not get the answers we seek.

"We will pray for the sick and say the words of absolution for the few, mostly older, men who are dying. We will not end the retreat. You are defying the will of the Gods by asking it." With that he vanished back into the tent. All the rest followed silently, ignoring calls from several of the onlookers who spoke to individual priests by name, imploring their aid.

Later that day Ahna and Sara were just arriving at a tent near the priests' compound where they were treating Ahna's friend Maezian when her mother, a slightly bemused expression on her face, ushered a nondescript stranger in his twenties wearing an unembroidered brown shirt and sash and faded blue pantaloons with leather shoes, not boots, into the sleeping space where they were getting out their supplies. She said, "Here is Mulynvi, girls, come to ask something of you."

"My children are ill," the man said without preamble. "My youngest son got the fever yesterday, the other two this morning. I want you to tell me how to care for them."

"We will come," said Ahna, touched by his concern. Most of the men would not show it if they did care, would send a woman, even a neighbor woman, to get help rather than ask for it themselves.

"Tell us where your tents are. We will come when we are done here."

"I... I cannot direct you to my tent," he stammered. "You must not come there! Please tell me what my wife and I can do to make them better."

Ahna frowned, then her brow cleared. "You are a priest, aren't you?" she asked. Mulynvi looked so alarmed at the question that she said, "No, don't answer that. It's all right. Stay and watch what we do for Maezian. We will give you medicines and your wife can do the same for your sons."

First the girls steeped a tea with willow bark, honey, camomile, and other herbs. "This is for the fever," Ahna explained. "It also has an expectorant to help loosen the congestion. We will give you the herbs. You use the willow bark and honey to keep the fever down, and the other herbs once the child starts coughing. For a small child, use only a little," she admonished, showing him exactly how much of each herb. "For a larger child, six to ten or eleven summers, use twice as much. For an adult, use three times as much. Do *not* give the tea more than four times a day and twice at night, or less than four hands' time apart, even if the fever is not under control. Too much can cause a child or an adult to go to sleep and never wake up.

"If your patient is coughing, keep him propped up in bed, and get him up several times a day to walk around, even if he is so weak you have to hold him up." The girls demonstrated with Maezian, who was able to help a little. As she walked around her coughing increased. Then they put her back in her furs and applied a hot boiled onion and camphor poultice to her chest; within just a couple of minutes she sat up and coughed gobs of thick, yellowy mucus into a bowl Sara was holding for her.

"The onions and camphor break up the congestion and help her cough the poisons out of her body," said Ahna. "Sitting up and getting up and walking around seem to help, too. You will know if a child needs this treatment if his cough becomes deep and rough and seems to shake his whole body, like Maezian's does. That means the congestion has gone down into the chest, and its the most deadly situation. You can also put your ear to the child's chest. If you can hear wheezing and bubbling when he breathes, you must to start using the poultice immediately, and apply it as often as necessary to allow the child to keep breathing freely. You should not have to use it for more than two or three days, though. The children either get better in that time, or they die."

The disguised priest asked her to repeat the directions, which she did, showing him the colored markers that identified the different herbs she had given him. Finally she gave him some onions. She hoped it would be enough because, though Sara said there were still onions in the gardens, she feared they would run out before the epidemic ended.

"Thank you," Mulynvi said, preparing to leave with the medications. He colored a little; "May the Gods bless you and your patients."

Ahna looked at Sara as he walked away. 'May the Goddess guide you and guard you and yours,' they said silently to his back.

Chapter 23

The winter fever that year had another way to kill. As the epidemic continued the healers, the women of the inner circle, and even some of those they had trained to tend the sick, began to die. Most had had the acute form of the disease and had recovered. Like Vladia, they plunged into nursing the sick the minute they were back on their feet, and there were too many sick. There was so much need. Few of the caregivers got enough rest; some didn't get any. Their coughs persisted, a new congestion began to build in their lungs, more subtle, less obviously debilitating, easier to ignore, but just as deadly if ignored.

Vladia's cough would not relent, but she insisted she was all right, and continued ministering to others despite her own exhaustion. Seven days after she started tending the sick, Jaromir found his wife dead in her furs. She was already cold.

Jaromir gathered her up and held her to him, emitting an agonized, despairing howl that brought his children running. They found him hunched around their mother's body, rocking back and forth, mute now, dry eyed. Redwolf and Ahna clung to each other, wailing, their tears wetting their night clothes. Sara came in and found them like that. She went to Jaromir and put her hand on his shoulder, trying to comfort him although the tears were running down her cheeks, too.

"The Goddess has her safe," she said haltingly. "She will be... born again. She will have happy life the next time... she was good person." Ahna gasped. She had warned Sara not to speak of these things, especially in front of the men. But to the Others these were not secrets. They were public beliefs held by all, the core of their way of life. To Sara death was an ending, but only of the moment. The gift of rebirth, the knowledge of a future life was what made it bearable, both for the dying and for those left behind.

Jaromir glanced at the concubine, not comprehending her words, perhaps not hearing them. He laid his wife back down in her furs, straightened the rumpled front of her sleeping shift, folded her hands and patted her hair into place. He paused to take one long last look at her, then pulled the coverlet over her. Without a word he got up and went back into his own sleeping quarters, apparently not even seeing his children, who now stood watching him. When Ahna tried to get him to come to breakfast he did not answer. When she took bread and tea in to him he lay in his furs, his face turned to the wall. He would not even acknowledge her presence.

There was no time to mourn, no time for ceremonies and processions. Ahna and Sara and some of the other young women carried Vladia's body, still clad in her simple night shift, to the sacred circle on the hilltop where the women went to communicate with the Goddess. With a few short prayers thanking the Lady for guarding Vladia's spirit until She gave her a new body they left it there, naked, in keeping with the teachings of the Goddess. If the clan stayed nearby long enough they would collect the stripped bones and put them in a cave with others; if not the bones would lie here and go slowly back to the Goddess as well.

Then they returned to their nursing duties. Her patients welcomed her. The word had spread about her successes, and they were grateful that she was in their tents, but Ahna's heart remained heavy. She could not shake the feeling that in some way all this really was her fault, and now the disease had taken her mother, too. It should have been her.

The next day, when Jaromir still refused even to acknowledge anyone or take food or even water, Ahna went in search of the Eldest. She found her at home, resting. Her daughter, Reova, had also died, but the onion poultice had saved Luliana, and she had become a martinet, insisting that her grandmother stay home and rest and accept treatment until her persistent cough was completely gone. The young woman greeted Ahna at the entrance to their tents, but when she explained her errand, her friend refused to let her see Ahshela.

"We have both lost our mothers now," she said apologetically, "you have lost a brother, and I have lost a child. I could not bear it if I lost my grandmother, too. Everyone 'needs' her, but her family needs her most of all. Please understand."

"I... I do understand," said Ahna. "We need my father, too." She started to turn away in resignation, but a voice from behind Luliana stopped her.

"Jaromir?" said Ahshela, coming out of her sleeping quarters. "What is wrong with him?"

"He will not eat or drink, or even speak or move from his furs, not since he found my mother yesterday morning," answered Ahna.

"Vladia?" cried the Eldest. "Not Vladia, too! Ahna, I'm so sorry!" Ahna glared at Luliana, who had been one of those that helped carry Vladia's body to its final resting place, and had promised to inform Ahshela of her death.

"Grandmother, you must not exert yourself!" Luliana scolded, a note of entreaty in her voice. "I did not tell you because I knew you would…"

"You knew it would matter to me," the Eldest interrupted with real anger. "My dearest living friend, and my second in command. I needed to know, Luliana! I appreciate your care of me, but if you want me to listen to you, you must show more respect for my needs." Her granddaughter hung her head, mumbling an apology.

"I will come," Ahshela said to Ahna. "We really cannot afford to lose Jaromir, too." To Luliana she said, "Don't worry. I will not overdo. Sitting down talking to the chief will not require exertion, and Ahna will feed us dinner, if I can get him to eat. I promise you that I will not go anywhere else and will come straight back to our tents when I am through."

"I will escort her back, or one of my brothers will," Ahna promised, smiling reassuringly at Luliana.

When Ahna and the Eldest entered the chief's tent, Ahna pointed out her father's private space, then went to find her brothers and gather her nursing supplies. Sara had already gone out with one of the other older girls from the women's circle. Moshel was in the work area, preparing carrots, broad beans and turnips. They were doing without onions in their food because every onion was needed for poultices. He smiled when Ahna said that Ahshela was with Jaromir.

"I need to care for some sick children this morning," she said. "Can you have something ready for the Eldest, and hopefully Father as well, at dinner time?"

Moshel grinned. "No problem. Redwolf has gone to get a leg of mutton from Lwenli. He killed a sheep yesterday. It will be our turn next. We'll cut off some small pieces and stew them with the vegetables for dinner, and roast the rest.

"You know, when we were talking about men being able to look after themselves during our break at the races I never thought I'd find myself doing this!" He swept his hand over the vegetables toward the pot of water heating on the fire. Ahna started to apologize for leaving him to do all the domestic chores, but he continued without a break.

"And I *really* never thought I'd enjoy it! I'm coming to respect all the work you women do. I'm learning a lot, including that our way of assigning duties by sex may be almost as limiting for the men as it is for the women." She grinned at him, then.

"I wish more of our men were like you, Moshel," she said. "I'm really glad you're my brother." He grinned back.

"It's an honor to have you for a sister, Healer Ahna. I wish there were more girls like you!"

"Oh, you might be surprised," she said enigmatically, thinking of the secrets of the women's circle. She picked up her nursing supplies and headed out the door.

Ahshela called to Jaromir from outside his closed curtains. Receiving no answer, she pushed them aside and walked in. The small sleeping cubby was neat, and smelled fresh. At least he was using the refuse pot, and someone was emptying it. The man lay on his furs, his face to the wall of the tent. He had apparently not moved. She suspected he meant to wait her out. She would see about that. She walked forward and settled, a little stiffly, to a seat on the furs beside him.

"I am so sorry about Vladia," she began. "She shouldn't have tried to do so much, but if she hadn't, she wouldn't have been the woman we loved. We were so lucky to have her, and she was lucky to have you, Jaromir. I know it is hard to lose her, but your children still need you. Your clan needs you, too. I need you. Please don't quit on us. That's not what Vladia would have done, nor what she would have expected of you."

The man didn't respond. He didn't acknowledge her presence in any way. He might have been dead, but she could see him breathing. As she watched she realized there was a tiny hesitation, almost a hitch, every little while at the end of an indrawn breath. He was not asleep. He was ignoring her. She thought a minute. There was one approach that just might work. Did she dare take the risk? She would be responsible for incalculable damage to her people if she was wrong, but she didn't think she was.

"You will be with her again, you know," she said conversationally. His body twitched involuntarily. That had made an impression.

"You've probably heard that the Others believe that men and women are equal in the eyes of their Goddess, and that every soul will be born again into another body." She paused, then took a deep breath and continued, her voice lower, more intimate. "I am breaking fifty summers of solemn vows by telling you this, but I trust that of all men, our secret will be safe with you. Jaromir, I, too, believe that we are all reborn, over and over, men as well as women. So did your mother, who was my dear friend, and so did Vladia. She is gone from this life, now, but you will be together again in a future life." She stopped speaking and sat watching his back. The silence stretched out. He almost seemed to have stopped breathing! Finally he stirred, rolled over, and stared at her.

"You don't believe in the priests' paradise for men only," he said, his voice hoarse and dry. "I don't think I do, either. No place could be paradise without her. Tell me why you trust the words of the Goddess any more than those of the Gods."

"It is not the traditions of the Goddess that have convinced us," she answered him, "it is common sense and our own observations of the world. Everything is reborn. Every spring the plants that died in the fall come back to life, either from their roots or from their seeds or spores. Animals have babies that have the same traits as their parents. How often have you known a mare or stallion to pass on their idiosyncrasies as well as their physical features to their foals?

"It is all part of a pattern that is necessary if life is to continue. The bodies of those that die, whether they are plants or animals, are recycled into the earth and used to feed the new generations."

Jaromir looked a little skeptical.

"Did you know that the Others bury fish guts and bones, or other animal and plant debris, in their gardens?" she asked. "That is one of the reasons their plants grow so much larger than similar ones in the wild. The materials rot in the soil and the result helps the plants grow. Then the fruits of the plants feed us! The grass in the meadows grows greenest where the cattle and horses have deposited their waste, made from the plants they eat. Everything that dies comes back to life. It will be that way as long as the balance is kept."

He shook his head. "The materials of life are used over and over, I know, but I don't see that that means our spirits, or souls, or whatever you want to call that which makes each of us ourselves, are reused."

"Everything else is reborn, or reused, as you say. Does it follow that the spirit of life, then, would just... vanish?" she countered. "When a person or animal, or even a plant - when anything dies it is obvious that something has gone, is missing from the remains, that was there while it was alive. That is the spirit, what the priests call the soul. If all the other parts of life are reused, it simply doesn't make sense that the Goddess, who we believe created all this, would waste the most important part, the essence of life. It is reused, too. Our souls are given new bodies. We are born again."

Jaromir thought that over for a while. "Even if that is true, I might be born as anyone anywhere," he finally said. "Who knows if Vladia and I would be born again at the same time, or near each other."

"It is said, in the lore of the Goddess," she answered him, "that as long as creatures stick to and care for their home territories they will be reborn in the same places. Their many lives are all tied to each other and to the land."

"But we are not now in our traditional territories. We keep moving into strange lands!"

"That is indeed a problem and, we believe, represents a terrible error on our part, because it badly upsets the balance. Perhaps, since we are nomads, we can hope that our spirits are tied to our clans as well as to the land. I do believe, if it's any consolation, that within a very few generations, if not sooner, we will be back in our ancestral territories."

Jaromir's eyebrows rose. "How? Why?"

"We are running out of places to conquer," she explained. "Only a little more than a hundred miles from here, our scouts tell us, the land ends in endless seas. When the clans reach the water, when there are no more communities of the Others ahead, and the other clans have wiped out all the ones on either side, we will be faced with a decision: learn to feed ourselves, to become farmers in the lands we have stripped of their husbandmen, or go home and resume our old lifestyle where we belong, on the steppes. Which do you think the people will choose?"

"They will choose to go home," he replied, suddenly if inexplicably certain.

"I think so, too," she said. "The Goddess has made us with a yearning for the place where we originated. Whether we will have learned anything is another matter."

"May I come in?" called Moshel from the other side of the curtain. He entered trying to suppress a grin when two voices told him 'yes'. "I brought some tea, he said, handing them each a steaming, fragrant cup. "Dinner will be ready when the sun is high," he said as he left the room.

"The men in this family are remarkable," Ahshela commented, "even the foster-sons!"

Jaromir set his tea aside, got up and poured some water from the pitcher by the door into the washbowl, then washed his face and hands, wiping them on the scrap of linen beside it. He rinsed his mouth directly from the pitcher, then took a long drink of the water.

He came and sat down beside Ahshela, giving her a quick companionable squeeze.

"Thank you for coming," he said. "Do I need to worship the Goddess to be reborn?"

The Eldest laughed. "You are still thinking as the priests would want you to," she said. "You would be born again if you had never heard of the Goddess, or if you denied Her every day of your life. It is the nature of things as She made them. Individuals cannot change the rules by their actions or their beliefs. They can only change the way they live: whether they keep the rules or break them."

He drank his tea, thinking. Finally he said, "I would like to know more about that. Right now I have a bargain for you." She looked a question at him.

"I have lost my wife, who meant as much to me as my life. I will soon lose my daughter, to marriage into a clan that will take her away forever. I have lost my youngest son, my older sons are already on their own, and Redwolf is becoming more independent and self-sufficient by the day. It seems likely that I will soon have my duties as chief taken away. That's why, when I found her like that, I lost my purpose in life. There was no reason to go on.

"I don't really want to die," he went on, "but I still need a reason to live. Please teach me how to treat those who are sick of this pestilence. I will take Vladia's place and help you and the girls with the nursing. That is a worthy purpose."

"Are you sure?" she asked. "You will make yourself a pariah in the eyes of most of the other men, and give Zynjaar more reason to escalate his campaign against you."

"I don't care what they think any more," Jaromir said. "There is a great need for caregivers and I am available."

Ahshela glanced at the pattern of light cast by the sun shining in through the vents in the tent ceiling.

"Come," she said, "it's high sun. Let's go get some dinner. I can't wait to try what the young men have prepared. We will talk about this. You must already know quite a lot, from the times you watched Vladia. Now you can help the girls. They will teach you much more."

Chapter 24

The wind picked up, slapping unsecured tent-flaps against the tents, throwing debris in Jaromir's eyes. He kept his head down and the hood of his windbreaker pulled over his face as he beat his way home against it, relieved when he stepped into the calm of the main living area. It howled around the outside, escalating, uncannily like the voices of the arguing clansmen at the meeting he had just left. A storm was coming.

A ten-day had passed since he had started helping his daughter and the concubine care for the sick. The epidemic still raged, and they had lost most of the older healers, but those that were left and the young ones had learned; their treatments were more effective now. Fewer of their patients died. The onions in the main gardens of the razed town had run out. Moshel and some of the younger warriors had ridden back to the community they had conquered two years earlier, taking three of the concubines with them. They searched the old gardens there for onions. The Goddess of growth and renewal was with them; they returned with a pack horse loaded down with the vegetables, and still more lives were saved.

Much more than half the camp had caught the fever. There were many new cases, but now there were also many who had recovered, who could not get the sickness again, at least not this year. The High Priest had come out of seclusion, the moon's retreat at an end, although he insisted that the priests must still continue to pay attention to the Gods rather than to their people. Zynjaar was stepping up his efforts to blame Jaromir and Ahna for the epidemic.

Hundreds had died, including most of the older members of the council and the women's circle, voices of wisdom and reason silenced and gone. The people were angry, helpless, fearful of the future as they had not been in their lifetimes; they wanted someone to blame. There were now many among the men who heeded the accusations of their highest religious authority.

Redwolf and Moshel were sitting on the rugs eating when Jaromir came in. There were three additional places set. Flatbread, roasted meat and even a few boiled turnips occupied the center space along with hot tea as well as beer and milk, but of course there were no greens. The girls did not have the strength or the time to gather wild vegetables, or even visit the overgrown gardens now that there were no more onions, and Moshel knew he was too ignorant to try to gather greens; he had no idea which ones were edible. The young men welcomed their senior, pointing to the basin with wash water and a towel that waited near the door and telling him to come eat. Neither Ahna nor Sara was there; they would be out very late again conquering the disease one patient at a time.

Jaromir folded cross-legged onto the rug at his usual place, and helped himself to meat and bread while his son poured him a cup of tea, spiking it with the pungent fermented mare's milk. He took a bite, chewed and swallowed, then set the remaining food down on the woven plate in front of him.

"We have a problem," he said. "Zynjaar came to the meeting tonight. He claimed he was reporting on the results of the priests' communications with the Gods, that They had told him personally that he was to give Their message to us. He announced that Ahna's behavior has made the Gods so angry that They will do nothing to help us, or to stop the epidemic. He is clever. He said the actions of a mere woman by themselves would not disturb the Gods so much. They are adamant, he claims, because I, the clan leader, sanction those actions. He insists I am making it worse by doing women's work myself: helping to treat the sick and comfort the bereaved, doing things like bringing water to tents where the entire family is too sick to do it themselves. He says they are demanding an extreme sacrifice. The Gods will only relent and end the epidemic if I am chastised, relieved of my duties and barred permanently from any position of leadership, if not banished, and Ahna herself is offered up to them."

"He... he wants to sacrifice Ahna?" asked Moshel incredulously. His foster-father nodded.

Redwolf choked, gagged, then scrambled across the floor to the entrance. The others could hear him heaving up his dinner outside.

Moshel looked as if he might follow, but fury quickly dominated his emotions. "That... that lying snake only wants revenge, and not even honorable revenge. He has lost his son under disgracing circumstances, so he wants to take away your daughter and put the blame on you! He must know that the Gods aren't really angry at her. If They wanted her life the fever would have killed her. It is taking enough who are perfectly innocent. Instead the Gods have given her the gift of healing others who are sick. As for censuring you for the work you have been doing, those are duties the priests themselves have been neglecting, and they are men. It doesn't even make sense. Surely no one will listen to him."

Redwolf returned, a little shamefaced, and resumed his seat, watching his father intently.

"Unfortunately, the men are listening to him," said Jaromir. "Not all of them, at least not yet. Most are saying some of what you just said. A few are even accusing him of seeking revenge, but he denies it vehemently, and of course it is known that priests cannot lie. He keeps going on about the weakness and tendency to evil of all women. He insists that Ahna has turned to evil and that, because she has refused to maintain the proper role of a woman of our clan, and I have allowed it, the Gods are angered and have brought all these ills upon us. He warns that things will only get worse until They are appeased, until the cause of Their anger has been destroyed. Most of the men have lost family members or fear they will, and many fear for their own lives and future as well. He will keep telling his lies, and the more he tells them the more people will believe them. When life-changing disasters happen most men need someone or something to blame, somewhere to vent their anger and frustration. He's giving them what they want. Unless we can think of some way to stop him this will rapidly get much worse."

"The most frightening possibility, in the long run," said Ahshela from the entryway, making them all jump, "is that he might be proved right." This provoked a chorus of protest from all three men.

"No, listen," she said, stepping further into the tent. She looked exhausted, the smudges under her eyes more pronounced, and she had to stop to catch her breath now and then, but her back was still straight and her eyes held fire. "You may be the only men in the camp who will listen. The disease will run its course, whether or not Zynjaar gets his way... whether or not Ahna is sacrificed. The number of new cases is already dropping, but this is not yet noticeable to most people. In a few more days it will be noticeable, and the number of deaths will decline as well. By the time the half moon outside is full this whole outbreak will be reduced to some residual coughing and a very black memory. That is why the high priest is pushing so hard now. If he manages to sacrifice Ahna soon, he will be able to say that his Gods approved that action and ended the epidemic. The men will believe him. He will have consolidated his power as the only conduit to the spiritual world for our people. He will also have sanctified the abomination of human sacrifice, particularly that of women, in the men's eyes. We must not allow it."

She took a deep breath, and immediately suffered a coughing fit. Redwolf rose to help her to a seat. An increasingly appalled silence followed her words. Jaromir broke it.

"If he does not succeed," he said, "we will be able to say that it was the healing skills and the nursing of the women, and Ahna's onion poultice, that saved lives and stopped the epidemic, while our 'spiritual leaders' did nothing. His priests have refused to do their duty in this emergency against all that is proper and right. He will lose face if his campaign to sacrifice Ahna fails." The Eldest nodded.

"Do you know of a way to stop him, short of killing him, which is against your laws?" asked Moshel finally.

Ahshela and the chief both shook their heads.

"No," said the chief. "He won't listen to reason. He has too much to lose now. I have no authority over religious matters and Zynjaar is fast convincing people this is a religious matter. I don't understand why his own priests are so willing to be a part of it, but apparently he has them well under control. I cannot think of a thing."

"Perhaps we could kidnap him and hold him somewhere until Marvulf gets here, marries Ahna and takes her away," suggested Moshel, not entirely seriously, "or maybe we can organize our supporters to delay him until then."

"He will not tolerate delay," said the Eldest, "for the reasons I have told you."

"We cannot wait for Marvulf." Redwolf spoke so seldom that his voice surprised them all. "He is not due for a ten-day yet. I don't think we have that much time." His father was temporarily rendered mute by his own bout of coughing, but he nodded vehemently. They had no time.

"I will go for him," Redwolf continued. "I will go now, tonight. It will take me two or three days to get back here with him. You and the council will have to keep Zynjaar from carrying out his threats until then."

"Maybe I should go," objected Moshel, looking closely at Redwolf. "You were really ill, and I'm not sure you're fully recovered."

"Thank you, Moshel," said Jaromir, "but I'm afraid it needs to be Redwolf. He is more familiar with the territory to the north and east of here, and since he is Ahna's brother and therefore blood kin to Marvulf by contract, he can ride into their camp and is more likely to be accepted by their clan. You would need to wait for an invitation, and they might not listen to you at all."

Moshel nodded.

"Besides," the chief added, "I need you here to speak to the younger warriors, who have not been as hard hit by this disaster as the family men. Redwolf is still a boy in their eyes, but you are a man. We will need as many of them as we can recruit if we are to hold off the priest and his supporters until Redwolf gets back." He turned to his son.

"I think you should start at first light," he said, "not tonight. There is a storm blowing up. Traveling at night is difficult enough. In the storm you could lose your way, or even be hurt. Sleep tonight. It is only fifty miles or so. With the right horses you should make it before dark tomorrow, easily."

Ahshela approved their plan and excused herself to go home, she said, to her own supper and her furs. Moshel accompanied her despite her protestations that it was unnecessary. Jaromir and Redwolf finished their meal, discussing the details, mapping out Redwolf's route for the morrow. There would be one large river to cross. He would have to go to the head of the estuary where it fed into the great bay to the east to find a place where he could swim it, even with the horses. His father warned him to go far enough upstream so he could not be swept down into the sea; the river had a very strong current, which would be stronger yet if this storm brought much rain. They dropped the subject when Ahna and Sara came in, seeing how tired and worn they were, not wanting to add to their troubles. Everyone went to bed when they were done with eating and a cursory cleanup.

*   *   *

The rain was still coming down in sheets beneath a grey, gloomy sky, driven by a wind only a little less fierce than the night before, when Redwolf tightened his saddle girths on Dark Streak, checked the roll of furs snuggly wrapped in a waterproof ground cloth of tightly woven linen treated with beeswax and tied behind his saddle, strapped on his saddlebags, and mounted. He took the lead of his second horse, Reliable, a solidly built brown gelding of no great speed but unmatched endurance, from his father, who huddled in his own waterproof in the rain, trying to suppress his unrelenting cough, determined to see his son off.

"Don't forget about the river," he admonished by way of goodbye. "It will surely be swollen and dangerous."

"Yes, Father, I know," smiled Redwolf, the hood of his waterproof pulled well forward against the rain so that most of his face was obscured. "The horses will take me across. I will go far enough upstream, I promise."

"Well, get going then," Jaromir forced himself to say; for some reason he was reluctant to let his son go, although the trip was necessary. They had no other options, nor could they afford to wait out the storm. "The Goddess be with you."

Inside his hood Redwolf frowned. Had he heard his father correctly? He couldn't have said that, could he? Then he shook off the question, nudged Dark Streak into a walk, and started him up the track to the north, Reliable following behind.

The wide trail was slick with mud that sucked at the horses' feet, causing them to slip without warning when their master urged them to the steady trot they normally used for covering long distances. Sliding like that could cause one of them to pull a muscle, or even fall. He had to keep to the slower pace. After a few miles he left the broad track through the valley for a narrower one that sloped up the rocky ridge to the east. He would have to cross three lines of hills before he reached the watershed of the great river at its mouth, some thirty miles to the northeast. The best route north was in the second valley over.

At the top of the ridge they were fully exposed to the storm. The wind whipped the horses' manes and tails and tore at his waterproof and his gear, finding crannies through which to force the driving rain. He got wetter and wetter despite his precautions, and the horses tucked in their tails and lowered their heads, plodding doggedly on. They dropped down the far side of the hill right into the teeth of the storm, picking their way slowly on the treacherous going, the rocky trail hardly visible at their feet. It was a little better when they reached the valley, for there were trees, and the hills themselves provided some shelter; it wasn't long enough before they had to start up the next steep slope.

That ridge passed the same as the last, slowly. By the time they were halfway down the other side, though, there came a notable lessening in the rain. When they reached the valley the wind had died to a breeze, and the sky was brightening as well. As they turned onto the track leading north at the base of the hill, the rain stopped altogether. Within only a few minutes the sun came out, approaching its midday high, its rays strong enough to draw wisps of mist from all over the sopping landscape. He had been traveling for more than half the day, and had only made about fifteen miles. He would have to

step up the pace considerably to reach the Red Wolf camp before
dark.

It proved impossible. He had to stop to let the horses rest and
graze. He entered an area of sunny meadows, one of the places that
the clans had deforested in earlier years. The grass was now tall and
gone to seed, but with plenty of new growth underneath.
Dismounting, he pulled off his horses' headstalls and the saddle. He
would ride Reliable when they went on. He did not bother to halter
them. Dark Streak would stay close to him, and the gelding would
stay close to the colt.

Redwolf got a drink at a clear spring that percolated out under a
rocky bank into a tiny pool, not wanting to drink from the storm-riled
river. He filled his water skin, then let the horses come to the pool for
their water. He spread his outer garments out on a rock to dry, and sat
on another, chewing on jerky, flat bread, and cheese, drinking from
his water skin and watching the horses taking the edge off their own
hunger.

He made much better time in the afternoon, although the track
he was following was still deep with mud and he had to watch
carefully for puddles that might conceal treacherous, tendon-straining
holes. Some of the time he could trot, a pace that covered roughly six
miles a hand-span. The sun was westering when he finally crossed the
last ridge and saw below him the northernmost reaches of the sea,
blue and white-capped to the south, and a wide valley stretching
away to low hills grey-green and misty with distance. At the foot of
the ridge the valley boasted a tree-lined river that flowed from the
north through an open, swampy estuary dotted with widely spaced
clumps of trees. The wetlands continued out of sight along the shore
of the sea, but were only about a half mile wide where the river
flowed through them.

When Redwolf reached the level ground he had less than three
hands of daylight left. His goal was still twenty miles away and on the
other side of a furious river. He had been here once before, two years
earlier with his father, to hunt water birds around the edges of the
swamp. Then their winter camp had been little more than ten miles
away. The river that fall was just as wide, but placid, at least to the

eye. Now it was a maelstrom. Leaves and branches and even whole trees floated by, rushing downstream much faster than he would have thought possible. Little waves and eddies gave further evidence of the storm beneath the surface. He rode upstream, eyeing the other shore, which seemed an inordinate distance away, though it was only about a hundred paces. He picked a spot about as far upstream from where the river entered the swamp as the river was wide, and watched while a floating tree traversed that distance. It only took a minute or two! 'We'll have to go at least a mile upriver, to be sure of getting across before we get swept into the swamp,' he thought. He rode on, considering his options.

They had been traveling so slowly that he had only made the one stop all day. His horses were hungry, not to mention himself, and even if he got across the river tonight, he would never make it the remaining twenty miles or so to the Wolf Clan before dark. It was beyond foolish to ride into a strange camp after dark; one's life might be forfeit without delay or consideration if one did. The river should go down at least a little overnight. Tomorrow it would be less wild, less dangerous, than it was now. He decided to camp on this side tonight and cross at first light tomorrow. If he reached Marvulf early enough they might even be able to start back immediately. Ah, the optimism of youth.

His decision made, Redwolf rode north along the river, looking both for a likely camping site and for a straight stretch of river where he could see the other side and perhaps pick out a landing area, far downstream from where he entered the water though it would have to be. Some little while before the sun set he found a likely little meadow beside the swollen river; he turned his horses loose to graze and then made camp. He was in his bedroll beside a comforting fire before full dark.

The river didn't appear much better in the morning. There was less debris in it, but the water had not gone down measurably; it was still brown with mud and eddies and wavelets all across its surface spoke of the angry currents beneath. There was no more time to wait. Redwolf secured his belongings on Dark Streak, fastened Reliable's lead to the back of his saddle with a quick-release knot in case of emergency, and went looking for a gently sloping spot from which to enter the river, a bad mistake. Finding what he wanted just a short way upstream, he rode out onto a gravel bar lit by the early sun and urged Dark Streak into the churning water.

The crossing went immediately and horribly wrong. Dark Streak had all four hooves in the water which, although only a couple of feet deep, was already pushing him hard enough so he had to work to keep his balance, and Reliable had just taken his first step into the river when the colt lurched forward; in the flood the unstable gravel was washing rapidly out from under the pressue of his feet. The sudden motion tossed Redwolf sideways in the saddle and caused Reliable to throw up his head, tugging on the tie rope. The shift and pull put Dark Streak more off balance. He scrambled to get his feet under him and the other horse, instead of following as he should have, flung himself back in earnest, his eyes showing white. The hard tug almost threw Dark Streak down on his side in the swiftly moving water.

Clinging precariously with his legs and one arm, Redwolf reached back and pulled the quick release, meaning to hold the rope in his hand, but the gelding yanked again and the rope burned through his palm and was gone. It was just as well. Relieved of the pressure from behind, Dark Streak managed to heave himself upright, get his hooves on the bottom and take another step into deeper water as his rider settled back into his seat.

Redwolf started to turn his horse back to the shore, meaning to get Reliable, who was clearly not going to enter the water on his own, although he had been trained, as all their horses were, always to stay close to the horse being ridden. Suddenly Dark Streak's right shoulder dropped down so far that his head and neck disappeared briefly under the water. Clinging again, Redwolf felt his horse find purchase on something and plunge violently up and forward, and then they were swimming, only the boy's torso and the horse's head above water, already well out in the river and headed directly downstream. He immediately swung his legs to the side, taking his weight off of Dark Streak's back so that his mount wouldn't have such a hard time keeping his head out of the water. Then he looked toward the bank, annoyed, to see Reliable trotting alongside the river, trying to keep even with them. Even as Redwolf spotted him, a thicket of brush that came right down to the water blocked the gelding's path. He stood watching them, and whinnied once, a long lonely call, but he made no further effort to follow them.

Redwolf looked at the far bank, then angled Dark Streak across the current toward it. There was no sense in going back after the other horse now. He didn't even think they could. He encouraged his colt as he had in the races; they were being swept along at an incredible rate, and the far shore came closer all too slowly. Dark Streak responded, putting everything he had into swimming.

By the time they were halfway across Redwolf felt his horse tiring, to his surprise; he'd been sure Dark Streak had more stamina than that. The young man started swimming himself, using his legs and one arm to assist their forward motion, trying to help. With dawning fear he watched the trees on the slowly approaching bank dwindle and disappear, to be replaced by cat tails and saw grass. They had entered the estuary.

They made it out of the main current of the river and into an eddy just as the swamp fell away and the river spread out into the open sea, but there was no place to land. They kept swimming, both nearly exhausted, along the edge of the swamp, looking for some place dry and solid, lifted and lowered by mercifully small waves coming in off the sea on their right. Shortly Redwolf spotted a few trees in the swamp ahead. Just as he saw the slight rise of land where they grew and the sand of the beach that fronted them, Dark Streak's hooves found bottom and Redwolf scrambled back into his saddle.

Only to jump off in dismay and reach for the bottom with his own feet. They were in chest deep water on the edge of a sandy slope, but Dark Streak seemed unable to move. His first attempt to take a step had almost ended in a fall. The water was clear, but Redwolf could not tell why his colt's right front would not bear his weight. Redwolf urged him forward again. He had to get the horse onto the land so he could examine the leg and perhaps treat the problem. He refused to accept what he already knew.

With Redwolf's encouragement and the help of the water supporting him, the game colt managed to roll his weight back on his hindquarters and hop forward on only his left foreleg, one short lunge at a time, until he was almost out of the water, when he halted for the last time and stood quivering in the bright sunshine, the little waves curling gently around his cannon bones. Redwolf lifted Dark Streak's right foreleg and, his heart sinking into his boots, surveyed the broken pastern from which the shiny, dripping black hoof dangled uselessly. Then he hugged his beloved horse, took off his saddle, saddlebags, and bridle, and carried them the few steps to shore, setting them down in the golden sand. Returning to Dark Streak, he hugged him again. "You swam all that way with a broken leg," he murmured into the wet black mane. "You are the toughest and bravest horse that ever was. You saved my life, and now I must take yours. It just isn't right!"

He leaned there a moment longer, but his horse's whole body was shaking with pain and exhaustion, his head low, his muzzle almost in the salty water. Redwolf pulled the bronze knife out of its sheath at his waist and, telling himself not to hesitate, to make the cut swift and deep, sliced across his colt's jugular. The horse hardly flinched; he was in shock and the knife was no more than a biting fly. Blood pumped into the water, the red stain widening, to be diluted and finally washed away by the waves along with Redwolf's tears. He gave Dark Streak a final pat and stepped back as his beautiful black colt sagged, then collapsed on his side in the shallow, sun-sparkled water and lay still. His father's parting words came back to him. "The Goddess be with you," he whispered.

Chapter 25

Mulynvi and his wife saved their two older sons, using Ahna's herbs and onion poultice. The youngest one died within the day, but the priest was grateful anyway; his wife was sure they would all have died without the treatments. Both adults caught the fever as well, but the young cleric had a mild case. He cared for his wife and remaining sons, and they all got better. When he felt up to it he went to a meeting that the high priest had called.

It was supposed to be a prayer meeting, but Zynjaar spent much of it restating his case against Jaromir. He was furious that the clan leader was now nursing the sick, carrying and heating water, and cooking for families whose female caretakers were too ill to do it themselves, even emptying night pots. Direct defiance of the word of the Gods, he called it. He went on and on about how vital it was that they take Ahna and sacrifice her immediately.

Next to Mulynvi, another priest spoke out of the corner of his mouth; "Your children, how are they doing?"

"Two will be fine," Mulynvi answered softly. "We lost the youngest." He glanced at his friend, whose face was flushed even in the dim light of the gathering tent.

"Are you all right, Fronzi?" he asked.

"I have the fever," his friend said. "So does my wife, and both of my children. My son is very, very sick."

"I have some medicines that might help," said Mulynvi. "My wife is still sick, though. Is there anyone who would help you nurse your wife and children?"

"My neighbor, I think," he said. "She has no children, although they have been married three years, and I don't think she has the fever."

"Send her to me," said Mulynvi. "I will show her how to do the treatments. Someone will have to ask the women for more onions."

"Onions?" Fronzi started to ask, but he was interrupted.

"Priests," bellowed Zynjaar, "are getting sick now because of Jaromir. Even here the pestilence is beginning to kill. The Gods are angry at us because we hesitate to do as they demand. We must take her now! Jaromir's followers cannot stop us, because they cannot harm us. If we take care not to raise our fists to them, but only go and take the woman, what can they do? We will be proven right, for the Gods will end the epidemic soon after the price They demand has been paid, you will see."

"It is not like she is one of the Others," Mulynvi said courageously. "She is a respected young woman of the clan. Sacrificing her would set a precedent we should consider most carefully."

"Respected? Respected by whom?" demanded Zynjaar. He was still bellowing. "She is abhorred by the Gods, she and all she represents!"

"We need medicine for our children now," one man in the middle of the room dared to say aloud. "They say she has medicine, and her nursing is very effective."

"You need prayers, not medicine," their chief exhorted them, apparently in an ungovernable rage. "She saves only women. Ask anyone out there. It is mostly girls and women that they treat, and that they save: worthless women, while the men die!"

"They say few men die; except for the old and the very young, most hardly get sick," his heckler contradicted.

"That's right," Zynjaar crowed, as if the speaker had just proved his point. "It is the women's behavior that is making the Gods so angry, women leaving their tents and their rightful work, meddling in other's lives, so of course it is the women who are most affected by the pestilence, but that doesn't change the fact that these so-called 'healers' treat women when there are men and boys that need treatment!"

His tone changed subtly. "I know some of you have been talking with the people. You have just admitted it. While you do so, at least do your duty; tell them that the Gods are adamant. We must sacrifice the blasphemous woman, and send her even more blasphemous father packing, before They will end this epidemic. I am going to the council meeting now, to repeat the message, to force the blind to see. Get back to your prayers; search in your hearts for messages from the Gods. No one has ever seen a pestilence as deadly as this one. The Gods are behind it, and only They can end it. You know I have heard correctly! You have only two choices. Obey Their edicts or be driven from the priesthood. We will go for her tomorrow or the next day at the latest."

Zynjaar went to the meeting, and repeated his arguments there, albeit in somewhat more circumspect tones. He particularly called attention to their chief's increasingly unmanly and improper behavior. Not only did Jaromir refuse to keep his women at home, he made his sons cook and clean for themselves while Ahna and Sara were out meddling in the business of others. The man himself now tended the sick and regularly did work that was only fit for women and children. It was so dishonorable it made him feel sick to talk about it, the High Priest said. It insulted all the men of the clan, lowering their stature in the Gods' eyes and their own.

Then he brought up an even greater crime of the clan leader; he allowed a concubine, a woman of the others, unclean animals that they were, to work with sick children not her own, even persuaded their parents to let her treat them.

"Until now Jaromir has always been a good leader, and followed our customs," he said. "No man in his right mind would so demean himself or his clan. I believe that evil girl has indeed put a spell on him!"

He reiterated the Gods' demands, and Their promise that, if those demands were met, the epidemic would end.

Yashihar stood to contradict him, saying that everyone knew Ahna and Sara had saved many of the children they treated, and that the epidemic would soon be over anyway. Then, with Ahshela's words in mind, Jaromir reminded his people that really virulent attacks of the winter fever such as this one usually ended with the same suddenness with which they began. Zynjaar sneered; likely words from the one who had caused it all, he said. He had had no such experience, he said. Look at all the folk who are still getting sick and dying, even the priests, he said.

"And as for those... girls saving children with their useless treatments, it is the sacrifices and prayers of your dedicated priests, continuing night and day as they have for the last moon, that have persuaded the Gods to relent and let some of the children live."

A warrior whose four children all lived because of the girls tried to say that Sara treated mostly the children of other concubines, and that the sick children that Ahna and Sara and the other young women of the women's circle did not get to in time had almost all died. The High Priest raised his voice and kept going right over him. "I tell you," he proclaimed, "you have aroused the ire of the Gods, and until you obey these commands They will not be appeased. You and your children will continue to die!" He turned and left the meeting.

The clans had never practiced human sacrifice as far as the men knew. The priests involved had not told anyone, not even their fellow priests, of the sacrifice of the elderly priestess of the Others the previous year. Zynjaar's insistence that the Gods demanded it now had already provoked a storm of controversy. The established warriors, hitherto so sure of their invincibility, but now fearing for their families and themselves and threatened with total disruption of their lives as the fever continued to kill, were listening to him. He promised a way out.

When Gylgan, one of the few remaining councilors, pointed out that taking the life of members of the clan was against the Gods' laws, except under strict rules of justified challenge and fair fight, Jumri said quite truthfully that those laws were intended only for men. No man would be punished if he beat his wife to death, or exposed an unwanted girl child, although normally men were not allowed even to touch other men's women. He repeated Zynjaar's argument that women were little more than animals, not really members of the clan, and if the Gods demanded Ahna's life, then it was a small price to pay to save the clan. The debate raged long into the night.

Chapter 26

Redwolf gathered up his gear and started inland. He needed to
rest, but he hated the thought of staying where he could see Dark
Streak's body lying in the water, so near, gone forever. He left the wet
sand of the beach for the dry, loose sand of the dune behind it,
struggling a little, his feet sinking and sliding in the loose pale gold
grains as the slope grew steeper. When he reached the top he looked
down the back of the dune, here dotted with clumps of coarse sea
grass, to the stand of trees he had seen from a distance. The ground
around the trees was solid and dry, but only ten paces beyond them
the swamp began. Well, rest and food first, he thought wearily, and
then find a way out of here.

He propped his saddle against the trunk of a tree, sat down in the
scant shade and leaned against the saddle, facing the swamp. He
delved into his saddle bags for something to eat. The flat bread and
cheese were soggy and inedible, but the dried beef was still good. He
reached back on his saddle for his water skin. It was not there.
Somehow it had come loose in the river. He looked around, knowing
even as he did that he would find no drinkable water on this scrap of
land. He surveyed the swamp while he chewed on the jerky, his tired
muscles slowly relaxing. It stretched as far as he could see in every
direction, cat tails and reeds, arrow plants and occasional water lilies,
bullrushes and tall, sharp-edged sawgrass, and water everywhere. To
the north, on the edge of vision, there was a misty suggestion of more
trees. Well, he would have to wade and swim. He closed his eyes.

When he opened them the sun was a little higher in the sky and
two people were standing looking down at him. He started to reach

for his knife. He did not yet have a sword, and the bow fastened to his saddle would be useless now. The strangers smiled and showed him their empty hands. They were dressed just alike, in snug leggings and looser shirts of a soft mottled brown and green material, belted with intricately braided hemp, and embroidered with spirals and shells around the neckline and sleeves. They had the same dark, almost black hair, also braided back out of the way, and the same olive-toned skin and brown eyes. Fastened to their belts were sheathed knives, shiny gourds with narrow necks that were incised with wavy lines, and some leather straps that Redwolf thought might be slings. The one with the necklace of shells was a woman. She smiled again and, untying the gourd from her belt, held it out to him. He took his hand off his knife, but he did not reach for the gourd. She took the gourd back, removed some kind of bark stopper from its neck, tipped it up and took a sip, then offered it to him again. He smiled at last and, accepting the gourd, drank the cool water that it contained.

They had to be some of the Others, and they surely they knew he was an enemy. Why were they being so kind to him? The young man, pointed behind Redwolf, then put his face in his hands, conveying sorrow. The strange words he uttered had to be condolences on the loss of his horse. Then the man turned and pointed the other way.

Looking beyond them for the first time, Redwolf saw a strange object, like a hollowed-out log more than three paces long, with pointed ends and branches with wide, flattened lobes where the leaves should be, lying at a slight angle at the edge of the water, one end in the swamp. Three more people, he thought two men and another woman, stood beside the weird log. The man in front of him was talking some more, asking a question, Redwolf thought. He pointed to Redwolf, then pointed to the log. Then he pointed out across the swamp to the north and made successive pointed shapes with his hands that looked like tents. Was he offering to take Redwolf to Marvulf's camp? No, that couldn't be. It seemed almost as unlikely that he was offering to take an enemy to his own tents, but that was the only explanation Redwolf could imagine.

The men of the Lion clan sneered at the Others because, supposedly, they were not fighters, and would even welcome strangers into their communities. Well, time to put it to the test. The Other reached out his hand, Redwolf grasped it, and the man pulled him to his feet. Redwolf turned and picked up his gear, then turned back to find the young couple walking away, the woman beckoning him to follow. He did.

When they reached the hollowed log the others had pushed it halfway into the water among the reeds and one of them was already kneeling in the end furthest out, using one of the curious branches to stabilize it. The young man from under the tree indicated the equipment in his arms, then pointed to himself. Redwolf held out the saddle and bridle and his saddle bags. The man took them, placing them in the front of the hollowed log where Redwolf could now see there were also several freshly killed geese. This was a hunting party, then.

The woman who had given him the gourd of water made sure she had his attention, then stepped carefully into the hollowed out space, her hands on each side of the log and her torso directly over her feet in the middle, and moved toward the back, turning with exaggerated care to kneel in front of the man that was already there, and picking up another of the odd branches. Then she nodded to Redwolf.

He imitated her, stepping into the middle of the hollow log, and held tightly to the sides as he realized how unstable it felt under his feet. He moved gingerly toward her, hesitating when she indicated with hand motions that he should stop, turn around, and kneel. He was sure that the log would roll when he tried to turn around, but finally he turned. It did seem as if the log wanted to tip, but the three people still on land had hold of it, and he found himself kneeling facing them in the spot they had indicated, still gripping the sides.

The rest of the Others then pushed the log further into the swamp. One at a time they got in, hardly rocking it at all. Finally the man from under the tree pushed the log all the way into the water, then stepped into it as if stepping across a tent floor, turned around, knelt and picked up his branch. The log didn't even quiver. Nor did it show any signs of sinking, although there were now six people kneeling in it. Redwolf decided it must be a boat. He had heard tales of boats that carried people on water. The two men in the front started using their branches to push the boat away from the solid land. The woman kneeling behind him put her hand on the wood beside him and said, "Dugout." When he didn't respond she patted it again and repeated "dugout." This time he responded by touching the log and saying the word. She said something that must have been "yes," and the woman kneeling in front of him nodded as well. Thus began an impromptu language lesson, limited because he could not see the face of either of his teachers, but nonetheless useful. The woman behind him was Tigua: the one in front Muriel. The man in front of her was Jornan. The branches with which they controlled the dugout were paddles. He told them he was Redwolf.

The Others used the paddles to push through the water, all four together as if they were dancing, propelling the dugout forward. Its pointed front cut through the bulrushes and reeds. They did not travel in a straight line. He realized after a very little while that they were keeping to the more open, watery areas and avoiding the most tangled and overgrown ones. Although their route wandered, the Others showed no hesitation; Redwolf was impressed because all the swamp looked exactly the same to him. They were headed steadily north. Before long he could see the tops of the distant trees, closer now. There were many more trees than had been behind his stretch of beach. He thought it was probably where the swamp became forest again.

He was wrong. It was not yet high sun when they approached another island, drawing up to a low bank where three more dugouts were pulled out of the water on the short grass. When everyone had climbed out, Redwolf having to have the boat steadied again or he would have found himself in the water, the Others pulled their conveyance onto the land as well, then emptied it of its cargo: the paddles, Redwolf's saddle, bridle, and saddle bags, three spear throwers and some light throwing spears, a small leather pack, and the carcasses of five geese.

The grassy banks were being grazed by a few sheep, and some brown and white milk goats browsed on the scanty brush and weeds beneath the nearer trees. He could see gardens behind a fence woven of tree branches. There must be a village nearby, but he could not see any houses.

The people from the boat beckoned him to follow and headed for the middle of the copse. As they approached, some of the 'brush' beneath the trees resolved itself into perhaps twenty man-made structures, neither houses nor tents. Cobbled together out of branches and small logs covered with intricately woven materials from the swamp, they appeared reasonably sturdy and weatherproof, though some were little more than closed lean-tos. There were more Others occupied with various tasks among the buildings. One woman just a couple of years older than Ahna, small by the standards of his people, dark complexioned and dark haired like the rest and dressed in the same fashion, came to meet them. She spoke to his companions from the canoe for a minute or two, then turned to him.

"Welcome to our camp," she said in his own tongue, lightly accented but perfectly clear. "I am Floriana. I hear you have lost your horse; I am sorry. Come and eat with us and dry your clothes."

"Thank you, but I have no time," Redwolf responded. "I am called Redwolf. How do you know my language?"

"I was... captive in one of your camps for two years before I ran away and came here," Floriana answered matter-of-factly. "What is your hurry? It is not good for you to remain wet when you have been sick."

"How did you know?" he asked.

"The hollows in your face speak of a recent fever," she answered, "and the way you clear your throat says you have had a cough. It may return if you keep abusing yourself!" He smiled. She sounded like somebody's mother.

She was. As he told her about his errand, they heard a child start to whimper, and Floriana turned to lift a sturdy, towheaded baby less than a year old from a basket, and sat down to nurse him. The contrast in their coloring told Redwolf the baby's father was probably one of his people rather than one of hers.

When he finished his brief explanation she called across the camp to Tigua.

"I'm sorry you cannot stay," she said, while she waited for the other woman. "Today is our harvest festival, and we would be glad to share the celebration with you. Since you must go, you should at least have some of the soup I have made to keep us until the feast later. It is there, on the fire, and there are bowls and spoons and a ladle beside it. Help yourself. Tigua and Jornan can take you to the mainland after you eat."

Floriana finished feeding her son while Redwolf got some of the delicious stew, rich with vegetables, mushrooms, shell-fish and bits of mutton. Tigua arrived, and the two women spoke at length.

"She wants to know where you are going."

"I was on my way to the Red Wolf camp, a clan of my people that have their tents set up about twenty miles east of the big river," he said. "I have to get help from them for an urgent problem in my own camp." The women talked a little more, and Tigua nodded to him and left.

"Tigua says it sounds like a story; she is sorry there is no time to hear it," Floriana repeated. "They will take you to the mainland, as near to the road east as they can. They will get the boat ready now," Floriana explained. "Jornan is worried that you will tell the other barbarians we are here, but I assured her that you would not." She lifted the sleepy child into a cleverly contrived crib of hollowed wood hanging from the branch of a tree.

"I won't, ever," he corroborated. Her smile was beautiful. "I knew you were different when Tigua said you were willing to learn some of our words. In the two years I spent with your people, while I was expected to learn your tongue, no one ever repeated a word from our language, not even names for plants that your healers didn't know; they would give the plant a new name rather than use ours for it." Redwolf nodded. The day was getting warmer, and his damp clothing was drying on him. He tried to clear the increasing congestion in his throat, and ended coughing.

"There," commented his new friend. "I was afraid of that. I will fix you some tea that will help. She went into another of the small structures, returning with a pair of gourd vessels with stoppers and leather straps. One she filled from the skin pot, saying a few words in her own tongue, and handed to him. "That will give you something nourishing for later," she said. The second she filled from a smaller skin of steaming water, then put the contents of a small packet into the gourd before sealing it shut. She handed him several more of the packets, which were made of cotton coated with beeswax and cleverly folded to keep moisture away from the contents.

"Take these with you," she said. "They are the herbs for your cough. Use half a packet in a cup of hot water. Let it steep several minutes before you drink it. The gourd has two doses in it: one for now and one for this evening."

"Thank you," he said again. They heard a call, and turned to see Tigua waving at them from across the expanse of grass between them and the boats.

"I wish you were staying longer," Floriana said. "It would be interesting to get to know one another. He nodded and then, taking a chance, gave her a hug. She grinned and hugged him back.

"Good luck, Redwolf. May the Goddess guard and guide you." She turned away, not wanting him to see how affected she really was by his going.

"Thank you again, Floriana." he called. He picked up his gear and jogged toward the people waiting by the boat.

When the sun was a little past the zenith the Others dropped Redwolf in a dry-floored open forest that came right to the edge of the swamp. They had come such a twisting route that the clansman could not have found his way back to the Others' island if he had wanted to. Tigua pointed northeast into the trees, and using the sun, indicated about a hand's time. He thought that must be how long it would take him to reach the road; the Others would surely not have brought him so close to the Red Wolf encampment even if they could.

They all got out except the man in the back, and Jornan unloaded his gear onto the bank. Tigua laughed when she saw the two gourds, then held out a third: the decorated water flask she had handed him when he first saw her. She also gave him a small but heavy packet which proved to contain food: compact squares of dried fruit and cracked grains stuck together with something sweet. "Honey bars," she said. He thought a moment, then bent and unhooked his carved wooden bow and embossed-leather quiver of bronze-tipped hunting arrows from his saddle. He held them out to her, but she shook her head 'no.' He nodded his emphatically, pushing the weapons toward her and saying, "Please, take them." One of the men said something then. She accepted the bow and quiver, said what he knew must be "thank you," and got back into the dugout. As they shoved off from the bank, she said something that he thought was probably a blessing from the Goddess. He couldn't repeat it, but he bowed a little and said, "The Goddess be with you, too." Her wide smile and wave made him hope she had understood. Then he tied the gourds to his belt by their thongs, put the straps connecting his saddle bags across one shoulder, swung his saddle a bit awkwardly to the other, and set off into the trees.

When the sun had dropped a hand's width he found the road, obvious by its straight route through the forest even though it was now little used and well grown with weeds and grass. He turned right onto it, thinking he could probably make the Red Wolf camp before the sun set. He knew he did not dare enter a strange clan's camp once the sun had gone down.

He almost made it. He stopped once after a couple of hand-spans to eat his soup and one of the honey bars. He had already drained his water bottle and refilled it at a little brook that crossed the path. The sun was low in the west but still shining through the trees behind him when he paused again and set down his gear. His throat was dry and scratchy; his intermittent cough had returned. And right here, in a little opening between the trees beside the road, was an extensive patch of blackberries, ripe fruit still clinging to the tips of the long, arching brambles. He got out the gourd of tea. He had drunk about half of it and eaten a double handful of berries when he heard, or thought he heard, a cough not his own. He looked around. At first he saw nothing. Then he caught sight of a pair of gleaming eyes, low to the ground under the trees on the other side of the road. And another. And several more! Then the first pair moved, and resolved itself into a young wolf, well camouflaged in the early evening shadows of the forest floor, crouched belly to the ground and creeping toward him.

It was an entire pack, he was sure. He had been lucky; the adults were holding off to give their pups a chance to hunt this easy prey. He did not move, knowing that when he did they would abandon their stealthy approach and attack. He looked for some possible way of escaping them. Most of the trees around him were very tall, with no branches for the first three or four paces at least, their trunks too big to be shinnied: no help there. About twenty feet away beside him was a tree he thought he could climb, a half-grown evergreen whose lowest boughs, dead though they were, were only a few feet off the ground. There were no wolves in that direction because of the dense patch of blackberries between him and the tree.

One of the older wolves gave a little bark; to Redwolf it sounded like 'go get it.' He plunged into the blackberries, sucking in a great gulp of air, his legs and heart pumping hard. The thorny brambles tangled his feet and stabbed relentlessly at his clothes and skin, but he plowed through regardless. The alternative would be much worse. A chorus of yips and barks greeted his sudden motion. He did not look, but he knew the wolves were coming fast. He tripped over a moss-covered log at the base of the tree, banging his shins and falling face first into the lowest branches. Ignoring a sharp twinge in his right knee, he grabbed the branch above his head and started to climb. Some of the yipping behind him changed to yelps of pain; blackberries were just as hard on wolves as they were on humans. The dead lower branches of the evergreen were almost as bad as the brambles for impeding progress, but he swarmed up them regardless, imagining sharp teeth in long jaws snapping at his heels.

When he had scrambled up through the first live branches, perhaps a bit more than two paces above the forest floor, he risked a look down. There were three adult wolves, their front feet planted on the rotting log, their tongues hanging out, looking up at him. One met his eyes and growled, but they did not try to come up after him. Their fur was unruffled; he thought they had probably gone around the blackberries. It was the reason he had had time to get away.

Out on the path were four more adult wolves and five well-grown puppies. They were having a grand time with his gear. Two of the young wolves were playing tug-of-war with his saddlebags, while a third yanked at the straps that held them together. Before very long the straps snapped. The two with the pouches settled down to explore their prizes. The third went back and forth, trying to horn in on one or the other. Finally he turned his attention to his siblings, who were tugging Redwolf's saddle across the ground by its flaps. Soon all three settled down to worry at its well-greased leather with razor-sharp baby teeth.

One of the adults beneath him had found the gourd that had held soup; it must have come detached during his scramble for the tree. The wolf cracked the gourd like a nut, then settled down with it between her paws, licking at its interior. Redwolf checked his belt, to find that the half-full water gourd and his knife were still there. In his pocket he found the rest of the honey bars. All well and good, but the packets of tea were in one of his saddle bags. Nothing he could do about that now.

He hunted around for a likely horizontal branch, spotted one just a little higher up, and climbed to it, settling down with his back to the trunk. He used his knife to take off a couple of smaller branches so he could rest more comfortably. Yes, he had wrenched his knee. Well, it would get a rest now. He didn't know how long the wolves would hang around, but they didn't look like going anywhere anytime soon. Briefly he wished for his bow; it would have been easy to pick the wolves off from here. Then he remembered Floriana's words about unnecessary killing. He had no interest in eating the wolves. There was no real reason to kill them; he was safe and could wait them out. Besides, his bow would have been on his saddle, and he was suddenly glad it was not receiving the destructive attentions of the young wolves. It had taken him a long time to make it and he was proud of the result.

After a few minutes two of the wolves below him ambled back through the woods to join the others on the overgrown road, but the one who had found the gourd didn't move. She was probably waiting for Redwolf to come down or fall off his perch.

It was a long night. He ate the honey bars and drank his water. The wolves were still there when it got dark, and he could hear them occasionally, snuffling or growling softly. He wouldn't dare go down before it got light, anyway. By then they should have given up and gone looking for other prey, but he would be a fool to try to share the forest floor with them at night. Sometime much later it rained, a brief shower, but enough to get him wet again. He lamented his waterproof, tucked in one of the saddlebags, or perhaps not, but at any rate far out of reach. Finally he dozed, to be wakened in the false dawn by a chorus of birds, not as varied as in the spring, but still notable. He stared at the old road and the forest floor as it got lighter. His saddle, bridle, saddlebags and, yes, his waterproof were in pieces, scattered over a wide area, but there was no sign of the wolves.

He moved to climb out of the tree, wincing as he put weight on his wrenched knee. It was very, very sore, and a little swollen, he thought. At least he *could* put weight on it. He eased himself down to the ground, and warily made his way around the blackberries to the road. He briefly examined his gear and was rewarded. One of the saddlebags had withstood the mauling; it was well chewed but still closed. His herbs were safe. The other had held his dried beef and other foods; it was in shreds. He found a straight, strong branch and trimmed it with his knife, then started down the road, limping a little despite his new walking stick, the saddlebag in his free hand. His knee was sore enough that he was almost glad he didn't have more to carry.

Less than two hundred paces on the forest ended, replaced by the stumps of trees over a wide area where the Red Wolves had been harvesting firewood. The clear-cut area went on as far as he could see. He plodded briskly ahead, following the road, glad he had stopped yesterday for the blackberries. If the wolves had come on him in this area his flesh would now be lining their stomachs. It was nearly full daylight when he crested a gentle rise and entered a region of overgrown fields and abandoned vineyards and orchards, with occasional patches of stumps. The road changed to flat stones laid next to each other as he passed between blackened ashy areas lumpy with the remains of walls and foundations where the town had been burned. He kept on doggedly. Soon he crossed another low rise and there in a wide, well-grazed valley about a mile away hundreds of felt tents cast long shadows toward him, black against the first rays of the rising sun. He hobbled down the hill. A huge herd of cattle were headed out from the fields surrounding the camp, accompanied by numerous boys on horseback and several busy herd dogs. The boys spotted him, but all stayed with their charges except one. He turned and trotted back toward the camp.

A little bit later Redwolf himself followed the road between the first row of tents. He'd finally made it!

Suddenly there were three men planted in front of him, hands on their sword or knife hilts, and more coming. He dropped his saddle bag and grasped his own knife; it would not do to appear pacifistic here. The men of the Red Wolf clan were fair-skinned and well-dressed, with clean embroidered clothes and well-rubbed boots, most sporting arm bands and other jewelry. He was all too aware of the poor impression he made with his tangled rust-colored hair, torn, still-damp and bloody clothing, scratched boots, and only a single, somewhat chewed saddle bag to show he might once have had a horse.

"Who are you?" demanded a tall, blond warrior who reminded Redwolf of Marvulf.

"My name is Redwolf…"

Swords and knives came out of sheaths all around him, headed for his throat.

Chapter 27

The main living area of Jaromir's tent would never have been described as small, but the gathering there filled it and spilled into the adjacent sleeping quarters, their privacy curtains tied back. Besides the chief and Moshel, Yashihar, Lwenli and their sons, Gylgan and one or two others of the council, there were numerous craftsmen who owed their children's or wive's lives, or both, to Ahna and the other healers, and many younger warriors like Havad and Elegin, Moshel's friends and acquaintances. These young men were still open minded enough to be little bothered by the 'improper' behavior of their chief and his family, and though not having been much affected directly by the epidemic, several had family members who were successfully nursed by the girls. Besides, they admired Ahna for her horse mastery and her performance in the races only two moons ago.

The discussion had been going on for some time. Ahna and Sara were still out about their nursing duties, but several of the older men present had brought a wife or concubine to the meeting. The women were keeping the participants supplied with hot drinks or beer or fermented mares milk, and woven plates with chunks of cheese and meat, flatbread and piles of nuts and dried fruit. They were lucky that the storehouse of the Others had seen them through this emergency when so many of their own food gatherers were incapacitated or otherwise occupied. So far, it was easier to feel well fed and comfortable than it was to come up with a viable solution to their problem. How were they to keep the priests and their cohorts from taking Ahna without breaking the prohibition against hurting priests or becoming embroiled in an illegal and ultimately clan-destroying fight with other members of their own clan?

They were meeting because the High Priest's campaign had gained converts, gathering in those who had lost sons despite the attention of the healers. Zynjaar was very good at playing to the men's fears and prejudices. Many now were willing to blame all their troubles on Ahna and Jaromir. Some of the men present tonight had attended a more general meeting earlier where it had been decided that Ahna would be taken the next morning so that she could be sacrificed at the most propitious time - midday - high sun. The chief of the Gods was the sun Himself.

Those who had been at the meeting reported that they had again argued that Marvulf would demand reparations if she was killed, especially as sacrificing her like an animal would be a huge insult to him and could begin a blood feud. Her supporters had repeated that Ahna was tirelessly nursing the sick, and that many she had nursed were recovering, a fact that seemed to contradict the notion that the Gods were angry with her. Even the priest Mulynvi spoke up, saying two of his three sons were alive because of her.

They were all shouted down by Zynjaar, his followers, and other men who were distraught at the loss of their loved ones and their women, feared for their own lives, and had an uncontrollable need to absolve themselves by finding someone else to blame. The priest's backers even took the chance of being challenged, calling Jaromir's supporters insulting names, saying they were further angering the Gods and destroying their clan by protecting the guilty ones.

Redwolf had been gone three days now, and privately the chief feared for his son. They had hoped he would return with Marvulf the previous day. When he had not everyone had been sure they would ride in before dark today, but there was neither word nor sign of them as the early dusk fell. Even among those that insisted they must just have been delayed, no one felt that they could be counted on to arrive in time to stop the High Priest now.

The only solution they could see was to sneak Ahna away that night, although most of the men of the clans believed that trying to travel beyond the tents at night was fraught with its own fearful dangers. They were not dangers Ahna's defenders were destined to face. Those who had been at the earlier meeting reported that the Dedicated, whose normal work when not fighting was guarding the ingathered livestock at night anyway, had agreed to build extra fires and watch the perimeter of the camp to prevent just such an attempt.

Moshel and Havad and a several of their friends excused themselves and went to escort Ahna and Sara home. The girls had promised Jaromir they would quit early this evening if he would; all three were exhausted from long days of nursing their neighbors and they were trying to look out for each other as best they could. The escort was necessary because no one wanted to take the risk that the priests might not wait, that they might take Ahna tonight. The young men saw no signs of trouble, heard only the gratitude of the clan's chief Leather Master, whose youngest son was now obviously on the road to recovery thanks to, as he said, "these lovely girls and their magical medications." When Moshel told him of the meeting, and that the priests were coming in the morning to take Ahna, and the difficulty her supporters were having producing a plan for her protection, he thought for a minute, then said,

"No one likes going against the priests or the Gods, but this thing that Zynjaar is advocating now just can't be right. Anyone can see that these girls and their treatments are not evil. The leatherworkers and metal workers almost all agree with me, and we will help as we can.

"You say the problem is that you aren't allowed to fight, but that really is the solution. A battle between clan members would be the worst thing that could happen; that is why we have such strict rules against fighting within the clan. So it's a good thing we don't need to fight. All we need to do is get between the priests and the girl, and stay there. Tomorrow morning, did you say? You can count on us."

The young people thanked him and started back to Jaromir's compound.

"What do you suppose he meant by 'all we need to do is get between the priests and the girl'?" asked Havad. They were walking along the dark lane, the young men in a tight circle around the girls, alert for any possible threats in the night.

"I think he must have meant just what you are doing now," said Ahna, enlightenment in her voice. "You have us surrounded. No one could get to me as long as you stayed around me like this, if they were not allowed to attack you."

"The priests are many; they could just shoulder us aside," objected Elegin. "The rules say an attack consists of raising hand or weapon against a person. Kicking is not allowed, either, but there is nothing against pushing with the body."

"Physically trying to move someone against their will, even without using hands, would be grounds for challenge for anyone except the priests," Havad said.

"If there were enough people around me to link arms," Ahna mused, "perhaps even to make a double circle with both circles linked, the priests would not be able to get through, and as long as you were unarmed and peaceful, no one else would even try."

"With the addition of the craftsmen, there are enough of us to surround Jaromir's entire tent," said one of the other young men jokingly.

"That is probably a good idea," ventured Ahna. "It would be just as well if the High Priest and his supporters couldn't even see me, or Sara, or any of the other women, since we are his targets. We could stay in the tents."

They were nearly back to Jaromir's compound now.

"Are we really going to suggest this?" asked Elegin. He still sounded skeptical.

"I will suggest it," said Moshel. He smiled at Ahna. "You're my sister."

The entire gathering had fallen into a glum silence when Ahna and Sara and the young men returned. Ahna and Sara went to help the women, and Moshel spoke briefly to Jaromir, who shook his head. Then he changed his mind and shrugged.

"What have we got to lose?" he asked. "Go ahead."

Moshel spoke to the now curious assembly. "The chief Leather Master and Ahna have come up with a suggestion," he said, "which might just work."

"Suggest away," said Yashihar. "Anything has to be better than what we have now."

"It will sound very strange," warned Jaromir's foster son. "We wouldn't have thought of it; we are too used to fighting to solve problems. The Leather Master pointed out that all we really need to do is stand between Ahna and the priests, to keep them and their allies from getting to her. We cannot fight without breaking the most basic laws of the clan, nor can we raise a hand to the priests unless they attack us first. But the other side must abide by these rules, too." There were nods all around; this ground they had been over many times. What was the young warrior getting at?

"Ahna noticed when we were walking back that we men were all around her in a circle," Moshel continued, "and no one outside the circle could get to her. If we all link arms and make a human wall around the tent the priests and their friends will have to break that barrier to get inside. They will have to become the aggressors if they want to take her." Murmurs of surprise and thoughtful frowns proliferated in the crowd.

"I think there are enough of us to make that a double wall," he went on, "especially since the leather masters and metal craftsmen have promised to join us. Ahna's onions have saved many of their children, and tonight the chief leather master told us they were against this idea of sacrificing one of our own, especially one who has worked so hard and done so much good."

"What makes you think such a silly idea would work?" said one of the older men, his tone almost a sneer. "It sounds like something a woman would think up."

"Only the priests will dare try to push us aside," Moshel explained. "Such an effort on anyone else's part would be seen as an attack, or at very least a serious personal insult worthy of challenge. We would have to take great care just to stand firm, and not in any way offer violence to the priests unless they lose their tempers and start striking at us, when they would clearly be in the wrong and could be arrested. Even then, it should be apparent that anything we do is only meant to restrain them. There are probably enough of us to have a small group of the warriors standing by for that purpose. Then we would not have to break the cordon to stop any priest that does transgress.

"Most priests are not known for their size or strength," he concluded. "I believe we could hold against them until they got tired of the effort and gave up."

"They have the Dedicated on their side," said one of the youngest of the warriors. "They are plenty strong. What's to keep them from simply shoving open a path for the priests?"

"The prohibitions against attacking, or even touching, other men of their own clan are stricter and more binding for the Dedicated than for any other of our folk," explained Yashihar. "Their very honor depends on their obeying such rules. This is necessary to keep peace within the clan precisely because the Dedicated tend to be stronger, and are decidedly shorter tempered and less under control, than other men. They would not even approach such a barrier as Moshel has proposed, if we aren't carrying weapons of war and are not acting in an aggressive fashion." He nodded to Moshel.

"I think it just might work."

The whole idea was so strange that nearly everyone else thought it would not work. Still, no one found any other loopholes in Moshel's reasoning, and no one had any other ideas, say nothing of better ones. They decided to try it. They agreed to gather at Jaromir's compound soon after sunrise, to be ready in case the priests came early. The meeting broke up.

Ahshela, barred yet again for her own well-being from tending the sick, visited Jaromir a little later that evening. The girls had retired, and the two old friends sat in the main living area, drinking chamomile tea and talking about the plans that had been made for Ahna's protection. The Eldest was intrigued and amused. The passive human barrier idea was something those who listened to the Goddess would approve; it was not the kind of response the men would normally even consider.

When that subject was exhausted they discussed the irony of the clan's decimation at the indirect hands of the Others; had they not been attacked by the clan warriors and most of their folk wiped out, Ester's people would not have been living so intimately with the pigs and chickens and probably wouldn't have contracted the virulent form of the winter fever at all.

"Of course the High Priest would likely say that the Dedicated were at fault and that the Gods are punishing them for not being thorough enough in wiping out all the Others," Jaromir said. "A strange argument," Ahshela commented, "given that none of the Dedicated have had any more than the most mild of cases." Jaromir laughed. "Facts that prove him wrong are meaningless to Zynjaar," he said.

Ahna rolled over in her furs and rearranged her pillow. She needed to sleep, but she could not get the conversation she had just overheard out of her head. She was beginning to accept that the Goddess really did not interfere directly in their lives despite their prayers and gifts to Her. Ahna often prayed to the Goddess, but she thought maybe those prayers were more to reinforce her own faith in Her laws than to get a tangible response. She could not believe the Mother would intervene directly in some matters, and yet do nothing to help the dying children, who certainly deserved Her attention if anyone did. Therefore she had to accept that her prayers would only be answered within herself.

Somehow this all made Ahshela's story about the Mother's teachings real; by upsetting the balance, her own clan had created the unusual circumstances that resulted in the epidemic. Their chosen way of life was the reason their children were dying. As her eyelids finally drifted down over her eyes Ahna concluded that the Goddess's laws really did make sense. To survive in the long run, a people had to understand the importance of the natural balance, and do all that they could to protect it from the shortsighted greed of those who did not care.

Chapter 28

"Hold!" commanded the tall blond, but he held the point of his own sword to Redwolf's chest.

"Tell us why we shouldn't kill you, stranger. The only reason you still live is because you look like us and speak our tongue, but you made a serious mistake giving us that name. We are the people of the Red Wolf, and you are not one of us. You insult our intelligence, naming yourself so."

Redwolf thought quickly. It obviously wouldn't do to insist that it *was* his name, but if he did not answer immediately they would kill him anyway.

"I am from the Lion clan," he began. "I am Jaromir Winter's son."

"Their chief! I don't believe it," snorted someone. "Look at his clothes. Where are his weapons, and his horses?"

"I lost my horses in the river twenty miles back," Redwolf explained. "It was flooded from the rains. My second horse refused to follow us across, and the horse I was riding... broke a leg in a pothole." His obvious distress made an impression on some of his listeners. Their horses were the centers of their lives; they all understood the wrenching loss of a favorite mount.

Skipping the part about the swamp and the Others, Redwolf told them of hunting for and finding the road again, meeting the wolves when he was almost to his destination and realizing they were hunting him, beating his way through the blackberry patch, climbing the tree, enduring the discomfort, the cold, and the rain, and coming down this morning to find his gear all shredded, excellent teething material for the wolf puppies that it was.

"What's left of my gear is still under that tree, no more than four miles west along the road," he concluded.

The knives and swords had mostly been lowered while he talked, and now the tall blond man glanced at the chew marks on Redwolf's saddle bag, then withdrew his own sword and sheathed it. His companions followed suit.

"You were apparently in haste to get here," he said. "Why? And what *is* your name?"

"I have an urgent message for Marvulf," Redwolf answered.

A number of boys had joined the now sizable group, and a youngster of about eleven summers left them, wriggling through the crowd until he reached the tall blond, whose brows had begun to lower again at what he saw as the stranger's continued refusal to tell them his name.

"I'll bet I know his name, Jaanyar," the tall towheaded boy said, grinning, "and why he won't tell it to you, too. Marvulf said that girl he is going to marry has a red-haired brother named Redwolf!"

There were exclamations from the men who had been the first to confront the outsider. The blond man laughed shortly.

"He did tell us, but we didn't believe him, Luugani," he said to the boy. "Run and get your brother. Our guest says he has an important message for him from the chief of the Lion clan." The boy took off, a couple of his friends racing after him, and Jaanyar turned back to the bedraggled young man.

"We owe you an apology, Redwolf, son of Jaromir," he said formally. "I hope you will find our error understandable, and forgive us." They had breached custom quite flagrantly by greeting an esteemed member of a clan soon to be allied with their own with bared swords and the threat of death. It would surely have meant blood feud if they had killed him, unarmed as he was. Their visitor had grounds for a challenge if he chose to use them.

"Of course I forgive you," said Redwolf. "I could wish my father had given me a more conventional name!"

The general laughter that followed this eased tensions all around.

"I would invite you to my tents for refreshment," Jaanyar said, gesturing to a large, handsomely embossed structure a short distance away, "but I am sure you want to find Marvulf now, so we'll go to meet him." He picked up the saddle bag, examined the well-chewed straps and flaps, and handed it to Redwolf. "You were lucky to get up that tree." Redwolf nodded; he knew. Whether it came from the Goddess or not, his luck was holding.

Shortly they saw Marvulf and his little brother coming toward them, now trailed by a whole gaggle of boys. Jaanyar said a formal farewell and went to his morning duties. Ahna's husband-to-be greeted Redwolf kindly, with patent surprise and concern.

"I'm glad to see you, but not on foot, nor in such straits, and I'm worried about any reason that could have brought you here with such obvious haste," he said, taking Redwolf's arm and encouraging him to lean on him. "Did Luugani hear rightly; your horse broke his leg?"

"He broke his pastern," Redwolf responded sadly. "His hoof was dangling, so he must have torn all the tendons as well. He did it when we were starting across the river, but he kept swimming as I directed anyway. I would have drowned in that flood for sure if he had not taken me across."

"Was it… It wasn't your black colt, was it?" Marvulf asked. At the younger man's nod his face fell.

"I'm so very sorry," he said. "He was a fine animal, and obviously had great courage as well."

Redwolf nodded again, then shook off the memory.

"Marvulf," he began, "you have to come back with me, today if possible, and marry Ahna and take her away!"

"Whoa," exclaimed Marvulf. "This sounds serious, but let's begin at the beginning. No, don't try to tell me now. We're here, and you need something hot to drink at the very least. I doubt you've had any breakfast either." He held the tent flap for Redwolf, then paused to send his brother and friends back to whatever they were doing before, saying, "No arguments. You can hear all about it later."

"I haven't eaten" answered his visitor, limping after him into the tent, where a portly older woman, shorter than average, wearing a full-fronted cotton apron over what was obviously a fine blue and gold linen dress, the half-length sleeves and flounced skirt heavily embroidered with horses in many colors and poses, her iron grey hair braided neatly around her head and topped by an embroidered blue cap rather than a scarf, held the traditional bowl of wash water for them.

"Redwolf, this is my foster-mother Vyarhe," said Marvulf. The woman gave him a wide smile, but said no more than "welcome to our tent."

"He has come a long way, and he hasn't had breakfast, or anything this morning," said Marvulf, rinsing his hands in his turn, and taking the towel from Redwolf to dry them. He led the younger man to the luxurious piles of furs and pillows surrounding the eating area, and signed for him to sit, while the woman disappeared through the tent flaps at the back of the chamber, into what Redwolf assumed was their work tent.

"Thank you," said his future brother-in-law, sitting down gratefully, his sore knee stretched out in front of him.

"I don't want to be rude," he continued, "but it is really necessary that we get back at once. I have been delayed and delayed. This is the third morning since I left our tents, and I'm afraid we may not make it back in time."

"What could possibly be so urgent?" asked Marvulf.

"It's a very long story," began Redwolf. "I will try to get the important parts now." Marvulf tensed and sat forward at his next words. "That priest, Srogaraad, tried to kidnap Ahna, over a moon and a half ago now. Moshel and our neighbors stopped him, but couldn't positively identify him, so Father had us set up a guard on her, day and night. Sure enough, he snuck into our tent and tried to rape her."

"I'll kill him," growled Marvulf.

"You'll have to find him, first," said Redwolf. "Moshel stopped him again - the brute had knocked me out, I'm ashamed to say - and this time he and my father got him tied up, and Father fetched the council, and they had a trial right there in our main living area in the middle of the night. They found him guilty and banished him and his father Zynjaar has been trying to get back at us ever since."

"Don't your people see through that, even if he is the High Priest?" asked Marvulf.

"I think they would ordinarily," said Redwolf, stopping again to cough, trying to clear his air passages, "but nothing is normal now. We have had a really bad time with the winter fever. I'm surprised you haven't heard; the word went out more than a moon ago to avoid our tents."

"It didn't come here," said Marvulf, staring at his guest in renewed concern.

"I had it right at the start," Redwolf reassured him, "and have been over it for well over a ten-day now. Ahna, who, by the way, is proving to be a talented healer, and our eldest and best healer, Ahshela, were certain that I could not bring it to you. I think this cough is because of that terrible river crossing, and maybe last night in the tree in the rain. I have some herbs in my saddle bag that really help, if your foster mother would be kind enough to make me some tea." Again he failed to mention the Others. There was nothing on their island that Marvulf's men could want, but he refused to take the chance, however slight, that the Red Wolf warriors might try to find and attack Floriana and her folk if they knew about them.

Vyarhe came in with flatbread, cheese, and some delicious smoked beef in a rich gravy seasoned with sage and rosemary, and hot drinks spiked with fermented mare's milk. Redwolf gave her a packet of the herbs. She exclaimed over the clever, waterproof wrapping and promised to brew the tea for him immediately. "When you're finished eating I will tend that knee," she added.

"How has the winter fever put Ahna at risk?" asked Marvulf when she had gone. "You said she was proving to be a good healer; that should protect her from your High Priest's attacks."

"It should," said Redwolf. "I hope it will long enough for us to get back. Zynjaar is very clever. He brought the child to our tents who was the first to get sick and the first to die. Father says he could not have done it on purpose, but I don't know... Anyway, he has started a rumor, except it is more of a campaign, blaming us for the disease, claiming that the Gods are angry because Father has allowed Ahna to do things, like riding competitions and racing, that only men are supposed to do. My little brother and my mother have both died; Zynjaar uses that as 'evidence' for his argument. As the epidemic got worse, and hundreds of people died, he kept increasing his attacks, insisting that Father was angering the Gods even more by allowing Ahna to use forbidden knowledge to treat the sick, and by his own insistence on helping those that need help, doing 'women's work'. Three days ago now the High Priest came to a council meeting and told the men that the Gods were demanding that my father be relieved of his position and Ahna herself be... sacrificed to Them, like a bull or a ram. He said They would continue to make the epidemic worse until these things were done."

Marvulf was shocked into openmouthed silence.

"Many people were outraged, including most of the council," Redwolf continued, "but many of the older council members have died, and most of the other men are, Father says, desperate for someone to blame for the epidemic, the deaths in their families, and the fear and uncertainty they feel. Ahshela warned us that Zynjaar will keep up the pressure until enough agree that he thinks he and the other priests can take Ahna without opposition. She is only a woman, after all."

"She is my promised woman!" snapped Marvulf, his anger increasing fast. "Aren't they afraid I would bring our warriors down on them if they paid me such an insult? I would, you know!"

"Zynjaar says the Red Wolves will be moving away from us in the spring, that you will not pursue blood feud."

"If that coward hurts Ahna, or causes her to be hurt, and especially if she is killed, he will find out how wrong he is a moment before my sword finds his heart! But I interrupted you. Is there more to your story?"

"The Eldest says that the epidemic has passed its peak," Redwolf went on, "and will soon be over, but the men will not be able to see that for some days yet. Zynjaar is determined to accomplish his revenge before then. If he succeeds, he will then say the epidemic ended because of his intercession with the Gods and Their pleasure in Ahna's sacrifice. Father says the men will believe him."

Marvulf looked sick. "If he succeeds, not only will we lose Ahna, he will have acquired great power, and the clans will be burdened with human sacrifice. What an ugly situation! I will kill him if he murders her, but it would be much better to prevent it. We must inform my father of this, and leave immediately."

'Immediately' hit a seventeen stone snag named Ryboryn Storm. Marvulf's father, a tall heavily muscled older version of Marvulf himself, was not inclined to believe in the seriousness of the situation. Priests in their own clan had little power and would not have dared suggest any radical change to even the religious observances which were their department. He didn't think Redwolf was a lier, but he suspected that Jaromir, who had lost so much recently, was overreacting to the essentially impotent threats of a political enemy. He thought privately that his eldest son and heir would not be going near the Lion camp until all risk of infection was gone, and maybe not then. He had never been enthusiastic about this hasty out-clan match, no matter how well born the girl. Any female that would ride in races must be enough out of the ordinary to be very uncomfortable to have around. He recognized that his son was truly enamored, but he had an eye to the future. He wanted a suitably compliant woman for his first daughter-in-law. Even were she really in danger, he could not see the need for unseemly and inconvenient haste just to save Ahna's life.

Aloud he reminded his son, who had brought him the story while Redwolf was getting cleaned up and having his knee tended before taking a much-needed nap, that there were tasks Marvulf himself was expected to perform, and that he would not be free to leave for the Lion camp until the moon was almost full, still nine days in the future.

"Surely that will be time enough," he said.

When Marvulf started to argue his father cut him off. "If we must, we will talk more about it at dinner," he said. "I can hear the whole story from the young man himself. Meanwhile I have a meeting to attend." As he left the tent, he added, "And you have duties, as well!"

Redwolf woke when Marvulf came into his sleeping quarters to tell him they would soon sit down to dinner. He rose hastily, thinking they should have been on their way by now, a little angry that Marvulf had let him sleep so long. He did feel a lot better, though. He combed his hair and tied it neatly back, then quickly donned the tan pants that Vyarhe had taken in at the waist and thighs for him and the rust-colored shirt with the gold embroidery that Marvulf had given him, commenting with a laugh that it matched his hair. He tightened his own braided belt with his knife in its sheath and pulled on his boots, from which the scratches had been mostly rubbed away.

He stepped out of Marvulf's sleeping place into the main tent, nodded briefly to the rather surprising gathering of men and boys, and continued out the door to the personal facilities. When he returned he had scrubbed his hands and face, but he ritually washed his hands in the basin held by a strange woman, who had snatched it up when she saw him come in. She glanced at the men, then whispered "Welcome, Redwolf. I am Marvulf's aunt Gracia. That big fellow, Rampat, is my husband." Redwolf smiled his thanks, thinking how pleasant she was.

He joined the gathering on the rugs. There were three older men besides Marvulf's father and his uncle Rampat, who wore the dark red and gold robes of a Red Wolf clan priest. The others were introduced as members of the clan council and friends of the leader. Marvulf himself was flanked by three of his younger brothers, including Peatli, whom Redwolf had met in the Lion camp, and five half-brothers. Luugani said, "Hey, Redwolf," trying to act nonchalant although he was still riding on the credit he had earned because he was the only one of his siblings besides Marvulf who had already met their visitor that day. Marvulf had told his prospective brother-in-law that his two next younger brothers were both fostered out in other clans, and that Peatli would begin his fostering at the winter solstice.

They all helped themselves to the delicious food. While they ate the younger boys pelted Redwolf with questions about his trip, the river, and the wolves, which he answered as best he could. By the time the serving women brought in the hot drinks everyone was feeling mellow with good food and drink, and Redwolf was itching to know why they were not at least preparing to leave. As the time passed his fears for his sister and his clan increased. He did not speak. He was still a boy and it would have been very bad manners for him to bring the subject up, at least until the men were done eating. He kept looking at Marvulf, who gave him slight nods that seemed to say, 'I know. Wait.' Redwolf waited.

When they sat back with their hot spiked tea, each with a little pile of honeyed fruits and nuts before him and Redwolf with another cup of the herbal remedy that kept his cough under control, Rampat said kindly,

"Now, young fellow, you've been patient, considering the trouble you had getting here, and I commend you for your very proper manners. My brother is reluctant to allow his eldest son to hare off to your camp on a mission he cannot believe is so urgent, especially since your people have had such a time with the winter fever, which we would just as soon did not visit our tents! Tell us the whole story, from the beginning, please."

Redwolf did so, starting with Marvulf's betrothal to Ahna, and Srogaraad's threat to prevent the marriage at all costs, which Marvulf himself had heard. He told of Srogaraad's attacks on Ahna and the trial and his banishment. He stressed Zynjaar's involvement at every turn of the tale. There were few interruptions or questions until he got to the part where the High Priest brought Ester to his mother's tents, and within two days the child was dead of the winter fever. He had told of his little brother dying, of the rapid spread and extreme deadliness of the fever, of his mother dying because she went back to nursing others too soon, and of Ahna's emergence as an important healer, along with other girls and young women, as many more of the older women died, when one of the councilors spoke.

"Just a minute," he said. "The priest brought the girl who carried the fever to you?" Redwolf nodded. "He must have known she was sick," another commented. "No offense, but I think Jaromir was a fool to have taken her in."

"Father said she showed no signs of illness, and Zynjaar had found her alone except for some animals. He said there was no way the High Priest, or anyone else, could have known she would get sick. She really did seem very healthy."

The two first-wives, exercising a privilege of their position, were standing near the opening to the work tent listening to the men's conversation while the second wives and concubines did the clearing up. Now Rampat glanced at his wife.

"Many times," he said, "when someone, especially a child, is coming down with the winter fever, they will seem to be more healthy and have more energy just before the fever strikes than is normal for them." Redwolf noticed that Gracia was nodding. "In our clan," her husband continued, "some of the priests are healers, and perhaps would have recognized that she would soon be ill. Is this Zynjaar a healer?"

"No," said Redwolf. "The priests have a duty to comfort and pray for the sick, and to help families that need it during illness or injury, but it is the older women, if anyone, who know healing. Since Zynjaar has been High Priest, though, the women have not dared to do more than the minimum for people, until this epidemic, because he is forever attacking them for doing anything beyond taking care of their own tents and families. He says that the Gods are angered if women take any part in public affairs, and even that any woman who demonstrates knowledge of herbs and healing beyond the most basic remedies is practicing witchcraft."

"What a fool," said another councilor. "Who does he think will heal the sick if his priests can't do it and he won't let the women do it, either?"

"He says," explained Redwolf, "that sickness is sent by the Gods to punish people for angering Them, and that he and his priests can intercede with the Gods through prayers and sacrifices to make the people well, provided they do what the Gods want. Of course, the only one who knows what the Gods want is the High Priest himself. He insists this is the way to deal with disease, injuries, or wounds. He says that what the women do is no more than palliative at best and that often it makes the Gods angrier, so that the disease or wound or whatever gets worse."

"How was it different this time?" asked Rampat.

"The priests have been in retreat all during the last moon, fasting and communing with the Gods, Zynjaar said, and would not break their isolation to resume their duties when the epidemic struck. In their absence the women have been openly tending the sick and have had some success at saving people who were very ill. I would have died if my sister and Sara had not come up with a poultice of onions and herbs that cleared the congestion from my chest."

Gracia took an involuntary step forward and Rampat sat up and said, "Onions. Really? Yes, I see where that might work. Whatever gave her that idea?"

"I don't know," said Redwolf, "but it does work. Ahna and the other women have saved many lives using it, but Zynjaar still insists that what they are doing is against the wishes of the Gods. So many have died that the men are listening to him."

"When did this 'retreat' of the priests start? Is it a normal thing for them to do?" asked a councilor.

"They do it every year," answered Redwolf, "but usually not until after the winter solstice, when it is cold enough to keep the sacrificial meat from spoiling. They started this retreat the day after Zynjaar brought Ester to us. He said he was out hunting to provide meat for their period of isolation when he found her."

"Convenient, if he wanted to avoid exposure," said Rampat. There were knowing nods, but no further comments.

"He said they were starting the retreat early because the Gods were restless, still upset over Ahna's racing and her 'unwomanly' behavior…"

"Did he mean her unwillingness to be raped and forced into marriage with his vicious son?" asked Marvulf, sarcasm lacing his voice.

Redwolf nodded. "He repeated that the Gods were angry at Father because he let his women get away with breaking Their laws and those of the clan. Of course, there are no such clan laws, but Zynjaar wants everyone to believe that his word is law, and too many do. Anyway, he said the sacrifices and fasting and prayers were necessary to placate the Gods and to find out what they wanted. He warned that something terrible would happen if the Gods were not appeased."

"This priest is not, after all, a fool," said Rampat. "He very cleverly set it up so that when people started to get sick he could say, 'I told you so,' and some people would believe him because of his apparent foreknowledge. It is a very good way to consolidate and increase his power."

"Do you believe all this, then?" asked his brother. "I do not. How many of your clan have died, Redwolf? More than four hundred?" His guest nodded. "No one," Ryboryn continued, "in a position of leadership could be so... so irresponsible, or cruel, as to deliberately bring such an epidemic down on his people just to accomplish some personal revenge. I realize that the one who was banished was his only son, but still..."

"Yes, I believe Redwolf," said Rampat, smiling at him. "Zynjaar probably did not know how virulent this form of the winter fever would prove to be, but even if he did there are a few people in the world who will do literally anything to consolidate and increase their power over others, not to mention that there are also those who will go to unbelievable lengths to get revenge on someone they think has wronged them. This High Priest is just the type."

"But... you did say he was demanding sacrifice of the girl?" the first councilor said. "Surely that is beyond anything that his people, or your clan council, would accept?" Rampat looked at Redwolf, then answered for him.

"Under ordinary circumstances I'm sure you would be right, but these are extraordinary circumstances. There must be many men in Jaromir's clan who are looking for someone, anyone, to blame. The priest's promise that the Gods will end the epidemic if the girl is sacrificed must seem like a floating log in a flood: something to grab on to."

"The evening before I left," Redwolf added, "our eldest healer said the epidemic was slowing down, that there were fewer new cases and would soon be fewer deaths, and that by the time this moon is full it will be over. If Zynjaar can succeed right away in having Ahna sacrificed and my father banished as he says the Gods demand, he will then be 'proven' right because the epidemic will end. He would have virtually total power over our clan, with the threat of human sacrifice to back him up. That is why it is important for us to go now. It took me so long to get here; I'm afraid we may already be too late!"

The men looked around at one another.

"Sacrifice of one of our own, even a woman, is an abomination that the clans have never practiced. It would be no good thing if this power-mad priest were to begin it, and worse if he managed to justify it," said the first councilor. The others nodded agreement.

"If Marvulf goes," Ryboryn asked his brother, "what is to keep him from contracting this very deadly winter fever?"

Rampat glanced at his wife again. She was shaking her head. "I think there is no danger of that if he and his companions limit their direct contact with the folk of the Lion clan to Jaromir's immediate family. They have all been free of the disease for at least a ten-day. I doubt that many other people in the clan can still transmit the disease, either, but there is no point in taking chances. Do not sleep in their tents, or handle anything of theirs if you can avoid it, Marvulf. You might also consider taking at least a ten-day to come back, to make sure that none of your companions are going to get sick. You will have an excellent healer with you if you should need her, and since you will have no very young, very old, or physically weakened people with you, I don't think there is any real risk. I am coming, by the way. You may need a priest, if only to marry you."

"Wonderful!" exclaimed Marvulf. "I was hoping you would."

"I still find it hard to believe that the majority of your clan would support such an action," Ryboryn said.

Redwolf had been thinking about this, because it seemed unbelievable to him, too. He thought he finally had the answer.

"It wouldn't take a majority, sir," he said. "It might not take very many at all, if there were enough others who remained neutral. Our priests are unarmed and are not allowed to fight. No one may raise a hand to a priest by clan law. To strike or attack a priest is punishable by banishment; to kill one is death. All they have to do is get all the priests together and go and get my sister. They would need a few warriors, in case someone did try to stop them. Their allies could then arrest those people."

"The boy is right; they would not need public opinion to be entirely on their side," corroborated Rampat. "The holdouts will come around after the fact, when the epidemic ends." The priest-healer had been watching Redwolf, who was trying to suppress his persistent cough, and still looked worn out.

"You know, brother," he now said, "if this were your son it would have taken an extraordinary emergency to persuade you to send him out into that storm after help from what are, essentially, strangers, especially if he had been very sick and was not yet fully recovered."

Marvulf's father looked at Redwolf, considering. Slowly he nodded. "Jaromir does have the reputation of being a sensible leader," he said. "You will start in the morning, then." Marvulf and Redwolf both opened their mouths, but the clan chief held up his hand.

"This day is too far gone for you to get there tonight," he pointed out, "and this young man is exhausted. He needs rest." He looked at the councilors a minute, then added, "I also think you should have an escort, and they will need some time to get ready." The councilors were nodding, as was Rampat. "You should get ready today, and leave at first light. If you push hard, you should be there by midday. If they have not already killed the girl, they will not do so before high sun."

"You must understand, Redwolf, that there is no prohibition in our clan against priests fighting or being challenged, or even being killed, if it is in fair fight," said Rampat. To his brother he said, "What role do you have in mind for this escort?"

"They will be there if needed, for whatever is needed," said his brother. "It may be they will be useful as intimidation, to prevent the priest and his cohorts from taking the girl. On the other hand, if this Zynjaar has succeeded in his ambitions, Marvulf would be well within his rights to challenge him according to our laws, and if the priest should fail to meet that challenge, which seems likely, then our laws state that he may be killed out of hand. The escort would then need to back you up, son, and get you all out of there. It is likely that some at least of the Lions would object to what they would see as the murder of their High Priest. You, however, would have revenged his

mortal insult to you of killing your contracted bride, and we would
also be rid of the problem of human sacrifice. If Jaromir isn't able to
take advantage of that situation to point out that the Gods obviously
didn't approve of Zynjaar's actions or They would have protected him,
then he isn't the leader I think he is."

"His brother gazed at him, amused. "How large an 'escort' do
you plan to send?" he inquired.

"Oh, I think Marvulf should invite about a hundred of his friends
to his wedding," said Ryboryn.

Rampat almost rolled on the rugs, he laughed so hard.

Redwolf was sent back to Marvulf's furs, although they had been
talking so long it was almost time to eat again. Marvulf went out to
round up a hundred young warriors who could take a few days away
from their other duties. Since warriors had few duties when no raids
were planned except for war games and hunting, and regular but
infrequent turns guarding the stock at night, it was not difficult.
Marvulf himself was in charge of training the newly initiated warriors;
that was the duty his father had not wanted him to leave. He decided
to take them along: all sixty-two of them, many of them fosterlings
from other clans, only a year or two older than Redwolf. It would be a
good chance for them to experience some military discipline first
hand without much risk of their having to fight. The rest of the
hundred were made up of unmarried young warriors around Marvulf's
age and some older fosterlings; they would not take any of the
Dedicated because there would be no need of their special services.

Marvulf and his father picked out the horses and cattle that
would go to Jaromir as their bride gift: among the finest they had, as
was proper. They planned a very early start, so the horses they were
going to ride and those they were taking along were put close to the
tent village in a separate field, handy for the morning. The cattle
would follow at a slower pace. They could not be expected to keep
up with a war band in a hurry.

Weapons and harness were checked, saddle bags were packed
with food and other necessities, water skins filled, and bedrolls and
waterproofs tied onto saddles. Clothes were picked out and readied
for the morning. Breakfast was planned to go and women were

warned to get up in time to serve hot drinks while it was still dark. The chief had said, 'first light.' He would be obeyed.

Redwolf woke up when Marvulf entered his private space. "Come and get some supper, little brother," he said, making Redwolf grin, "and then we will go to bed. Everything is ready for a very early start. If we switch horses frequently and push them when we can, we will reach your camp before high sun." He gave the young man a hand climbing to his feet, mindful of the sprained knee, which Gracia had poulticed and wrapped that morning. "I haven't had a chance to tell you how bad I feel about Ahndru and your mother," Marvulf said before he pulled aside the privacy curtain. "They were both remarkable people. If that priest could be shown to be responsible for their deaths I would kill him myself, even if we get there in time to save Ahna."

"Thank you," said Redwolf. "We will miss them terribly, especially my father. I'm not sure I believe in revenge any more, though. If Zynjaar did bring the sickness to our camp, it was because he wanted revenge. That's too much for me." Marvulf nodded, although he wasn't sure he understood. Justified revenge for egregious wrongs done to oneself or one's family was a long-established and honorable custom in the clans.

The next morning they rose while it was still full dark, dressed, visited the facilities, and returned to find Marvulf's father being served hot tea and fresh flatbread. Vyarhe brought them cups of tea with fermented mares' milk. They drank them standing up, taking bites of flatbread between swallows of tea. Ryboryn lectured his son at length about avoiding any chance of infection, and keeping the young warriors out of harms way as well, then said, "Well, it will soon be dawn. Be on your way. I trust I will see you all safely home in a ten-day. I've been pleased to meet you, Redwolf. Your father should be very proud of you. Don't dawdle. On your way, now!"

Bemused, the two young men picked up their loaded saddle bags and were hustled out through the tent flaps. They walked down the wide road between the rows of tents, a few other warriors joining them along the way. At the field they found many more warriors already assembled, tacking up their horses in the light of smoky torches held by siblings, or sometimes by a friend who was not going. Two of Marvulf's younger brothers appeared leading four horses, already saddled and bridled. The stars in the east began to fade. It was still very dark, but dawn was near.

"Those two are yours," Marvulf said, pointing to the pair that Luugani was leading. "The mare is Bright Banner. The gelding is Playboy." He went to check the girths on Golden Boy.

Redwolf looked over the mare and the gelding in the flickering light, beautiful horses, both dark bays, strong and well made with alert ears and kind eyes. "These must be some of your best," he said. "I don't need anything so fine."

"Perhaps not, but you will ride one of these, and the other will be your second," Marvulf insisted. "They are yours, anyway. They are part of the bride gifts I am bringing to your father. The mare is war-trained."

Redwolf thanked him then, and checked over his own gear. Bright Banner was wearing the gaudy saddle that Ahna and Firefly had won. He said nothing, correctly assuming that Marvulf meant Ahna to use it on the return trip. They were mounting their horses when Rampat rode up on a striking cream buckskin gelding, strongly made and well up to his rider's considerable weight. It was a memorable picture because his second horse was an exact match for the first.

The stars were all gone now except the morning star, which gleamed brightly on a limitless backdrop of indigo velvet. A line of light bloomed behind the tents on the eastern horizon. The torches seemed paler as their carriers retreated to the sidelines. Everywhere around them warriors were mounting and forming up by twos along the road. Marvulf's brothers handed them the leads to their seconds, said goodbye, and ran back out of the way. As they trotted up to the head of the column the three leaders passed a small herd of loose horses. Among the dark bays and browns Redwolf spotted the familiar red coat, arched neck and dished face of his sister's mare. "You're giving my father Firefly?" he asked.

"No," laughed Marvulf. "Not for anything! I win far too many bets with her. She still doesn't like me much, but Luugani rides her to perfection.

"I'm taking her for Ahna to ride back. I figured she'd like that."

"They both will," agreed Ahna's brother.

Chapter 29

Ahna's defenders gathered at Jaromir's tents in the misty post-
dawn freshness of a promising late fall day. Nothing happened. The
men had brought their women, and generous amounts of food and
drink, anticipating what proved to be a long wait. When all were
assembled they practiced taking their assigned places, mixing
younger and larger men among older ones and less well grown boys
until the line really did look impregnable. Havad was in charge of
eight warriors who stood to one side, ready to gently but firmly arrest
any priest or other person who used unacceptable force against
anyone in the line.

   When they were all clear as to their roles, they squatted or stood
in groups surrounding Jaromir's main tent and the annex, making sure
they could not be surprised. Ahna and the other women were kept
busy, first providing breakfast, and then serving drinks and snacks and
preparing food for later in the day.

   When half-high sun had passed and still nothing had happened a
few of the young warriors became restless, suggesting that maybe the
high priest and his followers had changed their minds. Jaromir and
Yashihar asked that they stay until at least high sun, promising them
fresh roast beef for dinner. They agreed and returned to their assigned
places with their stones or other games, singing songs of battle, or
telling each other outrageous stories. It began to feel much more like
a party than a serious matter. A hand-width before midday the
situation changed.

   They heard the sound of many feet first, then saw all the priests
of the clan, led by Zynjaar, march purposefully out of a side path and

turn in their direction. Behind them came most of the rest of the men of the camp, roughly matching the number of Ahna's protectors, grimly silent, led by a fully armed and armored phalanx of the Dedicated.

Ahna and the other women who had been serving snacks vanished into the tents, taking the food and drinking utensils with them. The defenders leaped to their places and quickly formed their double cordon, standing shoulder to shoulder, backs to the tent, arms locked at the elbows, the inner ring arranging themselves so that their bodies filled the spaces between the bodies of the men in front, strengthening the line. The priests stopped ten paces away, assessing this strange sight. It didn't take Zynjaar long to grasp the situation. He took a few steps closer.

"Stand aside," he ordered, his compelling voice firm. "You are illegally interfering with the pursuit of our priestly duty and the express wishes of the Gods."

"That must be another of your made-up laws," said Yashihar mildly from his place near the entrance to the tents. Since no one had ever seen anything like the cordon around the chief's tents, or heard of any laws about the duties of priests and what they could or could not do in their pursuit, Zynjaar's pronouncement hung there unsupported. He curbed his anger and turned to the Dedicated.

"Remove them," he demanded curtly. "They are not armed. Some of them are old men, others hardly more than boys. Surely you are strong enough to move this rabble out of the way."

"We would be happy to," said their leader, "except the laws against that are very clear and very strict. You are asking us to throw away our honor and put banishment in its place. Everyone knows, priest, that we may not even touch any man of our own clan without his permission, with very limited exceptions, all involving weapons. I see no weapons. Do you think these clever men are going to give us permission?"

Thwarted again, the High Priest tried another tack, turning back to the stolid ring of Ahna's defenders.

"It is your behavior that is dishonorable," he accused. "You are threatening to precipitate a fight between members of the clan, setting neighbor against neighbor, brother against brother. It would surely destroy us. No man should be willing to do that over a woman!"

The woman he referred to was watching the confrontation from the shadows behind the tent flaps, along with as many of the visiting women as could get to a viewing spot without being seen. Lwenli's wife was organizing the rest in the kitchen; she was sure the priests and their supporters would give up before long, and they would then be expected to serve dinner to all the defenders. They had baked huge platters of flat-bread, and a whole carcass of beef cut into joints was roasting over fires in all three hearths along with numerous cuts of mutton and pots of root vegetables; still she hoped there was enough food.

Ahna did not think the high priest would give up so easily; she remembered all too well how dogged in pursuit of her his son had been. She hoped Sara and the other young healers were all right today; they had gone out as usual to tend the sick early this morning. Sara had wanted to stay with her friend, but Ahna had convinced her that there was really nothing she could do here; the sick children needed her more. "Don't worry, I will still be here when you get back this evening," she had promised, though she wasn't at all sure it would be true.

"We have no weapons, as you yourselves have pointed out," Yashihar was answering Zynjaar. "We threaten no one. All we are doing is standing here. In case you are wondering," he added, indicating the warriors standing to one side, "Havad and his friends over there are prepared to arrest any priest or other individual who illegally raises hand or weapon to us, since we are not insulting or threatening anyone. We will stand here for as long as is necessary to prevent you from carrying out this abomination of human sacrifice, which none of us can believe really has been commanded by the Gods."

Zynjaar almost lost his temper. "We've been over that too many times already." He spoke loudly, shortly. "She is not a man, has no right to the same consideration as a man. She is only a woman!"

"You are not her father, or her husband, and neither are any of these others," Yashihar responded without raising his voice. "None of you has any right to touch her, say nothing about taking her life. That is murder, by our laws."

Zynjaar took himself in hand. "Hundreds of our people have died because of her," he proclaimed. "The Gods demand her sacrifice. A holy sacrifice cannot be murder."

Without giving Yashihar time to answer he turned and stepped back into the press of priests behind him. They gathered around him, and he told them what he wanted them to do. Some clearly thought he was crazy, but all he said was "make sure you do not hit them, or kick them, or in any way threaten them. Just get through that line."

The ensuing minutes would have been hilarious if the consequences hadn't had such disastrous potential. Fifteen or twenty of the priests, their long bronze robes now flapping in a rising breeze, approached the circle of defenders tentatively. Quite a few, however, stayed right where they were despite Zynjaar's angry, if low, commands. Of those who had obeyed him, several tried the direct approach. They walked up to men they knew in the double line and asked them, in the name of the Gods, to let them through. Little smiles and shaken heads were their only reward. Others tried to crawl between the defender's legs, and a few tried to climb the cordon as if it was a wall; in both cases, because they could not 'raise their hands', they were easily deterred. A couple of the largest tried to push their way through, but they couldn't budge the living barrier.

When even some of their own supporters could not suppress their laughter, the priests retreated, gathering around one of their members who was soliciting suggestions for ending this impasse. They were ready to give up and go back to their regular duties, many profoundly if secretly relieved, but the most determined of them, a tall, heavyset, nearly bald and truly imposing figure of a man who had once been a wrestler, suggested that the strongest among them form a wedge, with himself at the tip, and simply shove themselves against the barrier. Either they would break through, or the defenders would have to leave gaps somewhere else to reinforce the threatened section, and that would give the rest of the priests an opportunity to get inside and get the woman.

Inside the tent, Ahna spoke to Yashihar's wife and the others who were watching.

"I don't know what they're planning, but I think they're up to something. I've been thinking about a plan of our own in case they break through. The priests aren't even allowed to touch a married woman not their own wife; no man in the clan is. If the priests do get through the men, will you all form around me in a circle like the one outside and holler for your husbands to come in and make sure no one touches us?" The women gathered around were nodding in comprehension.

"Thank you," said Ahna fervently.

"No thanks needed," said an older woman. "If the High Priest succeeds in sacrificing you, none of us will ever be safe! That man hates women."

Exhorted anew by Zynjaar, and with a plan that at least some of them thought might work, the priests scattered out around the circle again, in pairs this time except for the six largest. These picked what they thought was the weakest point in the line, and, making a tight wedge of their bodies, leaned forward as one and pushed themselves against the massive back of their leader, who plowed into the cordon, his arms at his sides. The extra warriors looked at each other, and moved toward the threatened section.

"That's an attack!" Havad accused.

"It is not," barked the High Priest. "They are not raising their hands. You may not touch them!"

The warriors hesitated. The line bent inward, the defenders bracing with all they had, but already the observers could see that it would not be enough.

Chapter 30

Redwolf, Marvulf, Rampat and the young warriors of the Red
Wolf clan trotted up the last rise between them and the tents of the
Lion clan. They had pressed their horses, changing mounts every five
miles or so without stopping, maintaining a fast, ground-covering trot
wherever possible, even galloping for short stretches when the way
was flat and open, jumping off and using their own feet on the
steepest hills, pausing only briefly to let the horses drink. They had
not stopped once. The river had been placid and easily passed. Still
the sun was less than a hand short of its highest point when they
finally approached their goal.

From the top of the hill the crowd around Jaromir's tents was
clearly visible; there seemed to be something happening between a
closely spaced line of men circling the tents and a bunch of priests,
with the rest of the men of the clan looking on. Whatever it was, they
knew it could not be good. At Marvulf's command they dropped the
ground ties on their second horses and left them behind, setting their
tired mounts to a gallop down the gentle slope and in among the
myriad tents, whooping and cheering as if they were arriving for a
celebration. They did not want the Lion warriors to think they were
attacking, but they did want them to know they had come.

The swelling thunder of four hundred and twelve fast
approaching hooves and the incongruously joyful noise made by the
young Red Wolves distracted the priests; the wedge broke up.

"Keep pushing!" cried their leader, knowing victory was
imminent, but those at his back had turned to face this new threat,

and with the reduced weight against them his opponents were able to renew their stances and their grips. He could not get through.

Marvulf signaled his forces to a halt in the lane short of the crowd, silenced them with a chopping motion of his raised hand, and rode Golden Boy right between the High Priest and the cordon around the tent. Intimidated by the strange horsemen, the other priests beat a precipitous retreat, regrouping behind their leader, the wrestler still berating his fellows for abandoning him when they had all but won. The priest nearest him hissed at him to shut up.

"There's nothing stopping *that* lot from attacking us!" he warned.

The Red Wolf warriors sat straight and silent, their hands on the hilts of their weapons, Redwolf and Rampat in front, an imposing show of force even if their mounts were lathered and weary. Marvulf, more impressive yet on his tall golden stallion, glared around at the men of the Lion clan and mentally opted for pretended ignorance. Finding Jaromir in the line around the tents, he addressed the chief.

"What is going on, sir? Why is your entire clan outside your tents instead of attending to their daily chores? Why did it appear that there was conflict of some sort between you and the priests? I believe you told me that was against your laws."

Jaromir released the men on either side of him and stepped forward. "Welcome, Marvulf," he said, his relief at seeing his son and prospective son-in-law compounded by his surprise at the number of their companions; it was nearly enough to be considered a hostile invasion. He looked the column over more closely and his eyes acquired a decided twinkle. They might be warriors in name, but he doubted that many of them had ever been in a real fight. There could not be more than three in the entire band who had reached their twentieth summer.

"You come at a critical moment for our clan," the chief began. "Our High Priest, Zynjaar here, whom I believe you have not met, wishes to introduce human sacrifice to the rites performed by himself and his brethren in service to the Gods. He has chosen our Ahna to be his first victim."

"The Gods demand it!" stated Zynjaar in stentorian tones. "They have spoken to us." He waved a hand toward the crowd gathered beyond him. "The men of the clan agree."

"Apparently not all of them," snapped Marvulf, nodding to the circle of men that still stood solid around the tent. He addressed the rest of the Lions, the fury in his voice intensifying as he spoke.

"What *right* had any of you to condemn my bride? Only her father and myself may, by long-standing clan law, decide her fate. Anything else is murder, pure and simple. Do you all seek banishment?

"The whole idea of sacrificing Ahna or any other person is an abomination, an evil thing. It is... it *must be* wrong! I have never heard of any true Gods that would demand it, nor have any of the elders in my clan.

"I know that you have been afflicted by a devastating pestilence, but surely you can see that this is not a matter of the Gods," he went on. "It is a vicious attempt at petty and unjustified revenge instigated by your High Priest. He is using his powers of persuasion and the power of his office for his personal, incredibly dishonorable ends!"

Marvulf's heartfelt but ill-considered statement brought protests from both sides; even many of those who were suspicious of the priest's motives would not stand for such accusations from an outsider. The Red Wolf leader addressed Zynjaar's fellow priests.

"If I am wrong," he said, "if you really have the sanction of your Gods for this horror, then some of the rest of you must be able to confirm your High Priest's claims. I understand you have been fasting and communing with your Gods for an entire moon. I know priests will not lie. Can any of you stand before your people and your Gods and swear that They have told you, *you personally*, that They demand the sacrifice of Jaromir's daughter?"

"Well, speak up!" commanded Zynjaar. "Tell him the Gods have spoken to you, too."

The silence lengthened, and Zynjaar became visibly angrier. Finally Mulynvi stepped forward and confronted him.

"You yourself told us that we were not to fast, because we would weaken ourselves and become more susceptible to the disease. We

have prayed, oh, how we have prayed, but without fasting we have
naturally had no direct communion with the Gods." Several other
priests hastily added,

"But you have, Holy One. We do believe you have!"

Zynjaar turned to the crowd of clansmen and Dedicated behind
him. "Are you going to let these outclanners insult me and tell us how
to behave in our own tents? You shame the Lion! We would drive
these sniveling strangers off ourselves if it were permitted."

The Dedicated had joined Zynjaar's mob not from anger at
Jaromir or fear of the winter fever, or even the Gods, but because they
were bored with the long seasons of peace and hoping for some
action. They were constrained from fighting with their own folk by
clan laws as long as the other men did not offer them violence. There
were no rules, however, against fighting outsiders if they could be
construed to have attacked the Lion clan. By the customs of the clans,
certain insults ranked as attacks. Even the fact that the armed Red
Wolves had galloped in among the tents without specific invitation
might be called an attack. The Dedicated leader, who had observed
with growing malice that Marvulf's force was made up of teen age
boys, now called on his fellows to show these out-horde invaders and
insulters of their High Priest what real fighting men could do.

"We all know what you can do," shouted Jaromir, suddenly
fearful for the young men of Marvulf's clan. "It is far beneath your
dignity to attack untried warriors. These young friends of my son-in-
law came to attend his wedding. If you slaughter them it will certainly
start a blood feud with the entire Red Wolf clan."

The Dedicated were extreme killers, living for battle and barely
under control at the best of times; now they were itching for a fight.
Their leader called out, "Be quiet, old man. The priest is right. Your
recent behavior has indeed insulted our manhood and proven you
unfit to be our leader. We will not heed you any more. The Red
Wolves will never pursue a blood feud with us," he said to his
fellows.

"Let's get 'em!" Then he made sure the inexperienced warriors
would stay and fight by adding, "They're mounted. If they're smart,

they'll run away." An ominous susurrus of weapons sliding out of sheaths on both sides filled the air.

Into the middle of this incipient battle, right into the no-mans-land between the combatants, galloped five or six young women, they and their horses panting with the unaccustomed effort. Outraged warriors on all sides began yelling for them to get out of there; some of the Lion clan's men started forward to remove them by force. Yashihar stepped out of his place in the defensive cordon around the tent and used his command voice to get everyone's attention.

"There must be some real emergency if these sensible young women are acting so strangely," he declared when he could be heard. "Stop screaming at them and try listening to them!" At these words many of the men, on edge as they all were, began hunting around for a new source of danger.

"What is wrong?" Yashihar asked the girls. Luliana, Ahshela's granddaughter and at eighteen summers the eldest of the girls and one of the best young healers, dismounted and took a step forward. Her husband left the defensive cordon to stand beside her.

"We have found the place where the winter fever came from," she began, still a little breathless. "We were out seeking onions for poultices because we are running out again."

"This has nothing to do with why we are here today," shouted Zynjaar. "It is none of these women's business anyway; it is men's business." The anger in his voice escalated, disguising an undercurrent of fear. He pointed to Sara, seated on her horse among the other girls.

"Look, there is even a *concubine* among them. Everyone knows you can never trust the word of a concubine. Can't you see that this is more of Ahna's pernicious influence? Get these blasphemous young women out of here. Their men should see that they are severely punished for this inexcusable behavior."

"We want to hear what they have found," called several voices in both camps. "Let her speak." Zynjaar opened his mouth again, but closed it when other voices repeated loudly, "Yes, let her speak!"

"Sara remembered that there was a garden we had not searched near an abandoned farmstead. We went there and found onions. We also found the remains of six humans and some pigs, dead for at least a moon, scattered around the barn yard and under the edge of the trees. The Others always take care of their dead, but these were untended. They must have died at nearly the same time. There was no sign of violence, and we haven't heard that the warriors have recently killed any more others. We believe they died of the disease." She looked a question at her husband, who nodded.

"There have been no living others found since the raid last fall," he confirmed. "Is there a half burned barn at this farmstead?" She nodded. "That's near the field where we held our war games during midsummer moon," he went on. "There were many pigs and chickens around that old barn, but we saw no sign of Others, living or dead."

"We looked inside the end of the barn that was still standing," she told him. "People were living there until just recently. A medium-tent-sized space is closed off, with a fire pit, four sleeping areas with bedding, an eating area, cooking utensils and containers with the remains of grain and root vegetables. There were egg shells in a wicker bowl near the fire pit. Everything was very neat, except for the chicken's leavings."

"We never went near the barn," her husband said, "because of the unclean animals. It's a good place, close enough to the old town so we would not look for them there. They might have stayed hidden indefinitely as long as they only came out at night."

"Except they didn't know the risk they were taking, living with those animals," said Mulynvi, stepping forward again. "Our teachers told us why the pigs and chickens were declared unclean, why we keep the prohibition against eating them. Long ago, when the clans began moving south, one of our clans took a town that had many pigs and chickens. Some families brought the unfamiliar animals into their camp, fed them food scraps and garbage, and ate them in turn. There was a terrible epidemic of the winter fever that year, fast moving and deadly as this one has been, that started first in the households that had the new animals. It seems very likely to me that these girls have indeed found the source of the infection." Turning toward Zynjaar, he added, "If so, then I'm forced to believe you found the girl who brought the fever to us there, too, and not 'in the forest,' as you told us.

"If the bodies of the others were right out in the open, as these women say, you could not have seen the child without seeing them, too. They must have just died; it explains why the child was willing to come with you. You had to know they died of a disease.

"I have been afraid to speak out, but now I am ashamed. The medications and nursing methods of Jaromir's daughter Ahna and the other healers work. They saved the lives of two of my children, and other priests and their wives have used them to save children as well, while those who have had only prayers have died.

"It is hard for me to accept that someone in your position could have done this terrible thing only for revenge, and to increase your power over our people, but the notion that our Gods want us to practice human sacrifice is abhorrent. Marvulf Storm is right. By all the real evidence before us, the Gods must approve of Ahna. They have blessed her hands and heart with healing skills. Only a demon could demand the sacrifice of a young woman who has worked so hard and given so much to save our children."

Zynjaar had been standing as if frozen, listening to his hitherto well-ordered world crumble about his ears. Now he rallied.

"Lies! Blasphemy! You bear false witness!" he screeched. Getting his voice under control, he added, "No wonder priests' children are dying, when even those who wear robes persist in angering the Gods. They would never 'approve' of blasphemous, upstart women. We all know women are soulless, and must be kept strictly to their own tasks, for their good and ours. You are a traitor to the Gods and to us. We will drive you from the priesthood. You will die forever, with no hope of meeting the Gods, or joining your brethren in the afterlife!"

Mulynvi gave him a disgusted look, but said no more.

"My son died," called Fronzi, "my only son, although my neighbor used the medications as your wife explained to us, Mulynvi. Now all I have is a worthless daughter. The witch's treatments are useless. She is a blasphemer, and should be sacrificed as the Gods demand!" There were a few calls from the crowd of clansmen in support of his words, but many of the priests looked thoughtful, and remained silent.

"Didn't you say, Jaromir," Yashihar cut in, "that when Zynjaar brought the child of the Others to you, his words were that there was no one living where he found her except the pigs and chickens?" The chief nodded. "Priests take a vow not to lie, but it would not have been a lie if the Others with her were already dead!" the Horse Master pointed out.

Low discussions, even arguments, broke out all around. The men were still not ready to believe that their High Priest, one of their most important leaders, could have deliberately brought the terrible fever on them just to get revenge on Jaromir and Ahna, even if he had found the child at the old farmstead. He was, after all, always insisting that his people behave with propriety. This accusation was so far outside the realm of what was right as to be inconceivable. If proven, it would certainly mean loss of everything, including life, for the guilty person. No sane man would risk it. What's more, women were notoriously poor witnesses, much more likely to be wrong than the High Priest. A generous majority was still quite sure Zynjaar could not have known that the little girl presented a threat.

Except the Dedicated. No one knew better than they what men were capable of doing, and they did have their own honor. They glared at the priest, contempt darkening their hard faces. Some of them hawked into the dirt, as near to Zynjaar's feet as they could reach, the worst indignity these masters of insult could bring to bear.

"We will not be a party to this," declared the leader, he who had been urging them to attack Marvulf's friends only minutes before. They sheathed their weapons and stalked back to their tents.

Zynjaar began at once to exhort his followers to a renewed effort to take Ahna, but the momentum was gone; too many now had doubts who had earlier been firmly behind him. There were also the Red Wolf warriors to be considered, mounted and armed, although they, too, had put away their weapons. They were still under no obligation to refrain from attacking the Lions, provided they believed they had just cause. The threats and insults of the Lion clan Dedicated were enough, if they wished to use them.

Yashihar called for an immediate meeting of the council, right where they stood. All the remaining members were present on either one side or the other. He thanked the young women and sent them about their business while the council assembled. Marvulf dismounted, and Redwolf and Rampat left their horses and joined him and Jaromir near the tent, where the members of the defensive cordon had relaxed their stances, although they did not abandon their positions. Moshel came out of the circle to welcome Redwolf with a backslapping hug, something his father would have liked to do.

"What delayed you?" asked his foster brother.

"Long story; tell you later," Redwolf answered.

After only a few minutes of discussion between themselves, the council members turned to Marvulf and Jaromir. "Has the young man met the terms of your contract to your satisfaction?" Gylgan asked the clan chief. Jaromir had had no opportunity to look over the horses that Marvulf brought for him, but he thought they were probably fine, and he really didn't care, anyway. He nodded.

"Has Jaromir fulfilled his obligations to you?" the councilor then asked Marvulf.

"As long as my bride is healthy and ready to go, I am content," the young Red Wolf answered. He had not seen any of the livestock that Jaromir meant him to have, either. It wasn't important.

"Then, with only one dissenting," Gylgan continued, nodding to Jumri, "we have decided that you, Marvulf Storm, will marry the daughter of Jaromir Winter immediately and take her back with you to your own tents, today if possible."

"That's not going to happen!" declared Zynjaar. "There is no priest who will marry them."

Mulynvi stepped forward, avoiding his chief's angry glare.

"I will marry them," he offered.

Marvulf spoke before Zynjaar could. "That is very kind, and very brave, of you, sir, but we would not have you put yourself at further risk. This is my father's brother, Rampat, a priest of our clan. He has come as a witness and representative of my family, and he will perform the marriage ceremony." He looked at Jaromir. "Is my bride ready?" The clan chief nodded.

"Everything is ready," he said. "We need only a couple hands' time to gather the animals and load the pack horses."

"Then we will do as you ask." Marvulf told the council. "We will be married and gone today."

Again the High Priest tried to interrupt, but Gylgan held up his hand.

"This is a matter for the council, Zynjaar, because it affects far more than religious observances. Not all are agreed, but the majority of the council feels that your single-minded effort to introduce human sacrifice, and particularly the sacrifice of one of our own people, into the rituals has threatened the peace and integrity, possibly even the existence, of our clan. We can only believe that you have misinterpreted the desires of the Gods. Therefore we declare that this subject be dropped, permanently." He turned back to the men standing in front of the tents.

"We feel that these problems have been compounded by the loss of leadership in the council. Therefore we will have an election to fill out the council, and then hold formal hearings to look into these latest accusations against our High Priest, tomorrow if Marvulf and Ahna and the Red Wolves have gone. Be prepared to attend, please, Zynjaar."

The High Priest nodded curtly, then gathered his flock with a wave of his hand and herded them back toward their compound. A few of his closest friends and supporters followed.

Gylgan addressed the rest of the men of the clan.

"We are done here for now," he said. "You should all get back to your own business. The council will meet at the third hand after sunrise tomorrow, on the gathering ground or in the gathering tent. You will choose five new council members. Consider your choices carefully as you go about your work today."

The women brought out the food they had prepared, and most of the defenders found places around the yard to eat an impromptu meal. Jaromir thanked all those who had come to keep the priests from taking his daughter. Then Ahna herself stepped forward. She looked at the Horse Master, who nodded and smiled at her encouragingly.

"I know it is not my place to speak," she said, "but I want you to know how grateful I am, not only because you saved my life, but because you stood up to the destructive efforts of the High Priest and saved our clan from bloodshed and probable dissolution. I know you did not have to fight, but your actions were still as brave and praiseworthy as those of the finest warriors, particularly because they were so different from what you usually do. Thank you."

"Thank you," said the Leather Master, "for all you have done to save our children." The Lion men set up a cheer for her as she returned to her duties, but Marvulf was wearing a little frown.

While they ate the talk was about the hands just past. Everyone thought it had been an interesting experience, and had worked much better than they expected. Now that the pressure was off, they even thought of ways to prevent the human wedge approach from breaking their line. One suggestion was to have people lie in front of the cordon, preventing anyone from approaching close enough to apply any real pressure with their bodies, since walking on the prone people would be 'kicking'.

Marvulf and Rampat sent the Red Wolf warriors to collect their extra mounts and go camp in the meadow where the horse fair had been held, well away from possible exposure to the winter fever. He detailed two to bring the bride-gift horses and Firefly to the village pasture before they, too, joined their fellows, taking Golden Boy with them to be cared for after their hard ride.

"We will join you before supper," Marvulf told them, "and camp there tonight. Tomorrow we will start for home. You all did very well. Thank you."

Chapter 31

Ahna lifted her eyes briefly to her bridegroom when he took her hand from her father, and smiled faintly when she found he was smiling down at her. Then she turned her gaze back down, where it was supposed to remain until she made her vows. Jaromir had led her from her private space to stand here with Marvulf, before the priest of the Red Wolves and the few of their friends who would fit in their living space without crowding; no one wanted to risk exposing Marvulf and his Uncle Rampat to the winter fever. The visitors would touch nothing, and would only remain inside for the ceremony itself. The traditional hugs and kisses had been forbidden where the visitors were concerned.

Ahna could not help thinking how different it all was from the wedding she had envisioned just two short moons ago. There would be no celebrations, no three-day party. Except for Luliana, and of course Sara, none of her special friends could attend, and most of Marvulf's family were not here, either. She thought sadly of Ahndru, who as the youngest of the family would have had a unique role. Most of all she missed her mother. Sara had helped her don her wedding outfit after her father had insisted they at least take the time to dress for the occasion. An elaborate hairdo was also traditional, but they had simply brushed hers until it flowed shining down her back before putting on the headdress; she was rewarded when Marvulf whispered to her how much he liked it that way. Still, it would have meant so much more if it had been Vladia...

Marvulf, too, had a beautiful suit of soft, off-white linen, the short jacket beaded with tiny, multicolored shells, which he had tucked into his saddle bags. It came out a little rumpled, but he looked so handsome in it that no one minded. Ahshela and Luliana had been hastily fetched for the ceremony, and somehow managed to find some asters and fall roses for Ahna to carry. Lwenli brought his wife and sons, and Gylgan and Yashihar and their wives had stayed as witnesses and friends. Rampat, impressive in his red and gold robes, opened the ceremony with an invocation to the gods and goddesses of Marvulf's clan, asking specifically that the Goddess of Spring, She who influenced fertility, forgive the season in which this wedding was taking place and bless the young couple with many healthy children.

While Rampat was going over the duties expected of each individual in a marriage, Ahna was thinking of all the strange circumstances which had brought her to this day. It seemed to come back to the way her people lived; Srogaraad was unbalanced, but that might be partly because he was one of a people whose beliefs and entire lifestyle were out of balance. They needed strict rules to keep themselves from tearing each other apart, yet she couldn't believe the Goddess had made humans so innately violent. Certainly the Others were not that way. Sara's philosophy of life was so different from that of the clans that her people thought most nomads were like Srogaraad: sick in the head crazy.

Ahna had accepted that the Goddess did not interfere directly in their lives, and yet she could see Her hand in many of the things that had happened. She glanced at Marvulf out of the corner of her eye, and asked the Lady to help them both in their dealings with each other. Rampat was speaking to Marvulf. Ahna could look up now, and she did.

"Marvulf Storm, do you promise to provide for Ahna and her children, to feed them and house them and bring your sons up as good clansmen, giving attention to their wellbeing even before yourself?"

The tall blond stranger, for he was still a stranger, smiled down at her. "I do."

"Ahna, do you promise to care for Marvulf as your husband, to keep his tents and prepare his food, to nurse him in sickness, support him in all his endeavors and applaud his triumphs, to bear his children and care for them as well, to be loyal to him in all things, forsaking any other man including those of your own family, and to obey him exclusively and unquestioningly?" She looked into his eyes; she had no choice. "I do," she whispered.

"Who has the ring?" asked the priest. Redwolf, the youngest remaining member of Ahna's family, brought the plain gold band that Marvulf had given him earlier and handed it to the priest. Rampat blessed it, then handed it to Marvulf. Ahna held out her left hand, and Marvulf slid the ring onto her third finger.

"This ring is a symbol of your union, of your responsibilities to each other and of the good will of the Gods as long as you fulfill those responsibilities," admonished Rampat. "Let it be a reminder of the vows you have taken today. I pronounce you man and wife."

Marvulf kissed Ahna lightly, and they turned to receive the congratulations of the witnesses. Only Jaromir and Redwolf among the men kissed Ahna, although all the women did. Ahshela searched her face before she hugged her.

"Your mother would be very proud of you," she whispered. "You have grown so much, so fast. You are no longer a young girl who thinks more of what she wants than of what others need. I see the light of the Lady shining in you, though you may not feel it at this moment. You will be fine; I know it." Ahna gave her a grateful smile, though she felt more like crying. She was leaving everyone she loved, everyone she knew, behind, and it was happening so fast!

The men shook Marvulf's hand. He had brought the jewelry that was promised to Vladia as part of the bride gifts, and now he tried to give it to Jaromir. The chief told him to give it to Ahna.

"I have a better idea," Marvulf said, smiling at his bride. He turned and handed the carved horn box to Redwolf, whom he had been watching with Sara. "Ahna will have a wide choice of beautiful things to wear, including some of her mother's jewelry," he said with a grin. "Give these to *your* bride when you get around to marrying her. She has no father to gift her; perhaps she will allow me to play that role."

Redwolf laughed aloud. "You are far too young to be her father," he protested. He looked at Sara a moment, sobering. "Thank you," he said to Marvulf. "I will accept your generosity, and I have a request as well." His brother-in-law lifted an eyebrow.

"We would like to join you, after…" he looked at his father, "after we have dealt with all this mess. I think Father means to resign as chief, and he will not want to stay. I know I don't; there has been too much unpleasantness. We don't feel we belong here any more. I… Marvulf, I do not want to be a warrior, and I have no interest in the priesthood. I would rather work with leather and bone and wood. I am already good, and will get better."

Marvulf smiled. "We can always use makers of bows, and harness and armor," he said. "There are few enough with the talent or desire to do the work well. You will be more than welcome, and I know that my wife will be happier with some of her family around her. Please come, at once if you can."

"We will come. We have to contact my brothers first. They must be informed of all that has occurred, and Father will want to divide his herds among them. We'll come when our obligations here have been met."

Moshel joined them. "If it's all right I will ride with you when you go," he said to Marvulf. "I am going home. We will be going in the same direction, at least for a while. I assume that you do not mean to hurry." Marvulf shook his head. "I want to take my time, too, to be sure I do not carry the winter fever home with me. My fostering was to have been up at the solstice anyway. This seems a good time to go, while the weather is still cooperative." He, too, glanced at Jaromir. "He has given me permission. He says you will not be staying long anyway, Redwolf."

The young man nodded, although his spirits fell. He hadn't realized how much he counted on Moshel, or how close they had become. The dealings with the clan and the council, and even his older brothers, would be more difficult for his foster brother's absence. He said nothing, though, except to wish Moshel well.

Everyone went outside except Ahna, who had to change, and Sara. They went into the private quarters that now belonged to the concubine, and Sara hugged her friend hard. The bride's composure had finally failed her and she was in tears.

"It's all right," promised her friend. "He is a good man at heart, even if he is a barbarian. He will treat you better than most; perhaps one day you will even be able to teach him the ways of the Goddess."

"I will miss you so much," said Ahna, swallowing her tears.

"Not for long," laughed Sara. "Surely you know I will be coming with Redwolf and your father." For the first time a genuine smile of happiness lit Ahna's face.

"I should have known," she said, "but I guess I'm not thinking very clearly. It makes all the difference in the world." She hugged her friend again. "I can't wait."

Ahna changed and they wrapped her wedding outfit. Everything else that she was taking was already outside, waiting to go on the pack horses. When the dress was safely folded into a protective layer of linen she handed it to the her friend, saying, "You will need this before long, I hope, and I have no further need of it at all. It will have to be altered, but you are even better with a needle than I am." Tears filled Sara's eyes this time.

"If I were being married from my old home, I would have worn my mother's wedding dress," she explained, taking the package and storing it safely behind her everyday clothes. "I will wear yours with pride and gratitude, and keep it safe for our daughters." They shared a final hug.

The horses that were to go to Marvulf had been brought, and the older women and even a few of the men pitched in to get them packed. Ahna's tents and the bulkier household items were tied on a drag behind a stout gelding; everything else went into pack baskets and saddle bags. They were careful to take nothing that had been in use during the epidemic, but only the new items that had been stored against this day. It did not take long. Nomads that they were, the folk of the clans were expert at packing and moving. The sun had still a full hand between it and the horizon, short as the days had become, when they were ready to ride.

Ahna came out of her father's tents for the last time, in a new blouse and divided skirts and serviceable, half-high riding boots, her hair braided in a gleaming red-gold coronet beneath her gold-embroidered blue headscarf. She was greeted by a high-pitched whinny of joy.

"Firefly!" she exclaimed, and had to stop herself from running to the filly, who danced in the lane between the tents, straining toward her, tugging on the rein that Redwolf held in his hand. The excited horse tossed her head and called again. Ahna looked around for her new husband, found him standing right beside her, grinning. He raised his eyebrows questioningly. She could not kiss him in public; it simply wasn't done.

"Thank you," she said, then went to her mare, patting and laughing as Firefly snorted, sucked in the scent of her mistress, and nuzzled, ecstatic. Preparing to mount, Ahna noted the silver-trimmed prize saddle and new, intricately worked leather saddle bags almost in passing.

Marvulf had followed her to the horse, enjoying their reunion. Now he put his hands on her waist to lift her up. "You're welcome," he said quietly in her ear. "She is yours now, as you are mine." He boosted, and she swung her leg across Firefly's back, feeling like she was coming home. She adjusted her skirts, and gave the man standing beside her a heart-stopping smile. "Thank you," she murmured again. "Just wait until I get you alone!"

Epilogue

By the time the hunter moon was full it was obvious to everyone that the epidemic was over. There had been no new cases for days and nearly everyone who had been sick only a few days ago had recovered. It was also clear to Redwolf and Sara, Ahshela and the rest of his friends that Jaromir was dying, despite the best that Sara and the Eldest could do. He had resigned from his duties as chief, and thereafter devoted himself to helping the last victims of the winter fever, most of whom were in the priests' compound where the women healers were unable to go. He saved lives, but the effort was too much. Even the Others' cough remedy did not help.

Ahshela visited again that morning, bringing another herb she hoped might ease Jaromir's breathing. She had aged tremendously in the few weeks since the epidemic began. Her braided hair was thinner and almost transparent, it was so white. She seemed smaller, and for the first time frail, and she walked with a cane now, but her cough was gone and the indomitable spirit still shone in her eyes.

She and Redwolf and Sara sat on the rugs around Jaromir's furs, where he lay propped up against a wealth of cushions. Redwolf told her what he had already told his father and Sara: all about Floriana and the Others. He knew now, he said, that they were people as worthy of consideration as any in the clans, and that it was wrong to kill them as if they were less than animals. He told her of his long talks with Sara since his return, and how he now believed more in the Goddess of the Others than he did in Zynjaar's fickle gods. He said he meant to marry Sara when they were both ready, taking her for his first and only wife despite the prohibitions of his people. He also told them all that he would not be a warrior, or a priest, and that although he meant to be a saddle and bow maker, he would make no weapons except those intended for hunting.

Jaromir roused himself to give his son and his friends a wan smile, his thanks, and his blessings.

"Go to your sister when you can," he whispered. "Tell her... tell her I loved her."

Redwolf was sitting with his father that afternoon when the High Priest came to see Jaromir, to help him reconcile with the Gods before he died so that he would be received in the eternal halls of men, just doing his duty, Zynjaar said. Redwolf eyed the priest suspiciously, but had no authority to turn him away. Nevertheless, he refused to leave Jaromir's quarters, although Zynjaar tried to drive him out, saying he could not witness the ceremony because he had not yet been initiated. Redwolf compromised by standing just outside the open privacy curtain, intently watching the priest and his father.

Zynjaar lighted a lump of herbal incense and intoned some mumbo-jumbo, then bent close to the former leader and whispered.

"Before you die I want you to know that it was not the Gods who sent the pestilence to you," Zynjaar said. "It was Srogaraad. It was he who found the child in that pig sty near the razed town with her dead and dying folk all about her, he who sent me to fetch her to you. We knew you would be fool enough to take her in. He prayed to the Gods to make it as hard on you as possible, and his prayers have been answered. You have brought all this on yourself by your stupidity, refusing to give him your daughter. You stole my son, but now he and I have taken yours, and so much more.

"I have not said the words of absolution, the words that might help you find everlasting life in the halls of men, nor will I or any other priest ever say them for you. Die with the knowledge that you have lost everything because of your stubbornness, and that now you lose even your soul, forever."

A spark kindled in Jaromir's dimming eyes as the High Priest spoke. Very little could have caused him to fight to live longer, but Zynjaar's words did.

"Your gods," he croaked, his voice strained and low, "will not take my soul. It is given to the Goddess, and She will see me reborn again. You, High Priest Zynjaar, have instead destroyed your own soul. You have betrayed the duty entrusted to you by our entire clan. You have brought this calamity on all for your personal gain. This you admit by your own words. Even your Gods could not forgive such a transgression. Neither will our people. The council shall know of this."

"No," hissed Zynjaar, "they won't!" He snatched up a heavy fold of bedding furs and pressed it down over Jaromir's mouth and nose, taking care to keep his body between Redwolf and Jaromir so that the boy could not see what he was doing. But the dying man was stronger than the priest would have believed. He struck out with both hands, kicked wildly if feebly with both legs, and at once Redwolf was by his side, forcing the priest away and removing the coverlet from his father's face.

"Hold... him," croaked Jaromir. Redwolf spun around to see the priest leaving the tent. Without thought he dived forward and wrapped his long arms around Zynjaar's knees, bringing the older man crashing to the ground. He held on, crawling up the priest's legs to sit on him, getting hold of one arm and then the other and twisting them up behind his back in a very effective wrestling pin. "Sara," he called loudly, "bring me some rope!" Sara appeared in seconds, a ball of stout hemp twine from the work tent in her hand. She looked horrified at seeing the High Priest on the floor and Redwolf on top of him, but she gave her betrothed the twine, and he swiftly bound Zynjaar's hands, then tied his feet together at the ankles and tied them to his hands for good measure. Then he jumped up and went back to his father's side. "Get Yashihar... and Gylgan... right now," Jaromir commanded, still in a hoarse whisper. He coughed weakly, trying to clear his air passages.

"Run for Gylgan," Redwolf said to Sara, explaining where the councilor's tent stood. "I will get Yashihar." Without a glance at their captive writhing and spitting malfeasances on the rugs in the main living area, the young people ran. When they came back only a bit later, each with a councilor in tow, they found several neighbors standing looking down at the priest, who was alternately begging and commanding them to let him go. No one had moved to do so. One of the younger warriors grinned at them as they hurried toward Jaromir's private space. "He swears almost as well as his son," he said. "We could hear him in our tents."

Lwenli was sitting on the furs beside his former chief, holding some crushed camphor leaves beneath his nose. The pungent odor seemed to help. The two councilors joined him, crouching down where they could hear the dying man.

With frequent pauses to get his breath, Jaromir told them word for word what Zynjaar had said about where the pestilence had come from and who was responsible for deliberately bringing it to the camp. "He admitted it. With his own words he has condemned himself," Jaromir concluded. "Take this to the full council." He closed his eyes as Yashihar took his hand, and all three men assured him that they would do as he asked. Justice would be done. He did not speak again.

Redwolf stood beside his father and watched him breathe his last. When Yashihar closed Jaromir's sightless eyes and the three men rose to their feet, the young man drew rein on his emotions and said,

"What my father didn't tell you was that Zynjaar tried to kill him. Apparently Father told him he was going to send for you. The ba... the High Priest tried to smother him with his own furs. I saw him struggling and dragged Zynjaar away. I had to tackle him and tie him up to keep him from leaving. Father told me to hold him."

"You did well, son," said Yashihar. "You have done extraordinarily well under extremely trying circumstances these past two moons. You may not be officially a man, but I know many men who would have been unable to do as well. I am sorry for all your losses." They moved out into the main living area, and stood looking down at Zynjaar, who glared back, coughing.

"We will take charge of this miscreant now and let you care for your own," Gylgan said kindly. "Your parents are a terrible loss to the whole clan as well as to you. My wife will come over in a little while to help the girl," he indicated Sara, hovering almost out of sight in the work tent opening, "ready your father for burial."

"He wanted his body to be exposed, in the fashion of those that follow the Goddess," Redwolf said. "He wants to be reborn; he hopes that he and my mother will find one another again."

A couple of the men raised eyebrows in surprise, then looked thoughtful. Yashihar only nodded. Zynjaar shouted "Blasphemy! You cannot permit this... this abomination." His explosion brought on another coughing fit.

"Shut up," said Gylgan. "You are the abomination here. Your deliberate and deadly betrayal of your people is a worse blasphemy than any other I have ever heard of, and so it shall be known to all. Your word has no weight now, nor will it ever again. We have been guilty, ourselves, of believing in you. We'll not listen any more!"

The young women of the Women's society carried Jaromir's body to the holy place, where they laid him naked among the hundreds of bodies of the women and children who had died in the epidemic, most already little more than bones. On the recommendation of Ahshela, they allowed Redwolf to help carry his father's body and take part in the ceremony, giving thanks to the Goddess for the life just ended, asking Her to care for Jaromir's spirit until he was given a new body, and closing with praise for the Goddess and Her cycle of birth and death and rebirth which made life possible.

Zynjaar was tried immediately, and with the testimony of Lwenli and the two councilors and Redwolf's description of his attempt to kill Jaromir, was finally found guilty, both by the council and by a convocation of senior priests. He was stripped of his robes and sentenced to forfeit all his considerable wealth to the many families who had lost supporting members in the epidemic, and banishment. He had to be helped to leave the camp, and died within days of lung congestion, alone in the hills. Mulynvi was chosen High Priest in his place, both by the other priests and by the council, as being the only one of them who had seen clearly and had the courage to speak.

The priesthood was rededicated to the service of the people, and the priests themselves seemed willing, even eager to learn healing from the women, although they continued to insist that females were soulless and it was natural and right for women to be subservient. Except for fertility, they vehemently denied the importance of the Goddess. The women's circle still had secrets that must be kept.

www.ingramcontent.com/pod-product-compliance
Lightning Source LLC
Chambersburg PA
CBHW021446240626
47153CB00001B/319